PENGUIN BOOKS

MAIGRET AND THE GHOST

Georges Simenon was born at Liège in Belgium in 1903. At sixteen he began work as a journalist on the *Gazette de Liège*. He has published over 212 novels in his own name, many of which belong to the Inspector Maigret series, and his work has been published in thirty-two countries. He has had a great influence upon French cinema, and more than forty of his novels have been filmed.

Simenon's novels are largely psychological. He describes hidden fears, tensions and alliances beneath the surface of life's ordinary routine which suddenly explode into violence and crime. André Gide wrote to him: 'You are living on a false reputation – just like Baudelaire or Chopin. But nothing is more difficult than making the public go back on a too hasty first impression. You are still the slave of your first successes and the reader's idleness would like to put a stop to your triumphs there . . . You are much more important than is commonly supposed'; and François Mauriac wrote, 'I am afraid I may not have the courage to descend right to the depths of this nightmare which Simenon describes with such unendurable art.'

Simenon has travelled a great deal and once lived on a cutter, making long journeys of exploration round the coasts of Northern Europe. A book of reminiscences, *Letter to My Mother*, was published in England in 1976. He is married and lives near Lausanne in Switzerland.

[illegible]

[illegible]

Georges Simenon was born at Liège in Belgium in 1903. At sixteen he began work as a journalist on the *Gazette de Liège*. He has published over [illegible] novels in his own name, many of which belong to the [illegible] series, and his work has been published in [illegible] countries. He has had a great influence upon [illegible] cinema, and more than [illegible] of his novels have been filmed.

Simenon's novels are largely psychological. He describes hidden fears, tensions and alliances beneath the surface of life's ordinary routine, which suddenly explode into violence and crime. André Gide wrote to him: 'You are living on a false reputation – just like Baudelaire or Chopin. But nothing is more difficult than making the public [illegible] on a [illegible] impression. You are still the slave of your first successes and the reader's idleness would like to put a stop to your progress [illegible] You are much more important than is commonly supposed'; and François Mauriac wrote, 'I am afraid I may not have the courage to descend right to the depths of this nightmare which Simenon describes with such genius.'

Simenon has travelled a great deal and once lived on a cutter, making long journeys of exploration round the coasts of Northern Europe. A book of his reminiscences, entitled *Letter to My Mother*, was published in England in [illegible]. He is married and [illegible] Switzerland.

GEORGES SIMENON

*

MAIGRET AND THE GHOST

MAIGRET AND THE HOTEL MAJESTIC

THREE BEDS IN MANHATTAN

MAIGRET AND THE GHOST

PENGUIN BOOKS

Penguin Books Ltd, Harmondsworth, Middlesex, England
Penguin Books, 625 Madison Avenue, New York, New York 10022, U.S.A.
Penguin Books Australia Ltd, Ringwood, Victoria, Australia
Penguin Books Canada Ltd, 2801 John Street, Markham, Ontario, Canada L3R 1B4
Penguin Books (N.Z.) Ltd, 182–190 Wairau Road, Auckland 10, New Zealand

Maigret and the Hotel Majestic first published in France 1942
under the title *Maigret et les caves du Majestic*

Translation first published in Great Britain by Hamish Hamilton 1977

Three Beds in Manhattan first published in France 1946
under the title *Trois chambres à Manhattan*

Translation first published in Great Britain by Hamish Hamilton 1976

Maigret and the Ghost first published in France 1964
under the title *Maigret et le fantôme*

Translation first published in Great Britain by Hamish Hamilton 1976

Published in Penguin Books 1982

Reproduced, printed and bound in Great Britain by
Hazell Watson & Viney Ltd, Aylesbury, Bucks
Filmset in Sabon
by Rowland Phototypesetting Ltd
Bury St Edmunds, Suffolk

CONTENTS

MAIGRET AND THE HOTEL MAJESTIC

Translated by Caroline Hillier

1

Prosper Donge's Puncture

A car door slamming. The first thing he heard each day. The engine ticking over outside. Charlotte was probably saying good-bye to the driver? Then the taxi drove off. Footsteps. The sound of the key in the lock and the click of the electric light switch.

A match being struck in the kitchen and the slow 'pfffttt' as the gas came alight.

Charlotte climbed slowly up the newly built staircase, having been on her feet all night. She crept noiselessly into the room. Another light switch. The light came on, a pink handkerchief with wooden tassels at the corners making a makeshift shade.

Prosper Donge kept his eyes firmly closed. Charlotte undressed, glancing at herself in the wardrobe mirror. When she got to her bra and girdle, she sighed. She was as plump and pink as a Rubens, but had a passion for constricting herself. When she had finished undressing, she rubbed the marks on her skin.

She had an irritating way of getting into the bed, kneeling on it first so that the mattress dipped to one side.

'Your turn, Prosper!'

He got up. She dived quickly into the warm hollow he had left, pulled the bedcovers up to her eyes and lay there unmoving.

'Is it raining?' he asked, running water into the basin.

A muffled groan. It didn't matter. The water was icy to shave in. Trains rumbled past below.

Prosper Donge got dressed. Charlotte sighed from time to time because she couldn't get to sleep with the light on. Just as he stretched out his right hand to the switch, with his other hand already on the doorknob, she muttered thickly: 'Don't forget to go and pay the money for the wireless.'

There was hot coffee on the stove – too hot. He drank it

standing up. Then, with the gestures of someone who does the same things every day, at the same time, he wrapped a knitted scarf round his neck, and put on his hat and coat.

Finally he wheeled his bicycle along the passage and out of the door.

The air was always damp and cold at that hour of the morning, and the pavements were wet although it hadn't rained; the people sleeping behind their closed shutters would probably waken to a warm, sunny day.

The street, with detached houses and little gardens on either side, ran steeply downhill. There was an occasional glimpse, through the trees, of the lights of Paris far down below.

It was no longer dark. But it wasn't yet light. The sky was bluish mauve. Lights came on in a few windows and Prosper Donge braked sharply as he reached the level crossing which was shut and which he crossed by the side gates.

After the Pont de Saint-Cloud, he turned left. A tug with its chain of barges was whistling angrily to be allowed into the lock.

The Bois de Boulogne . . . Lakes reflecting a whiter sky, with swans stirring awake . . .

As he reached the Porte Dauphine, Donge suddenly felt the ground become harder under his wheels. He went on a few metres, jumped off and saw that his back tyre was punctured.

He checked the time by his watch. It was ten to six. He began to walk quickly, pushing his bike, and his breath hung in the air as he panted along, with a burning sensation in his chest from the effort.

Avenue Foch . . . The shutters of the private houses were all still closed . . . Only an officer trotting along the ride followed by his orderly . . .

Getting lighter behind the Arc de Triomphe . . . He was hurrying along . . . getting very hot now . . .

Just at the corner of the Champs-Élysées, a policeman in a cape, near the newspaper kiosk, called out: 'Puncture?'

He nodded. Only three hundred metres more. The Hotel Majestic, on the left, with all its windows still shuttered. The street lights barely shed any light now.

He turned up the Rue de Berri, then the Rue de Ponthieu. There was a little bar open. And two houses farther along, a door which passers-by never noticed, the back entrance of the Majestic.

A man was coming out. He appeared to be in evening dress under his grey overcoat. He was bareheaded. His hair was plastered down and Prosper Donge thought it was Zebio, the dancer.

He could have glanced into the bar to see if he was right, but it didn't occur to him to do so. Still pushing his bike, he started down the long grey corridor, lit by a single light. He stopped at the clocking-on machine, turned the wheel, and put a card in at his number, 67, his eyes on the little clock which said ten past six. Click.

It was now established that he had arrived at the Majestic at 6.10 a.m. – ten minutes later than usual.

That was the official statement made by Prosper Donge, still-room chef at the big Champs-Élysées hotel.

He had continued to behave, he said, as on any other morning.

At that hour, the great basement with its twisting corridors, innumerable doors and grey-painted walls like those of a ship's gangway, was deserted. Here and there you could see a feeble light from a yellowish bulb, which was all the light there was at night, shining through the glass partitions.

There were glass partitions everywhere, with the kitchens on the left, and the pastrycook's kitchen beyond. Opposite was the room called the guests' servants' hall, where the senior staff and guests' private servants, chambermaids and chauffeurs ate. Then farther on, the junior staff dining-room, with long wooden tables and benches like school benches.

Finally, overlooking the basement like the bridge of a ship, a smaller glass cage, where the book-keeper kept a check on everything which left the kitchens.

As he opened the door of the still-room, Prosper Donge had the impression that someone was going up the narrow staircase which led to the upper floors, but he didn't pay any attention to the fact. Or so he stated later.

He struck a match, just as Charlotte had done in their little house, and the gas went 'pfffttt' under the smallest percolator, which he heated first for the few guests who got up early.

Only when he had done this did he go to the cloakroom. It was a fairly large room, down one of the corridors. There were several basins, a greyish mirror, and tall, narrow metal lockers round the walls, each with a number.

He opened locker 67 with his key. Took off his coat, hat and scarf. He changed his shoes because he liked wearing softer, elastic-sided shoes during the daytime. He put on a white jacket.

A few minutes to go . . . At half past six, the basement burst into life . . .

Upstairs, they were all still asleep, except the night porter, who was waiting to be relieved in the deserted foyer.

The percolator whistled. Donge filled a cup with coffee and started up the staircase, which was like one of those mysterious staircases in the wings of a theatre which lead to the most unexpected places.

Pushing open a narrow door, he found himself in the cloakroom in the foyer; no one would have known the door, covered by a large mirror, was there.

'Coffee!' he announced, putting the cup on the cloakroom counter. 'All right?'

'OK!' the night porter grunted, coming to get it.

Donge went downstairs again. His three women helpers, the Three Fatties as they were called, had arrived. They were rough types, all three ugly – and one of them old and cantankerous. They were already noisily clanking cups and saucers in the sink.

Donge continued his daily routine, ranging the silver coffee pots in order of size – one, two or three cups . . . Then the little milk jugs . . . teapots . . .

He caught sight of Jean Ramuel, looking dishevelled, in the book-keeper's glass booth.

'Hmm . . . Spent the night here again!' he said to himself.

For the past three or four nights, Ramuel, the book-keeper, had slept at the hotel instead of going home to Montparnasse.

Officially, this was not allowed. There was a room with three or four beds in it at the end of the corridor, near the door leading to the wine cellars. But in theory the beds were for the use of members of the staff who needed to rest between their hours of work.

Donge waved his hand in greeting to Ramuel, who replied equally casually.

Then it was time for the head chef – vast and full of pomp – to arrive back from the market with his van which he parked in the Rue de Ponthieu for his assistants to unload.

By half past seven there were at least thirty people scurrying about in the basements of the Majestic, and bells began to ring, service-lifts began to descend and were loaded before ascending with their trays, while Ramuel speared pink, blue and white chits on the metal prongs on his desk.

Then it was time for the day porter, in his light blue uniform, to take up his post in the foyer, and for the post clerk to sort the letters in his little cubbyhole. The sun was probably shining out in the Champs-Élysées, but down in the basement they were only aware of the buses rumbling overhead, making the glass partitions tremble.

At a few minutes past nine – at four minutes past nine precisely, it was later established – Prosper Donge came out of his still-room and a few seconds later went into the cloakroom.

'I had left my handkerchief in my coat pocket . . .' he stated when interrogated.

At all events he found himself alone in the room with its hundred metal lockers. Did he open his? There were no witnesses. Did he look for his handkerchief? Possibly he did.

There were in fact not a hundred but only ninety-two lockers, all numbered. The last five were empty.

Why did it occur to Prosper Donge to open locker 89, which didn't belong to anyone and was therefore not locked?

'It was automatic . . .' he said later. 'The door was ajar . . . I didn't think . . .'

In the locker was a body which had been pushed in upright and which had fallen over on itself. It was the body of a woman of about thirty, very blonde – peroxide blonde in fact – wearing a dress of fine black wool.

Donge didn't cry out. He turned very pale, and going up to Ramuel's glass cage, bent to whisper through the grille.

'Come here a minute . . .'

The book-keeper followed him.

'Stay here . . . Don't let anyone in . . .'

Ramuel bounded up the stairs, burst into the foyer cloakroom and saw the porter talking to a chauffeur.

'Is the manager here yet?'

The porter gestured with his chin towards the manager's office.

Maigret paused outside the revolving door, and was about to tap his pipe on his heel to empty it. Then he shrugged and put it back in his mouth. It was his first pipe of the day – the best.

'The manager is expecting you, Superintendent . . .'

There were few signs of life in the foyer as yet. An Englishman was arguing with the post clerk and a young girl walked through on grasshopper-long legs carrying a hatbox which she had probably come to deliver.

Maigret went into the office and the manager shook his hand silently and pointed to a chair. There was a green curtain across the glass door, but if one pulled it back a little one could see everything that went on.

'A cigar?'

'No thank you . . .'

They had known each other for a long time. There was no need to say much. The manager was wearing striped trousers, a black jacket and a tie which seemed to have been cut from some rigid material.

'Here . . .'

He pushed a registration form towards his visitor.

OSWALD J. CLARK, INDUSTRIALIST, OF DETROIT, MICHIGAN (USA). TRAVELLING FROM DETROIT.

ARRIVED ON 12 FEBRUARY.

ACCOMPANIED BY: MRS CLARK, HIS WIFE; TEDDY CLARK, AGED 7, HIS SON; ELLEN DARROMAN, AGED 24, GOVERNESS; GERTRUD BORMS, AGED 42, MAID.

SUITE 103.

The telephone rang. The manager answered impatiently. Maigret folded the form in four and put it in his wallet.

'Which of them is it?'

'Mrs Clark . . .'

'Ah!'

'The hotel doctor, whom I telephoned as soon as I had informed the Police, and who lives just round the corner in the Rue de Berri, is already here. He says Mrs Clark was strangled some time between 6 and 6.30 a.m.'

The manager was plunged in gloom. There was no need to tell an old hand like Maigret that it was a disaster for the hotel and that if there was any way of hushing it up . . .

'The Clark family have been here a week then . . .' murmured the Superintendent. 'What sort of people are they?'

'Well heeled . . . Very . . . He's a great, tall, silent American, about forty . . . Forty-five perhaps . . . His wife – poor thing! – seems to be French . . . Twenty-eight or nine . . . I didn't see very much of her . . . The governess is pretty . . . The maid, who also looks after the child, is very ordinary, rather surly . . . Ah! . . . I nearly forgot to tell you . . . Clark left for Rome yesterday morning . . .'

'Alone?'

'From what I can gather, he is in Europe on business . . . He has a ball-bearing factory . . . He has to visit various European capitals and he decided to leave his wife, son and staff in Paris for the time being . . .'

'What train did he get?' Maigret asked.

The manager picked up the telephone.

'Hullo! Porter? . . . What train did Mr Clark catch yesterday . . . Suite 103, yes . . . Wasn't there any luggage to go to the station? He only took a grip? . . . By taxi? . . . Désiré's taxi? . . . Thank you . . .

'Did you get that, Superintendent? He left at eleven o'clock yesterday morning in a taxi, Désiré's taxi, which is nearly always parked outside the hotel. He took only one small bag with him . . .'

'Do you mind if I make a call myself? . . . Hullo! Judicial Police, please, Mademoiselle . . . Police Headquarters? . . . Lucas? Get over to the Gare de Lyon . . . Check on the trains to Rome from 11 a.m. yesterday . . .'

He continued giving instructions, while his pipe went out.

'Tell Torrence to find Désiré's taxi . . . Yes . . . Which is usually outside the Majestic . . . Find out where he took a fare, a tall thin American he picked up outside the hotel yesterday . . . That's it . . .'

He looked for an ashtray in which to empty his pipe. The manager handed him one.

'Are you sure you won't have a cigar? . . . The nanny is in a great state . . . I thought it best to tell her . . . And the governess didn't sleep at the hotel last night . . .'

'What floor is the suite on?'

'On the second floor . . . Looking out over the Champs-Élysées . . . Mr Clark's room, separated from his wife's by a sitting-room . . . Then the child's room, the nanny's and the governess's . . . They wanted to be all together . . .'

'Has the night porter left?'

'He can be reached by telephone, I know, because I had to contact him one day. His wife is the concierge at a new block of flats in Neuilly . . . Hullo! . . . Can you get me . . .'

Five minutes later they knew that Mrs Clark had gone to the theatre alone the evening before, and that she had got back a few minutes past midnight. The nanny had not gone out. The governess on the other hand had not dined at the hotel and had been out all night.

'Shall we go downstairs and have a look?' Maigret sighed.

The foyer was busier now, but no one had any idea of the drama which had taken place while they were still asleep.

'We'll go this way . . . I'll lead the way, Superintendent . . .'

As he spoke, the manager frowned. Someone was coming through the revolving door, letting in a shaft of sunlight. A young woman in a grey suit came in and, as she passed the post desk, asked in English: 'Anything for me?'

'That's her, Superintendent – Miss Ellen Darroman . . .'

Fine silk stockings, with straight seams. The well-groomed look of someone who had dressed with care. She didn't look at all tired, and the brisk February air had brought colour to her cheeks.

'Do you want to talk to her?'

'Not yet . . . Wait a minute . . .'

And Maigret went over to an inspector he had brought with him, who was standing in a corner of the foyer.

'Don't let that girl out of your sight . . . If she goes into her room, stand outside the door . . .'

The cloakroom. The tall mirror turned on its hinges. The Superintendent followed the manager down the narrow staircase. A sudden end to all the gilt, potted plants and elegant bustle. A smell of cooking rose to meet them.

'Does this staircase go to all the floors?'

'There are two of them . . . leading from the cellar to the attics . . . But you have to know your way around to use them . . . For instance, upstairs, there are little doors exactly the same as the other doors, but with no number on. None of the visitors would ever guess . . .'

It was nearly eleven o'clock. There were not fifty, but more like a hundred and fifty people now, scurrying about in the basement, some in cooks' white hats, others in waiters' coats, or cellarmen's aprons, and the women, like Prosper Donge's Three Fatties, doing the rough work . . .

'This way . . . Careful you don't get dirty or slip . . . The passages are very narrow . . .'

Through the glass partitions everyone stared at them, and particularly at the Superintendent. Jean Ramuel was busy catching each chit handed up to him as its bearer flew past, and casting an eagle eye over the contents of the trays.

It was a shock to see the unexpected figure of a policeman standing on guard outside the cloakroom. The doctor – who was very young – had been warned that Maigret was coming, and was smoking a cigarette while waiting.

'Shut the door . . .'

The body was lying on the floor in the middle of the room, surrounded by the metal lockers. The doctor, still smoking, muttered: 'She must have been attacked from behind . . . She didn't struggle for very long . . .'

'And her body wasn't dragged along the ground!' Maigret added, examining the dead woman's black clothes. 'There are no traces of dust . . . Either the crime was committed here, or she was carried, by two people probably, because it would be difficult in this labyrinth of narrow corridors . . .'

There was a crocodile handbag in the locker in which she had been found. The Superintendent opened it, and took out an automatic, which he slipped into his pocket, after checking the safety catch was on. There was nothing else in the bag except a handkerchief, a powder compact, and a few banknotes amounting to less than a thousand francs.

Behind them the basement was humming like a beehive. The service-lifts shot up and down, bells rang ceaselessly and they could see heavy copper saucepans being wielded behind the glass partitions of the kitchens, and chickens being roasted in their dozens.

'Everything must be left in place for the Public Prosecutor's Department to see,' Maigret said. 'Who found the body? . . .'

Prosper Donge, who was cleaning a percolator, was pointed out to him. He was tall, with the kind of red hair usually referred to as carroty, and looked about forty-five to forty-eight. He had blue eyes and his face was badly pockmarked.

'Has he been here long?'

'Five years . . . Before that he was at the Miramar, in Cannes . . .'

'Reliable?'

'Extremely reliable . . .'

There was a partition separating Donge and the Superintendent. Their eyes met through the glass. And a rush of colour flooded the face of the still-room chef, who like all redheads, had sensitive skin.

'Excuse me, sir . . . Superintendent Maigret is wanted on the telephone . . .'

It was Jean Ramuel, the book-keeper, who had hurried out of his cage.

'If you'd like to take the call here –'

A message from Headquarters. There had only been two express trains to Rome since eleven o'clock the day before. Oswald J. Clark had not travelled on either of them. And the taxi driver, Désiré, whom they had managed to contact on the telephone at a bistro where he was one of the regulars, swore he had taken his fare, the day before, to the Hotel Aiglon, in the Boulevard Montparnasse.

Voices, from the staircase, one of them the high-pitched voice of a young woman protesting in English to a room waiter who was trying to bar her way.

It was the governess, Ellen Darroman, who was bearing down on them.

2

Maigret Goes Bicycling

Pipe in mouth, bowler on the back of his head, and hands in the pockets of his vast overcoat with the famous velvet collar, Maigret watched her arguing vehemently with the hotel manager.

And one glance at the Superintendent's face made it clear that there would not be much sympathy lost between him and Ellen Darroman.

'What's she saying?' he sighed, interrupting, unable to understand a single word the American woman said.

'She wants to know if it's true Mrs Clark has been murdered, and if anyone has telephoned to Rome to let Oswald J. Clark know; she wants to know where the body has been taken and if . . .'

But the girl didn't let him finish. She had listened impatiently, frowning, had thrown Maigret a cold glance and had gone on talking faster than ever.

'What's she saying?'

'She wants me to show her the body and . . .'

Maigret gently took the American girl's arm, to guide her towards the cloakroom. But he knew she would shy away from the contact. Just the kind of woman who exasperated him in American films! A terrifyingly brisk walk. All the kitchen staff were gaping at her through the glass partitions.

'Do come in,' murmured the Superintendent, not without irony.

She took three steps forward, saw the body wrapped in a blanket on the floor, remained stock still and started jabbering away in English again.

'What's she saying?'

'She wants us to uncover the body . . .'

Maigret complied, without taking his eyes off her. He saw her start, then immediately recover her composure in spite of the horrifying nature of what she saw.

'Ask her if she recognizes Mrs Clark . . .'

A shrug. A particularly disagreeable way of tapping her high heel on the floor.

'What's she saying?'

'That you know as well as she does.'

'In that case, please ask her to go up to your office and tell her that I have a few questions to ask her.'

The manager translated. Maigret took the opportunity of covering the dead woman's face again.

'What's she saying?'

'She says "no".'

'Really? Kindly inform her of my position as head of the Special Squad of the Judicial Police . . .'

Ellen, who was looking straight at him, spoke without waiting for this to be translated. And Maigret repeated his interminable: 'What's she saying?'

'*What's she saying?*' she repeated, imitating him, overcome by unjustifiable irritation.

And she spoke in English again, as if to herself.

'Translate what she's saying for me, will you?'

'She says that . . . that she knows perfectly well you're from the police . . . that . . .'

'Don't be afraid!'

'That one only has to see you with your hat on and your pipe in your mouth . . . I'm so sorry . . . You wanted me to tell you . . . She says she won't go up to my office and that she won't answer your questions . . .'

'Why not?'

'I'll ask her . . .'

Ellen Darroman, who was lighting a cigarette, listened to the manager's question, shrugged again and snapped a few words.

'She says she's not under any obligation to answer and that she will only obey an official summons . . .'

At which the girl threw a last look at Maigret, turned on her heel and walked, with the same decisive air, towards the staircase.

The manager turned somewhat anxiously towards the Superintendent, and was amazed to see that he was smiling.

He had had to take off his overcoat, because of the heat in the basement, but he hadn't abandoned his bowler or his pipe. Thus accoutred, he wandered peacefully along the corridors, with his hands behind his back, stopping from time to time by one of the glass partitions, rather as if he were inspecting an aquarium.

The huge basement, with its electric lights burning all day long, did in fact strike him as being very like an oceanographical museum. In each glass cage there were creatures, varying in number, darting to and fro. You could see them constantly appearing and disappearing, heavily laden, carrying saucepans or piles of plates, setting service-lifts or goods-lifts in motion, forever using the little instruments which were the telephones.

'What would someone from another planet make of it all? . . .'

The visit from the DPP had only lasted a few minutes, and the examining magistrate had given Maigret a free hand as usual. The latter had made several telephone calls from Jean Ramuel's book-keeper's cage.

Ramuel's nose was set so crookedly, that one always seemed to be seeing him in profile. And he looked as though he was suffering from a liver complaint. When his lunch was brought to him on a tray, he took a sachet of white powder from his waistcoat pocket and dissolved it in a glass of water.

Between one and three o'clock, the pace was at its most hectic, everything happening so fast that it was like seeing a film run off in fast motion.

'Excuse me . . . Sorry . . .'

People were constantly bumping into the Superintendent, who continued his walk unperturbed, stopping and starting, asking a question now and then.

How many people had he talked to? At least twenty, he reckoned. The head chef had explained to him how the kitchens were run. Jean Ramuel had told him what the different coloured slips of paper meant.

And he had watched – still through the glass partitions – the guests' servants having their lunch. Gertrud Borms, the Clarks' nanny, had come down. A large, hard-faced woman.

'Does she speak French?'

'Not a word . . .'

She had eaten heartily, chatting to a liveried chauffeur who sat opposite her.

But what amazed him most of all was the sight of Prosper Donge, all this while, in his still-room. He looked exactly like a large goldfish in its bowl. His hair was a fiery red. He had the almost brick-red complexion redheads sometimes have, and his lips were thick and fish-like.

And he looked exactly like a fish when he came to press his face up against the glass, with his great, round, bewildered eyes, probably worried because the Superintendent hadn't spoken to him yet.

Maigret had questioned everyone. But he had hardly seemed to notice Prosper Donge's presence, although it was he who had discovered the body, and he was therefore the principal witness.

Donge, too, had his lunch, on a little table in his still-room, while his three women bustled round him. A bell would ring about once a minute to indicate that the service-lift was coming down. It arrived at a sort of hatch. Donge seized the slip of paper on it, and replaced it with the order on a tray, and the lift went up again to one of the upper floors.

All these seemingly complicated operations were in fact quite simple. The large dining-room of the Majestic, where two or three hundred people would then be having lunch, was immediately over the kitchens, so most of the service-lifts went there. Each time one of them came down again, the sound of music was wafted down with it.

Some of the guests had their meals in their rooms, however, and there was a waiter on each floor. There was also a grill-room on the same floor as the basement, where there was dancing in the afternoons from about five o'clock.

The men from the Forensic Laboratory had come for the body, and two specialists from the Criminal Records Office had spent half an hour working on locker 89 with cameras and powerful lights, looking for fingerprints.

None of this seemed to interest Maigret. They would be sure to inform him of the result in due course.

Looking at him, you would have thought he was making an amateurish study of how a grand hotel functions. He went up the narrow staircase, opened a door, then immediately closed it again, because it led to the large dining-room, which was filled with the sound of clinking cutlery, music and conversation.

He went up to the next floor. A corridor, with doors numbered to infinity and a red carpet stretching into the distance.

It was clear that any of the guests could open the door and make their way to the basement. It was the same as with the entrance in the Rue de Ponthieu. Two car attendants, a porter, and commissionaires guarded the revolving door leading from the Champs-Élysées, but any stray passer-by could get into the Majestic by using the staff entrance and no one would probably have noticed he was there.

It is the same with most theatres. They are rigidly guarded at the front, but wide open on the stage-door side.

From time to time people went into the cloakroom in their working clothes. Shortly afterwards they could be seen leaving, smartly dressed, in their hats and coats.

They were going off duty. The head chef went to the back room for a nap, which he did every day between the lunch and dinner shifts.

Soon after four there was a loud burst of music from near at hand in the grill-room, and the dancing began. Prosper Donge, looking exhausted, filled rows of minute teapots, and microscopic milk jugs, and then came anxiously up to the glass partition once more, casting nervous glances in Maigret's direction.

At five o'clock his three women went off duty and were replaced by two others. At six he took a wad of bills and a sheet of paper, which was obviously his accounts for the day, to Jean Ramuel. Then he in turn went into the cloakroom, came out in his street clothes and fetched his bicycle, the puncture having been repaired by one of the bell-boys.

Outside it was now dark. The Rue de Ponthieu was congested. Prosper Donge made for the Champs-Élysées, weaving his way between taxis and buses. When he was almost at the Étoile, he suddenly did an about-turn, bicycled back to the Rue de Ponthieu, and went into a radio shop, where he handed over three hundred odd francs to the cashier as one of the monthly instalments which he had contracted to pay.

Back to the Champs-Élysées. Then on to the regal calm of the Avenue Foch, with only the occasional car gliding silently past. He pedalled slowly, with the air of one who has a long way to go yet – an honest citizen pedalling along the same route at the same time every day.

A voice from behind, speaking quite close to him: 'I hope you don't mind, Monsieur Donge, if I go the rest of the way with you?'

He braked so violently that he skidded and almost collided with Maigret on his bicycle. For it was Maigret who was bicycling along beside him, on a bike which was too small for him, which he had borrowed from a bell-boy at the Majestic.

'I can't think,' Maigret continued, 'why everyone who lives in the suburbs doesn't go by bicycle. It's so much more healthy and agreeable than going by bus or train!'

They were entering the Bois de Boulogne. Soon they saw the shimmer of street-lights reflected in the lake.

'You were so busy all day that I didn't like to disturb you in your work . . .'

And Maigret, too, was pedalling along with the regular rhythm of someone who is used to bicycling. Now and then there was the click of a gear.

'Do you know what Jean Ramuel did before he came to the Majestic?'

'He was a bank accountant . . . The Atoum Bank, in the Rue Caumartin . . .'

'Hmm! . . . The Atoum Bank . . . Doesn't sound too good to me . . . Don't you think he has rather a shifty look about him?'

'He's not very well . . .' Prosper Donge mumbled.

'Look out . . . You were nearly on the pavement . . . There's something else I'd like to ask you, if you won't think it impertinent . . . You're the still-room chef . . . Well, I was wondering what made you take up that profession . . . I mean . . . I feel it isn't a vocation, that one doesn't suddenly say to oneself at fifteen or sixteen: "I'm going to be a still-room chef . . ."

'Look out . . . If you swerve like that you'll get mown down by a car . . . You were saying? . . .'

Donge explained, in a dejected voice, that he had been a foster child, and that until he was fifteen he had lived on a farm near Vitry-le-François. Then he had gone to work in a café in the town, first as an errand-boy and then as a waiter.

'After doing my military service, I wasn't very fit, and I wanted to live in the South of France . . . I was a waiter in Marseilles and Cannes. Then they decided, at the Miramar, that I didn't look right to wait at table . . . I looked "awkward", was the word the manager used . . . I was put in the still-room . . . I was there for years and then I took the job of still-room chef at the Majestic.'

They were crossing the Pont de Saint-Cloud. After turning down two or three narrow streets they reached the bottom of a fairly steep incline, and Prosper Donge got off his bike.

'Are you coming any farther?' he asked.

'If you don't mind. After spending a day in the hotel basement, I can appreciate even more your desire to live in the country . . . Do you do any gardening?'

'A little . . .'

'Flowers?'

'Flowers and vegetables . . .'

Now they were going up a badly surfaced, badly lit street, pushing their bicycles; their breath came more quickly, and they didn't talk much.

'Do you know what I discovered while I was nosing about in the basement and talking to everyone I could see? That three people, at least, slept in the hotel basement last night. First, Jean Ramuel . . . It appears . . . it's rather amusing . . . it appears that he has an impossibly difficult mistress and that she periodically shuts him out of the house . . . For the last three or four days she's done it again and he's been sleeping at the Majestic . . . Does the manager know?'

'It's not officially allowed, but he turns a blind eye . . .'

'The professional dancing-partner slept there too . . . the one you call Zebio . . . A strange bloke, isn't he? To look at, he seems too good to be true . . . He's called Eusebio Fualdès on the studio portraits in the grill-room . . . Then, when you read his identity papers you discover that he was born in Lille, in spite of his dark skin, and that his real name is Edgar Fagonet . . . There was a dance, yesterday evening, in honour of a filmstar . . . He was there until half past three in the morning . . . It seems that he's so poor that he decided to sleep at the hotel rather than get a taxi . . .'

Prosper Donge had stopped, near a lamp-post, and stood there, his face scarlet, his expression anxious.

'What are you doing?' Maigret asked.

'I'm there . . . I . . .'

Light filtered under the door of a little detached house of millstone grit.

'Would it be a great nuisance if I came in for a moment?'

Maigret could have sworn that the poor great oaf's legs were trembling, that his throat was constricted and that he felt ready to faint. He finally managed to stutter: 'If you like . . .'

He opened the door with his key, pushed his bike into the hall, and announced, in what was probably his usual way: 'It's me!'

There was a glass door at the end of the passage, leading to the kitchen; the light was on. Donge went in.

'This is . . .'

Charlotte was sitting by the stove, with her feet on the hob, and was sewing a shrimp-pink silk petticoat, lolling in her chair.

She looked embarrassed, took her feet off the stove and tried to find her slippers under the chair.

'Oh! There's someone with you . . . Please excuse me, Monsieur . . .'

There was a cup with some dregs of coffee on the table, and a plate with some cake crumbs.

'Come in . . . Sit down . . . Prosper so rarely brings anyone home . . .'

It was hot. The wireless – a smart new one – was on. Charlotte was in her dressing-gown, with her stockings rolled down below the knee.

'A superintendent? What's going on?' she said anxiously, when Donge introduced Maigret.

'Nothing, Madame . . . I happened to be working at the Majestic today, and I met your husband there . . .'

At the word husband, she looked at Prosper and burst out laughing.

'Did he tell you we were married?'

'I imagined . . .'

'No, no! . . . Sit down . . . We're just living together . . . I think we're really more like friends than anything else . . . Aren't we, Prosper? . . . We've known each other so long! . . . Mind you, if I wanted him to marry me . . . But as I always say to him, what difference would it make? . . . Everyone who knows me knows I was a dancer, and then a night-club hostess, on the Riviera . . . And that if I hadn't got so fat, I wouldn't have needed to work in the cloakroom in a club in the Rue Fontaine . . . Oh, Prosper . . . did you remember the payment on the wireless?'

'Yes, it's all done . . .'

An agricultural programme was announced on the radio and Charlotte switched it off, noticed that her dressing-gown was open and pinned it together with a large nappy pin. Some leftovers were heating in a pan on the stove. Charlotte wondered whether to lay the table. And Prosper Donge didn't know what to do or where to go.

'We could go into the sitting-room . . .' he suggested.

'You forget there's no fire there . . . You'll freeze! . . . If you two want to talk, I can go up and get dressed . . . You see, Superintendent, we play a sort of game of musical chairs . . . When I get back, he goes out . . . When he gets back it's almost time for me to go, and we just about have time to have something to eat together . . . And even our days off hardly ever seem to coincide, so that when he has a free day he has to get his own lunch . . . Would you like a drink? . . . Can you get him something, Prosper? . . . I'll go up . . .'

Maigret hurriedly interrupted: 'Not at all, Madame . . . Do please stay . . . I'm just off . . . You see a crime was committed this morning, at the Majestic . . . I wanted to ask your . . . your friend a few questions, as the crime occurred in the basement, at a time when he was almost the only person down there.'

He had to make an effort to continue the cruel game, because Donge's face – did he look like a fish, or was it a sheep? – Donge's face expressed so much painful anguish. He was trying to keep calm. He almost succeeded. But at the cost of how much inner turmoil?

Only Charlotte seemed unmoved, and calmly poured out the drinks in small gold-rimmed glasses.

'Something to do with one of the staff?' she said with surprise, but still unperturbed.

'In the basement, but not one of the staff . . . That is what is so puzzling about the whole affair . . . Imagine to yourself a hotel guest, from one of the luxury suites, staying at the Majestic with her husband, her son, a nanny and a governess . . . A suite costing more than a thousand francs a day . . . Well, at six o'clock in the morning she is strangled, not in her room, but in the cloakroom in the basement . . . In all probability, the crime was committed there . . . What was the woman doing in the basement? Who had lured her down there, and why? . . . Especially at a time when people of that sort are usually still fast asleep . . .'

It was barely noticeable: a slight knitting of the brows, as if an idea had occurred to Charlotte and was immediately dismissed. A quick glance at Prosper who was warming his hands over the stove. He had very white hands, with square fingers, covered with red hairs.

But Maigret continued relentlessly: 'It won't be easy to find out what this Mrs Clark had come down to the basement to do . . .'

He held his breath, forced himself to remain motionless, to look as if he were studying the oilcloth tablecloth. You could have heard a pin drop.

Maigret seemed to be trying to give Charlotte time to regain her composure. She had frozen. Her mouth was half open, but no words came out. Then they heard her make a vague noise which sounded like: 'Ah!'

Too bad! It was his job. His duty.

'I was wondering if you knew her . . .'

'Me?'

'Not by the name of Mrs Clark, which she has only been called for a little over six years, but under the name of Émilienne, or rather Mimi . . . She was a hostess, in Cannes, at the time when . . .'

Poor plump Charlotte! What a bad actress she was. Looking at the ceiling like that as if she were racking her memory. Making her eyes look much too rounded and innocent!

'Émilienne? . . . Mimi? . . . No! I don't think . . . You're sure it was Cannes?'

'In a club which was then called La Belle Étoile, just behind the Croisette . . .'

'It's strange . . . I don't remember a Mimi . . . Do you, Prosper?'

It was a miracle he didn't choke. What was the point of forcing him to talk, when his throat was constricted as if by a vice?

'N – no . . .'

Nothing had outwardly changed. There was still that pleasant homely smell in the kitchen, the walls of the little house exuding a reassuring warmth, still the familiar smell of meat braising on a bed of golden onions. The red-and-white-checked oilcloth on the table. Cake crumbs. Like most women who have a tendency to grow fat, Charlotte probably went in for orgies of solitary cake-eating.

And the shrimp-pink silk petticoat!

Then suddenly, the tension evaporated. For no apparent reason. Someone coming in would probably have thought that the Donge family were quietly entertaining a neighbour.

Only none of them dared say a word. Poor Prosper, his skin pitted as a sieve with pock marks, had shut his periwinkle-blue eyes and was standing swaying by the stove, looking as though he would fall on the kitchen floor at any minute.

Maigret got up with a sigh.

'I'm so sorry to have disturbed you . . . It's time I . . .'

'I'll come to the door with you . . .' Charlotte said quickly. 'It's time I got dressed anyway . . . I have to be there at ten, and there's only one bus an hour in the evenings . . . So . . .'

'Good night, Donge . . .'

'Goo –'

He possibly said the rest, but they didn't hear him. Maigret found his bicycle outside. She shut the door. He nearly looked through the keyhole, but someone was coming down the road and he didn't want to be caught in that position.

He braked all the way down the hill, and stopped in front of a bistro.

'Can you keep this bicycle for me, if I send for it tomorrow morning?'

He swallowed the first thing that came to hand and went to wait for the bus at the Pont de Saint-Cloud. For more than an hour Police Sergeant Lucas had been telephoning frantically, trying in vain to locate his boss.

3

Charlotte at The Pélican

'There you are at last, Monsieur Maigret!'

Standing in the doorway of his flat in the Boulevard Richard-Lenoir, the Superintendent couldn't help smiling, not because his wife called him 'Monsieur Maigret', which she often did when she was joking, but at the warm smell which came to meet him and which reminded him . . .

It was a long way from Saint-Cloud and he lived in a very different milieu to that of the unmarried Donge couple . . . But nevertheless, on his return he found Madame Maigret sewing, not in the kitchen, but in the dining-room, her feet not on the cooker but on the dining-room stove. And he could have sworn that here too there were some cake crumbs tucked away somewhere.

A hanging lamp above the round table. A cloth with a large round soup tureen in the middle, a carafe of wine, a carafe of water, and table-napkins in round silver rings. The smell coming from the kitchen was exactly the same as that from the Donges' stew . . .

'They've rung three times.'

'From the House?'

That was what he and his colleagues called Police Headquarters.

He took off his coat with a sigh of relief, warmed his hands over the stove for a minute, and remembered that Prosper Donge had done exactly the same a short while ago. Then he picked up the receiver and dialled a number.

'Is that you, Chief?' asked Lucas's kindly voice at the other end of the line. 'All right? . . . Anything new? . . . I've got one or two small things to report, which is why I'm still here . . . First, about the governess . . .

'Janvier has been shadowing her since she left the Majestic . . . Do you know what Janvier says about her? . . . He says that in her country she must be a gangster, not a governess . . .

'Hullo! . . . Well I'll give you a brief run-down of what happened . . . She left the hotel soon after talking to you . . . Instead of taking the taxi the doorman had called for her, she jumped into a taxi which was passing and Janvier was hard put to it not to lose her . . .

'When they got to the Grands Boulevards, she leapt down the métro . . . then twice doubled back on her tracks. Janvier didn't give up and followed her to the Gare de Lyon . . . He was afraid she might take a train, because he hadn't enough money on him . . .

'The Rome Express was about to leave from Platform 4 – in ten minutes' time. Ellen Darroman looked in all the compartments . . . Just as she was turning back, disappointed, a tall, very elegant bloke arrived, carrying a bag . . .'

'Oswald J. Clark . . .' said Maigret, who was looking vaguely at his wife, while listening. 'She obviously wanted to warn him . . .'

'According to Janvier, it appears that they met rather as good friends than as an employer and his employee . . . Have you seen Clark? He's a great tall, lanky devil; muscular, with the open, healthy face of a baseball player . . . They went along the platform arguing, as if Clark was still thinking of going . . . When the train started, he still hadn't made up his mind, because it looked for a minute as though he was going to jump into the train.

'Then they went out of the station. They hailed a taxi. A few minutes later, they were at the American Embassy, in the Avenue Gabriel . . .

'They then went to the Avenue Friedland, to see a consulting barrister, a *solicitor* as they call it . . .

'The solicitor telephoned the examining magistrate, and three-quarters of an hour later all three of them arrived at the Palais de Justice and were taken at once to the magistrate's office . . .

'I don't know what went on inside, but the magistrate wanted you to telephone him as soon as you got back . . . It seems it is very urgent . . .

'To conclude Janvier's story, after leaving the Palais de Justice, our three characters went to the Forensic Laboratory to identify the body officially . . . Then they went back to the Majestic and there, Clark had two whiskies in the bar with the solicitor while the young woman went up to her room . . .

'That's all, Chief . . . The magistrate seems very anxious to have a word with you . . . What time is it? He'll be at home until eight; Turbigo 25–62 . . . Then he's having dinner with some friends, whose number he gave me . . . Just a minute . . . Galvani 47–53 . . .

'Do you need me any more, Chief? Good night . . . Torrence will be on duty tonight . . .'

'Can I serve the soup?' Madame Maigret asked, sighing, shaking little bits of cotton off her dress.

'Get my dinner-jacket first . . .'

As it was after eight, he dialled Galvani 47–53. It was the number of a young Deputy. A maid answered and he could hear the sound of knives and forks and an excited buzz of conversation.

'I'll go and call the Magistrate . . . Who is speaking? Superintendent Négret? . . .'

Through the open door of the bedroom, he could see the wardrobe and Madame Maigret taking out his dinner-jacket . . .

'Is that you, Superintendent? . . . Hum . . . Ha . . . You don't speak English, do you? . . . Hullo! Don't ring off . . . That's what I thought . . . I wanted to say . . . Hum! . . . it's about this case, naturally . . . I think it would be better if you didn't concern yourself with . . . I mean not directly . . . with Mr Clark and his staff . . .'

A slight smile hovered round Maigret's mouth.

'Monsieur Clark came to see me this afternoon with the governess . . . He's a man of some standing, with important connections . . . Before he came to see me, I had had a call from the American Embassy who gave me a very good account of him . . . So you see what I mean? . . . In a case like this, one must be careful not to make a mistake . . .

'Monsieur Clark was with his solicitor and insisted on his statement being taken down . . .

'Hullo! Are you still there, Superintendent?'

'Yes, sir, I'm listening . . .'

The sound of forks in the background. The conversation had ceased. No doubt the Deputy's guests were listening attentively to what the magistrate was saying.

'I'll put you briefly in the picture . . . Tomorrow morning my clerk can let you have the text of the statement . . . Monsieur Clark did have to go to Rome, then on to various other capitals, for business reasons . . . He had recently become engaged to Miss Ellen Darroman . . .'

'Excuse me, sir. You said engaged? I thought Monsieur Clark was married . . .'

'Yes, yes . . . That doesn't mean that he didn't intend getting divorced shortly . . . His wife didn't know yet . . . We can therefore say engaged . . . He took advantage of the trip to Rome to . . .'

'To spend a night in Paris first with Miss Darroman . . .'

'Quite. But you're wrong, Superintendent, to indulge in sarcasm. Clark made an excellent impression on me. Morals aren't quite the same in his country as in ours, and divorce over there . . . Well, he made no secret of how he had spent the night . . . In your absence, I referred the matter to Inspector Ducuing for verification, to make doubly sure, but I'm certain Clark wasn't lying . . . Under the circumstances, it would be unfortunate if . . .'

Which meant, in fact:

'We are dealing with a man of the world, who has the protection of the American Embassy. So in the circumstances, don't interfere, because you're likely to be tactless and offend him. See the people in the basement, the maids and so on. But leave Clark to me – I'll deal with him myself!'

'I understand, sir! Of course, sir . . .'

And turning to his wife:

'You can serve the soup, Madame Maigret!'

It was nearly midnight. The long corridor at Police Headquarters was deserted, and so dimly lit that it seemed to be filled with a dense smog. Maigret's patent-leather shoes, which he seldom wore, creaked like those of a first-time communicant.

In his office, he began by raking the stove and warming his

hands, then, pipe in mouth, he opened the door of the inspectors' office.

Ducuing was there, busy telling Torrence a story which seemed to be amusing them both highly; both men were in great good humour.

'Well, lads?'

And Maigret sat down on a corner of the wooden, ink-stained table, tapping the ash from his pipe on to the floor. He could relax here. The two inspectors had had beer sent up from the Brasserie Dauphine and the Superintendent was pleased to see they hadn't forgotten him.

'You know, Chief, that man Clark's an odd bloke . . . I went to have a good look at him in the Majestic bar, so that I could see him at close quarters and register his appearance . . . And at that point I thought he looked the typical businessman, rather a tough customer in fact . . . Well, now I know how he spent last night, and I can assure you he's a bit of a lad . . .'

Torrence couldn't help eyeing the Superintendent's gleaming white shirt-front, adorned with two pearls, which he didn't often see him wearing.

'Listen . . . First he and the girl dined in a cheap restaurant in the Rue Lepic . . . You know the kind I mean . . . The proprietor noticed them, because he doesn't often get asked for real champagne . . . Then they asked where there was a merry-go-round . . . They had difficulty in explaining what they wanted . . . He finally directed them to the Foire du Trône . . .

'I caught up with them again there . . . I don't know if they had a ride on the merry-go-round, but I imagine they did . . . They also had a go at the rifle range, I know, because Clark spent over a hundred francs there, much to the amazement of the good lady running it . . .

'You know the kind of thing . . . Wandering through the crowd, arm in arm, like two young lovers . . . But now we're coming to the best part . . . Listen . . .

'You know Eugène the Muscle-Man's booth? At the end of his show he threw down the gauntlet to the crowd . . . There was a sort of colossus there who took up the challenge . . . Well . . . our Clark took him on . . . He went to get undressed behind a filthy bit of canvas and made short work of the said colossus . . . I imagine the girl was applauding in the front row of the crowd . . . Everyone was shouting:

'"Go it, the Englishman! . . . Bash his face in!"

'After which our two lovers went dancing at the Moulin de la Galette . . . And at about three they were to be seen at the Coupole, eating grilled sausages, and I imagine they then went quietly off to bye-byes . . .

'The Hotel Aiglon has no doorman. Only a night porter who sleeps in his little room and pulls the door-pull without bothering too much about who comes in . . . He remembers hearing someone talking in English at about four in the morning . . . He says no one went out . . .

'And that's it! Don't you think it's rather an odd evening for people who are supposed to be staying at the Majestic?'

Maigret didn't answer one way or the other, and, glancing at his wrist-watch, which he only wore on special occasions (it was a twentieth wedding anniversary present), got up from the table where he'd been sitting.

'Good night, children . . .'

He was already at the door, when he came back to finish his glass of beer. He had to walk two or three hundred yards before he found a taxi.

'Rue Fontaine . . .'

It was 1 a.m. Night life in Montmartre was in full swing. A Negro met him at the door of the Pélican and he was obliged to leave his coat and hat in the cloakroom. He hesitated a bit, as if unsure of himself, on entering the main room, where rolls of coloured thread and streamers were flying through the air.

'A table by the cabaret? . . . This way . . . Are you alone?'

He was reduced to muttering under his breath to the maître d'hôtel, who hadn't recognized him: 'Idiot!'

The barman however had spotted him at once, and was whispering to two hostesses who were propping themselves up at the bar.

Maigret sat down at a table and, as he couldn't drink beer there, ordered a brandy and water. Less than ten minutes later the proprietor, who had been discreetly summoned, came to sit down opposite him.

'Nothing out of order, I hope, Superintendent? . . . You know I've always abided by the rules and . . .'

He glanced round the room, as if to see what could have caused this unexpected visit from the police.

'Nothing . . .' Maigret replied. 'I felt in need of entertainment . . .'

He pulled his pipe out of his pocket, but saw from the proprietor's face that it would be out of place there, and put it back, sighing.

'If you need any information of any kind . . .' the other said, winking. 'But I know all my staff personally . . . I don't think there's anyone here at present who could be of interest to you . . . As for the customers, you can see for yourself . . . The usual crowd . . . Foreigners, people up from the provinces . . . Look! That man over there with Léa is a Deputy . . .'

Maigret got up and walked heavily over to the stairs leading to the toilets. These were in a brightly lit basement room, with bluish tiles on the walls. Wooden telephone booths. Mirrors. And a long table on which were numerous toilet articles: brushes, combs, a manicure set, every conceivable shade of powder, rouge and so on . . .

'It's always the same when you dance with him. Give me another pair of stockings, Charlotte . . .'

A plump young woman in an evening dress was sitting on a chair and had already taken off one stocking. She sat there with her skirt hitched up, inspecting her bare foot, while Charlotte rummaged in a drawer.

'Size 44, sheer ones, again?'

'Yes, that will do. I'll take those. If a bloke doesn't know how to dance, he ought at least . . .'

She caught sight of Maigret in the glass and went on putting on her new stockings, glancing at him occasionally as she did so. Charlotte turned round. She, too, saw the Superintendent, who saw her turn visibly paler.

'Ah! It's you . . .'

She forced a laugh. She was no longer the same woman who had put her feet on the hob and who stuffed herself with pastries, in the little house in Saint-Cloud.

Her blonde hair was dressed with so much care that the waves seemed permanently glued in place. Her skin was a sugary pink. Her rounded figure was sheathed in a very simple black silk dress, over which she wore a frilly little lace apron of the kind usually only worn by soubrettes in the theatre.

'I'll pay for those with the rest, Charlotte . . .'

'Yes, all right . . .'

The girl realized that the stranger was only waiting for her to go and, as soon as she had her shoes on again, she hurried upstairs.

Charlotte, who was making a show of tidying the brushes and combs, was finally forced to ask: 'What do you want?'

Maigret didn't answer. He had sat down on the chair left vacant by the girl with the laddered stockings. As he was in the basement he seized the chance of filling his pipe, slowly, with immense care.

'If you think I know anything, you're mistaken . . .'

It is a strange fact that women who have a placid temperament are the ones who show their emotions the most. Charlotte was trying to keep calm, but she couldn't prevent the waves of colour mounting to her face, or her hands moving so clumsily over the toilet articles that she dropped a nail-polisher.

'I could see, from the way you looked at me, just now, when you visited our house, that you thought . . .'

'I take it you never knew a dancer or night-club hostess called Mimi, is that correct?'

'No, never!'

'And yet you were a bar-girl in Cannes for a long time . . . You were there at the same time as this Mimi . . .'

'There isn't only one night club in Cannes, and you don't meet everyone, you know . . .'

'You were at the Belle Étoile, weren't you?'

'What if I was?'

'Nothing . . . I just wanted to come and have a chat with you . . .'

They were silent for at least five minutes, because a customer came down, washed his hands, combed his hair, then asked for a cloth to polish his patent-leather shoes with. When he had finally left a five-franc piece in the saucer, the Superintendent continued: 'I feel great sympathy for Prosper Donge . . . I feel sure he's the nicest man in the world . . .'

'Oh yes! You don't know how good he is!' she cried fervently.

'He had a miserable childhood and he seems to have always had to struggle for . . .'

'And do you know he didn't pass any exams at school and everything he's learnt he's taught himself? . . . If you look in his still-room you'll find books which people like us don't usually read . . . He's always had a passion for learning things . . . He always dreamt of . . .'

She suddenly stopped, tried to regain her composure.

'Did I hear the telephone ring?'

'No, I don't think so . . .'

'What was I saying?'

'That he always dreamt of . . .'

'Oh well! There's no secret about it. He would have liked to have had a son, make someone of him . . . He chose badly with me, poor lad, because since my operation I can't have children.'

'Do you know Jean Ramuel?'

'No. I know he's the book-keeper and that he's not very well, that's all. Prosper doesn't tell me much about the Majestic . . . Not like me; I tell him everything that happens here . . .'

Having reassured her, he tried to make a bit of headway again.

'You see, what struck me was . . . I oughtn't to tell you this . . . it's officially a secret . . . But I feel sure it won't go any further . . . Well, the automatic which was found in this Mrs Clark's handbag had been bought the day before at a gunsmith's in the Faubourg Saint-Honoré . . . Don't you think that that's very odd? There's this rich, married woman, a mother of a family, who arrives from New York and stays in a luxury hotel in the Champs-Élysées, and who suddenly feels the need to buy a gun . . . And note that it wasn't a pretty little lady's pistol, but a proper weapon . . .'

He avoided her eye, looked at the gleaming toecaps of his shoes, as if amazed at his own smartness.

'Now we know that this same woman slipped down a back staircase a few hours later, to get to the hotel basement . . . One is bound to think that she had a rendezvous . . . And to conclude that it was in view of this rendezvous that she had bought her gun. Suppose for a moment that this woman, who is now so respectable, had a stormy past in days gone by and that someone who knew her at that time had tried to blackmail her . . . Do you know if Ramuel ever lived on the Riviera? . . . Or a certain professional dancing-partner called Zebio? . . .'

'I don't know him.'

He could tell, without looking at her, that she was on the point of bursting into tears.

'And there's one other person – the night porter – who could have killed her, because he went down to the basement at about six in the morning . . . It was Prosper Donge who heard him going up the back stairs . . . Not to mention any of the room waiters . . . It's a great pity that you didn't know Mimi in Cannes . . . You could have given me details of all the people she knew then . . . Oh well! I would have liked not to have had to go to Cannes . . . I'm bound to be able to find some of the people who knew her, down there . . .'

He got up, tapped out his pipe, felt in his pocket for some change for the saucer.

'You don't need to do that!' she protested.

'Good night . . . I wonder what time there's a train . . .'

As soon as he got upstairs, he paid his bill and rushed across the street to the bar opposite, a café frequented by employees from all the night clubs in the district.

'The telephone, please . . .'

He got on to the exchange.

'Judicial Police, here. Someone from the Pélican will probably ask you for a Cannes number. Don't connect them too quickly . . . Wait till I get to you . . .'

He leapt into a taxi. Rushed to the telephone exchange and made himself known to the night supervisor.

'Give me some headphones . . . Have they asked for Cannes?'

'Yes, a minute ago . . . I found out whose number it was . . . It's the Brasserie des Artistes, which stays open all night . . . Shall I put them through?'

Maigret put on the headphones and waited. Some of the telephone girls, also wearing headphones, stared at him curiously.

'I'm putting you through to Cannes 18–43, Mademoiselle . . .'

'Thank you . . . Hullo! The Brasserie des Artistes? . . . Who's speaking? . . . Is that you, Jean? . . . It's Charlotte here . . . Yes! . . . Charlotte from the Belle Étoile . . . Wait . . . I'll shut the door . . . I think there's someone . . .'

They heard her talking, probably to a customer. Then the sound of a door being shut.

'Listen, Jean dear . . . It's very important . . . I'll write and explain . . . No, I don't think I'd better! It's too risky . . . I'll come and see you later, when it's all over . . . Is Gigi still there? What? Still the same . . . You must be sure to tell her that if anyone questions her about Mimi . . . You remember? . . . Oh no, you weren't there then . . . Well, if she's asked anything at all about her . . . Yes! She knows nothing! . . . And she must be particularly careful not to say anything about Prosper . . .'

'Prosper who?' asked Jean on the other end of the line.

'Never you mind . . . She doesn't know anyone called Prosper, do you hear me? . . . Or Mimi . . . Hullo! Are you there . . . Is there someone else on the line? . . .'

Maigret realized that she was scared, that it had perhaps occurred to her that someone was listening to the conversation.

'You understand, Jean dear? . . . I can rely on you? . . . I'm hanging up because there's someone . . .'

Maigret also took off his headphones, and relit his pipe, which had gone out.

'Did you learn what you wanted to know?' asked the supervisor.

'Indeed, yes . . . Get me the Gare de Lyon . . . I must find out what time there's a train for Cannes . . . Provided I've got . . .'

He looked at his dinner-jacket in irritation. Provided he had time to . . .

'Hullo! . . . What did you say? . . . Seventeen minutes past four? . . . And I get there at two in the afternoon? . . . Thank you . . .'

Just time to hurry back to the Boulevard Richard-Lenoir and to laugh at Madame Maigret's ill humour.

'Quick, my suit . . . A shirt . . . Socks . . .'

At seventeen minutes past four he was in the Riviera express, sitting opposite a woman who had a horrible pekinese on her lap and who kept looking sideways at Maigret, as though suspecting him of not liking dogs.

At about the same time, Charlotte was getting into a taxi, as she did each night. The driver dealt mostly with customers from the Pélican and took her home free.

At five, Prosper Donge heard a car door slamming, the sound of the engine, footsteps, the key in the door.

But he didn't hear the usual 'Pfffttt' of the gas in the kitchen. Without pausing on the ground floor, Charlotte rushed upstairs and banged the door open, panting: 'Prosper! . . . Listen! Don't pretend to be asleep . . . The Superintendent . . .'

Before she could explain, she had to undo her bra and take off her girdle, so that her stockings were left dangling round her legs.

'Look, it's serious! Well get up then! . . . Do you think it's easy talking to a man who just lies there! . . .'

4

Gigi and the Carnival

For the next three hours, Maigret had the unpleasant feeling that he was floundering in a sort of no man's land between dream and reality. Perhaps it was his fault? Until after Lyon, as far as about Montélimar, the train had rolled through a tunnel of mist. The woman with the little dog, opposite the Superintendent, didn't budge from her seat, and there were no empty compartments.

Maigret couldn't get comfortable. It was too hot. If he opened the window, it was too cold. So he had gone along to the restaurant car and, to cheer himself up, had drunk some of everything – coffee, then brandy and then beer.

At about eleven, feeling sick, he told himself he'd feel better if he ate something and ordered some ham and eggs, which were no improvement on the rest.

He was suffering from his sleepless night, the long hours in the train; he was in a very bad temper in fact. After leaving Marseilles, he fell asleep in his corner, with his mouth open, and started awake, stupid with surprise, when he heard Cannes announced.

There was mimosa everywhere, under a brilliant 14th July sun, on the engines, on the carriages, on the station railings. And crowds of holidaymakers in light clothes, the men in white trousers . . .

Dozens of them were pouring out of a local train, wearing peaked caps, with brass instruments under their arms. He was hardly out of the station before he ran into another band, already rending the air with martial notes.

It was an orgy of light, sound, colour. With flags, banners and oriflammes flying on all sides, and everywhere, the golden yellow mimosa, filling the whole town with its all-pervading, sweetish scent.

'Excuse me, Sergeant,' he asked a festive-looking policeman, 'can you tell me what it's all about?'

The man looked at him as though he had landed from the moon.

'Not heard of the Battle of Flowers?'

Other brass bands were winding through the streets, making for the sea, which could be seen from time to time, lying, pastel blue, at the end of a street.

Later he remembered a little girl dressed as a pierrette, being dragged hurriedly along by her mother, probably in order to get a good place for the pageant. There would have been nothing unusual about it if the little girl hadn't worn a strange mask over her face, with a long nose, red cheeks and drooping Chinese moustache. Trotting along on her chubby little legs . . .

He had no need to ask the way. Going down a quiet street towards the Croisette he saw a sign: BRASSERIE DES ARTISTES. A door farther on: HOTEL. And he saw at a glance what kind of hotel it was.

He went in. Four men dressed in black, with rigid bow ties and white dickeys, were playing *belote*, while waiting to go and take up their positions as croupiers in the casino. By the window, there was a girl eating sauerkraut. The waiter was wiping the tables. A young man, who looked as though he was the proprietor, was reading a newspaper behind the bar. And from outside, from far and near, on all sides, came echoes of the brass bands, and a stale whiff of mimosa, dust kicked up by the feet of the crowd, shouts and the honking of hooters . . .

'A half!' grunted Maigret, at last able to take off his heavy overcoat.

He found it almost embarrassing to be as darkly clad as the croupiers.

He had exchanged glances with the proprietor as soon as he came in.

'Tell me, Monsieur Jean . . .'

And Monsieur Jean was clearly thinking . . .

'That one's probably a cop . . .'

'Have you had this bar a long time?'

'I took it over nearly three years ago . . . Why?'

'And before that?'

'If it's of any interest to you, I was barman at the Café de la Paix, in Monte Carlo . . .'

Barely a hundred metres away, along the Croisette, were the luxury hotels: the Carlton, the Miramar, the Martinez, and others . . .

It was clear that the Brasserie des Artistes was a backstage prop, as it were, to the more fashionable scene. The whole street was the same in fact, with dry-cleaning shops, hairdressers, drivers' bistros, little businesses in the shadow of the grand hotels.

'The bar's open all night, is it?'

'All night, yes . . .'

Not for the winter visitors, but for the casino and hotel staff, dancers, hostesses, bell-boys, hotel touts, go-betweens of all kinds, pimps, tipsters, or night-club bouncers.

'Anything else you want to know?' Monsieur Jean asked curtly.

'I'd like you to tell me where I can find someone called Gigi . . .'

'Gigi? . . . Don't know her . . .'

The woman eating sauerkraut was watching them wearily. The croupiers got up: it was nearly three o'clock.

'Look, Monsieur Jean . . . Have you ever had any trouble over fruit machines or anything like that? . . .'

'What's that to do with you?'

'I ask because if you've ever been convicted, the case will be much more serious . . . Charlotte's a good sort . . . She telephones her friends to ask their help, but forgets to tell them what it's about . . . So if one has a business like yours, if one's already been in a spot of trouble once or twice, one generally doesn't want to become incriminated . . . Well – I'll telephone the vice squad and I'm sure they won't have any difficulty telling me where I can find Gigi . . . Have you got a token?'

He had got up, begun walking towards the telephone booth.

'Excuse me! You spoke of becoming incriminated . . . Is it serious?'

'Well, a murder's involved . . . if a Superintendent from the special squad comes down from Paris, you can take it . . .'

'Just a minute, Superintendent . . . Do you really want to see Gigi?'

'I've come more than a thousand kilometres to do so . . .'

'Come with me then! But I must warn you that she won't be able to tell you very much . . . Do you know her? . . . She's useless for two days out of three . . . When she's found some dope, I mean, if you get me? . . . Well, yesterday . . .'

'Yesterday, it so happened that, after Charlotte's telephone call, she found some, didn't she? Where is she?'

'This way . . . She's got a room somewhere in town, but last night she was incapable of walking . . .'

A door led to the staircase of the hotel. The proprietor pointed to a room on the landing.

'Someone for you, Gigi!' he shouted.

And he waited at the top of the stairs until Maigret had shut the door. Then went back to his counter, shrugged, and picked up his newspaper, looking a little worried despite himself.

The closed curtains let in only a luminous glow. The room was in a mess. A woman lay on the iron bed, with her clothes on, her hair awry, her face buried in the pillow. She began asking in a thick voice: '. . . d'you want?'

Then a very bleary eye appeared.

'. . . been here before?'

Pinched nostrils. A wax-like complexion. Gigi was thin, angular, brown as a prune.

'. . . time is it? . . . Aren't you going to get undressed? . . .'

She propped herself up on one elbow to drink some water, and stared at Maigret, making a visible effort to pull herself together, and, seeing him sitting gravely on a chair by her bed, asked: 'You the doctor? . . .'

'What did Monsieur Jean tell you, last night?'

'Jean? . . . Jean's all right . . . He gave me . . . But what business is it of yours?'

'Yes, I know. He gave you some snow . . . Lie down again . . . And he spoke to you about Mimi and Prosper.'

The bands still blaring outside, coming closer and then dying away, and still the stale scent of mimosa, with its own indefinable smell.

'Good old Prosper! . . .'

She spoke as if she were half asleep. Her voice occasionally took on a childish note. Then she suddenly screwed up her eyes and her brow became furrowed as if she were in violent pain. Her mouth was slack.

'You got some, then?'

She wanted some more of the drug. And Maigret had the unpleasant feeling that he was extracting secrets from someone who was sick and delirious.

'You were fond of Prosper, weren't you?'

'. . . He's not like other people . . . He's too good . . . He shouldn't have fallen for a woman like Mimi, but that's always the way . . . Do you know him?'

Come on now! Make an effort. Wasn't that what he, Maigret, was there for?

'It was when he was at the Miramar, wasn't it? . . . There were three of you dancing at the Belle Étoile . . . Mimi, Charlotte and you . . .'

She stuttered solemnly: 'You mustn't say unkind things about Charlotte . . . She's a good girl . . . And she was in love with Prosper . . . If he'd listened to me . . .'

'I suppose you met at the café, after work . . . Prosper was Mimi's lover . . .'

'He was besotted, he was so much in love with her . . . Poor Prosper! . . . And afterwards, when she . . .'

She sat up suddenly, suspicious: 'Is it true that you're a friend of Prosper's?'

'When she had a baby, you mean? . . .'

'Who told you that? I was the only person she wrote to about it . . . But it didn't start like that . . .'

She was listening to the music, which was drawing nearer once more.

'What's that?'

'Nothing . . .'

The flower-decked wagons filing along the Croisette as guns were fired to announce the start. The blazing sun, calm sea, motorboats cutting circles through the water and small yachts gracefully swooping . . .

'Are you sure you haven't got any? . . . You won't go and ask Jean for some? . . .'

'It began when she left with the American?'

'Did Prosper tell you that? . . . Give me another glass of water, there's a good bloke . . . A Yank she met at the Belle Étoile, who fell in love with her . . . He took her to Deauville, then Biarritz . . . I must admit Mimi knew how to do things properly . . . She wasn't like the rest of us . . . Is Charlotte still working at the Pélican? . . . And look at me! . . .'

She gave a dreadful laugh, disclosing villainous teeth.

'One day, she just wrote that she was going to have a baby and that she was going to make the American think it was his . . . What was he called now? . . . Oswald. Then she wrote again to tell me that it nearly went wrong because the baby had hair the colour of a carrot . . . Can you imagine it! I wouldn't want Prosper to know that . . .'

Was it the effect of the two glasses of water she had drunk? She pulled one leg after the other out of bed, long, thin legs which would attract few male glances. When she was standing upright, she appeared tall, skeleton-like. What long hours she must spend pacing up and down the dark pavements or loitering at a café table before she got any results . . .

Her stare became more fixed. She examined Maigret from head to toe.

'You're from the police, eh?'

She was getting angry. But her mind was still cloudy and she was making an effort to clear her thoughts.

'What did Jean tell me? . . . Ah! . . . And who brought you here anyway? . . . He made me promise not to talk to anyone . . . Admit it! . . . Admit you're from the police . . . And I . . . Why should it matter to the police, if Prosper and Mimi . . .'

The storm broke, suddenly, violently, sickeningly: 'You dirty bastard! . . . Swine! . . . You took advantage of me being . . .'

She had opened the door, and the sounds from outside could be heard even more clearly.

'If you don't get out at once, I'll . . . I'll . . .'

It was ridiculous, pathetic. Maigret just managed to sidestep the jug she threw at his legs, and she was still hurling abuse after him as he went down the stairs.

The bar was empty. It was too early still.

'Well?' Monsieur Jean asked, from behind his counter.

Maigret put on his coat and hat, and left a tip for the waiter.

'Did she tell you what you wanted?'

A voice, from the stairs: 'Jean! . . . Jean! . . . Come here – I must tell you . . .'

It was poor wretched Gigi, who had padded down in her stockings and now pushed a dishevelled head round the door of the bar.

Maigret thought it better to leave.

On the Croisette, in his black coat and bowler hat, he must have looked like a provincial come to see the carnival on the Côte d'Azur for the first time. Masked figures bumped into him. He had difficulty disentangling himself from the brass bands. On the beach, a few winter visitors ignored the festival and were sunbathing: their near-naked bodies already brown, covered with oil . . .

The Miramar was down there, a vast yellow structure with two or three hundred windows, with its doorman, car attendants and touts . . . He nearly went in . . . But what was the use?

Didn't he already know everything he needed to know? He no longer knew if he was thirsty or drunk. He went into a bar.

'Have you got a railway timetable?'

'Trains to Paris? There's an express – first, second and third class – at 20.40 hours . . .'

He drank another half litre. There were hours to fill in. He couldn't think what to do. And later, he had nightmare memories of those hours spent in Cannes, amidst the carnival.

At times, the past became so real to him that he could literally see Prosper, with his red hair, great candid eyes, pitted skin, coming out of the Miramar by the little back door and hurrying across to the Brasserie des Artistes.

The three women, who would be six years younger then, would be there having lunch or dinner. Prosper was ugly. He knew it. And he was passionately in love with Mimi, the youngest, and prettiest, of the three.

His burning glances must have made them laugh heartlessly, at first.

'You shouldn't, Mimi,' Charlotte must have intervened. 'He's a good sort. You never know how it may turn out . . .'

Then the Belle Étoile, in the evening. Prosper never set foot inside. He knew his place. But he met them in the early morning to eat onion soup at the café . . .

'If a man like that loved me, I would . . .'

Charlotte must have been impressed by his humble devotion. And Gigi wasn't yet on cocaine.

'Don't take any notice, Monsieur Prosper! . . . She pretends to make fun of you, but at heart . . .'

And they had been lovers! Had lived together perhaps. Prosper spent most of his savings on presents. Until the day when a passing American . . .

Had Charlotte told him, later, that the child was definitely his?

Good, kind Charlotte – She knew he didn't love her, that he still loved Mimi, and yet she was living with him, happily, in their little house in Saint-Cloud.

While Gigi slipped farther and farther . . .

'Some flowers, Monsieur? . . . To send to your little girl-friend . . .'

The flowerseller spoke ironically, because Maigret didn't look like a man who has a little girl-friend. But he sent a basket of mimosa to Madame Maigret.

Then, as he still had half an hour before the train left, a kind of intuition made him telephone Paris. He was in a little bar near the station. The musicians from the bands now had dusty trousers. Whole carriage-loads of them were leaving for near-by stations, and the fine Sunday afternoon was drawing drowsily to a close.

'Hullo! Is that you, Chief? . . . You're still in Cannes?'

He could tell from Lucas's voice that he was excited.

'Things have been happening here . . . The examining magistrate is furious . . . He's just telephoned to know what you are doing . . . Hullo? They made the discovery only three-quarters of an hour ago . . . It was Torrence, who was on duty at the Majestic, who telephoned . . .'

Maigret stood listening to his account in the narrow booth, and grunted from time to time. Through the window, he could see, in the light from the setting sun which filled the bar, the musicians in their white linen trousers and silver-braided caps, and now and then one of them would jokingly sound a long note on his bombardon or trombone, while the golden liquid sparkled in their glasses.

'Right! . . . I'll be there tomorrow morning . . . No! Of course . . . Well if the magistrate insists, you'll have to arrest him . . .'

It had only just happened, then. Downstairs at the Majestic . . . Thé dansant time, with music drifting along the passageways . . . Prosper Donge like a great goldfish in his glass cage . . . Jean Ramuel, yellow as a quince, in his . . .

From what Lucas said – but the inquiry had not yet begun – the night porter had been seen going along the corridors, in his outdoor clothes. No one knew what he was doing there. Everyone had enough to do himself without bothering about what was happening elsewhere.

The night porter was called Justin Colleboeuf. He was a quiet, dull little man, who spent the night alone in the foyer. He didn't read. There was no one to talk to. And he didn't go to sleep. He sat there, on a chair, for hour after hour, staring straight ahead of him.

His wife was the concierge at a new block of flats in Neuilly.

What was Colleboeuf doing there at half past four in the afternoon?

Zebio, the dancer, had gone to the cloakroom to put on his dinner-jacket. Everyone was going about his business. Ramuel had come out of his booth several times.

At five o'clock, Prosper Donge had gone along to the cloakroom. He took off his white jacket and put on his own jacket and coat, and collected his bicycle.

Then a few minutes later a bell-boy went into the cloakroom. He noticed that the door of locker 89 was slightly open. The next minute the whole hotel was alerted by his yells.

In the locker, folded over itself, in a grey overcoat, was the body of the night porter. His felt hat was at the back of the cupboard.

Like Mrs Clark, Justin Colleboeuf had been strangled. The body was still warm.

Meanwhile, Prosper Donge, on his bike, peacefully passed through the Bois de Boulogne, crossed the Pont de Saint-Cloud, and got off his bicycle to go up the steep road to his house.

'A pastis!' Maigret ordered, as there didn't seem to be anything else on the counter.

Then he got into the train, his head as heavy as it had been when he was a child, after a long day in the country, in the blazing sun.

5

Spit on the Window

They had been travelling for some time. Maigret had already taken off his jacket, tie and stiff collar, as the compartment was once again too hot; it was as though hot air, and the smell of the train, was oozing from everywhere – woodwork, floor, seats.

He bent to unlace his shoes. Not content with his free first-class pass, he had taken a couchette; too bad if anyone objected. And the guard had promised him that he would have his compartment to himself.

Suddenly, as he was still bending over his shoes, he had the unpleasant feeling that someone was looking at him, from close to. He looked up. There was a pale face peering through the window from the corridor. Dark eyes. A large mouth, badly made up, or rather enlarged, by two streaks of red applied at random, which had then run.

But the most noticeable thing about the face was its expression of dislike, hatred. How had Gigi got there? Before Maigret could put on his shoe again, the girl's face puckered in disgust and she spat on to the window, in his direction, then went back down the corridor.

He remained impassive, and got dressed. Before leaving the compartment, he lit a pipe, as if for moral support. Then he went down the corridor, from carriage to carriage, assiduously looking in each compartment. The train was a long one. Maigret walked through at least ten coaches, bumped into the partitions, had to disturb fifty or more people.

'Sorry . . . Sorry . . .'

He came to where the carpet ended. The third-class compartments. People were dozing six to a side. Others were eating. Children stared into space.

In a compartment with two sailors from Toulon who were going 'up' to Paris, and an old couple who were nodding off, mouths agape, the woman clutching her basket on her lap, he found Gigi, huddled in a corner.

He hadn't noticed, earlier, in the corridor, how she was dressed. He had been so surprised that he had only taken in that it wasn't the Gigi of the Brasserie des Artistes, with her wandering gaze and slack mouth.

Wrapped in a cheap fur coat, her legs crossed, revealing down-at-heel shoes and a large ladder in her stocking, she stared straight ahead of her. Had she succeeded, on her own, in dragging herself out of the comatose state in which she had been that afternoon? Had someone given her something to take? Or possibly a new dose of cocaine had revived her?

Maigret made no move. He watched her for a while, trying to sign to her; she still took no notice. So he opened the door.

'Would you come out for a minute?'

She hesitated. The two sailors were staring at her. Make a scene? She shrugged and got up to join him, and he shut the door.

'Haven't you had enough?' she hissed at him. 'You should be pleased with yourself, shouldn't you! You should feel proud of yourself! You took advantage of the fact that a poor girl was in the state I was in . . .'

He saw that she was about to cry, that her garishly painted mouth was trembling, and turned away.

'And you didn't lose any time in locking him up, did you!'

'Tell me, Gigi. How do you know Prosper has been arrested?'

A weary gesture.

'Haven't you heard? I thought the telephone tapping would see to that . . . It doesn't matter if I tell you, because you'll soon know . . . Charlotte telephoned Jean . . . Prosper had just got back from work when a taxi full of cops arrived and took him away . . . Charlotte's in a terrible state . . . She wanted to know if I'd talked . . . And I did talk, didn't I? I told you enough to . . .'

A violent jolt of the train made her fall against Maigret, and she recoiled in horror.

'I'll be even with you yet! I swear! Even if Prosper did kill that dirty bitch Mimi . . . I'll tell you something, Superintendent . . . On my honour, the honour of a prostitute, a slut who has nothing to lose, I swear to you that if he's condemned to death, I'll find you and plug you full of holes . . .'

She paused for a moment, scornfully. He didn't say anything. He felt it wasn't an empty threat, that she was just the type, in fact, to wait for him on some lonely street corner and empty her automatic into him.

The two sailors were still watching them from the compartment.

'Good night,' he sighed.

He went back to his compartment, got undressed at last and lay down.

The dimmed light was shedding a vague blue glow on the ceiling. Maigret lay there with his eyes shut, frowning.

One question kept worrying him. Why had the examining magistrate ordered Prosper Donge's arrest? What had the magistrate, who had not left Paris, and who did not know Gigi, or the Brasserie des Artistes, learnt? Why arrest Donge rather than Jean Ramuel or Zebio?

He felt vaguely apprehensive. He knew the magistrate.

He hadn't said anything when he saw him arrive at the Majestic with the public prosecutor, but he had made a face, because he had worked with him in the past.

He was a man of integrity, certainly, a good, family man even, who collected rare editions of books. He had a fine square-cut, grey beard. Maigret had once had to make a raid on a gambling den with him. It was in the daytime, when the place was empty. Pointing to the large baccarat tables shrouded under dust-covers, the magistrate had asked ingenuously: 'Are those billiard tables?'

Then, with the same naïveté of a man who has never set foot in a low dive, he had been amazed to discover three exits into three different streets, one of them leading via the basement to another building. He was even more astonished to learn from the account books that certain players were given large advances, because he didn't know that in order to make people play, you have first to get them hooked.

Why had the magistrate, whose name was Bonneau, suddenly decided to have Donge arrested?

Maigret slept badly, waking up each time the train stopped, the noise and jolting of the carriages becoming mixed with his nightmares.

When he got out of his compartment, at the Gare de Lyon, it was still dark and a fine, cold rain was falling. Lucas was there, with his coat collar turned up, stamping his feet to keep himself warm.

'Not too tired, Chief?'

'Have you got someone with you?'

'No . . . If you need a police inspector, I saw one of our men in the railway office . . .'

'Go and get him . . .'

Gigi got out, shook hands in a friendly way with the two sailors, and shrugged as she went past the Superintendent. She had gone a few steps when she suddenly came back.

'You can have me followed if you want . . . I can tell you in advance that I'm going to see Charlotte . . .'

Lucas came back.

'I couldn't find the inspector . . .'

'Never mind . . . Come on . . .'

They took a taxi.

'Now, let's hear what's happened . . . Why has the magistrate . . .'

'I was going to tell you . . . He summoned me as soon as the second crime had been committed and he had sent some men to arrest Donge . . . He asked me if we had any news, if you'd telephoned and so on . . . Then he handed me a letter, with a nasty smile . . . An anonymous letter . . . I can't remember the exact words . . . It said that Mrs Clark, who was once a chorus girl called Mimi, had been Donge's mistress, that she had a child by him and that he had often threatened her . . . You look as though you're put out, Chief?'

'Go on . . .'

'That's all . . . the magistrate was delighted . . .

'So you see it's a straightforward story!' he concluded. 'Common blackmail . . . And as Mrs Clark no doubt didn't want to pay up . . . I'll go and interrogate Donge shortly in his cell . . .'

'He's there already?'

But the taxi had pulled up at the Quai des Orfèvres. It was half past five in the morning. A thick yellow mist rose from the Seine. Maigret slammed the car door.

'He's at the station? . . . Come with me . . .'

They had to go round the Palais de Justice to get to the Quai de l'Horloge; they went on foot, without hurrying.

'Yes . . . The magistrate telephoned me again at about nine in the evening to say that Donge had refused to speak . . . It appears that he said he would only talk to you . . .'

'Did you get any sleep last night?'

'I got two hours, on a sofa . . .'

'Go and get some rest . . . Be at Headquarters at about midday . . .'

And Maigret went into the Central Police Station. A police van was coming out. There had been a raid at the Bastille and about thirty women had been brought in, some of them new ones without identity cards, and they were sitting round the vast, badly lit room. There was a barrack-room smell, and the air was thick with raucous voices and obscene jokes.

'Where is Donge? . . . Is he asleep?'

'He hasn't slept a wink . . . You'll see for yourself . . .'

The separate boxes were shut by doors with bars, as in a stable. In one of them a man sat, with his head in his hands – a barely discernible figure silhouetted against the darkness.

The key turned in the lock. The hinges creaked. The tall, drooping man got up, as though coming out of a dream. His tie and shoelaces had been taken away. His red hair was unkempt.

'It's you, Superintendent . . .' he whispered.

And he rubbed his eyes with his hand, as if to make sure that it was really Maigret who was there.

'I gather you wanted to speak to me?'

'I thought it would be best . . .'

And he asked, with a childish innocence: 'The magistrate isn't cross? . . . What could I have told him? . . . He was sure I was guilty . . . He even showed my hands to his clerk, saying they were strangler's hands . . .'

'Come with me . . .'

Maigret hesitated a moment. What was the point of making him wear handcuffs? They must have put them on to bring him to the station. The marks were still on his wrists.

One behind the other, they went along strange corridors, which had little resemblance to those in the Majestic basement. Under the vast Palais de Justice to the Judicial Police building, where they suddenly emerged in a brightly lit passage.

'In here . . . Have you had anything to eat?'

The other indicated that he hadn't. Maigret, who was hungry too, and also thirsty, sent the man on duty to fetch beer and sandwiches.

'Sit down, Donge . . . Gigi is in Paris . . . She must be with Charlotte, by now . . . Cigarette?'

He didn't smoke them, but he always kept cigarettes in his drawer. Prosper clumsily lit one, like someone who has suddenly, in the space of a few hours, lost all his self-assurance. He was troubled by his gaping shoes, the absence of a tie, and the smell which, after only one night in the cells, emanated from his clothes.

Maigret stirred up the fire. All the other offices had central heating, which he loathed, and he had managed to keep the old iron stove which had been there for twenty years.

'Sit down . . . they're bringing us something to eat . . .'

Donge was hesitating as to whether to tell him something, and when he finally decided to speak, stammered in an anguished voice: 'Did you see the little boy?'

'No . . .'

'I saw him for a moment in the foyer of the hotel . . . I can swear to you, Superintendent, he's . . .'

'Your son. I know.'

'You should see him! His hair's as red as mine. He has my hands, my large bones . . . They used to laugh at me, when I was a child, because of my big bones . . .'

The beer and sandwiches arrived. Maigret ate standing up, pacing to and fro across his office, while outside, the sky over Paris began to grow lighter.

'I can't . . .' Donge finally sighed, timidly putting his sandwich back on the plate. 'I'm not hungry . . . Whatever happens, they won't take me back at the Majestic now, or anywhere else . . .'

His voice shook. He was waiting for Maigret to help him, but the Superintendent let him flounder on.

'Do you think I killed her, as well?'

As Maigret didn't answer, he nodded miserably. He wanted to explain it all now, persuade his interrogator; but he didn't know where to begin.

'You see I never had much to do with women . . . In our trade . . . And always working down in the basement . . . Some of them burst out laughing when I showed I was fond of them . . . With a face like mine, you see . . . Then, when I knew Mimi, at the Brasserie des Artistes . . . There were three of them . . . You know about that . . . And it's odd how it turns out, isn't it? If I had chosen one of the other two . . . But no! I had to fall in love with her! Crazily in love! Superintendent . . . Madly in love! She could have done anything she liked with me! . . . And I thought she'd agree to marry me one day . . . Well, do you know what the magistrate said to me last night? . . . I can't remember what he said, exactly . . . It made me feel ill . . . He said that what I had really been interested in was the money she brought in . . . He took me for a . . .'

Maigret looked out of the window, to spare him further embarrassment, watching the Seine turn palely silver.

'She left with this American . . . I hoped that he'd desert her when he returned to America and that she'd come back to me . . . Then one day we heard that he'd married her . . . The news made me ill . . . It was Charlotte who out of the goodness of her heart, looked after me . . . I told her I couldn't live in Cannes any longer . . . Every street brought back memories . . . I looked for a job in Paris . . . Charlotte offered to come with me. And you may find it hard to believe, but for a long time we lived together as brother and sister . . .'

'Did you know that Mimi had had a child?' Maigret asked, emptying his pipe into the coal bucket.

'I didn't know anything, except that she was living somewhere in America . . . It was only when Charlotte thought I was better . . . In time, you see, we had become a real couple . . . One evening, a neighbour burst into our house; he was beside himself . . . His wife was about to have a baby, much earlier than had been expected . . . He was frantic . . . He asked us to help . . . Charlotte went over . . . The next day, she said to me, "Poor old Prosper . . . What a state you would have been in, if . . ."

'And then, I don't know quite how it happened . . . bit by bit, she told me that Mimi had a child . . . Mimi had written to Gigi to tell her . . . She had explained that she had used the child as an excuse to make him marry her, although it was definitely mine . . .

'I went to Cannes . . . Gigi showed me the letter, because she'd kept it, but she refused to give it to me and I think she burnt it . . .

'I wrote to America . . . I begged Mimi to give me my son, or at the very least to send me a photograph of him . . . She didn't reply . . . I didn't even know it was the right address . . .

'And I kept thinking: Now my son will be doing this . . . Now he's doing that . . .'

He was silent, choking with emotion, and Maigret pretended to be busy sharpening a pencil, while doors began to bang in the corridors.

'Did Charlotte know you'd written?'

'No. I wrote the letter at the hotel . . . Three years passed . . . One day I was looking at some of the foreign magazines guests leave on their tables . . . I got a shock seeing a photograph of Mimi with a little boy of five . . . It was a newspaper from Detroit, Michigan, and the caption said something like: "The elegant Mrs Oswald J. Clark and her son who have just returned from a cruise in the Pacific . . ."

'I wrote again . . .'

'What did you say?' Maigret asked, in an even tone.

'I don't remember. I was going mad. I begged her to reply. I said . . . I think I said I'd go over there, that I'd tell everyone the truth or that if she refused to give me my son, I'd . . .'

'Yes?'

'I swear I wouldn't have done it . . . Yes, I may have threatened to kill her . . . When I think that for a week she was living over my head, with the boy, and that I never suspected . . .

'I only discovered by chance . . . You saw the guests' servants' hall . . . Names don't exist for us, down in the basement . . . We know that Room no. 117 has chocolate in the morning and that no. 452 has eggs and bacon . . . We know the maid from Room no. 123 and the chauffeur from no. 216 . . .

'It was silly . . . I went into the guests' servants' hall . . . I heard a woman speaking English to a chauffeur and she said the name Mrs Clark . . .

'As I don't speak English, I got the book-keeper to ask her . . . He asked her if she was talking about a Mrs Clark from Detroit, and if she had her son with her . . .

'When I learnt they were there, I tried, for a whole day, to catch sight of them, either in the foyer, or in the corridor on their floor . . . But it's difficult for us to go where we want . . . I didn't succeed . . .

'Don't get me wrong . . . I don't know if you'll understand . . . If Mimi had asked to come and live with me again, I couldn't have . . . Don't I love her any more? . . . That may be it . . . I only know that I wouldn't have the heart to leave Charlotte, who's been so kind to me.

'Well, I didn't want to upset things for her . . . I wanted her to find a way to give me back my son . . . I know Charlotte would be only too happy to bring him up . . .'

Maigret looked at him at that moment, and was struck by the intensity of Prosper Donge's emotion. If he hadn't known he had only drunk a half litre – and had not even finished that! – he would have thought he was drunk. The blood had rushed to his face. His eyes shone – great, protruding eyes. He wasn't crying, but he drew great sobbing breaths.

'Have you got any children, sir?'

It was Maigret's turn to turn away, because it was Madame Maigret's great sorrow that she hadn't got children. It was something he tried not to talk about, himself.

'The magistrate talked all the time . . . According to him, I had done this and that, for such and such a reason . . . But it wasn't like that . . . After spending all my free time for the whole day prowling along the corridors of the hotel, in the vain hope of seeing my son . . . I didn't know what I was doing any longer . . . And the telephone ringing all the time, and the serving-lifts, and my three helpers, and the coffee-pots and milk-jugs to fill . . . I sat down in a corner . . .'

'In the still-room, you mean?'

'Yes. I wrote a letter . . . I wanted to see Mimi . . . I remembered that at six o'clock in the morning I was nearly always alone downstairs . . . I begged her to come . . .'

'You didn't threaten her?'

'Possibly, at the end of the letter . . . Yes, I must have written that if she didn't come within three days, I would do what was necessary . . .'

'And what did you mean by "what was necessary"?'

'I don't know . . .'

'Would you have killed her?'

'I couldn't have done it.'

'You would have kidnapped the child?'

He gave a pathetic, almost half-witted smile.

'Do you think that would be possible?'

'Would you have told her husband everything?'

Prosper Donge's eyes opened wide in horror.

'No! . . . I swear to you! . . . I think . . . Yes I think that if it had come to the worst, I would have killed her rather than do that, in a moment of anger . . . But that morning, I had a puncture when I got to the Avenue Foch . . . I got to the Majestic nearly quarter of an hour late . . . I didn't see Mimi . . . I thought that she had come and that, as she couldn't find me, she had gone back to her suite . . . If I had known her husband had left, I would have gone up by the back stairs . . . But there again, we in the basement know nothing about what's going on above our heads . . . I was worried . . . That morning, I can't have seemed myself . . .'

Maigret suddenly interrupted him.

'What made you go and open locker 89?'

'I can tell you why . . . And it proves I'm not lying, at any rate to anyone from the police, because if I'd known she was dead, I wouldn't have acted as I did . . . It was about a quarter to nine when the waiter on the second floor sent down the order for no. 203 . . . On the slip there was – you can check it, because the management keep them – there was: one hot chocolate, one egg and bacon and one tea.'

'Which meant?'

'I'll explain. I knew that the chocolate was for the boy, the egg and bacon for the nurse . . . So there were only two of them there . . . Every other day at that time there was an order for black coffee and toast for Mimi . . . So, I put the black coffee and toast on the tray too . . . I sent the lift up . . . A few minutes later the coffee and toast were sent back . . . It may seem odd to you to attach so much importance to these details . . . But don't forget that in the basement that's about all we see of what people are doing . . .

'I went to the telephone.

'"Hullo! Didn't Mrs Clark want her breakfast?"

'"Mrs Clark isn't in her room . . ."

'Please believe me, Superintendent . . . The magistrate didn't believe me . . . I was certain that something had happened.'

'What did you think had happened?'

'Oh well! . . . I thought of the husband . . . I thought that if he had followed her . . .'

'Who took the letter up for you?'

'A bell-boy . . . He assured me he had given it to the right person . . . But those boys lie all the time . . . It comes from being with such an odd lot of people . . . And then Clark could have found the letter . . .

'So – I don't know if anyone saw me, but I opened nearly all the doors in the basement . . . Of course no one takes much notice of anyone else, so perhaps no one noticed me . . . I went into the cloakroom . . .'

'Was the door of locker 89 really open?'

'No. I opened all the empty lockers . . . Do you believe me? . . . Will anyone believe me? . . . No, they won't, will they? . . . And that's why I didn't tell the truth . . . I was waiting . . . I hoped no one would pay any attention to me . . . It was only when I saw that I was the only one you weren't questioning . . . I've never felt so awful as I did that day, while you walked up and down in the basement without saying a single word to me, without seeming to see me! . . . I didn't know what I was doing . . .I forgot the instalment I had to go and pay . . . I came back again . . . Then you joined me in the Bois de Boulogne and I knew you were on my track . . .

'The next morning, Charlotte said when she woke me up: "Why didn't you tell me you had killed her? . . ."

'So you see, if even Charlotte . . .'

It was broad daylight, and Maigret hadn't noticed. A stream of buses, taxis and delivery vans was going across the bridge. Paris had come to life again.

Then, after a long silence, and in an even more miserable voice, Prosper Donge mumbled: 'The boy doesn't even speak French! . . . I asked . . . You couldn't go and see him, Superintendent? . . .'

And suddenly frantic: 'No! You're not going to let him go away again? . . .'

'Hullo! . . . Superintendent Maigret? . . . The boss's asking for you . . .'

Maigret sighed, and went out of his office. It was time to make his report. He was in the head of the Judicial Police's office for twenty minutes.

When he got back, Donge was sitting there unmoving, leaning forwards with his arms crossed on the table and his head on his arms.

The Superintendent was worried in spite of himself. But when he touched the prisoner's arm, he slowly looked up, with no attempt to hide his pockmarked face, which was wet with tears.

'The magistrate wants to question you again in his office . . . I advise you to repeat exactly what you have told me . . .'

An inspector was waiting at the door.

'Forgive me if . . .'

Maigret took some handcuffs out of his pocket and there was a double click.

'It's the regulation!' he sighed.

Then, alone in his office once more, he went to open the window and breathed in the damp air. It was a good ten minutes before he went into the inspectors' office.

He appeared fresh and rested again, and asked in his usual way: 'All right, children?'

6

Charlotte's Letter

There were two policemen sitting on the bench, leaning against the wall, their arms crossed on their chests, and their booted legs stretched out as far as possible, barring the way down the corridor.

A low murmur of voices came through the door beside them. And all along the corridor were other doors flanked by benches, on most of which sat policemen, some with a handcuffed prisoner between them.

It was midday. Maigret was smoking his pipe, waiting to go into examining magistrate Bonneau's office.

'What's that?' he asked one of the policemen, pointing to the door.

The reply was as laconic, and as eloquent, as the question: 'Jeweller's in the Rue Saint-Martin . . .'

A girl, sitting slumped on the bench, was staring despairingly at the door of another magistrate. She blew her nose, wiped her eyes, and twisted her hands, tugging at her fingers in a paroxysm of anxiety.

The grim tones of Monsieur Bonneau's voice grew more distinct. The door opened. Maigret automatically stuffed his pipe, which was still warm, into his pocket. The boy who came out, who was at once seized on by the policemen again, had the insolent air of an inveterate ne'er-do-well. He turned back to say to the magistrate with heavy sarcasm: 'I'll be happy to come and see you any time, sir!'

He saw Maigret, and frowned; then, as if reassured, winked at the Superintendent. The latter's face, at that moment, had the abstracted look of someone who vaguely remembers something without quite knowing what it is.

He heard, from behind the door, which had been left open: 'Ask the Superintendent to come in . . . You can go now, Monsieur Benoit . . . I won't need you any more this morning . . .'

Maigret went in, still clearly searching his memory. What was it that had struck him about the prisoner who had just left the magistrate's office?

'Good morning, Superintendent . . . Not too tired, I hope? . . . Please sit down . . . I don't see your pipe . . . You may smoke . . . Well, how was your trip to Cannes?'

Monsieur Bonneau wasn't a spiteful man, but was obviously delighted to have succeeded where the police had failed. He tried unsuccessfully to hide the gleam of satisfaction which glinted in his eye.

'It's funny that we both learnt the same things, I in Paris, without leaving my office, and you on the Côte d'Azur . . . Don't you think?'

'Very funny, yes . . .'

Maigret had the polite smile of a guest who is forced by his hostess to have a second helping of a dish he detests.

'Well, what are your conclusions on the affair, Superintendent? . . . This Prosper Donge? . . . I have his statement here . . . It seems he merely repeated to me what he'd already told you this morning . . . He admits everything, in fact . . .'

'Except the two crimes,' Maigret said quietly.

'Except the two crimes, naturally! That would be too good to be true! He admits that he threatened his ex-mistress; he admits that he asked her to meet him at six in the morning in the basement of the hotel, and his letter can't have been very reassuring because the poor woman went straight out to buy a gun . . . Then he tells us this story of his punctured tyre which made him late . . .'

'It isn't a story . . .'

'How do you know? . . . He could have made a puncture in his tyre when he got to the hotel . . .'

'But he didn't . . . I've found the policeman who called out to him about his tyre that morning, at the corner of the Avenue Foch . . .'

'It's only a detail,' said the magistrate hurriedly, not wanting to have his beautiful reconstruction undermined. 'Tell me, Superintendent, have you looked into Donge's past history?'

The glint of satisfaction was now clearly visible in Monsieur Bonneau's eye, and he couldn't help stroking his beard in anticipation.

'I dare say you haven't had time. I made it a point of interest to consult the records . . . I was given his dossier and I discovered that our man, so docile in appearance, is not a first offender . . .'

Maigret was forced to look contrite.

'It's strange,' went on the magistrate, 'we have these records right above us, on the top floor of the Palais de Justice, and we so often forget to consult them! . . . Well, at the age of sixteen, we find Prosper Donge, who has a job as a washer-up in a café in Vitry-le-François, stealing fifty francs from the till, making off and being caught in a train on his way to Lyon . . . He promises to be good, of course . . . He narrowly escapes being sent to a remand home and is put on probation for two years . . .'

The odd thing was that, while the magistrate was saying all this, Maigret kept thinking: 'Where the devil did I see that . . . ?'

And he wasn't thinking of Donge, but of the boy who had come out as he went in.

'Fifteen years later, in Cannes, three months' suspended sentence for criminal assault, and insulting behaviour to a policeman . . . And now, Superintendent, perhaps it's time I showed you something . . .'

At which he held out a bit of squared paper like that sold in small shops or used as bill chits in small cafés. The text was written in violet ink, with a spluttery pen, and the writing was that of an ill-educated woman.

It was the famous anonymous letter which had been sent to the magistrate, informing him about Prosper and Mimi's affair.

'Here is the envelope . . . As you see, it was posted between midnight and six in the morning in the postbox in the Place Clichy . . . Place Clichy, you note . . . Now, take a look at this exercise book . . .'

A rather grubby school exercise book, covered with grease marks. It contained cooking recipes – some cut from newspapers and stuck in, others copied out.

This time, Maigret frowned, and the magistrate couldn't disguise a triumphant smile.

'You would agree that it's the same writing? . . . I felt sure you would . . . Well, Superintendent, this exercise book was taken from the dresser in a kitchen which you already know, in Saint-Cloud – at Prosper Donge's house, in fact – and these recipes were copied out by a certain Charlotte . . .'

He was so pleased with himself that he made a show of apologizing.

'I know the police and ourselves don't always see things in quite the same light . . . At the Quai des Orfèvres, you have a certain sympathy for a particular kind of person, for certain irregular situations, which we as magistrates have difficulty in sharing . . . Admit, Superintendent, it is not always we who are wrong . . . And tell me why, if this Prosper is the upright man he appears, his own mistress, this Charlotte who also pretends to be such a good sort, should send me an anonymous letter to destroy him?'

'I don't know . . .'

Maigret seemed completely bowled over.

'This case can be tidied up quite quickly now. I've sent Donge to the Santé prison. When you've interrogated the woman, Charlotte . . . As for the second crime, it can easily be explained . . . The poor night porter . . . Colleboeuf, I believe? . . . must have been party to the first crime . . . At any rate he knew who the murderer of Mrs Clark was . . . He couldn't rest all day . . . And finally no doubt, tortured by indecision, he came back to the Majestic to warn the murderer that he was going to denounce him . . .'

The telephone rang.

'Hullo! Yes . . . I'll come at once . . .'

And to Maigret: 'It's my wife, to remind me that we have some friends coming to luncheon . . . I will leave you to your inquiry, Superintendent . . . I think you now have enough leads to go on . . .'

Maigret was almost at the door, when he came back, with the look of someone who has at last pinned down what he had been trying to remember for some time.

'About Fred, sir . . . It *was* Fred-the-Marseillais you were interrogating when I arrived, wasn't it?'

'It's the sixth time I've interrogated him without discovering the names of his accomplices . . .'

'I met Fred about three weeks ago, at Angelino's in the Place d'Italie . . .'

The magistrate stared at him, clearly unable to see the relevance of this remark.

'Angelino, who has a "club" frequented by rather dubious types, has been going with the sister of Harry-the-Squint for a year . . .'

The magistrate still didn't understand. And Maigret said modestly, effacing himself as much as his massive frame would allow: 'Harry-the-Squint has had three sentences for house-breaking . . . He's an ex-bricklayer whose speciality is tunnelling through walls . . .'

And, with his hand on the door: 'Didn't the burglars in the Rue Saint-Martin get in by the basement by tunnelling through two walls? . . . Good-bye, sir . . .'

He was in a bad mood, all the same. That letter from Charlotte . . . And looking at him, you would have sworn that it wasn't only anger, but that he was also a little sad.

He could have sent an inspector. But would an inspector have been able to get the feel of the house as well as he could?

A large, new, luxury building, painted white and with a wrought-iron gateway, in the Avenue de Madrid, by the Bois de Boulogne. The concierge's lodge to the right of the hall, with a glass door, furnished like a proper reception room. Three or four women dozing on chairs. Visiting cards on a tray. Another woman, whose eyes were red, who opened the door and asked: 'What do you want?'

The door of a further room was open and there was a corpse lying on the bed, hands folded, a rosary clasped in the fingers, with two candles fluttering in the dim light and box-wood in a bowl of holy water.

They spoke in low tones. Blew their noses. Walked on tiptoe. Maigret made the sign of the cross, sprinkled a little holy water over the body, and stood there for a minute silently contemplating the dead man's nose, which the candle threw into strange relief.

'It's terrible, Superintendent . . . Such a good man, without an enemy in the world!'

Above the bed, in an oval frame, a large photograph of Justin Colleboeuf, in his sergeant-major's uniform, taken at the time when he still had a large moustache. A croix de guerre with three palms and the military medal were fixed to the frame.

'He was in the regular army, Superintendent . . . When he got to retiring age, he didn't know what to do to keep himself occupied and insisted on doing work of some kind . . . He was nightwatchman at a club in the Boulevard Haussmann for a while . . . Then someone suggested the job of night porter at the Majestic to him, and he took that . . . You see he was someone who needed very little sleep . . . At the barracks he used to get up nearly every night to go the rounds . . .'

Her neighbours, or possibly relations, nodded sympathetically.

'What did he do in the daytime?' Maigret asked.

'He got back at quarter past seven in the morning, just in time to put out the dustbins for me, because he didn't let me do any of the heavy work . . . Then he stood in the doorway and had a pipe while he waited for the postman, and had a little chat with him . . . The postman had been in the same regiment as my husband, you see . . . Then he went to bed till midday . . . That was all the sleep he needed . . . When he'd had lunch, he walked across the Bois de Boulogne to the Champs-Élysées . . . Sometimes he went into the Majestic to say hullo to his colleague on duty there during the day . . . Then he had his usual in the little bar in the Rue de Ponthieu and got back at six o'clock, and left again at seven to go on duty at the hotel . . . He was so regular in his habits that people round here could set their clocks by the time when they saw him go by . . .'

'Is it a long time since he gave up wearing a moustache?'

'He shaved it off when he left the army . . . I thought he looked very funny without it . . . it made him seem less important . . . He even looked smaller somehow . . .'

Maigret inclined his head once more in the direction of the dead man and crept away on tiptoe.

He wasn't far from Saint-Cloud. He was impatient to get there and yet at the same time, for some unknown reason, he was stalling for time. A taxi went past. Oh well! He held up his arm . . .

'To Saint-Cloud . . . I'll explain where . . .'

It was drizzling. The sky was grey. It was only three o'clock but it might have been evening. The houses, in their bare little gardens, with their leafless winter trees, looked desolate.

He rang the bell. It wasn't Charlotte but Gigi who came to the door, while Donge's mistress peered from the kitchen to see who was there.

Still glowering balefully at him, Gigi let him in without saying a word. It was only two days since Maigret had last been there and yet it seemed to him that the house looked different. Perhaps Gigi had brought some of her own chaos with her. The unwashed lunch things were still on the kitchen table.

Gigi was wearing one of Charlotte's dressing-gowns, which was much too big for her, over her nightdress, and an old pair of Prosper's shoes on her bare feet. She was smoking a cigarette, and squinting through the smoke.

Charlotte, who had got up as he went in, was at a loss for words. She hadn't washed. Her skin looked blotchy, and without a bra, her bosom sagged.

He wondered who would speak first. They were giving each other anxious, suspicious looks. Maigret sat down, unabashed, with his bowler on his knee.

'I had a long talk with Prosper this morning,' he said at last.

'What did he say?' Charlotte hurriedly asked.

'That he didn't kill Mimi, or the night porter . . .'

'Ah!' Gigi cried triumphantly. 'What did I tell you!'

Charlotte couldn't take it in. She seemed at a loss. She wasn't made for drama and seemed perpetually to be looking for something to cling to.

'I also saw the magistrate. He has been sent an anonymous letter concerning Prosper and Mimi . . .'

No reaction. Charlotte was still staring at him with curiosity, her lids heavy, her body limp.

'An anonymous letter?'

He handed her the recipe book which he had brought with him.

'It's your writing in this book, isn't it?'

'Yes . . . Why?'

'Would you be good enough to take a pen? . . . preferably an old one which splutters . . . And paper . . . and ink . . .'

There was a bottle of ink and a penholder on the dresser. Gigi looked from Maigret to her friend in turn, as if ready to intervene the moment she sensed danger.

'Make yourself comfortable . . . And write . . .'

'What shall I write?'

'Don't write anything, Charlotte! You can't trust them . . .'

'Write – There's no danger, I promise you – *"Sir, I am taking the liberty of writing to you about the Donge affair, which I read about in the newspaper . . ."*

'Why do you spell newspaper with a "u"?'

'I don't know . . . What should I put?'

On the anonymous letter which he had in his hand, there was a 'z'.

'. . . *"The American woman isn't really an American woman; she was a dancer and her name was Mimi . . ."*'

Maigret shrugged impatiently.

'That will do,' he said. 'Now, take a look . . .'

The writing was exactly the same. Only the spelling mistakes were different.

'Who wrote that?'

'That's exactly what I would like to know . . .'

'You thought it was me?'

She was choking with anger, and the Superintendent hurriedly tried to calm her.

'I didn't think anything . . . What I came to ask you is who, besides you and Gigi, knew about Prosper and Mimi's affair, and particularly about the child? . . .'

'Can you think of anyone, Gigi?'

They thought for a long time, indolently. They seemed to be aimlessly drifting in the untidy house, which had suddenly taken on a sordid aspect. Gigi's nostrils quivered from time to time, and Maigret realized that it wouldn't be long before she was out searching frantically for a fix.

'No . . . Except us three . . .'

'Who was it who got Mimi's letter at the time?'

'It was me,' said Gigi, '. . . and before I left Cannes, I found it in a box where I kept some souvenirs . . . I brought it with me . . .'

'Let me see . . .'

'Provided you promise . . .'

'Of course, you fool! Can't you see I'm trying to get Prosper out of the mess.'

He felt concerned, irritable. He had begun to have a vague feeling that there were mysterious complications to the affair, but he had not the slightest clue to tell him what they might be.

'Will you promise to give it back?'

He shrugged again, and read:

> My dear old Gigi,
>
> Phew! I've made it! I've made it at last! You and Charlotte laughed when I told you I'd get out of there one day and that I'd be a real lady.
>
> Well, ducky, I've done it . . . Oswald and I were married yesterday, and it was a funny kind of wedding, because he wanted it to be in England, where it's quite different from in France. In fact I sometimes wonder at times if I'm really married.
>
> Let Charlotte know. We'll be sailing for America in three or four days' time. We don't know exactly when we'll be sailing, because of the strike.
>
> As for poor Prosper, I think it would be best not to tell him anything. He's a nice boy, but a bit simple. I don't know how I managed to stay with him for nearly a year. It must have been my year for being kind . . .
>
> But still, he's done me a good turn, without knowing it. Keep this to yourself. No point in telling Charlotte – she's a great sentimental fool.
>
> I've known for some time that I was pregnant. You can imagine the face I made when I knew. I rushed to see a specialist before telling Oswald . . . We did some calculations . . . Well, it's quite definite that the baby can't be Oswald's . . . So it's poor Prosper who . . . Don't ever let him know! He might get a rush of paternal feeling!
>
> It would take too long to tell you everything . . . The doctor has been very decent about it . . . By cheating a bit as to the date of birth (we'll have to pretend it's a premature delivery), we've succeeded in convincing Oswald that he's going to be a father.
>
> He took it very well. Contrary to what one might think when one first meets him, he's not at all cold. In fact when we're by ourselves he's like a child, and the other day, when we were in Paris, we visited all the pleasure gardens and rode on the roundabouts . . .
>
> Well, I'm now Mrs Oswald J. Clark of Detroit (Michigan), and

from now on I shall speak English all the time, because Oswald, if you remember, doesn't know a word of French.

I think of you two sometimes. Is Charlotte still just as worried about getting fat? Does she still knit all the time? I bet she'll finish up behind the counter in a haberdasher's shop in the provinces!

As for you, my old Gigi, I don't think you'll ever grow respectable. As the client in the white gaiters said so comically – you remember, the one who gulped down a whole bottle of champagne in one go? – you've got vice in the blood!

Say hullo to the Croisette for me and don't burst out laughing when you look at Prosper and imagine him being a father without knowing it.

I'll send you some postcards.

Love and kisses,

Mimi.

'May I take this letter with me?'

It was Charlotte who intervened.

'Let him, Gigi . . . It can't make it any worse . . .'

And as she showed the Superintendent out: 'Look! . . . Couldn't I get permission to go and see him? He has the right to have his meals sent in from outside, hasn't he? . . . Could you . . .'

And she blushed and held out a thousand franc note to him.

'If he could have a few books too . . . He used to spend all his free time reading . . .'

Rain. A taxi. The street-lamps coming alight. The Bois de Boulogne which Maigret had crossed on his bike, side by side with Donge.

'Put me down by the Majestic, will you?'

The porter followed him a little anxiously as he crossed the foyer without speaking, and took Maigret's coat and hat in the cloakroom. The manager had also seen him, through the crack in his curtains. Everyone knew Maigret – followed him with their eyes.

The bar? Why not? He was thirsty. But he was attracted by a muffled sound of music. Somewhere in the basement a band was softly playing a tango. He went down a staircase carpeted with thick carpet, into a bluish haze. People were eating cakes at little tables. Others were dancing. A waiter came up to the Superintendent.

'Bring me a half, please . . .'

'We don't . . .'

Maigret gave him a look and he hurriedly scribbled something on a chit . . . The bills which . . . Maigret watched where it went . . . At the back of the room, to the right of the band, there was a sort of hatch in the wall . . .

On the other side were the glass cages, the still-room, the kitchens, the sculleries, the guests' servants' hall, and, right at the end, near the clocking-on machine, the cloakroom with its hundred metal lockers.

Someone was watching him – he could feel it – and he noticed Zebio dancing with a middle-aged woman covered in jewels.

Was it an illusion? It seemed to Maigret that Zebio's look was trying to tell him something. He turned and saw with a shock that Oswald J. Clark was dancing with his son's governess, Ellen Darroman.

They both seemed utterly oblivious of their surroundings. They were caught up in the ecstasy of new-found love. Solemn, hardly smiling, they were alone on the dance-floor, alone in the world, and when the music stopped they stood there without moving for a minute before going back to their table.

Maigret then noticed that Clark was wearing a thin band of black material on the lapel of his jacket – his way of wearing mourning.

The Superintendent's fist tightened on Mimi's letter to Gigi which was in his pocket. He had a terrible desire to . . .

But hadn't the magistrate told him not to get involved with Clark, who was no doubt too much of a gentleman to grapple with a policeman?

The tango was followed by a slow foxtrot. A frothy half followed the route the waiter's order had taken previously – in the opposite direction. The pair were dancing again.

Maigret suddenly got up, forgot to pay for his drink, and hurried to the foyer.

'Is there anyone in Suite 203?' he asked the porter.

'I think the nanny and the boy are up there . . . But . . . If you'd like to wait while I telephone . . .'

'No, please don't do that . . .'

'There's the lift, on your left, sir.'

Too late. Maigret had made for the marble staircase and was slowly starting up the stairs, grunting as he went.

7

'What's He On About?'

Maigret was assailed for a moment by a strange thought, which however he soon forgot. He had reached the second floor of the Majestic and stopped for a moment to get his breath back. On his way up he had met a waiter with a tray, and a bell-boy running up the stairs with a bundle of foreign newspapers under his arm.

On this floor there were smartly dressed women getting into the lift, who were probably going down to the thé dansant. They left a trail of scent behind them.

'They are all in their proper places,' he thought to himself. 'Some behind the scenes and the others in the lounges and foyer . . . The guests on one side and the staff on the other . . .'

But that wasn't what was bothering him, was it? Everyone, round him, was in his allotted place, doing the right thing. It was normal, for instance, for a rich foreign woman to have tea, smoke cigarettes and go out for fittings. It was natural for a waiter to carry a tray, a chambermaid to make beds, a liftman to operate a lift . . .

In short, their functions, such as they were, were clearly defined, settled once and for all.

But if anyone had asked Maigret what he was doing there, what would he have answered?

'I am trying to get a man sent to prison, or even executed . . .'

It was nothing. A slight dizziness, probably caused by the over-luxurious, almost aggressively luxurious setting, and the atmosphere in the tea-room . . .

209 . . . 207 . . . 205 . . . 203 . . . Maigret hesitated for a moment and then knocked. His ear to the door, he could hear a child's voice saying a few words in English, then a woman's voice

sounding more distant, and, he imagined, telling him to come in.

He crossed a little hall and found himself in a sitting-room with three windows overlooking the Champs-Élysées. By one of the windows an elderly woman, dressed in a white apron like a nurse, was sitting sewing. It was the nanny, Gertrud Borms, made to look even more severe by the glasses she wore.

But the Superintendent paid no attention to her. He was looking at a boy of about six, dressed in plus-fours and a sweater which fitted snugly round his thin frame. The boy was sitting on the carpet, his few toys round him, including a large toy boat, and cars which were exact replicas of various real makes. There was a picture book on his knee which he was looking at when Maigret went in, and after glancing briefly at the visitor, he bent over it again.

When he recounted the scene to Madame Maigret, the Superintendent's description went something like this: 'She said something like, "You we you we we well . . ."

'And to gain time, I said very quickly: "I hope that I'm correct in thinking this is Monsieur Oswald J. Clark's suite? . . ."

'She went on again: "You we you we we well", or something of the sort.

'And meanwhile, I was able to get a good look at the boy. A very big head for his age, covered, as I had been told, with hair of a fiery red. The same blue eyes as Prosper Donge – the colour of periwinkles or of certain summer skies . . . A thin neck . . .

'He started talking to his nanny, in English, too, looking at me as he did so, and to me it still sounded like: "You we we you we we well . . ."

'They were evidently asking themselves what I wanted and why I was standing there in the middle of the room. I didn't know myself why I was there. There were flowers worth several hundred francs in a Chinese vase . . .

'The nanny finally got up. She put her work down on the chair, picked up a telephone and spoke to someone.

'"Don't you understand any French, little one?" I asked the child.

'He merely gazed at me with eyes full of suspicion. A few

seconds later, an employee in a tailcoat came into the suite. The nanny spoke to him. He then turned to me.

'"She wants to know what you want?"

'"I wanted to see Monsieur Clark . . ."

'"He isn't here . . . She says he is probably downstairs . . ."

'"Thank you very much . . ."'

And that was that! Maigret had wanted to see Teddy Clark and he had seen him. He went back downstairs thinking about Prosper Donge, shut in his cell at the Santé. Automatically, without thinking, he went on down to the tea-room and, as his beer had not yet been cleared away, he sat down again.

He was in a state of mind he knew well. It was rather as if he were in a daze, although he was conscious of what was happening round him, without attaching any importance to it, without making any effort to place people or things in time or space.

Thus he saw a page go up to Ellen Darroman and say a few words to her. She got up and went to a telephone booth, in which she only remained for a few seconds.

When she came out, she immediately looked round for Maigret. Then she rejoined Clark and said something to him in a low voice, still looking at the Superintendent.

In that instant, Maigret had a sudden very definite feeling that something disagreeable was about to happen. He knew that the best thing to do would be to leave at once, but he didn't go.

He would have found it hard to explain why he stayed there, if called on to do so.

It wasn't because he felt it was his professional duty. There was no need to stay at the thé dansant any longer – he was out of his element there.

That was precisely it – but he couldn't have put it into words.

The magistrate had arrested Prosper Donge without consulting him, hadn't he? And moreover he had forbidden him to concern himself with the American?

That was tantamount to saying: 'That is not your world . . . You don't understand it . . . Leave it to me . . .'

And Maigret, plebeian to the core, to the very marrow of his bones, felt hostile towards the world which surrounded him here.

Too bad. He would stay all the same. He saw Clark looking at him in turn, then Clark frowned, and, no doubt telling his companion to stay where she was, got up. A dance had just begun. The blue lighting gave way to pink. The American made his way between the couples and came and stood in front of the Superintendent.

To Maigret, who couldn't understand a word of English, it still sounded like: 'Well you well we we well . . .'

But this time the tone was aggressive and it was clear that Clark was having difficulty controlling himself.

'What are you saying?'

And Clark burst out even more angrily.

That evening, Madame Maigret said, shaking her head: 'Admit it! You did it on purpose! I know that way you have of looking at people! You'd make an angel lose his temper . . .'

He didn't admit anything, but there was a twinkle in his eye. Well, what *had* he done anyway? He had stood there in front of the Yankee, with his hands in his jacket pockets, staring at him as if he found the spectacle curious.

Was it his fault? Donge was still uppermost in his mind – Donge who was in prison, not dancing with the very pretty Miss Ellen. No doubt sensing that a drama was about to unfold, she had got up to join them. But before she reached them, Clark had hit out furiously at Maigret's face, with the clean clockwork precision one sees in American films.

Two women having tea at the next table got up screaming. Some of the couples stopped dancing.

Clark seemed to be satisfied. He probably thought that the matter was now settled and that there was nothing further to add.

Maigret didn't even deign to run his hand over his chin. The impact of Clark's fist on his jaw had been clearly audible, but the Superintendent's face remained as impassive as if he had been lightly tapped on the head.

Although he hadn't planned it that way, he was delighted at what had happened, and couldn't help smiling when he thought of the examining magistrate's face.

'Gentlemen! . . . Gentlemen! . . .'

Just as it seemed that Maigret would launch himself at his

adversary and that the fight would continue, a waiter intervened. Ellen and one of the men who had been dancing grabbed hold of Clark on either side and tried to restrain him, while he still went on talking.

'What's he on about?' Maigret grumbled calmly.

'It doesn't matter! . . . Gentlemen, will you please kindly . . .'

Clark went on talking.

'What's he saying?'

Then, to everyone's surprise, Maigret began negligently to play with a shiny object which he had taken from his pocket and the fashionable women stared in amazement at the handcuffs, which they had so often heard about but never actually seen.

'Waiter, would you be good enough to translate for me? . . . Tell this gentleman that I am obliged to arrest him for insulting an officer of the law while in the course of his duty . . . And tell him too that if he is not prepared to follow me quietly, I shall have regretfully to use these handcuffs . . .'

Clark didn't flinch. He didn't say another word and pushed Ellen, who was clinging to his arm and trying to follow him, aside. Without waiting for his hat or coat he followed closely on the Superintendent's heels, and as they crossed the foyer, followed by a small crowd of onlookers, the manager saw them from his office, and raised his hands to heaven in horror.

'Taxi! . . . To the Palais de Justice . . .'

It was dark now. They went up the stairs, along corridors, and stopped outside Monsieur Bonneau's door. Maigret then adopted a humble and contrite attitude which Madame Maigret knew well and which infuriated her.

'I am so sorry, sir . . . I have been obliged, much to my regret, to put Mr Clark, who you see here, under arrest . . .'

The magistrate had no idea what had happened. He imagined that Maigret suspected the American of having murdered his wife and the night porter.

'Excuse me! Excuse me! On what grounds have you . . .'

It was Clark who answered and to Maigret the words still sounded like a senseless jingle.

'What's he saying?'

The poor magistrate raised his eyebrows and frowned. His own knowledge of English was far from good and he had difficulty himself in following what the American was saying. He mumbled something, and sent his clerk to fetch another clerk who sometimes acted as interpreter.

'What's he on about?' Maigret muttered from time to time.

And Clark, irritated beyond measure by this, burst out, clenching his fists and imitating the Superintendent: 'What's he saying? . . . What's he saying? . . .'

There had followed another tirade in English.

The interpreter sidled into the room. He was a little bald man, disarmingly humble and timid.

'He says he's an American citizen and that it's intolerable that policemen . . .'

Judging by his tone of voice, Clark had little respect for the police . . .

'. . . that policemen should be allowed to follow him about everywhere . . . He says an inspector has been constantly at his heels . . .'

'Is that true, Superintendent?'

'He is probably right, sir.'

'. . . He says another policeman was following Miss Ellen . . .'

'It's very likely . . .'

'. . . And you burst into his hotel suite, in his absence . . .'

'I knocked politely on the door and asked the good lady who was there in the politest way in the world if I could see Monsieur Clark . . . After which I went down to the thé dansant to have a glass of beer . . . It was then that this gentleman saw fit to shove his fist in my face . . .'

Monsieur Bonneau was in despair. As if the affair wasn't complicated enough anyway! They had managed to keep the press out of it until now, but after the fracas in the tea-room there would be journalists besieging the Palais de Justice and Police Headquarters on all sides . . .

'I cannot understand, Superintendent, why a man like you, with twenty-five years' experience . . .'

And then he nearly lost his temper, because instead of listening to him, Maigret was playing with a bit of paper which he'd taken out of his pocket. It was a letter, written on bluish paper.

'Monsieur Clark certainly went too far. Equally, it is true to say that for your part you omitted to show the tact one would have expected of you in circumstances which . . .'

It had worked. Maigret had to turn away to hide his satisfaction. Clark had become hypnotized by the piece of paper and finally walked up to him and held out his hand.

'Please –'

Maigret appeared surprised, and gave the American the piece of paper he was holding. The magistrate understood less and less, and suspected, not without reason, that the Superintendent was up to something.

Then Clark went up to the interpreter and showed him the letter, gabbling away as he did so.

'What's he saying?'

'He says he recognizes his wife's handwriting and wants to know how you came to be in possession of a letter from her . . .'

'Please explain, Monsieur Maigret,' Monsieur Bonneau said coldly.

'I beg your pardon, sir . . . It's a document I've just been given . . . I wanted to show it to you, and add it to the dossier . . . Unfortunately Monsieur Clark took it before . . .'

Clark was still talking to the interpreter.

'What's he saying?' said the magistrate, catching the disease.

'He wants me to translate the letter . . . He says if someone has rifled through his wife's things, he will lodge a complaint with his embassy and that . . .'

'Translate . . .'

Maigret, his nerves taut, started filling his pipe, and went over to the window, where he could see the gas lights shining like stars through their misty haloes.

The poor interpreter, his bald pate covered in sweat, translated Mimi's letter to her friend Gigi word by word, wondering as he did so if he dared continue, so horrified was he. The magistrate had drawn closer to read over his shoulder, but Clark, more peremptory than ever, had motioned him aside, saying: 'Please –'

He had the air of one guarding his property, as though he wanted to prevent anyone from taking the letter, or from trying to destroy it, or from missing out anything in the translation. He pointed to each word with his finger, demanding the exact meaning.

Monsieur Bonneau, in total despair, went over to join the Superintendent, who was smoking his pipe with seeming indifference.

'Did you do this on purpose, Superintendent?'

'How could I foresee that Monsieur Clark would thrust his fist in my face?'

'This letter explains everything!'

'With perfect cynicism!'

Good grief! The magistrate had sent Prosper Donge to prison without any proof that he was guilty. And he was perfectly prepared to send Charlotte, Gigi or any of the rest of them to join him!

The interpreter and Clark stood leaning over the table, where the green-shaded lamp shed its circle of light.

Finally Clark stood up. He banged his fist on the table, muttering something which sounded like: 'Damned!'

Then he reacted very differently to what one might have expected. He remained calm, and didn't look at any of them. His face had set, and he stared into space. After remaining like that for a long time, during which the poor interpreter looked as though he was trying to gather his courage to apologize to him, he turned round, saw a chair in a corner of the room, and went and sat down, so calmly and simply, that his very simplicity seemed almost tragic.

Maigret, who had been watching him from a distance, could see beads of sweat literally breaking out on the skin above his upper lip.

And Clark, at this moment, was a bit like a boxer who has just received a knock-out blow but who is kept upright by the force of inertia and instinctively looks for some support before going down for good.

There was complete silence in the magistrate's office and they could hear the sound of a typewriter in a neighbouring room.

Clark still made no move. He sat in his corner with his elbows on his knee, his chin in his hands, staring at his feet in their square-toed shoes.

A long time later, they heard him muttering: 'Well! . . . Well! . . .'

And Maigret quietly asking the interpreter: 'What's he saying?'

The magistrate took the line of pretending to look at his papers. The smoke from Maigret's pipe rose slowly in the air, seeming to drift towards the circle of light round the lamp.

'Well . . .'

Clark's thoughts were far away. God knew where. He finally looked up, and they wondered what he would do next. He took a heavy gold cigarette case out of his pocket, opened it, took out a cigarette and snapped the case shut again. Then, turning to the interpreter, he said: 'Please . . .'

He wanted a match. The interpreter didn't smoke. The Superintendent handed him a box of matches, and as he took it, Clark glanced at him and gave him a long look, which said a great deal.

When he stood up, he must have felt weak, because his body seemed to sway a little. But he was still quite calm. His features were expressionless once more. He began by asking a question. The magistrate looked at Maigret as if waiting for him to answer.

'He asks if he may keep this letter?'

'I would rather it were photographed first. It won't take more than a few minutes. We can send it up to the Criminal Records Office . . .'

Translation. Clark appeared to understand, nodded his head, and handed the letter to the clerk, who bore it off. Then he went on talking. It was maddening not to be able to understand. The shortest speech seemed to go on for ever and the Superintendent kept wanting to interrupt to ask what he was saying.

'First of all, he wants to consult his solicitor, because what he has just learnt was totally unexpected and it changes everything . . .'

Why did Maigret feel moved at these words? At this great healthy man who three days before had been riding on roundabouts with Ellen, and only a few hours before had been dancing the tango in a haze of blue light . . . and who had now received a much more shattering blow than the one he had dealt the Superintendent . . . And, like Maigret, he had barely flinched . . . He had sworn briefly . . . Banged his fist on the table . . . Remained silent for a while . . .

'Well . . . Well! . . .'

It was a pity they couldn't understand each other. Maigret would have liked to have been able to talk to him.

'What's he saying now?'

'That he now wants to offer a reward of a thousand dollars to the police officer who discovers the murderer . . .'

While this was translated, Clark looked at Maigret as if to say: 'You see what a good sport I am . . .'

'Tell him, that if we win them, the thousand dollars will go to the police orphanage . . .'

It was odd. It was as though they were now competing to see who could be most polite. Clark listened to the interpreter, and nodded.

'Well . . .'

Then he began speaking again, this time in the tone of a businessman conducting his affairs.

'He supposes – but he doesn't want to do anything before having seen his solicitor – that an interview between him and this man – Prosper Donge – will be necessary . . . He asks if he might be permitted to do this and if . . .'

It was the magistrate's turn to nod gravely. And in another minute they would all have been exchanging compliments.

'After you . . .'

'Please . . .'

'No, really . . .'

Clark then asked some more questions, turning frequently to Maigret.

'He wants to know, sir, what will happen about the punch-up, and if there will be any repercussions. He doesn't know what consequences such an act might have in France . . . In his country . . .'

'Well, tell him I have no recollection of the event he mentions . . .'

The magistrate looked anxiously towards the door. It was too good to be true! He was afraid some new incident would come to disturb this marvellous harmony. If only they would hurry up and bring back the letter which . . .

They waited. In silence. They had nothing more to say to each other. Clark lit another cigarette, after having signed to Maigret to lend him his matches.

At last the clerk came back with the dreaded piece of blue paper.

'It's been copied, sir . . . May I?'

'Yes, give the letter to Monsieur Clark . . .'

Clark slipped it carefully into his wallet, put the wallet in his breast pocket, and forgetting he had come without his hat, looked round for it on the chairs. Then he remembered, smiled stiffly and said good night to them all.

When the interpreter had also gone, and the door was shut, Monsieur Bonneau coughed two or three times, walked round his desk, and picked up some papers which he then didn't know what to do with.

'Hum! . . . Was that what you wanted to happen, Superintendent?'

'What do you think, sir?'

'I believe it is I who am asking the questions.'

'I'm so sorry . . . Of course! You see, I have the feeling that it won't be long before Monsieur Clark remarries . . . And the child is definitely Donge's son . . .'

'The son of a man who is in prison and who is accused of . . .'

'. . . various crimes, yes,' Maigret sighed. 'But the boy is nevertheless his son. What can I do under the circumstances . . .'

He, too, looked for his hat, which he had left at the Majestic. He felt very odd leaving the Palais de Justice without it, so he took a taxi back to the Boulevard Richard-Lenoir.

The bruise on his chin had had time to turn black. Madame Maigret spotted it at once.

'You've been fighting again!' she said, laying the table. 'And, of course, you're minus a hat! . . . What was it this time? . . .'

He felt satisfied, and smiled broadly as he took his table-napkin out of its silver ring.

8

Maigret Dozing

And it wasn't at all bad either to be sitting comfortably at his desk, with the stove purring away at his back, and the window on the left curtained with lace-like morning mist, while in front of him was the black marble Louis-Philippe mantelpiece, the hands of the clock permanently stuck at noon for the last twenty years; on the wall a photograph in a black and gilt frame of a group of gentlemen in frock-coats and top hats, with improbable moustaches and pointed beards: the association of secretaries of the Central Police Station, when Maigret was twenty-four!

Four pipes arranged in order of size on his desk.

A RICH AMERICAN WOMAN STRANGLED
IN THE BASEMENT OF THE MAJESTIC.

The headline ran across the front page of an evening paper of the day before. To journalists, of course, all American women are always rich. But Maigret's smile broadened on seeing a photograph of himself, in his overcoat and bowler hat, and with his pipe in his mouth, looking down at something which wasn't shown in the picture.

SUPERINTENDENT MAIGRET EXAMINES THE CORPSE.

But it was a photograph which had been taken a year before, in the Bois de Boulogne, when he had in fact been looking at the body of a Russian who had been shot with a revolver.

Some more important documents, in manila folders.

Report from Inspector Torrence as to inquiry regarding Monsieur Edgar Fagonet, alias Eusebio Fualdès, alias Zebio, aged twenty-four, born in Lille.

'Son of Fagonet, Albert Jean-Marie, foreman at the Lecoeur Works, deceased three years ago;

'. . . and Jeanne Albertine Octavie Hautbois, wife of the above, aged 54, housewife.

'The following information was given to us, either by the concierge at no. 57 Rue Caulaincourt, where Edgar Fagonet lives with his mother and sister, or by neighbours and shopkeepers in the area, or on the telephone by the Police Station in the Gasworks district of Lille.

'We have also been in touch by telephone with the "Chevalet Sanatorium" in Megève, and have personally seen the manager of the Imperia cinema, in the Boulevard des Capucines.

'Although opinion must be reserved until further verification has been carried out, the information below appears to be correct.

'The Fagonet family, of Lille, led a decent life, and occupied a bungalow in the modern part of the Gasworks district. It appears that the parents' ambition was to give Edgar Fagonet a good education, and in fact the latter went to the Lycée at the age of eleven.

'Shortly afterwards he had to leave it for a year to go to a sanatorium on the island of Oléron. His health then apparently restored, he continued his studies, but they were constantly interrupted from that time on owing to his weak constitution.

'When he was seventeen, it was found necessary to send him to a high altitude, and he spent four years at the Chevalet Sanatorium, near Megève.

'Doctor Chevalet remembers Fagonet well; he was a very good-looking boy and had a lot of success with certain of the female patients. He had several affairs while he was there. It was also there that he became an accomplished dancer, because the rules at the establishment were very informal, and it appears that in general the patients were intent upon pleasure.

'Turned down permanently by the recruiting board.

'At twenty-one, Fagonet returned to Lille, just in time to close his father's eyes. The father left a few small savings, but not enough to feed his family.

'Fagonet's sister, Émile, aged nineteen, has a bone disorder which renders her virtually disabled. Additionally, she is of below average intelligence, and needs constant care.

'It appears that at this time Edgar Fagonet made serious attempts to find regular employment, first in Lille and then in Roubaix. Unfortunately his interrupted education was a handicap. On the other hand, although cured, his constitution prevented him from doing manual labour.

'It was then that he came to Paris, where he could be found a few weeks later in a sky-blue uniform, working at the Imperia cinema, which was the first to employ young men instead of usherettes, and which also took on a number of poor students.

'It is difficult to get precise information on this point because those involved have proved discreet, but it appears certain that many of these young men, shown to advantage in their uniforms, made FRUITFUL conquests at the Imperia!'

Maigret grinned because Torrence had found it necessary to underline the word 'fruitful' in red ink.

'At any rate one of Fagonet's first acts – his friends were now beginning to call him Zebio, because of his Latin-American appearance – was to bring his mother and sister to Paris and install them in a three-room flat, in the Rue Caulaincourt.

'He is considered by the concierge and by neighbours to be a particularly dutiful son, and it is often he who goes out to do the shopping in the mornings.

'It was through colleagues at the Imperia that he learnt, about a year ago, that the Majestic was looking for a professional dancing-partner for its tea-room. He applied, and was taken on after a few days' trial. He then adopted the name Eusebio Fualdès, and the hotel management have no complaints to make on his account.

'According to the staff, he is a rather timid, sentimental and shy boy. Some of them call him "a proper girl".

'He doesn't talk much, and conserves his strength, because he's apt to have relapses and has several times had to go and lie down on a bed in the basement, especially when he has had to stay late because of gala evenings.

'Although he gets on well with everyone, he doesn't seem to have any friends and is not much inclined towards gossip.

'It is thought that his monthly earnings, including tips, must be in the region of two thousand to two thousand five hundred francs.

'That just about sums up life in the household in the Rue Caulaincourt.

'Edgar Fagonet doesn't drink, doesn't smoke, and doesn't take any drugs. His poor health prevents him doing so.

'His mother is a woman from the North of France – stocky and energetic. She has often spoken – to the concierge for one – about getting a job herself, but the fact that she has to look after her daughter has always prevented this.

'We have tried to find out if Fagonet has ever been to the Côte d'Azur. We can't get any precise information on this point. Some say he stayed there for a few days, about three or four years ago, while he was still at the Imperia, with a middle-aged woman. But the information is too vague to be admitted as evidence.'

Maigret slowly filled pipe no. 3, filled the stove, and went to have a look at the Seine, which was tinged with gold by a pale winter sun. Then he sighed comfortably and sat down again.

Report by Inspector Lucas concerning Ramuel, Jean Oscar Adelbert, aged forty-eight, living in a furnished flat at no. 14, Rue Delambre (XIVe).

'Ramuel was born in Nice, of a French father, now deceased, and an Italian mother, whom we cannot trace and who seems to have gone back to her own country some time ago. His father was a market-gardener.

'At eighteen, Jean Ramuel was book-keeper to a wholesaler in Les Halles in Paris, but we have been unable to get precise information about this, because the merchant died ten years ago.

'Enlisted voluntarily at nineteen. Left the army with the rank of quartermaster-sergeant at twenty-four and entered the service of a broker whom he left almost immediately to work as junior accounts clerk in a sugar refinery in Egypt.

'He stayed there three years, came back to France, took various jobs in the city sector of Paris and tried his luck on the Stock Exchange.

'At thirty-two, he embarked for Guayaquil, in Ecuador, to

work for a Franco-English mining company. He was commissioned to go and sort out the accounts, which seemed to be in a mess.

'He was away for six years. It was there that he met Marie Deligeard, on whom we have little information and who was most probably engaged in a somewhat disreputable profession in Central America.

'He returned with her. The company headquarters having been transferred to London, we have little information about this period.

'The couple then lived for some time fairly comfortably in Toulon, Cassis and Marseilles. Ramuel tried his hand at some property and land deals, but didn't have much success.

'Marie Deligeard, whom he introduces as Madame Ramuel, although they aren't married, is a loud-mouthed, vulgar woman who is quite prepared to make scenes in public and who takes a malicious pleasure in making a spectacle of herself.

'They have frequent rows. Sometimes Ramuel leaves his companion for several days, but it's always she who has the last word.

'Ramuel and Marie Deligeard then came to Paris, and took quite a comfortable furnished flat in the Rue Delambre: bedroom, kitchen, bathroom and hall, at a rent of eight hundred francs a month.

'Ramuel took a job as an accountant in the Atoum Bank, in the Rue Caumartin. (The bank has now crashed, but Atoum has started a carpet business in the Rue des Saints-Pères, in the name of one of his employees.)

'Ramuel left the bank before the crash, and almost immediately saw an advertisement and applied for the post of book-keeper at the Majestic.

'He has been there three years. The management are quite satisfied with him. The staff don't like him, because he's excessively strict.

'On several occasions, when he's had a tiff with his companion, he has stayed for days at the hotel without going home, sleeping on a makeshift bed. He has nearly always had telephone calls on these occasions, or else the woman has come to fetch him from the basement herself.

'The staff can't believe their eyes, because she seems to inspire absolute terror in him.

'Note that Jean Ramuel returned to the communal life in the flat in the Rue Delambre yesterday.'

A quarter of an hour later, the old usher knocked softly on Maigret's door. Receiving no answer, he pushed the door quietly open and crept in on tiptoe.

The Superintendent seemed to be asleep. He was sprawled in his chair, with his waistcoat unbuttoned and a burnt-out pipe in his mouth.

The usher was about to cough to let him know he was there when Maigret mumbled, without opening his eyes:

'What is it?'

'A gentleman to see you . . . Here's his card.'

Maigret still seemed reluctant to shake off his drowsiness and he stretched out his hand without opening his eyes. Then he sighed and, putting the visiting card down on his desk, picked up the telephone.

'Shall I bring him in?'

'In a minute . . .'

He had barely glanced at the card: ÉTIENNE JOLIVET, ASSISTANT MANAGER OF CRÉDIT LYONNAIS, O BRANCH.

'Hullo! . . . Would you ask Monsieur Bonneau, the examining magistrate, to be good enough to give me the name and address of Monsieur Clark's solicitor . . . Solicitor . . . yes . . . that's right . . . Then get him for me on the telephone . . . It's urgent . . .'

For more than quarter of an hour, the dapper Monsieur Jolivet, in striped trousers, black jacket and hat as rigid as reinforced concrete, remained sitting very upright on the edge of his chair, in the gloomy waiting-room at Police Headquarters. His companions were an evil-looking youth and a streetwalker who was recounting her adventures in a raucous voice.

'. . . For a start, how could I have taken his wallet, without him noticing? . . . These provincials are all the same . . . They daren't tell their wives what they've spent in Paris and so they pretend they've been robbed . . . It's lucky the vice squad superintendent knows me . . . That's proof that . . .'

'Hullo! . . . Monsieur Herbert Davidson? . . . How do you do,

Monsieur Herbert Davidson. Superintendent Maigret here . . . Yes . . . I had the pleasure of meeting your client Monsieur Clark yesterday . . . He was most kind . . . What's that? . . . No . . . not at all! . . . I've forgotten all about it . . . I'm telephoning because I got the impression that he was prepared to help us in so far as he was able . . . You say he's with you at the moment? . . .

'Could you ask him . . . Hullo! . . . I know that in the circles he moves in, particularly in the United States, the partners in a marriage lead fairly separate lives . . . Nevertheless he may have noticed . . . No, just a minute . . . Wait, Monsieur Davidson, you can translate for him afterwards . . . We know that Mrs Clark received at least three letters from Paris during the last few years . . . I want to know if Monsieur Clark saw them . . . And I also particularly want to know if by any chance she received any more letters of the same kind . . . Yes . . . I'll hang on . . . thank you . . .'

And he heard a murmur of voices at the other end of the line.

'Hullo! . . . Yes? . . . He didn't open them? . . . He didn't ask his wife what they were? . . . Naturally! How very strange . . .'

He would like to see Madame Maigret getting letters without showing them to him!

'About one every three months? . . . Always in the same handwriting? . . . Yes . . . A Paris postmark? . . . Just a minute, Monsieur Davidson . . .'

He went and opened the door of the inspectors' room, because they were making a terrible noise.

'Shut up, you lot!'

Then he came back.

'Hullo! . . . Fairly substantial sums? . . . Would you be good enough, Monsieur Davidson, to make a written note of these details and send it to the examining magistrate? . . . No! Nothing else . . . I apologize . . . I don't know how the papers got hold of it, but I can assure you I had nothing to do with it . . . Only this morning I sent away four journalists and two photographers who had been lying in wait for me in the corridor at Police Headquarters. Please give my regards to Monsieur Clark . . .'

He frowned. When he had opened the door of the inspectors'

room just now, he had thought he recognized? . . . He looked in again, and there, sitting on the table, were a reporter and his photographer colleague.

'Listen, my young friend . . . I think I was shouting loud enough for you to hear just now . . . If a single word of what I said appears in your rag, you'll never get another scrap of information out of me . . . Understand?'

But he was half smiling as he went back to his room and rang for the usher.

'Bring in Monsieur . . . Monsieur Jolivet . . .'

'Good morning, Superintendent . . . Forgive me for bothering you . . . I thought I ought . . . When I read the paper yesterday evening . . .'

'Please sit down . . .'

'I should add that I didn't come here on my own initiative, but after consultation with our head manager, who I telephoned first thing this morning . . . The name Prosper Donge struck me, because I happened to have seen the name somewhere recently . . . I should explain that it's my job at the O Branch to pass the cheques . . . They go through automatically, of course, because the customer's account has been checked previously . . . I just glance at them . . . Attach my stamp . . . However, as a large sum of money was involved . . .'

'Just a minute . . . Do you mean Prosper Donge was a customer of yours?'

'He had been for five years, Superintendent. And before that, even, because his account was transferred to us at the beginning of that period by our Cannes branch . . .'

'Can I ask you a few questions . . . It will make it easier for me to get my ideas in order . . . Prosper Donge was a customer at your Cannes branch . . . Can you tell me the size of his account at that date?'

'A very modest account, like that of most of the hotel employees who are customers of ours . . . However, one must remember that as they get their board and lodging free, if they are careful, they can put aside the greater part of their earnings . . . It was so in Donge's case and he paid about a thousand to fifteen hundred francs into his account each month . . .

'In addition to that, he had just got twenty thousand francs from a bond he had asked us to buy for him . . . So in fact he had about fifty-five thousand francs on arrival in Paris . . .'

'And he went on paying in small amounts?'

'Well – I've brought a list of his transactions with me. There's something very worrying about it, as you will see . . . The first year, Donge, who was living in a flat in the Rue Bray, near the Étoile, paid in about another twelve thousand francs . . .

'The second year, he made withdrawals and didn't pay in. He changed his address. He went to live in Saint-Cloud, where I gathered from the cheques he wrote, he was having a house built . . . Cheques to the estate agent, to the carpenter, to the decorators, to the builders . . .

'So by the end of that year, as you can see from this statement, he only had eight hundred and thirty-three francs and a few centimes left in his account . . .

'Then, three years ago, that is a few months later . . .'

'Excuse me – You said *three years ago* . . . ?'

'That's right . . . I'll give you the exact dates in a minute . . . Three years ago, he sent a letter notifying us that he had moved and asking us to note his new address: 117b Rue Réaumur . . .'

'Just a minute . . . Have you ever seen Donge in person?'

'I may have seen him, but I don't remember . . . I'm not at the counter. I have a private office where I only see the public through a sort of spy-hole . . .'

'Have your employees seen him?'

'I asked several of the staff that this morning . . . One of the clerks remembers him, because he was also having a house built in the suburbs . . . He told me he remembered remarking that Donge had left his house almost before it had been built . . .'

'Could you telephone this man?'

He did so. Maigret took the opportunity of stretching, like someone who is still half asleep, but his eyes were alert.

'You were saying . . . Let me see . . . Donge changed his address and went to live at 117b Rue Réaumur . . . Will you excuse me a moment?'

He disappeared in the direction of the inspectors' office.

'Lucas . . . Jump in a taxi . . . 117b Rue Réaumur . . . Find out all you can about Monsieur Prosper Donge . . . I'll explain later . . .'

He came back to the assistant branch manager.

'What transactions did Donge make after that?'

'It's that that I wanted to see you about. I was horrified, this morning, when I looked at his account, and even more horrified when I saw the last entry . . . The first American cheque . . .'

'Excuse me – the what?'

'Oh – there were several! The first American cheque, drawn on a bank in Detroit and made out to Prosper Donge, was dated March, three years ago, and was for five hundred dollars . . . I can tell you what that was worth, exactly, at the time . . .'

'It doesn't matter!'

'The cheque was paid into his account. Six months later another cheque for the same amount was sent to us by Donge, asking us to pay it in and credit it to his account . . .'

The assistant manager suddenly became worried by the Superintendent's complacent expression, and the fact that he no longer appeared to be listening to him. And Maigret's thoughts were far away. It had suddenly occurred to him that if he hadn't telephoned the solicitor before seeing his visitor, if he hadn't asked certain questions when he was speaking to him, it would all have looked as though it was sheer chance . . .

'I'm listening, Monsieur – Monsieur Jolivet isn't it?'

He had to look at the visiting card each time he said it.

'Or rather, I already know what you are going to tell me. Donge continued to receive cheques from Detroit, at the rate of about one every three months . . .'

'That is correct . . . But . . .'

'The cheques amounted to how much altogether?'

'Three hundred thousand francs . . .'

'Which remained in the bank without Donge ever drawing any money out?'

'Yes . . . But for the last eight months, there has been no cheque . . .'

Ah! Hadn't Mrs Clark been on a cruise in the Pacific, with her son, before coming to France?

'During this time, did Donge continue to pay small amounts into his account?'

'I can't find any trace of any . . . Of course any such payments would have been derisory compared with the cheques from America . . . But I'm just coming to the worrying part . . . The letter the day before yesterday . . . It wasn't me who dealt with it . . . It was the head of the foreign currency department – you'll see why in a minute . . . Well, we got this letter from Donge the day before yesterday . . . Instead of containing a cheque as usual, it asked us to make one out for him, payable to the bearer, at a bank in Brussels . . . It's a common procedure . . . People going abroad often ask us to give them a cheque payable at another bank, which avoids complications with letters of credit and also avoids the necessity of carrying large sums in cash . . .'

'How much was the cheque for?'

'Two hundred and eighty thousand French francs . . . Nearly all the money in his account . . . In fact there is now only a little under twenty thousand francs in Donge's account . . .'

'You made out the cheque?'

'We sent it to the address he gave, as requested . . .'

'Which was?'

'Monsieur Prosper Donge, 117b Rue Réaumur, as usual . . .'

'So the letter would have been delivered yesterday morning?'

'Probably . . . But in that case, Donge can't be in possession of it . . .'

And the assistant manager brandished the newspaper.

'He can't have got it, because, the day before yesterday, at just about the time when we were making out the cheque, Prosper Donge was arrested!'

Maigret leafed rapidly through the telephone directory and discovered that 117b Rue Réaumur, where there were several numbers, also had a telephone in the concierge's lodge. He dialled the number. Lucas had arrived there a few minutes earlier.

He gave him brief instructions.

'A letter, yes, addressed to Donge . . . The envelope is stamped with the address of the O Branch of the Crédit Lyonnais . . . Hurry, old chap . . . Call me back . . .'

'I think, Superintendent,' said the assistant branch manager solemnly, 'I did right to . . .'

'Yes! Yes!'

But he no longer saw the poor fellow, and paid not the slightest attention to him. He was miles away, as if in a dream, and had to keep moving objects about, stirring up the stove, walking to and fro.

'An employee from the Crédit Lyonnais, sir . . .'

'Tell him to come in . . .'

As he spoke, the telephone rang. The bank clerk remained standing nervously in the doorway, staring at his assistant manager in horror, wondering what he could possibly have done to be summoned to the Quai des Orfèvres.

'Lucas?'

'Well, Chief, the building isn't a residential block. It's only offices, most of them with only one room. Some of them are rented by provincial businessmen who find it useful to have a Paris address. Some of them practically never set foot in the place and their mail is forwarded on to them. Others have a typist to answer the telephone . . . Hullo! . . .'

'Go on.'

'Three years ago, Donge had an office here for two months, at a rent of six hundred francs a month . . . He only came here two or three times . . . Since then he has sent a hundred francs to the concierge each month to forward his mail . . .'

'Where is it forwarded to? . . .'

'Poste Restante to the Jem bureau, 42 Boulevard Haussmann . . .'

'To what name?'

'The envelopes are ready typed and Donge sends them in advance . . . Wait – it's a bit dark in the lodge . . . Yes, put the light on, mate . . . Here we are . . . J. M. D. Poste Restante, Jem, 42 Boulevard Haussmann . . . That's all . . . Private bureaux are allowed to accept letters addressed with initials only . . .'

'Did you keep your taxi? . . . No? . . . Idiot! Jump in a cab . . . What time is it? . . . Eleven . . . Get over to the Boulevard Haussmann . . . Did the concierge send on a letter yesterday morning? . . . He did? . . . Hurry, then . . .'

He had forgotten the two men, who didn't know what to do and were listening in bewilderment. His thoughts had raced ahead so fast that he almost found himself asking: 'What are you two still doing here?'

Then he suddenly calmed down.

'What do you do at the bank?' he asked the clerk, who started in surprise.

'I'm on current accounts.'

'Do you know Prosper Donge?'

'Yes, I know him . . . That is, I've seen him several times . . . You see he was having a house built in the suburbs at one time, and so was I . . . Only I chose a plot of land at . . .'

'Yes – I know . . . Go on . . .'

'He used to come in from time to time to draw out small amounts for the workmen who didn't have bank accounts and wouldn't accept cheques . . . He found it very tiresome . . . I remember we discussed it . . . We said everyone should have a bank account as they do in America . . . It was difficult for him to get there, because he had to be at the Majestic from six in the morning until six at night, and the bank was shut by then . . . I told him . . . the assistant manager won't mind, because we do it for some of our customers . . . that he could just telephone me and that I would send him the money to be signed for on receipt . . . I sent him money like that to the Majestic two or three times . . .'

'Have you seen him since?'

'I don't think so . . . But I had to go to Étretat for two summers running, to run the branch there . . . He could have come in then . . .'

Maigret pulled open a drawer of his desk, took out a photograph of Donge and laid it on the desk without saying a word.

'That's him!' said the bank clerk. 'You couldn't miss his face. It appears – so he told me – that he had smallpox as a child and the farm people he was living with didn't even call in a doctor . . .'

'Are you sure that's him?'

'As sure as I am of anything!'

'And you'd recognize his writing?'

'I would certainly recognize it,' the assistant manager put in, annoyed at being relegated to second place.

Maigret handed them various bits of paper, with writing by different people on them.

'No! . . . No! . . . That's not his writing . . . Ah! . . . Wait a minute . . . There's one of his 7s . . . He had a very characteristic way of writing his 7s . . . And his Fs too . . . That's one of his Fs . . .'

The writing they were pointing at was indeed Donge's; it was one of the slips he scrawled when people ordered so many coffees, coffee with croissants, tea, portions of toast or cups of chocolate.

The telephone remained silent. It was just midday.

'Well, thank you very much, gentlemen!'

What on earth was Lucas doing at the Jem bureau? He was quite capable of having taken a bus, to save the taxi fare!

9

Monsieur Charles's Newspaper

Apart, they might still have passed. But standing together by the entrance to Police Headquarters, they looked as if they were waiting at a factory gate, and made a pathetic, grotesque pair. Gigi perched on her thin legs, in her worn rabbit-skin coat, her eyes wary, defying the policeman on duty at the entrance and peering to see who it was whenever she heard anyone coming; and poor Charlotte, who hadn't had the heart to do her hair or put on make-up, with her large moon-like face blotched and red because she'd been crying and was still sniffling. Her nose was bright red, and looked like a small red ball in the middle of her face.

She was wearing a decent black cloth coat, with an astrakhan collar and band of astrakhan round the hem. She held limply on to a large glacé kid bag. Without the ghoulish presence of Gigi, and the red gleaming in the middle of her face, she might have looked fairly presentable.

'There he is!'

Charlotte hadn't budged, but Gigi had been walking frenziedly to and fro. And now she had seen Maigret arriving, with a colleague. Too late, he saw the two women. It was sunny out on the quay, with a touch of spring in the air.

'Excuse me, Superintendent . . .'

He shook hands with his colleague . . .

'Have a good lunch, old chap . . .'

'Can we talk to you for a minute, Superintendent?'

And Charlotte burst into tears, stuffing her handkerchief which was rolled in a ball into her mouth. People in the street turned round. Maigret waited patiently. Gigi said, as if to excuse her friend: 'The magistrate sent for her and she's just been seeing him . . .'

Oh dear – Monsieur Bonneau. He had a right to do so, of course. But all the same . . .

'Is it true, sir, that Prosper has . . . has admitted everything?'

This time Maigret smiled openly. Was that all the magistrate had been able to think up? That corny trick used by junior policemen? And that great goose Charlotte had believed him!

'It's not true, is it? I knew it wasn't! If you knew what he said to me! . . . To listen to him you'd think I was the lowest of the low . . .'

The policeman on duty at the entrance was looking at them with amusement. It was a curious sight – Maigret besieged by the two women, one of them crying and the other peering at him with no attempt to hide her antagonism.

'As if I'd write an anonymous letter accusing Prosper, when I'm sure he didn't kill her! . . . If it had been a revolver, now, I might just have believed it . . . But not strangling someone . . . And particularly not doing it again the next day to some poor man who hadn't done anything . . . Have you discovered anything else, then, Superintendent? Do you think they'll keep him in prison?'

Maigret signed to a taxi which was passing.

'Get in!' he told the two women. 'I was going on an errand – you can come with me . . .'

It was quite true. He had at last had a telephone call from Lucas, who had drawn a blank at the Jem bureau. He had asked him to meet him in the Boulevard Haussmann. And he had just had the idea that he might . . .

Both the women tried to sit on the flap seats, but he made them sit on the back seat and he himself sat with his back to the driver. It was one of the first fine days of the year. The streets of Paris lay gleaming in the sun, and everyone looked more cheerful.

'Tell me, Charlotte, is Donge still paying his savings into the bank?'

He felt irritated with Gigi, who frowned each time he opened his mouth, as if suspecting a trap. She was clearly longing to say to her friend: 'Look out! . . . Think before you answer . . .'

But Charlotte exclaimed: 'Savings! Poor love! . . . We haven't saved anything for a long time now! . . . Since we've had this house weighing us down, and that's a fact! . . . It was supposed to cost forty thousand francs at the most, according to the estimates ... First the foundations cost three times as much as they expected, because they found a subterranean stream ... Then, when the walls were being built, there was a building strike which brought everything to a stop just as winter began ... Five thousand francs here ... Three thousand francs there ... They fleeced us on all sides! If I told you how much the house had cost us to date you wouldn't believe it! I don't know the exact figure, but it must be more than eighty thousand, and there are still some things which haven't been paid for ...'

'So Donge hasn't any money in the bank?'

'He hasn't even got an account ... He hasn't had one for ... wait a minute ... for about three years now ... I remember because one day the postman brought a money order for about eight hundred francs ... I didn't know what it was ... When Donge got back he told me he had written to the bank to close his account ...'

'You can't remember the date?'

'What's that got to do with you?' asked Gigi, who couldn't refrain from adding her sour note.

'I know it was in the winter, because I was busy breaking the ice round the pump when the postman came ... Wait ... I went to the market in Saint-Cloud that day ... I bought a goose ... So it must have been a few days before Christmas ...'

'Where are we going?' grumbled Gigi, looking out of the window.

Just at that moment, the taxi stopped in the Boulevard Haussmann, just before the Faubourg Saint-Honoré. Lucas was standing on the pavement and goggled as he saw Maigret follow the two women out of the cab.

'Wait a second ...' the Superintendent told them.

He drew Lucas aside.

'Well?'

'Look ... You see that sort of narrow shop, between the suitcase shop and the ladies' hairdresser? That's the Jem bureau ... It's run by a revolting old man whom I couldn't get any information from ... He wanted to shut the bureau and go off to lunch, pretending it was his lunch hour ... I forced him to stay ...

He's furious . . . He insists that I've no right without a warrant . . .'

Maigret went into the shop, which was so poorly lit it was almost dark, and cut in two by a dirty wooden counter. Small wooden pigeon-holes, also filthy, lined the walls and these were full of letters.

'I'd like to know . . .' the old man began.

'I'll ask the questions, if you don't mind,' Maigret growled. 'You get letters addressed by initials, I believe, which is not allowed by the official poste restante, so your clientele must be a pretty bunch . . .'

'I pay my licence,' the old man promptly objected.

He wore glasses with heavy lenses, behind which darted rheumy eyes. His jacket was dirty and the collar of his shirt frayed and greasy. A rancid smell emanated from his body and filled the whole shop.

'I want to know if you have a register where you note the real name of your clients against the initials . . .'

The man snickered.

'D'you think they'd come here if they had to give their names? . . . Why not ask them for identity papers?'

It was somewhat unpleasant to think of pretty women coming furtively into the shop, which had served as a go-between for so many adulterous couples, and many other shady transactions.

'You got a letter yesterday morning addressed with the initials J. M. D. . . .'

'It's possible. I've already said so to your colleague. He even insisted on checking that the letter was no longer here . . .'

'So, someone came to collect it. Can you tell me when?'

'I've no idea, and even if I had, I doubt if I'd tell you . . .'

'You realize I may come and close down your shop one of these days?'

'Other people have said the same to me, and my shop, as you call it, has been here for the last forty-two years . . . If I counted up all the husbands who've come to shout at me, and who've even threatened me with their sticks . . .'

Lucas had been quite right in saying he was revolting.

'If it's all the same to you, I'll put up the shutters and go and have my lunch . . .'

Where could the old brute possibly have lunch? Surely he hadn't got a family – wife and children? It seemed far more likely that he was a bachelor, with his special place at some dingy restaurant in the neighbourhood, with his napkin in a ring.

'Have you ever seen this man?'

Maigret refusing to be hustled, produced Donge's photograph again, and curiosity gained the upper hand over the man's ill humour. He bent to peer at it and had to hold it within a few centimetres of his face. His expression didn't change. He shrugged.

'I don't remember seeing him . . .' he mumbled, as if disappointed.

The two women were waiting outside, in front of the narrow shop window. Maigret called Charlotte in.

'And do you recognize her?'

If Charlotte was acting, she was doing it remarkably well; she was looking round as if shocked and embarrassed, which was hardly surprising in such surroundings.

'What is . . . ?' she began.

She was terrified. Why had she been brought here? She looked round instinctively for Gigi, who came in of her own accord.

'How many people are you going to bring in here then?'

'You don't recognize either of them? You can't tell me whether it was a man or a woman who came to collect the letter addressed to J. M. D., or when the letter was collected?'

Without replying, the man seized a wooden shutter and started to hang it in front of the door. There was no option but to beat a hasty retreat. Maigret, Lucas and the two women found themselves outside on the pavement, under the chestnut trees with their new spring buds.

'You two can go now! . . .'

He watched them go off. Gigi had barely gone ten metres before she started violently haranguing her companion whom she was dragging along at a pace little suited to Charlotte's dumpy figure.

'Any news, Chief?'

What could Maigret say? He was brooding, anxious. The

spring weather seemed to make him irritable rather than relaxed.

'I don't know . . . Look . . . Go and have some lunch . . . Stay in the office this afternoon . . . Tell the banks – in France and Brussels – that if a cheque for two hundred and eighty thousand francs has been presented . . .'

He was only a few metres from the Majestic. He went down the Rue de Ponthieu, and into the bar near the staff door of the hotel. They served snacks there and he ordered some tinned cassoulet, which he ate morosely, alone at a little table at the back, near two men who were hurriedly downing a snack before going to the races and who were talking about horses.

Anyone who followed him that afternoon, would have been hard put to it to decide what exactly he was doing. Having finished his meal, he had some coffee, bought some tobacco and filled his pouch. Then he went out of the bar and stood on the pavement for a while, looking around.

He probably hadn't formulated any precise plan of action. He ambled slowly into the Majestic and along the back corridor, and stood by the clocking-on machine, rather like a traveller with hours to wait at a station, putting coins into the chocolate machines.

People brushed past him, mostly cooks, with cloths round their necks, nipping out to have a quick drink at the bar next door.

As he went farther along the corridor, the heat grew more intense, and there was a strong smell of cooking.

The cloakroom was empty. He washed his hands at a basin, for no reason, to pass the time, and spent a good ten minutes cleaning his nails. Then, as he was too hot, he took off his overcoat and hung it in locker 89.

Jean Ramuel was sitting in state in his glass cage. In the still-room opposite, the three women were working at an accelerated pace, with a new cook in a white jacket who had replaced Prosper.

'Who's that?' Maigret asked Ramuel.

'A temp, whom they've engaged until they find someone . . . He's called Monsieur Charles . . . So you've come to take a little stroll round, Superintendent? . . . Excuse me a minute . . .'

It was hectic. The luxury clientele ate late, and the chits were piling up in front of Ramuel, waiters were dashing past, all the telephones were ringing at once and the service-lifts were shooting up and down non-stop.

Maigret, still wearing his bowler, wandered about with his hands in his pockets, stopping by a cook who was thickening a sauce as if it fascinated him, watching the women wash up, or peering through the glass partitions into the guests' servants' hall.

He went up the back stairs, as he had done on his first visit, but stopped on all the floors this time, without hurrying, and still looking rather disgruntled. As he went down again, he was joined by the manager, who was out of breath.

'They've just told me you were here, Superintendent . . . I don't suppose you've had lunch? . . . May I offer . . .'

'I've eaten, thank you . . .'

'May I inquire if you've any news? . . . I was so taken aback when they arrested that Prosper Donge . . . But are you sure you won't have anything? . . . A brandy, perhaps? . . .'

The manager was growing more and more embarrassed, finding himself on the narrow staircase with Maigret, who obstinately refused to show any reaction. At times the Superintendent seemed as slumberous and thick-skinned as a pachyderm.

'I had hoped the press wouldn't get on to the affair . . . You know, for a hotel, what . . . As for Donge . . .'

It was hopeless. Maigret offered him no help as he stumbled on. He had started going downstairs again, and they had now reached the basement.

'A man I would have cited as of exemplary character, only a few days ago . . . Because as you can imagine, we get all sorts in a hotel like this . . .'

Maigret was glancing from one glass partition to another, or as he would say, from one aquarium to another. They finally ended up in the cloakroom, by the famous locker 89, where two human lives had come definitely to an end.

'As for that poor Colleboeuf . . . Forgive me if I'm boring you . . . I've just thought of something . . . Don't you think it would need unusual strength to strangle a man in broad daylight, only a few metres from numerous people – I mean so that the victim had no chance to cry out or struggle? . . . It would be possible now, because everyone's rushing about making a din . . . But at half-past four or five in the afternoon . . .'

'You were in the middle of lunch, I imagine?' Maigret murmured.

'It doesn't matter . . . We're used to eating when we can . . .'

'Do please go and finish your meal . . . I'm just going . . . I'll just see . . . If you'll excuse me . . .'

And he ambled off down the passage again, opening and shutting doors, and lighting his pipe, which he then allowed to go out.

His steps kept bringing him back to the still-room, and he began to know the occupants' every movement, and muttered between his teeth: 'So . . . Donge is there . . . He's there from six o'clock onwards every day . . . Good . . . He had a cup of coffee at home, which Charlotte prepared when she got in . . . OK then . . . When he gets here, I imagine he pours himself a cup as soon as the first percolator's hot . . . Yes . . .'

Did it make any sense?

'He usually takes a cup of coffee up to the night porter . . . Yes . . . In fact, that day, it was probably because it was already after ten past six and Donge still hadn't come up that Justin Colleboeuf came down . . . So . . . Well . . . for that or some other reason . . . Hmm!'

In fact they weren't filling the silver coffee-pots that had been used at breakfast, but little brown glazed pots, each with a tiny filter on top.

'. . . Breakfasts go up all morning, more and more of them . . . OK . . . Then Donge has a bit to eat himself . . . They bring him something on a tray . . .'

'Would you mind moving a little to the right or left, Superintendent? . . . You're blocking my view of the trays . . .'

It was Ramuel, who had to oversee everything from his glass cage. He even had to count all the cups leaving the still-room as well, then?

'I'm so sorry to have to ask you . . .'

'Not a bit! Not a bit!'

Three o'clock. The pace slackened a bit. One of the cooks had just fetched his coat to go out.

'If anyone wants me, Ramuel, I'll be back at five . . . I've got to go to the tax office . . .'

Nearly all the little brown coffee-pots had come down again. Monsieur Charles came out of the still-room and went along the passage leading to the street, after having glanced curiously at the Superintendent. The women must have told him who he was.

He came back a few minutes later with an evening paper. It was a little after three. The women were washing up at the sink, up to their elbows in hot water.

Monsieur Charles however sat down at his little table and made himself as comfortable as possible. He spread out the paper, put on his glasses, lit a cigarette and began to read.

There was nothing odd about this, but Maigret was staring at him as though thunderstruck.

'Well,' he said, smiling at Ramuel, who was counting his chits, 'there's a break now, is there?'

'Until half past four, then it starts up again with the thé dansant . . .'

Maigret went on standing in the corridor for a short while longer. Then suddenly a bell rang in the still-room, Monsieur Charles got up, said a few words into the telephone, reluctantly left his paper and went off along the corridor.

'Where's he off to?'

'What time is it? Half past three? It's probably the storekeeper ringing him to give him his coffee and tea supplies.'

'Does he do that every day?'

'Yes, every day . . .'

Ramuel watched Maigret, who was now calmly wandering into the still-room. He did nothing spectacular – merely opened the drawer of the table, which was an ordinary deal one. He found a small bottle of ink, a penholder and a packet of writing paper. There were also some stumps of pencils and two or three postal order counterfoils.

He was shutting the drawer when Monsieur Charles came back, carrying some packets. Seeing Maigret bending over the table, he misinterpreted his action.

'You can take it . . .' he said, meaning the newspaper. 'There's nothing in it! . . . I only read the serial and the small ads.'

Maigret had guessed as much.

'There it was then . . . Prosper Donge sitting peacefully at his table . . . the three women over there splashing about in the sink . . . He . . .'

The Superintendent was looking less and less ponderous and sleepy every minute. With the air of a man who has suddenly remembered that he has an urgent job to do, and without saying good-bye to anyone, he walked rapidly towards the cloakroom, seized his coat, put it on as he came out and a minute later had hurtled into a taxi.

'To the financial section of the Public Prosecutor's Department,' he directed the driver.

A quarter to four. There might still be someone there. If all went well, there was a chance that by tonight . . . before the day was out . . .

He turned round. The taxi had just driven past Edgar Fagonet, alias Zebio, who was walking towards the Majestic.

10

Dinner at the Coupole

The operation was carried out with such brutal effectiveness that even an ancient antique dealer, rotting away at the back of his dark little shop like a mole, came to the door, dragging his feet over the floorboards.

It was a few minutes to six. The dingy shops in the Rue des Saints-Pères were feebly lit, and outside in the street there lingered a bluish twilight.

The police car shot round the corner with enough blasts on the horn to unnerve all the antique dealers and little shopkeepers in the street.

Then, with a squeal of brakes, it drew into the kerb, as three men jumped out, looking purposeful, as if summoned by an emergency call.

Maigret walked up to the door, alone, just as the pale, terrified face of a shop assistant came and glued itself to the glass, like a transfer. An inspector went up the side alleyway to check that the shop had no other entrance, and the policeman who remained on the pavement outside looked more like a caricature than a real inspector, with his large drooping moustache and baleful, suspicious eyes, for which reason he had been purposely chosen by Maigret.

In the shop, whose walls were hung with Persian carpets, giving it an air of opulent tranquillity, the assistant tried to appear calm.

'Did you want to see Monsieur Atoum? . . . I'll see if he's in . . .'

But the Superintendent had already brushed the poor creature aside. He had spotted a glow of reddish light, coming from an opening in the carpets at the back of the shop, and could hear the murmur of voices. He found himself on the threshold of a small room, no bigger than a tent made of four carpets and furnished with a sofa covered with bright leather cushions, and a table inlaid with mother-of-pearl on which were cups of Turkish coffee.

A man had stood up and was about to leave, and seemed as ill at ease as the clerk. Another man was lying on the sofa smoking a gold-tipped cigarette, and said a few words in a foreign tongue.

'Monsieur Atoum, I believe? . . . Superintendent Maigret of the Judicial Police . . .'

The visitor hurriedly departed and there was a slam as the door of the shop closed behind him. Maigret sat himself composedly on the edge of the sofa, examining the little Turkish coffee cups with interest.

'Don't you recognize me, Monsieur Atoum? . . . We spent a whole half day together once, let me see . . . my goodness, it must be nearly eight years ago now . . . A splendid journey! . . . The Vosges, Alsace! If I remember rightly, we parted company near a frontier-post . . .'

Atoum was fat, but had a young face and magnificent eyes. He was richly dressed, with rings on his fingers, and heavily scented, and reclined rather than sat on the sofa. The small room, lit by a mock alabaster lamp, seemed more like something in an Oriental bazaar than a Parisian street.

'Let me see – what was it you had done on that occasion? . . . Nothing much, as far as I can remember . . . But as your papers weren't in order, the French Government thought it would be a good idea to offer you a little trip to the border . . . You came back that evening, of course, but appearances were saved and I think you then found protection . . .'

Atoum seemed quite unperturbed by all this, and remained staring at Maigret with cat-like calm.

'After that you became a banker, because in France you don't necessarily have to have a clean slate to handle people's money . . . You've had various little difficulties since, Monsieur Atoum . . .'

'May I be allowed to ask, Superintendent . . .'

'What I'm doing here, you mean? Well, frankly, I don't know. I've got a car and men outside. We may all go for a little ride . . .'

Atoum's hand remained perfectly steady, as he lit a cigarette, having offered one to Maigret, who refused.

'Or I could go peacefully off, leaving you here . . .'

'Depending on what?'

'The way you answer one small question . . . I know how discreet you are, so I've taken a few precautions to help you overcome this, as it were . . . When you were a banker, you had a clerk who was your right-hand man, your trusted confidant – you note I don't say accomplice – called Jean Ramuel . . . Well – I'd like to know why you parted with such a trusted helper, why, to be more precise, you booted him out? . . .'

There was a long silence while Atoum reflected.

'You're mistaken, Superintendent . . . I didn't get rid of Ramuel; he left of his own accord, for reasons of health, I think it was . . .'

Maigret got up.

'Too bad! In that case it'll have to be the first alternative . . . If you'd be good enough to come with me, Monsieur Atoum . . .'

'Where are you going to take me?'

'Back to the border . . .'

A smile hovered over the oriental's lips.

'But we'll try a different border this time . . . I think I'd like to make a little trip to Italy . . . I'm told that you left that country in undue haste and that you forgot to carry out a five-year sentence for forgery and passing counterfeit cheques . . . So . . .'

'Sit down, Superintendent . . .'

'You think it won't be necessary for me to get up again in a hurry, then?'

'What do you want with Ramuel?'

'Perhaps to give him his deserts. What do you think?'

And changing his tone abruptly: 'Come, Atoum! I've no time to waste today . . . I have no doubt Ramuel's got a hold over you . . .'

'I admit that if he were to talk inadvisedly, he could cause me a great deal of trouble. Banking affairs are complex. He would stick his nose into everything . . . I wonder if I wouldn't do better to choose Italy . . . Unless you can give me some assurance . . . That if, for example, he speaks of certain things, you won't pay any attention to them, since that's all in the past and I'm now an honest businessman . . .'

'It's within the realm of possibility . . .'

'In that case I can tell you that Ramuel and I parted company after a somewhat stormy exchange of words . . . I had discovered, in fact, that he was working in my bank on his own behalf, and that he had committed a number of forgeries . . .'

'I suppose you kept the documents?'

Atoum batted his eyelids, and confessed in a whisper: 'But he has kept others, you see, so . . .'

'So you've got a mutual hold over each other . . . Well, Atoum, I want you to give me those documents immediately . . .'

He still hesitated. Italian or French prison? He finally got up, and lifted the hanging behind the sofa, revealing a little safe set in the wall, which he opened.

'Here are some bills of exchange on which Ramuel copied, not only my signature, but also that of two of my customers . . . If you find a little red book among his things, in which I noted various transactions, I would be grateful if you . . .'

And, as he crossed the shop after Maigret, he hesitated a moment and then, pointing to a magnificent Kerman carpet: 'I wonder if Madame Maigret would like that design . . .'

It was half past eight when Maigret walked into the Coupole and made for the part of the vast room where dinner was being served. He was alone, his hands in his pockets, as usual, and his bowler on the back of his head. He seemed to have nothing on his mind except looking for a free table.

Then he suddenly saw a small man already installed with a grill and a half of beer in front of him.

'Hullo, Lucas! . . . Is this place free?'

He sat down at Lucas's table, smiling in anticipation at the thought of his dinner and then got up to give his coat to a waiter. An aggressive and common-looking woman sitting at the table next to him, with a half lobster of impressive dimensions, shouted in a disagreeable voice: 'Waiter! . . . Bring some fresh mayonnaise . . . This smells of soap . . .'

Maigret turned towards her, and then to the man at her side, and said with a show of genuine astonishment: 'Why – Monsieur Ramuel! . . . What a coincidence meeting you here! . . . Would you do me the honour of introducing? . . .'

'My wife . . . Superintendent Maigret, of the Judicial Police . . .'

'Delighted to meet you, Superintendent . . .'

'Steak and chips, and a large beer, please, waiter!'

He glanced at Ramuel's plate, and saw that he was eating some noodles, without butter or cheese.

'Do you know what I think?' he said suddenly, in a friendly tone of voice. 'It seems to me, Monsieur Ramuel, that you've always been unlucky . . . It struck me the first time I saw you . . . There are some people for whom nothing will go right, and I've noticed that it is just those same people who on top of all that fall prey to the most disagreeable illnesses and accidents . . .'

'He'll use what you say as an excuse for his horrible nature!' interrupted Marie Deligeard, sniffing the new mayonnaise she had just been brought.

'You're intelligent, well educated and hard-working,' continued the Superintendent, 'and you should have made your fortune ten times over . . . And the strange thing is, that you nearly succeeded several times in gaining a marvellous position for yourself . . . In Cairo, for instance . . . Then in Ecuador . . . Each time, you had a rapid success, and then had to go right back to the beginning again . . . What happens when you get an excellent job in a bank? . . . You are unlucky enough to land up with a crooked banker – Atoum – and are obliged to leave . . .'

The people dining at the neighbouring tables had no idea what they were talking about. Maigret spoke in a cheerful, friendly tone of voice and attacked his steak with relish, while Lucas kept his nose buried in his plate and Ramuel appeared to be preoccupied with his noodles.

'In fact, I wasn't expecting to meet you here, in the Boulevard Montparnasse, as I thought you'd already be on the train to Brussels . . .'

Ramuel said nothing, but his face became even more yellow, and his fingers tightened on his fork. His companion shouted at him: 'What? Hey – you were going to Brussels and hadn't said anything to me about it? What's up, Jean? . . . Another woman, eh?'

And Maigret said blandly: 'I assure you, Madame, that it's got nothing to do with a woman . . . Don't worry . . . But your husband . . . I mean your friend . . .'

'You can call him my husband . . . I don't know what he's told you on that score, but we're well and truly married . . . I can prove . . .'

She fumbled frantically in her bag and pulled out a tightly folded, torn and faded bit of paper.

'There you are! . . . It's our marriage certificate . . .'

The text was in Spanish, and it was covered in Ecuadorian stamps and seals.

'Answer me, Jean! . . . What were you going to Brussels for?'

'But . . . I had no intention . . .'

'Come, Monsieur Ramuel . . . Forgive me – I had no intention of causing a family row . . . When I learnt that you had taken nearly all your money out of the bank and had asked for a cheque for two hundred and eighty thousand francs, to be drawn on Brussels . . .'

Maigret hurriedly bit into a mouthful of deliciously crisp chips, because he was having difficulty not to smile. A foot had been placed on his, and he realized it was Ramuel's – silently begging him to be quiet.

It was too late. Forgetting her lobster, forgetting the dozens of people dining round them, Marie Deligeard, or Madame Ramuel rather, if the bit of paper could be believed, shrieked: 'Did you say two hundred and eighty thousand francs? . . . Do you mean he had two hundred and eighty thousand francs in the bank and kept me short? . . .'

Maigret looked pointedly at the lobster and half-bottle of twenty-five-franc Riesling . . .

'Answer me, Jean! . . . Is it true? . . .'

'I've no idea what the Superintendent's talking about . . .'

'You've got a bank account?'

'I repeat, I haven't got a bank account, and if I did have two hundred and eighty thousand francs . . .'

'What do you mean by saying that, then, Superintendent?'

'I'm so sorry, Madame, to upset you like this. I thought you knew about it, that your husband hid nothing from you . . .'

'Now I understand!'

'What do you understand?'

'His attitude, recently . . . He was too kind . . . Fawning on me

. . . But I thought it didn't seem natural . . . It was all part of the plan, wasn't it?'

People were turning to stare at them in amusement, because all this could be heard at least three tables away.

'Marie! . . .' Ramuel begged.

'You were making your pile in secret, were you, and letting me go without, while you got ready to leave . . . One fine day you'd have left, just like that! . . . I'd find myself all alone in a flat with the rent not even paid! . . . None of that, my little lad! . . . You've tried to sneak away twice already, but you know perfectly well it didn't work . . . You're sure there's no woman tucked away somewhere, Superintendent? . . .'

'Look, Superintendent, don't you think it would be better if we continued this conversation somewhere else? . . .'

'No, no. Not a bit!' Maigret sighed. 'Besides . . . I'd like . . . Waiter! . . .'

He pointed to the silver dish with a domed cover, which was being wheeled on a trolley between the tables.

'What have you got in your machine there?'

'A side of beef . . .'

'Good! Give me a slice, will you? A little beef, Lucas? . . . And some chips, please, waiter . . .'

'Take away my lobster – it's not fresh!' Ramuel's companion interrupted. 'Give me the same as the Superintendent . . . So the dirty beast had money tucked away all the time, and . . .'

She had become so heated she had to touch up her face, waving a doubtful pink powderpuff over the tablecloth.

And under the table, there was frantic activity – Ramuel quietly kicking her to make her shut up, and she pretending not to understand and stabbing him viciously with her heel in return.

'You'll pay for this, you beast! . . . Just you wait . . .'

'Look, I'll explain it all, in a minute . . . I don't know why the Superintendent thinks . . .'

'And you, you're sure you're not mistaken? . . . I know what you police are like . . . When you can't find out anything and are floundering about in the dark, you invent something just to make people talk . . . I hope that's not what you're doing?'

Maigret looked at his watch. It was half past nine. He gave

Lucas a quiet wink, and Lucas coughed. Then Maigret leant confidentially towards Ramuel and the woman.

'Don't move, Ramuel . . . Don't make a scene, it won't help . . . Your right-hand neighbour is one of our men . . . And Sergeant Lucas has been following you since this afternoon and it was he who telephoned me to let me know you were here . . .'

'What do you mean?' stuttered Marie Deligeard.

'I mean, Madame, that I wanted to let you eat first . . . I'm afraid I have to put your husband under arrest . . . And it will be better for everyone if we do it quietly . . . Finish your meal . . . We'll go out together in a minute – all good friends . . . We'll get a taxi and go for a little ride to the Quai des Orfèvres . . . You can't imagine how peaceful the offices are at night . . . Some mustard, please, waiter! . . . And some gherkins, if you've got any . . .'

Marie Deligeard went on attacking her food with venom, giving her husband a terrible look from time to time, her brow furrowed with a deep scowl, which was hardly conducive to making her look any prettier or more prepossessing. Maigret ordered a third glass of beer and leant across to Ramuel, murmuring confidentially: 'You see, at about four o'clock this afternoon, I suddenly remembered that you had been a quartermaster-sergeant . . .'

'You always said you were a second-lieutenant!' the odious woman spat, not missing a trick.

'But it's very smart, Madame, being a quartermaster-sergeant! . . . It's the quartermaster-sergeant who does all the writing for the company . . . So, you see, I remembered my military service, which was a long time ago, as you can imagine . . .'

Nothing could prevent him enjoying his chips. They were sensational – crisp outside and melting within.

'As our captain came to the barracks as little as possible, it was our quartermaster-sergeant who signed all the passes and most other documents, in the captain's name, of course . . . And the signature was so well done that the captain could never tell which signatures he had written himself and which were the work of the quartermaster-sergeant . . . Do you see what I mean, Ramuel?'

'I don't understand . . . And as I imagine you're not going to try to arrest me without a proper warrant, I'd like to know . . .'

'I've got a warrant from the Financial Section of the Public

Prosecutor's Department . . . Does that surprise you? . . . It happens quite often, you see . . . One is busy on a case . . . Without meaning to, one uncovers something else, which happened many years ago and which everyone has forgotten . . . I've got some bills in my pocket, given to me by a man called Atoum . . . You won't have any more to eat? . . . No dessert, Madame? . . . Waiter! . . . We'll each pay for our own, don't you think? . . . What do I owe you, waiter? . . . I had a steak, something from the trolley, oh yes, some beef, three portions of chips and three beers . . . Have you got a light, Lucas?'

11

Gala Evening at Police Headquarters

The dark porch, then the great staircase, with a dim light at infrequent intervals, and finally the long corridor with its many doors.

Maigret said cheerfully to Marie Deligeard, who was out of breath: 'We've arrived, Madame . . . You can get your breath back . . .'

There was only one light on in the corridor, and two men were walking along deep in conversation – Oswald J. Clark and his solicitor.

At the end of the corridor was the waiting-room, which was glassed in on one side, to allow the police to come and watch their visitors if necessary. There was a table with a green cloth.

Green velvet armchairs. A Louis-Philippe clock on the mantel-piece – exactly like the one in Maigret's office and in no better working order. Black frames on the walls with photographs of policemen who had fallen on the field of glory.

Two women in armchairs, in a dark corner – Charlotte and Gigi.

In the corridor, on a bench, Prosper Donge – still without his tie and shoelaces – sitting between two policemen.

'This way, Ramuel! . . . Come into my office . . . And Madame, would you be good enough to wait in the waiting-room for a minute, please? Will you show her the way, Lucas?'

He opened the door to his office. He was smiling at the thought of the three women left alone in the waiting-room, no doubt exchanging worried and angry glances.

'Come in, Ramuel! . . . You'd best take off your overcoat, because it looks as though we'll be here for some time . . .'

A green-shaded lamp on the table. Maigret took off his hat and coat, chose a pipe from his desk and opened the door of the inspectors' room.

It was as if Police Headquarters, usually so empty at night, had been stuffed with people for the occasion. Torrence was sitting at his desk, wearing a felt hat. He was smoking a cigarette, and sitting on a chair facing him was a little old man with a ragged beard, who was busily staring at his elastic-sided shoes.

Then there was Janvier who had seized the chance to write up his report, and who was keeping an eye on a middle-aged man, who looked like an ex-NCO.

'Are you the concierge?' Maigret asked him. 'Would you come into my office for a minute?'

He stood aside to let him go in first. The man held his cap in his hand and didn't at first see Ramuel, who was standing as far from the light as possible.

'You're the concierge at 117b Rue Réaumur, aren't you? . . . Some time ago a man called Prosper Donge rented one of your offices and since then you have continued to send on his mail to him . . . Here . . . Do you recognize Donge?'

The concierge turned towards Ramuel in his corner, and shook his head, saying: 'Hm . . . Er . . . Frankly . . . no! I can't say I do . . . I see so many people! . . . And it was three years ago, wasn't it? . . . I don't know if I remember rightly, but I have a vague idea that he had a beard . . . But perhaps the beard was someone else . . .'

'Thank you . . . You can go now . . . This way . . .'

One done. Maigret opened the door again and called: 'Monsieur Jem! . . . I don't know what your real name is . . . Would you come in, please . . . And would you be good enough to tell me . . .'

There was no need to wait for an answer this time. The little old man started with surprise on seeing Ramuel.

'Well?'

'Well what?'

'Do you recognize him?'

The old man was furious.

'I'll have to go and give evidence at the trial, I suppose? And they'll leave me to rot for two or three days in the witness's room, and who'll look after my shop during that time? . . . Then, when I'm in the witness box I'll be asked a lot of embarrassing questions, and the lawyers will say a lot of things about me which will ruin my reputation . . . No thank you, Superintendent!'

Then he suddenly added: 'What's he done?'

'Well – he's killed two people for a start – a man and a woman . . . The woman was a rich American . . .'

'Is there a reward?'

'A pretty large one, yes . . .'

'In that case, you can write . . . I, Jean-Baptiste Isaac Meyer, businessman . . . Will there be many witnesses sharing the reward? . . . Because I know what happens . . . The police make fine promises . . . Then, when it comes to the point . . .'

'I'll write: ". . . *formally recognize in the man presented to me as Jean Ramuel the person with whom I dealt at my private correspondence bureau under the initials J. M. D. . . .*" Is that correct, Monsieur Meyer?'

'Where shall I sign?'

'Wait! I'll add: ". . . *And I confirm that the said person came to collect a final letter on . . .*" Now you can sign . . . You're a cunning old devil, Monsieur Meyer, because you know very well that all this will bring you a good deal of publicity and that everyone who hadn't already heard of your bureau will be rushing to contact you . . . Torrence! . . . Monsieur Meyer can go now . . .'

When the door had shut behind him, the Superintendent read the repellent old man's statement with satisfaction. A voice made him start. It came from a dark corner of the room – only the lamp on the desk was lit.

'I protest, Superintendent, you . . .'

Then Maigret suddenly seemed to remember that he had forgotten something. He began by pulling the unbleached cotton blind across the window. Then he looked at his hands. This was a Maigret that few people knew, and those who did, didn't often boast about it afterwards.

'Come here, my little Ramuel . . . Do as I say, come here! . . . Farther! . . . Don't be afraid! . . .'

'What do . . . ?'

'You see, since I've discovered the truth, I've had a terrible desire to . . .'

As he spoke, Maigret's fist shot out and landed on the accountant's nose, as, too late, Ramuel raised his arm.

'There! . . . It's not really in order, of course, but it does one good . . . Tomorrow, the judge will interrogate you politely and everyone will be nice to you because you'll have become the star attraction of the court . . . Those gentlemen are always impressed by a star performer . . . If you see what I mean . . . There's some water in the basin, in the cupboard . . . Wash yourself, because you look disgusting like that . . .'

Ramuel, bleeding profusely, washed himself as well as he could.

'Let me see! . . . That's better! . . . You're almost presentable . . . Torrence! . . . Lucas! . . . Janvier! . . . Come on, lads . . . Bring in the ladies and gentlemen . . .'

Even his colleagues were surprised to find him much more elated than he usually was, even at the end of a difficult case. He had lit another pipe. The first to enter, between two policemen, was Donge, who held his handcuffed hands clumsily in front of him.

'Have you got the key?' Maigret asked one of the men.

He unlocked the handcuffs, and an instant later they snapped shut round Ramuel's wrists, while Donge stared at him with almost comic stupefaction.

The Superintendent then noticed that Donge had neither tie nor shoelaces, and he ordered Ramuel's laces and his little black silk bow tie to be taken away.

'Come in, ladies . . . Come in, Monsieur Clark . . . I know you can't understand what we're saying . . . But I'm sure Monsieur Davidson will be kind enough to translate . . . Has everyone got a chair? . . . Yes, Charlotte, you can go and sit next to Prosper . . . But I must ask you not to be too effusive for the time being . . .

'Is everyone here? . . . Shut the door, Torrence!'

'What has he done?' Madame Ramuel asked in her coarse voice . . .

'Please sit down too, Madame! . . . I hate talking to people who are standing up . . . No, Lucas! . . . Don't bother to put on the ceiling light . . . It's cosier like this . . . What has he done? . . . He's gone on doing what he's been doing all his life: committing forgeries . . . And I bet that if he's married you and spent so many years with a poisonous creature like you, saving your presence, it's because you've got a hold over him . . . And you've got a hold over him because you knew what he was up to in Guayaquil . . . There's a cable on its way there, and another for the company headquarters in London. I know in advance what the answer will be . . .'

And Marie chipped in in her vile voice: 'Why don't you answer, Jean? . . . So the two hundred and eighty thousand francs and the trip to Brussels were true, then! . . .'

She had sprung up like a jack-in-the-box, and rushed towards him.

'Scoundrel! . . . Thief! . . . Scum! . . . To think . . .'

'Calm yourself, Madame . . . It was much better that he didn't tell you anything because if he had done so, I would have been obliged to arrest you as an accomplice, not only in the forgery but in a double crime . . .'

From then on, an almost comic note was added to the proceedings. Clark, who kept his eyes on Maigret, kept leaning across to his solicitor to say a few words in English. Each time, the Superintendent looked at him, and he was sure that the American must be saying, in his own language: 'What's he saying?'

However, Maigret continued: 'As for you, my poor Charlotte, I have to tell you something which Prosper perhaps told you on the last evening he spent with you . . . When you thought he was better and told him about Mimi's letter and the story of the child, he wasn't better at all . . . He didn't say anything, but set to work during the rest period, in his still-room, as Ramuel has explained, writing a long letter to his old mistress . . .

'Don't you remember, Donge? . . . Don't you remember the details?'

Donge didn't know what to reply. He couldn't understand what was going on and kept looking round him with his great sky-blue eyes.

'I don't understand what you mean, sir . . .'

'How many letters did you write?'

'Three . . .'

'And on at least one of the three occasions, weren't you disturbed by a telephone call? . . . Weren't you summoned to go to the storekeeper to collect your rations for the next day? . . .'

'Possibly . . . Yes . . . I think I probably was . . .'

'And your letter stayed on your table, just opposite Ramuel's booth . . . Unlucky Ramuel's booth . . . Ramuel who, all his life long, has committed forgeries without ever winning a fortune . . . Who did you give your letters to to take them to the post?'

'The lift-boy . . . He took them up to the hall, where there was a post-box . . .'

'So Ramuel could easily have intercepted them . . . And Mimi . . . Forgive me, Monsieur Clark . . . She is still Mimi to us . . . After Mrs Clark, I should say, had received some letters from her ex-lover, in Detroit, in which he wrote mainly about his son, she then received other, more menacing letters, in the same handwriting and still signed Donge . . . But these letters demanded money . . . The new Donge wanted to be paid to keep silent . . .'

'Oh sir! . . .' cried Prosper.

'Be quiet, man! . . . and for the love of God try to understand! . . . Because it's all very complex, I assure you . . . And it's proof yet again that Ramuel never had any luck . . . First he had to write to Mimi that you had changed your address, which was easy, because you hadn't said much in your letters about your new way of life . . . Then he rented the office in the Rue Réaumur in the name of Prosper Donge . . .'

'But . . .'

'There is no need of any proof of identity to rent an office and you are given any mail which arrives addressed to you . . . Unfortunately the cheque Mimi sent was made out to Prosper Donge, and banks do ask for your papers to be in order . . .

'I repeat that Ramuel is an artist in that line . . . But first of all he had to know that you would be having half to three-quarters of an hour off, in the still-room, opposite his glass booth, under his very eyes, so to speak, and that you would spend the break writing your letters . . .

'He suddenly sees you writing a letter to your bank to close your account and asking them to send the balance to Saint-Cloud . . .

'But it wasn't this letter which reached the Crédit Lyonnais. It was another letter, written by Ramuel, still in your handwriting, merely giving a change of address . . . In future, any letters to

Donge were to be addressed to 117b Rue Réaumur . . .

'Then the cheque is sent in . . . To be paid into the account . . . As for the eight hundred odd francs that you got in Saint-Cloud, it was Ramuel who sent them to you in the bank's name . . .

'A cleverly worked out bit of dirty business, as you can see! . . .

'So clever in fact that Ramuel, distrusting the address in the Rue Réaumur, took the additional precaution of having his post sent to a box number . . .

'Who would be able to get on his tracks now?

'Then suddenly, the unexpected happened . . . Mimi comes to France . . . Mimi is staying at the Majestic . . . Any minute now, Donge, the real Donge, may meet her and tell her that he has never tried to blackmail her, and . . .'

Charlotte couldn't take any more. She was crying, without quite knowing why, as she might have done when reading a sad story or seeing a sentimental film. Gigi whispered in her ear: 'Don't! . . . Don't! . . .'

And no doubt Clark was still mumbling to his solicitor: 'What's he saying?'

'As for Mrs Clark's death,' Maigret continued, 'it was accidental . . . Ramuel, who had access to the hotel register, knew she was at the Majestic . . . Donge didn't know this . . . He learnt of it by chance on overhearing a conversation in the guests' servants' hall . . .

'He wrote to her . . . He fixed a rendezvous for six in the morning and probably wanted to demand that he should be given his son, beg her on his knees, beseech her . . . I'm sure that if they had met, Mimi would have run rings round him again . . .

'He didn't know that, thinking she was about to meet a blackmailer, she had bought a gun . . .

'Ramuel was worried. He didn't leave the Majestic basement. The little note Donge had sent via a bell-boy had escaped his notice . . .

'And there it was! . . . A punctured tyre . . . Donge is a quarter of an hour late . . . Ramuel sees the young woman wandering along the corridor in the basement and guesses what has happened, and is afraid that everything will come out . . .

'He strangles her . . . Pushes her in a locker . . .

'He soon realizes that everything will point to Donge, and that there is nothing, in fact, which could possibly incriminate him . . .

'To make doubly certain of this, he writes an anonymous letter, in Charlotte's handwriting . . . Because there are several notes from Charlotte in the drawer in the still-room . . .

'I repeat, he's a consummate artist! Meticulous! . . . He takes care of every detail! . . . And when he realizes that poor Justin Colleboeuf has seen him . . . When Colleboeuf comes to tell him that he feels duty bound to denounce him to the police, he commits another crime, with no trouble at all, and one which can easily be attributed to Donge . . .

'That is all . . . Torrence! . . . Use a damp towel on that scum – his nose is beginning to bleed again . . . He slipped just now and banged his face on the corner of the table . . .

'Have you anything to say, Ramuel?'

Silence. Only the American was still asking: 'What's he saying?'

'As for you, Madame . . . What shall I call you? . . . Marie Deligeard? . . . Madame Ramuel? . . .'

'I prefer Marie Deligeard . . .'

'That's what I thought . . . You weren't mistaken in thinking he hoped to leave you soon . . . No doubt he was waiting until there was a nice round sum in the bank . . . Then he could go and look after his liver abroad, alone, a long way from your ranting and raving . . .'

'No!'

'With all due respect, Madame! . . . with all due respect! . . .'

And suddenly: 'Constables . . . Take the prisoner to the cells . . . I hope that tomorrow examining magistrate Bonneau will be good enough to sign a warrant and that . . .'

Gigi was standing in a corner, perched on her stilt-like legs, and all the emotion had given her such a craving for drugs that she felt dizzy, and her nostrils fluttered like a wounded bird's wings.

'Excuse me, Superintendent . . .'

It was the solicitor. Clark stood behind him.

'My client would like there to be a meeting between you, Monsieur Donge and himself, in my office, as soon as possible, to discuss . . . discuss the child who . . .'

'D'you hear that, Prosper?' cried Gigi triumphantly, from her corner.

'Would tomorrow morning suit you? . . . Are you free tomorrow morning, Monsieur Donge? . . .'

But Donge couldn't speak. He had suddenly cracked. He had thrown himself on Charlotte's ample bosom and was crying, crying his heart out, as the saying goes, while, a little embarrassed, she soothed him like a child.

'Pull yourself together, Prosper! . . . We'll bring him up together! . . . We'll teach him French . . . We'll . . .'

Maigret – God knows why – was rummaging through the drawers of his desk. He remembered that he had put some little sachets he had taken during a recent raid in one of them. He took a sachet out, hesitated a moment, and then shrugged.

Then, as Gigi was almost fainting, he brushed past her. His hand touched hers.

'Ladies and gentlemen, it's one o'clock . . . If you'll be so good . . .'

'*What's he saying*,' Clark seemed still to be asking, at the end of his first encounter with the French police.

They learnt the following morning that the cheque for two hundred and eighty thousand francs had been presented at the Société Générale in Brussels, by a man called Jaminet, who was a bookmaker by trade.

Jaminet had received it by airmail from Ramuel, under whose command he had been when he was doing his military service, as a corporal.

Which didn't prevent Ramuel denying everything to the last.

Or from being lucky for the first time in his life, because owing to his poor state of health – he fainted three times during the final hearing – his death sentence was commuted to transportation with hard labour for life.

Nieul-sur-Mer, 1939

THREE BEDS IN MANHATTAN

Translated by Lawrence G. Blochman

1

At three o'clock in the morning he couldn't stand it any longer. He got up and started dressing. At first he considered going out in his slippers, without a tie, and with the collar of his overcoat turned up, like the dawn and midnight dog-walkers, but thought better of it. When he reached the courtyard of this house, which even after two months he could not bring himself to look upon as home, he glanced up and saw that he had forgotten to turn out his light. Well, let it burn; he didn't have the courage to climb the stairs again.

He wondered how far along they were, up there in J.K.C.'s apartment, next to his. Had Winnie started to vomit yet? Probably, accompanied by groans, softly at first, then louder. She would wind up with an interminable fit of sobbing.

As his footsteps echoed in the nearly empty streets of Greenwich Village, he was still thinking of those two who had once more wrecked his sleep. He had never seen them. He did not even know what the letters J.K.C., painted in green on the door next to his, stood for. He had noted one morning through the half-open door that the floor was painted a glossy black, which made the bright red furniture all the more startling.

He knew a few fragmentary facts about the couple, but he could not link them together to make sense. He knew, for instance, that J.K.C. was a painter, and that Winnie lived in Boston. He could not imagine, however, what possible profession allowed her to come to New York on Friday evenings only, on no other day of the week, and never for a whole week-end. She always came by taxi a few minutes before eight o'clock, apparently from the train terminal, for the time never varied.

Winnie's voice was sharp and piercing when she arrived; she put on her second voice later. Combe could hear her walking back and forth as she talked with all the volubility of a new arrival. Then they would dine in the studio. Every week the dinner would be delivered from an Italian restaurant a quarter of an hour before the girl came.

J.K.C. talked little and in muffled tones. Despite the thinness of the walls, he was almost impossible to understand. On the other evenings, when he telephoned to Boston, only an occasional phrase came through. And why was it that he never telephoned before midnight, sometimes long after one in the morning?

'Hello. Long-distance . . . ?'

And Combe would know that he was in for a long session. He always understood the word 'Boston', but he never caught the exchange. J.K.C. called person to person, so Combe knew that the girl's name was Winnie, but could not hear her last name. It began with a *P*, apparently, and had an *o* and an *l* in it, but that was all that came through – except the long, muted murmuring that followed.

It was exasperating, but not so exasperating as the Friday evenings. What did they drink with their dinner? Something strong, no doubt, which they drank neat. Winnie's voice quickly lost pitch and gained resonance, and Winnie lost all restraint and inhibitions. Combe would never have imagined that passion could produce such unbridled, animal-like violence.

And all the while the unknown J.K.C. remained calm and self-controlled, speaking in soft, even tones that seemed touched with just a trace of condescension.

After each new tempest she demanded more to drink, and Combe could picture the studio a shambles, with fragments of broken glasses glittering on the glossy black floor.

Tonight Combe had gone out without waiting for the inevitable sequence, the hurried trips to the bathroom, the hiccups, the retching, the vomiting, the tears, and finally the endless wail of a stricken animal – or a hysterical woman.

Why did he continue to think of her? Why, as a matter of fact, had he left his room? He had been promising himself that one Saturday morning he would manage to be in the hallway or on the stairs when she left. No matter how stormy the night, she always awoke at seven. She needed no alarm clock. She didn't even wake her artist friend, for there was no sound of voices. There were only vague sounds in the bathroom, perhaps a kiss on the forehead of the sleeping J.K.C., then the door would open and close softly. Combe could imagine her quick steps on the sidewalk as she ran for a taxi to take her to the terminal, but he could not decide how she would look. Would the wild night have left its traces on her face, a droop to her shoulders, a huskiness in her voice?

It was the morning woman he would have liked to see, not the evening woman, just off the train, full of poise and self-assurance as she swept into the studio as if she were dropping in on casual friends. Yes, he was interested in the morning woman, who stole off alone into the awakening day, while the man slept on in his selfish calm, unaware that his clammy forehead had been brushed by a kiss . . .

Combe had been walking aimlessly. He came to a corner that was vaguely familiar. A night club was closing, its last-gasp customers spewing out to the kerb, optimistically waiting for taxis. Two men at the corner apparently could not bear to say good night to one another; they parted, shook hands again, parted again, and came back drunkenly to reaffirm everlasting friendship.

Combe suddenly felt that he too had just emerged from a night club instead of a warm bed. He was strangely exhilarated, although he had not had a drink all evening. Instead of the caressing warmth of night-club music, he had spent the evening in the cold loneliness of his room, made even lonelier by the love cries that filtered through the wall.

He forced himself to the reality of his street corner. A yellow cab had finally stopped in front of the night club, had been assailed by a dozen prospective fares, and had escaped with difficulty – but empty. The street lights festooned the almost deserted avenues with their garlands of softly glowing globes. At the corner a brilliantly lighted show window thrust itself aggressively into the half-gloom, a long glass cage that vulgarly challenged the dark human shadows on the sidewalk to bring their loneliness inside. Combe went in.

He surveyed the stools anchored in front of the endless counter of cold plastic. He watched two drunken sailors trying to bid each other good night with much hand-shaking and unintelligible language. He slid onto a stool without realizing that he had taken a seat next to a woman. A white-coated Negro counterman stood in front of him, waiting for his order. He looked around. The place smelled of the morning after, of dead carnival, of night people who can never make up their minds to go to bed; it also had that curiously typical New York smell of quietly impersonal nonchalance and brutal individualism.

He ordered at random – grilled sausages. Then he turned to look at his neighbour. The counterman had just slid a platter of bacon and eggs in front of her, but she ignored the food, calmly returning Combe's evaluating glance. She took her time lighting a cigarette, then carefully examined the imprint of her rouged lips on the tip. Then: 'Are you French?' she asked in French – without an accent, he thought at first.

'How did you guess?'

'I don't know. I sensed it as soon as you came in, even before you spoke.' With a nostalgic smile she added, 'Parisian?'

'Parisian indeed – from Paris.'

'Which quarter?'

His eyes grew misty for an instant; he wondered if she had noticed it. 'I had a villa in Saint-Cloud. Do you know Saint-Cloud?'

She smiled and, imitating the monotone of a dispatcher for the Seine river boats, she announced, 'Pont de Sèvre, Saint-Cloud, Point-du-Jour . . .' Then, lowering her voice, she said, 'I lived in Paris for six years. Do you know the Auteuil church? My flat was practically next door, at the corner of Rue Mirabeau, a few steps from the Molitor swimming pool . . .'

He was listening, but he was trying to relate this throwback from Paris to the reality of a night in New York. How many people were there in this all-night coffee pot? Perhaps a dozen, separated not only by empty stools but by an emptiness that was difficult if not impossible to define, an emptiness that seemed to emanate from each of the customers. They were linked only by two Negro waiters in soiled white coats who made frequent trips to a hole in the wall from which they extricated plates containing hot edibles of some sort, which they slid along the counter to some anonymous but hungry character.

In spite of the blazing lights, there was a pall of greyness hanging over the lunch counter, a bleak loneliness that defied the glare. The blinding neon tubes might hurt the eyes, but they could not dissipate the night that these men brought in with them from the outer darkness.

'Aren't you eating?' he asked, chiefly because the silence had become embarrassing.

'I'm in no hurry.'

She smoked the way American girls smoked in magazine ads and in the movies: the same pout of the lips, the same angle of the wrist, the same way of throwing her fur back from her shoulders to show her black silk dress to advantage, the same way of crossing her sheer-sheathed legs.

He had no need to turn towards the girl to catalogue her fine points. There was a long mirror that ran the length of the counter so that they could look straight ahead and see their images sitting side by side. The reflections were certainly unflattering, and perhaps even a little distorted.

'You're not eating either,' the girl said. 'Have you been in New York long?'

'About six months.' Why did he find it necessary to introduce himself? A touch of vanity, naturally, which he regretted as soon as he had said, 'I'm François Combe.'

Perhaps he had not said it with the easy grace he had intended. In any case, she did not seem impressed – even though she had lived for six years in Paris. Strange . . . 'Were you living in Paris recently?' he added.

'Let's see . . . not for the last three years, really. I passed through on my way from Switzerland, but I didn't stay long.' After a brief pause she added, 'Have you been to Switzerland?' Then, without waiting for a reply, she continued, 'I spent two winters in a sanatorium in Leysin.'

Her last words made him look at her for the first time as a woman. Before he could analyse his reaction, she went on with a superficial gaiety that touched something deep inside him.

'It's not as terrible as people think. Not for those that get out, anyhow. They told me I was definitely cured.'

She crushed out her cigarette in an ashtray and again he looked at the blood-like stain of her lipstick. Why, in that fraction of a second, did his thoughts revert to the Winnie he had never seen? Perhaps it was because of her voice. He had not noticed it before, but this woman, whose name he did not know, did indeed have a voice like Winnie's – but the Winnie of the tragic moments, the Winnie of the lower, sonorous voice, the Winnie of the wounded animal.

It was like Winnie's voice, but different – more subdued, perhaps, more muted, like a scar that was not quite healed, a pain that lies constantly below the conscious, but that remains a cherished part and parcel of oneself . . .

She had just ordered something from the coloured waiter, and Combe frowned because she had used the same intonation, the same facial expression, the same seductive fluidity of speech she had used when she spoke to him. 'Your eggs are getting cold,' he said.

What was he hoping for? Why did he suddenly want to get away from this glass cage with its blurred reflection of their dual image? Did he really expect her to go home with him, just as if they really knew one another?

She began to eat her eggs at last, with exasperatingly slow gestures. She put down her fork while she shook pepper into a glass of tomato juice she had just ordered. It was all like a slow-motion film. One of the sailors was being sick in a corner (just as Winnie was no doubt doing at this moment). His buddy was helping him with touching concern. The waiters watched with complete indifference.

Time dragged on. An hour passed and Combe still knew nothing about this woman. He was becoming annoyed by her delaying tactics. Somehow he had got it into his mind that fate had decreed since time immemorial that she and he would leave the place together, arm in arm, and that her senseless, stubborn resistance was robbing them of the little time allotted to them.

During the hour, Combe found answers to some of the questions that had been puzzling him – her accent, for one. While her French was impeccably correct, there was a curious little intonation that showed through occasionally and that he could not define. He finally asked her if she was an American, and she replied that she had been born in Vienna.

'My name is Catherine,' she said. 'When I was a little girl, they called me Kathleen. Here in America they call me Kay. Have you ever been to Vienna?'

'I have.'

'Oh.' For the first time he noted that her expression reflected his own curiosity. After all, she knew no more about him than he did about her. It was past four in the morning. People were still coming into the lunch counter from time to time, coming from Lord knows where to haul themselves to the summit of a stool with weary sighs.

She was still eating. She ordered a frightful-looking cake, covered with gaudy frosting, which she ate with maddening slowness, dipping the tip of her spoon into the technicolour mess to carry away only a microscopic bit at a time. When she had finally finished, he was hopefully about to call for the bill, when she ordered coffee. And as the coffee was scaldingly hot, there was more delay.

'Could you give me a cigarette? I've finished mine.'

He knew that she would smoke it to the last inch, and perhaps ask for another one. He was surprised by his own impatience. What did he expect, anyhow? Once they left the counter, wouldn't she merely offer her hand and say good night?

At last they were outside. There was nobody in sight except a man who was obviously asleep propped against the subway entrance. She did not suggest a taxi. She walked along the sidewalk, just as if the sidewalk would lead her to her chosen destination.

After they had walked about a hundred yards, during which she had stumbled a few times because of her too high heels, she hooked her hand into the crook of Combe's arm, just as though the two of them had been walking the streets of New York at five in the morning since the beginning of time.

*

He was to remember every detail of that night, although while he was living them they seemed so incoherent that they were not real.

Fifth Avenue stretched endlessly before them, but it was so different at this pre-dawn hour that he did not recognize it until they had walked a dozen blocks and come upon a little church that he knew. Kay stopped.

'I wonder if it's open,' she said. Then, with a curious touch of nostalgia in her voice, 'I want so much for it to be open.'

She made him try all the doors. They were all locked.

'So it's closed.' She sighed and took his arm again.

A few blocks farther on she said, 'My shoe hurts.'

'Shall we take a taxi?'

'No, let's walk.'

She had not told him her address and he had not dared ask her. It was a strange feeling to be walking like this through the vastness of the great city without the slightest idea of where they were going or what was going to happen to them in the next few hours – few minutes, even. He glimpsed their reflection in a shop window they were passing. Perhaps because she was tired she was leaning on him a little, and for an instant the dark image in the window was that of two lovers, a picture that only last night would have made him sick with loneliness. For the past several weeks he had found himself gritting his teeth every time he passed two people who were so obviously a couple that an aura of loving intimacy seemed to surround them. And yet here they were, he and Kay, who to the passer-by must also appear to be a couple. A funny couple, indeed.

'Would you like to drink some whisky?' she asked suddenly.

'I thought all bars were closed at this hour.'

She was already in pursuit of her latest whim. She guided him around a corner into a cross street, stopped, backtracked. 'No, it's not here. It's the next block ...'

She knocked nervously on two wrong doors before one was opened a crack by a startled man with a mop in his hand. Behind him was an empty bar and chairs stacked on tables. She cross-examined the man with a mop until she got the address she was seeking. After another fifteen minutes of trial and error, they found themselves in a basement room where three men sat at a bar, gloomily drinking.

Kay seemed to know the place. She called the barman 'Jimmy'. A few minutes later she remembered that his name was Teddy and went into a long explanation to the bored Ganymede. She asked about some people who had once come in with her. The bartender merely stared at her with unseeing eyes.

It took her nearly half an hour to finish her scotch, and then she wanted another one. She lit another cigarette – always the last one.

'We'll go as soon as I smoke this one,' she promised.

She grew more voluble. Once outside, her grip on Combe's arm was tighter. She nearly stumbled over a kerb. She spoke of her daughter. She had a daughter somewhere in Europe; where, or why the girl was not with her mother, Combe never knew.

As they reached the Forties, through the cross streets they could see the lights of Broadway paling in the coming dawn. It was nearly six o'clock. They had walked a long way and they were both weary. Combe asked suddenly, 'Where do you live?'

She stopped short. At first he thought she was angry, but when he looked into her eyes – he still didn't know exactly what colour they were – he saw that she was troubled, perhaps in deep distress. She dropped his arm, took several quick steps as though she was running away, then stopped again. When he had caught up with her, she looked him squarely in the eyes. Her mouth hardened as she said: 'Since this morning, I don't live anywhere.'

Why was he so touched that he wanted to cry? They were standing in front of a shop window. His legs were so tired his knees shook; there was the bitterness of a sleepless night in his mouth and an aching emptiness in his head. Had the two whiskies done something to his nerves?

It was ridiculous. They stood there, watching each other to see who would make the first move, both of them moist-eyed. With a stupidly sentimental gesture he seized both her hands.

'Come,' he said. Then, after an instant, he added, 'Come, Kay.' It was the first time he had called her by name.

'Where will we go?' It was not an objection; it was a docile question.

He had no answer. He couldn't take her to his place, to that barn that he hated, to the room that hadn't been cleaned for a week, to a bed that hadn't been made.

They started walking again. Now that she had confessed she had nowhere to go, he was afraid of losing her. He listened. She was telling him a complicated story full of names that meant nothing to him but that she pronounced as though everybody must know them.

'I was sharing an apartment with Jessie. I wish you knew Jessie. She's the most seductive woman I've ever known. About three years ago, her husband Ronald got a very important job in Panama. Jessie tried hard to live with him down there, but her health wouldn't stand it. She had to come back to New York – with her husband's permission, of course – and we took an apartment together in the Village, not far from where you and I met . . .'

He was listening, but he was also examining the problem of a place where they could lay their heads on the same pillow. They were still walking, although they were so tired they could neither of them feel their legs any more.

'Jessie had a lover,' Kay continued, 'a Chilean named Enrico. He's married, with two children, but he was about to get a divorce so that he could marry Jessie. Do you follow me?'

He nodded. He was rather far behind, but he was following.

'Somebody must have written or cabled to Ronald – and I think I know who it was – so this morning Ronald arrived unexpectedly. Enrico's pyjamas and bathrobe were still hanging in the cupboard. I had just gone out, so I missed the scene. It must have been terrible. Ronald is a man who is usually very calm, but I can imagine what he must be like when he is really furious . . . Anyhow, when I came home at two in the afternoon, the door was locked. Our next-door neighbour heard me knocking, and gave me a letter that Jessie had left for me. I have it in my bag . . .'

She opened her bag but couldn't look for the letter while they were crossing Sixth Avenue. Then Combe stopped under a vulgar neon-violet sign reading, 'Ivy Hotel'.

He nudged Kay into the lobby and spoke to the night clerk in a subdued, half-frightened voice. He finally picked up the key and its big, dangling brass disc. The clerk took them up in a tiny lift, built for two, that smelled a little like an outhouse. Kay squeezed his arm and said in French, 'Ask him to get us some whisky. I'm sure he can.'

It took him several minutes to realize that she had addressed him by the familiar 'tu', which was practically like calling him 'darling'.

This was the hour at which Winnie usually arose from J.K.C.'s warm love couch to tiptoe into the bathroom.

The room at the Ivy was just as drab and dusty as the daylight that had begun to filter through the curtains. Kay had dropped into a chair, thrown her fur back from her shoulders, and kicked off her black suede shoes with the too high heels. She held a glass in her hand and was sipping her drink slowly, staring into space. Her handbag was open on her lap. There was a run, like a long scar, in one stocking.

'Pour me another drink, will you, dear? It's the last one, I swear it.'

She was already visibly a little giddy. She drank her whisky more quickly than usual, then sat for a moment shut up within herself, far, very far away from the room and from the man who waited without knowing exactly what he was waiting for. At last she stretched her legs – her big toes showed through the flesh pink of her stockings – and stood up.

She first turned her head away for a fraction of a second. Then very simply, so simply that the gesture might have been planned ages ago, she took two steps towards the man, threw her arms around his shoulders, raised herself on her toes, and planted her lips firmly against his.

The drone of a vacuum cleaner sounded in the hotel corridors. Downstairs the night clerk was getting ready to go home.

2

For an instant he was almost relieved to find her no longer beside him, a perplexing sentiment that a few minutes later seemed not only incredible but even shocking. Since it had not been a conscious thought, he could with almost complete honesty deny to himself that he had been guilty of disloyalty.

The room was dark when he awoke, the darkness pierced by spears of ruddy light hurled between the curtains by the neon signs in the street. He had stretched out his hand and touched only the cold sheets. Had he really been glad, had he truly and consciously believed that things would be easier and simpler if they ended thus? Apparently not, because when he saw the crack of light under the bathroom door, his heart had given a gay flip.

The sequence of events that followed left little impression on his memory; things had happened so smoothly and naturally. He had got out of bed, he remembered, because he wanted a cigarette. She must have heard him for she reached out from under the shower and opened the bathroom door.

'Do you know what time it is?' she asked gaily.

Strangely ashamed of his nakedness, he had reached for his shorts. 'No, I don't know.'

'Half-past seven in the evening, my dear old Frank.'

Nobody had ever called him old Frank before, and the name struck a light note that vibrated in his whole being for hours. He had the marvellous feeling of being a juggler, and that life was nothing more than three or four featherweight balls to be kept in the air simultaneously. Whatever had happened before was of no importance. Nothing would matter in the future. He remembered saying, 'How the devil am I going to shave?'

And she had said, with only a touch of sarcasm, 'I really don't know, but if I were you, I would call room service and have a bell-boy go out and get me a razor, some blades, and some shaving cream. Do you want me to call?'

She was having the time of her life. She was one of those persons who could wake up without an ache or a wrinkle, while he had not really achieved full wakefulness. For him the present was so new that it was not quite real. He remembered the most recent past – the time she had said, 'You're not really fat, you know.'

He replied very seriously, 'I take care of myself. I'm not too old for sports.' He was within an inch of flexing his muscles and swelling his chest.

The room was still strange. They had gone to bed as night was fading; they had wakened to night returning. He was afraid to leave her now, for fear that she too would disappear with the day they had not yet seen together, and that he would never find her again. Something stranger still: neither of them had thought of a good-morning kiss for the other.

She was studying the run in her stocking that he had noticed before they went to bed. She said gravely, 'I must buy some stockings.' She moistened her finger and applied it to the nylon scar.

He said awkwardly, 'Would you lend me your comb?'

The street outside, which had been so dead when they came in, was fully awake to a noisy, glaring, blaring life – bars and restaurants side by noisy side. Their oasis of ambiguous privacy was all the more precious when they considered the carnival madness from which they were briefly isolated.

As he rang for the lift, he asked, 'Are you sure you haven't forgotten anything?'

She nodded. They got into the lift. A bored, gloomy girl in uniform had replaced the night man who had brought them up at dawn. In another hour the night man would doubtless be back on duty. He would have understood everything . . .

Combe dropped his key nonchalantly on the desk while Kay went on a few steps, as poised and unconcerned as a wife or at least a mistress of long standing.

'Keeping the room?' asked the day clerk.

'Yes.' Combe's affirmative was uttered quickly without thinking, partly because Kay was listening, partly because of a superstitious fear of tempting fate by trying to forecast the future.

What did he know of the future, after all? Nothing. He knew no more about Kay than she knew about him, no more than they had known on the night before, perhaps less. And yet never had two beings, two human bodies, so savagely sought mutual annihilation in fusion, so furiously shared the hunger of desperation.

He could not remember at which moment they had sunk into exhausted sleep. He awoke once in broad daylight. He had studied her face, still marked with unspoken sorrow, her body spread-eagled, one foot and one arm hanging over the edge of the bed. Gently he had lifted them back into place, and she had not even opened her eyes.

In the street again, they turned their back on the glaring purple sign of the Ivy Hotel. Kay took his arm again, as she had during the endless walk from the Village to the Times Square region. Now that he thought of it, he resented her having taken his arm so readily, the arm of a stranger.

'Maybe we should eat,' she said with a little laugh.

'Dinner, you mean?'

She laughed outright. 'Don't you think we should start with breakfast?'

He didn't know. He no longer knew who he was, how old he was, where he was. He no longer recognized the city he had crossed and crisscrossed for six months, bitterly, hopefully, tensely, hopelessly. The overwhelming power of the metropolis, its incoherence, its impersonal wonder, suddenly struck him. They were being buffeted by the street crowds as they walked, battled like ping-pong balls, and it all seemed to amuse Kay. This time it was she who was leading them, and he asked, as if it was the most natural question in the world, 'Where are we going?'

'To the cafeteria in Rockefeller Center to get a bite to eat.'

They threaded their way through the complex of Radio City. Kay guided them through the endless corridors of grey marble, and for the first time he was jealous. It was ridiculous, but there it was. He was jealous.

'Do you come here often?' he asked.

'Once in a while. When I'm in the neighbourhood.'

'With whom?'

'Idiot!'

In a single night, even less than a night, they had miraculously achieved the cycle that most lovers take weeks, sometimes months, to complete.

He was surprised to find himself eyeing the countermen, even the bus boys, trying to discover how well known she was in the cafeteria. If she had come there often with other men, he was sure that he would notice some sign of recognition. Why? He was not in love with Kay. He was certain that he was not in love with her. He already bristled when she fumbled in her bag for a cigarette, stained the end with her lipstick, fumbled for her lighter. He knew that she would light another as soon as she had finished the first, that she would dawdle over her coffee, and that he would want to scream when she insisted on smoking still another before beginning the agonizingly slow ritual of applying fresh lipstick while her lips pouted at the tiny mirror of her compact.

He sat through it all, nevertheless. He could not imagine any other course. He waited, resigned to this routine, resigned perhaps to many other things still to come. He caught sight of himself in a mirror across the room and recognized his smile as something from the past, a smile at once childish and tense, the smile of his college days, when he was not sure just how far some new sentimental adventure would lead him.

He was no longer a college boy. He was forty-eight years old, something he had not yet told her. They had not yet discussed the question of age. Should he tell her the truth? Or should he say that he was forty-two?

Perhaps the matter would never come up. Perhaps they would no longer be interested in each other in another hour. Or half-hour.

Perhaps that was why they had been living in slow motion since they first met, dawdling, postponing, because neither of them had as yet caught a glimpse of any possible future . . .

They were in the street again. No doubt about it, they felt most at home in the street. Their mood changed immediately. The magic, lighthearted comradeship they had found by accident returned the moment they were again caught up in the noise and confusion of traffic.

People were lining up in front of the cinemas. Gaudily uniformed doormen guarded the padded portals of night clubs. They passed them all by. They zigzagged aimlessly through the crowds until she turned to him with a smile he recognized instantly. It was the smile that had started everything. He wanted to anticipate her words, to say yes before she could open her mouth. He knew what she was about to say, and, knowing that he knew, she skipped the opening question and answer.

'Just one,' she said. 'Shall we?'

They turned into the first bar they came to. It was a cosy little place, so made-to-order for lovers that it seemed to have been purposely placed on their path. Kay gave her companion a look that said, 'You see?' Then, holding out her hand, she said, 'Give me a nickel.'

Without understanding, he produced the coin and she made off at once for the jukebox in the corner. She frowned as she studied the list of records with its array of shiny buttons. He had never seen her so gravely pensive. At last she found what she was looking for, pushed a button, and came back to climb on her bar stool.

'Two scotches.'

A vague smile of anticipation hovered over her lips as she listened for the first notes of her song, and for the second time he felt a pang of jealousy. With whom had she heard the tune she had sought so intently? He must have been staring stupidly at the bartender, for she said, 'Listen, darling. Don't make a face like that.'

The machine in the corner, after a preliminary series of clicks, had garlanded itself with a halo of orange light and began crooning in a soft, insinuating voice one of the half-whispered melodies that had been cradling the loves of thousands of Americans for the past half-year or so.

She had taken his arm. She squeezed it. She smiled, and for the first time he noticed how white her teeth were; too white, perhaps; their whiteness bespoke fragility. He was about to speak, when she placed a finger across his lips and said, 'Shh.'

After a moment she asked, 'Give me another nickel, will you?'

To listen to that same record, over and over, they were to consume considerable scotch and exchange few words.

'Doesn't this bore you?'

No, no. Nothing bored him. On the contrary, he wanted to stay with her. He had the curious feeling that he would be lost without her, and he dreaded the possibility of their separation. And yet he was in the grip of the same impatience, an almost physical sensation, that had disturbed him at the cafeteria.

The music had finally got under his skin too, with a kind of gentle, wistful tenderness, but he still wanted it to end. He told himself that when this one was finished they would go. Why must Kay interrupt their aimless wandering with such long pauses?

She asked, 'What would you like to do?'

He didn't know. He had no idea what time it was. He had no desire to come down to earth, to resume the routine of daily living, yet he was plagued by an indefinable uneasiness that prevented him from abandoning himself to the moment.

'What about going down to the Village? Would you mind?'

Why should he mind? He was at once very happy and very unhappy.

Outside, he saw her hesitate for an instant, and he knew why. It was surprising how each was aware of the slightest nuance of change in the other's mood. She was wondering if they would take a taxi. The question of money had never come up between them. She did not know whether he was rich or poor, and she had been startled, a moment earlier, by the size of the bill at the bar.

He raised his arm and a yellow cab stopped at the kerb on which they were standing. Like thousands and thousands of other couples at this same hour, they slid into the sweet gloom of a car. A rainbow of bright, dancing colours whirled by each side of the driver's back.

She took off one glove and slipped her bare hand into his. They sat without speaking all the way to Washington Square. They had left the noisy anonymity of New York behind them and it was hard to believe they were in the same city. The quiet neighbourhood might have been a small town anywhere in the world.

There were few people on the sidewalks and not many shops. A couple appeared from a side street, and it was the man who was awkwardly pushing the pram.

'I'm so glad you wanted to come down here with me. I've been so happy here.'

He was frightened. He wondered if she was going to tell him the story of her life. Sooner or later the time would come when she would talk about herself and he would have to talk about himself. But this was not the moment. She stopped talking. She had a way of leaning against his arm that he found tenderly charming, and now he was learning another of her gestures: she would brush her cheek against his, just a fleeting touch, so quick that he was scarcely aware of it.

'Shall we turn left here?'

They were just five minutes' walk from his place, from the room where, he suddenly remembered, he had left the light burning. He laughed to himself at the thought. She felt it. He had known her less than twenty-four hours and already he could hide nothing from her.

'Why are you laughing?'

He was about to tell her, but changed his mind at the thought she would want to see the place.

'I wasn't laughing. Not really.'

She stopped at the corner of a street in which the houses were only three or four storeys high. 'Look,' she said.

She nodded at a house with a white front. Four or five windows were lighted. 'That's where I used to live with Jessie.'

She nodded again, at an Italian restaurant with red-and-white-checked curtains, just beyond a Chinese laundry. 'We used to eat there often, just the two of us.'

She counted the windows. 'There, third floor, second and third windows from the right. It's quite small, you know; just one bedroom, the living-room and a bathroom.'

He had been expecting to be hurt, and he was. He resented being so vulnerable and he took it out on her. His voice was almost a snarl as he demanded, 'What did you do when Enrico came to see your friend Jessie?'

'I slept on the sofa in the living-room.'

'Always?'

'What do you mean?'

So he was right to be suspicious. She had answered a question with a question, and only after hesitating. She was obviously embarrassed.

Remembering the paper-thin wall that separated him from J.K.C. and his Winnie, he was furious. 'You know very well what I mean.'

'Let's walk,' she said.

They walked in silence, as though they had nothing more to say to one another. Then, 'Shall we go in here?'

It was a little bar, another little bar that she must know well, since it was in her street. What difference? He said yes, and regretted it immediately. This was not the cosy little bar, exciting in its intimacy, that they had left only minutes before. It was much too big, much too dreary. The bar itself was filthy, the glasses unattractive, to say the least, if not downright dirty.

'Two scotches,' she said. 'Neat.' Then, 'Give me a nickel anyhow.'

Here too was the mechanical monster with a bellyful of records, but she couldn't find the softly confidential words of love that she was seeking. She pushed another button to kill time, while a half-tight stranger tried to barge in on their conversation.

Kay turned her back on him. They sipped their pale, lukewarm whisky.

'Let's get out of here.'

When they were on the sidewalk again, she said, 'You know, I've never slept with Ric.'

He was about to sneer because she called him Ric instead of Enrico, but why bring that up now? She had certainly gone to bed with other men . . .

'He did try one night – but even then, I'm not sure,' she went on.

Why didn't she shut up? Didn't she realize that the best thing she could say at this point was nothing? Or perhaps she was torturing him deliberately. He thought of shaking off the hand that was still hooked into his arm, and walking on alone, his hands in his pockets except when he wanted to light a cigarette – or, even better, his pipe, which he had not yet flaunted before this girl.

'I don't want you to imagine things,' she continued, 'so I want you to know the truth. Ric is a South American, understand? One night – oh, it must have been two months ago, in August. *Tiens*, you must know how hot an August night can be in New York. Or have you ever lived through a New York August? The little apartment was like an oven . . .'

Why was she evoking images that he would prefer not even to entertain? He would have liked to order her to shut up. Was there no shame in a woman? Instead, he said nothing. They were walking around Washington Square . . .

'He was beautifully built,' she was saying, 'but he behaved very well. He never took off his pants.'

'And you?'

'What about me?'

'What did you take off?'

'I? Nothing – that I remember. I guess I was wearing my dressing-gown. Jessie and I were both wearing dressing-gowns.'

'But you were naked under your dressing-gown?'

'Probably.' She didn't seem to know what he was talking about. She was so much in control of the situation that she stopped in the middle of the square to point.

'I forgot to show you Mrs Roosevelt's hotel,' she said. 'That's it, over there. When he was in the White House, the President used to sneak away to spend a few days over there. He used to get away from the Secret Service even . . .' She came back to her subject. 'That night . . .'

He could have twisted her wrist to shut her up – but he didn't.

'That August night, I wanted to take a shower, so I had to go through their room. Ric had been terribly restless, I don't know why. Well, I think I do know, now that I think back about it. He said we were all silly to act like prudes in New York in summer. He said we should all be comfortable – that we might as well take off all our clothes, the three of us, and take our shower together. Do you understand?'

'So you took your shower?' he said disdainfully.

'I took my shower – alone – and I locked the door. Ever since, I have refused to go out with him unless Jessie came along.'

'But you *had* gone out with him without Jessie?'

'Yes. Why not?'

He said nothing. With the most honest air in the world, she asked, 'What are you thinking about?'

'About nothing. About everything.'

'Are you jealous of Ric?'

'No.'

'Listen. Do you know the No. 1 Bar? No. 1 Fifth Avenue?'

He was suddenly very tired. Several times he had been so fed up with walking the streets of New York with her that he had been ready to leave her on the slightest pretext. What were they doing together anyhow, bound and riveted like two people who had always been in love and who were destined to love each other for all eternity?

Rico . . . Enrico . . . whatever his name . . . a trio for the shower. She must have been lying. He felt that she was lying. He was sure of it, in fact. How could she have resisted such a mad proposal? She was lying, not to deceive him, but openly, to fill a pathological need to lie, just as she had a built-in need to ogle every man who passed, to buy with a smile the flattering glance of a bartender, a counterman, or a taxi driver. *Did you see the way he was looking at me . . . ?* She had said this about the taxi driver who had driven them from Times Square to Greenwich Village, and who had probably been thinking of nothing more sexual than the size of the tip he might expect . . .

He followed her into a room suffused with a dim, rose-tinted light. He noted an ethereal gentleman seated at a piano, nonchalantly allowing his long, pallid fingers to wander over the keyboard, releasing notes that rose like incense to fill the air with heavy nostalgia. She halted near the doorway while she told him, 'Leave your coat in the cloakroom.'

As though he didn't know!

It was she who led the way behind the *maître d'hôtel*, radiant, an excited smile on her lips. She must have thought of herself as beautiful. He did not. What he found most attractive about her were the certain signs of wear in her face, the tiny lines like onionskin which at times tinged her eyelids with mauve, the occasional hints of weariness that weighed down the corners of her mouth.

'Two scotches.'

She had to speak to the *maître d'hôtel*, to subject him to what she imagined to be her powers of seduction. With great solemnity she asked him useless questions – what numbers of the evening's show they had missed, what had become of the singer who had been there last month.

She lighted a cigarette, naturally, pushed her fur slightly away from her shoulders, tilted her head back, and sighed with pleasure. She asked: 'Are you unhappy?'

'Why shouldn't I be happy?'

'I don't know. But at this very minute I have a feeling that you hate me.'

How sure she must be of herself to have stated the truth so simply and so bluntly! Sure of what? Why didn't he suddenly get up and go home? Why was he staying with her? To him she was neither seductive nor beautiful. She was not even young. She wore the patina of many adventures. Perhaps it was this patina that drew him to her . . .

'Will you excuse me for a minute?'

With long, easy strides she moved to the pianist, bent over him with a smile that was once more the smile of a woman determined to charm, who would be hurt if a beggar to whom she gave a dime should refuse her a look of admiration.

She returned to the table beaming, her eyes sparkling ironically; it was for him, or at least for them, that she had used her charm this time. The pale fingers moved over the keyboard with a new rhythm now, and it was the melody of the little bar that now trembled in the rose-tinted dimness. She listened with her lips half parted, the smoke from her cigarette drifting upward past her eyes like incense.

As soon as the music had stopped, she arose, picked up her gloves, her lighter and cigarette case, and commanded, 'Pay. Let's go.'

As he fumbled in his pocket, she took several steps, then came back.

'You always overtip. Forty cents is plenty here.' It was the final mark of possession, a take-over without argument. He did not even try to argue. Nor did he at the cloakroom, where she said, 'Leave her a quarter.'

Outside she said, 'There's no use taking a taxi.'

A taxi to where? Was she so sure they were going on together? She may have heard him telling the clerk that he would keep the room at the Ivy. Perhaps it was instinct; anyhow, he was convinced that she did know. At least she asked his advice. 'Shall we take the subway?'

'Not right away. I'd rather walk a little.'

They were standing at the foot of Fifth Avenue, as they had the night before, and he felt a strong desire to do the same things all over again, to walk uptown beside her, to turn the same corners, perhaps even to stop at the same strange cellar where they had drunk their first whisky together. He knew that she was tired, and that walking in high heels was no fun. The idea of mild revenge, of making her suffer a little, was not displeasing to him. Besides, he wondered if she would protest. It would be a kind of experiment.

'All right. Let's walk,' she said.

Had the time come for them to talk? He both hoped and feared that it was. He was in no hurry to learn more about Kay's life, but he did want to talk about his own. He wanted her particularly to know who he was, for, consciously or not, he did not enjoy being taken for just anyone, even being loved as just anyone. The night before she had not blinked an eye when he told her his name. Perhaps she had not heard clearly. Or perhaps she had not connected the name of a man she had met in a Manhattan all-night hash house with the name she must have seen in big letters on the kiosks of the Paris boulevards.

As they passed a Hungarian restaurant, she asked, 'Have you ever been to Budapest?'

He said that he had, but she obviously did not care. She had gone on talking without waiting for his reply, and it was apparent that his turn had not yet come.

'What a grand city, Budapest!' she said. 'I think I was happier there than anywhere else in the world. I was sixteen.'

He frowned at the word 'sixteen'. He was afraid another Enrico was about to rise between them.

'Mother and I were living alone. I must show you a picture of my mother. She was the handsomest woman I've ever seen.'

He wondered if she might not be rambling on just to keep him from speaking. What sort of man did she think he was, anyhow? Whatever she thought, she was obviously wrong. And yet she still clung to his arm without the slightest hint of reservation.

'My mother was a very fine pianist. You must have heard her name, for she played in all the capitals of Europe. Miller, Edna Miller. That was my maiden name, and the name I took back after I was divorced. It was Mother's maiden name too. Mother would never get married on account of her art. Does that shock you?'

'Me? No.' He wanted to tell her that he was not in the least shocked because he was a great artist himself. He, however, did get married, and it was on account of that . . .

He closed his eyes. When he reopened them, he saw himself as someone else might have seen him, perhaps in even sharper outline, walking up Fifth Avenue with a woman clinging to his arm, a woman he did not know and with whom he was going Lord knows where.

She continued, 'Am I boring you?'

'On the contrary.'

'Are you really interested in hearing about my girlhood?'

Should he try to shut her up or ask her to go on? He didn't know any more. He did know that when she spoke he felt a dull pain on the left side of his chest. Why? Could it be because he wished that his life had begun only last night? Perhaps. But it didn't matter. Nothing mattered now, because he had suddenly decided to struggle no longer.

He listened. He walked. He studied the long line of street lights marching off into infinity. He saw the taxis go by silently, always with a couple inside. No longer did he ache to be one of a couple, to have a woman clinging to his arm.

'Let's go in here for a moment; do you mind?'

It was not a bar this time; it was a drugstore. She smiled, and he understood the smile. She felt as he did, that this marked another step in their growing intimacy: she was buying a few indispensable toilet articles.

She let him pay, and he was happy, just as he was happy to hear the clerk call her 'Madam'.

'Now we can go home,' she said.

'Without one last scotch?' he asked ironically, and immediately regretted the tone.

'No more scotch,' she announced gravely. 'Tonight I'm practically a girl of sixteen. Do you mind?'

It was ridiculous that the common violet sign above the entrance to the Ivy Hotel should be a source of pleasure, like homecoming. It was ridiculous that a welcoming nod from the shabby, beaten old night clerk should be an even greater pleasure, or that he could be thrilled by the banality of a hotel and two pillows waiting on a bed that had been turned down.

'Take off your overcoat,' she said, 'and sit down.'

He obeyed, subtly moved. She too seemed moved. Or was she? There were moments when he hated her, and some moments, like this one, when he wanted to cry on her shoulder.

He was tired but relaxed. He waited, a faint smile on his lips, a smile she caught and understood. She stooped to kiss him for the first time that day, not with the carnal hunger of their first embrace, nor with the violence born of despair. It was a gentle kiss. She advanced her lips slowly, paused at the instant of contact, then bore down tenderly. He closed his eyes. When he reopened them, he saw that she had closed hers, too. He was grateful.

'Don't move, now. Let me fix everything.'

She switched out the ceiling light, leaving only the shaded lamp on the night table. Then she went to the cupboard for the bottle of whisky they had opened the night before.

'This isn't the same thing.' She felt she had to explain.

She poured the whisky carefully into two glasses, added the water as solemnly as though she were following a recipe. She set one glass beside him, brushing his forehead with a caress as she passed.

She kicked off her shoes and curled up in a big chair like a little girl.

'Are you happy?' she asked. She sighed. Then, in a voice he had never heard before, she added, 'I'm happy.'

They were only a few feet apart, yet they both knew that the gap would not be closed now. They looked at each other through half-closed lids, pleased at the responsive, peaceful glow each found in the other's eyes.

Was she about to start talking? She parted her lips, but only to sing, or rather to croon the melody that had become theirs. And the commonplace little tune became so deeply moving that tears came to his eyes and he was filled with a great warmth. She knew it, too. She knew everything. She held him to her with each note, with her warm contralto that grew husky at times. Skilfully she prolonged their pleasant awareness of being alone together, of being cut off from the world.

When she stopped, the street sounds again flowed into the silence. They listened in surprise. Then she repeated, much more softly than before, as though not to frighten destiny away, 'Are you happy?'

Did he really hear her next words, or were they merely echoing inside him?

'Myself, I've never been so happy in all my life.'

3

It was a curious sensation. She was speaking and he was affected by what she said. But not for a single instant did he lose his lucid objectivity. He told himself, 'She's lying!'

He was sure of it. Perhaps she was not making up the story – although he would not have put it beyond her – but she was certainly lying by distortion, exaggeration, or omission.

She poured herself a second drink, then a third. He knew now that this was her hour and that it was the whisky that kept her going. He could imagine her on other nights with other men, drinking to keep up her animation, talking, talking endlessly in that husky, exciting voice of hers. Did she tell them all exactly the same story with the same sincerity? He was surprised to find that he didn't care and that he did not hold it against her.

She told him about her husband, a Hungarian, Count Larski, to whom she was married when she was nineteen. She was a virgin, she said, and went on at some length about his brutality on their wedding night. This too was a lie, or at least a half-truth; apparently she had forgotten that a little earlier she had spoken of an adventure she had had when she was seventeen. He didn't mind the lies half so much as he did the images she evoked. He didn't like her debasing herself in his eyes with a shamelessness that bordered on defiance.

Was it the whisky that made her talk this way? At one moment of cold judgment he told himself, *This is a three-o'clock woman, a woman who never wants to go to bed, who has to keep her emotions at fever pitch by any means, who must drink, smoke, and talk until from sheer nervous exhaustion she falls into the arms of a man.*

And he had not the slightest urge to run away. The more lucid he became, the more he realized that Kay was indispensable to him. And he was resigned to the fact. That was the exact word – resigned. Whatever he might find out about her in the future, he was not going to fight against the truth that he needed her.

Why didn't she stop talking? It would have been so simple. He would have put his arms around her. He would have whispered, 'None of this matters, since we're starting all over again.' Starting a life from zero. Two lives. Two lives from zero.

From time to time she would pause.

'You're not listening.'

'Of course I'm listening.'

'You're listening, but you're thinking of something else at the same time.'

Yes, he was thinking of himself, of her, of everything. He was not only himself, but someone else watching himself. He could love her and still judge her implacably.

'We lived in Berlin for two years,' she went on. 'My husband was attached to the Hungarian Embassy. My daughter was born in Berlin, or more exactly in Swansee on the shores of the lake. Her name is Michele. Do you think Michele is a pretty name?' Without waiting for an answer, she continued, 'Poor Michele! She's living with one of her aunts, a sister of Larski's who never married and who lives in a huge chateau a hundred kilometres from Buda . . .'

He didn't like that huge, romantic chateau, although it may very well have been true. He wondered how many men she had told this story to. He scowled and she noticed it.

'Am I boring you with the story of my life?'

'Not at all.'

This was something he'd have to sit through, like the last cigarette, which jangled his nerves to the finger tips. His happiness seemed to exist only in the future, and he was anxious to be done once and for all with the past and even the present . . .

'Then he was named first secretary to Paris and we had to live at the embassy because the ambassador was a widower and he needed an official hostess . . .'

She was lying again. Or had she been lying that night at the lunch counter, when she told him that she had lived near the Auteuil church at the corner of Rue Mirabeau. The Hungarian Embassy in Paris was never in Rue Mirabeau.

'Jean was really first-rate,' she went on. 'One of the most intelligent men I've ever met.'

He was jealous. Why did she have to bring up another name?

'He was a great lord in his own country. You don't know Hungary –'

'Yes, I do.'

'You can't. You're too French. I'm Viennese and have Hungarian blood in my veins from my grandmother's side, and even I could never get used to Hungary. When I say "a great lord", I don't mean one of your modern lords, but a great lord of the Middle Ages. I've seen him horsewhip his servants. Once when we were driving through the Black Forest, our chauffeur nearly turned us over. Jean made him stop the car, dragged him out, knocked him down, and stamped on his face. Then he turned to me and said calmly, "Too bad I don't have a revolver on me. The lout might have killed you."'

And still Combe lacked the courage to say, 'For heaven's sake, shut up!'

She was belittling herself by talking and he was belittling himself by listening.

'I was pregnant at that time, which partly explains his brutal fury. He was so jealous that even a month before my baby was born he watched me from morning to night. He wouldn't let me go out alone. He locked me up in the apartment. Even better, he locked up all my shoes and clothes in one room and carried the key around with him . . . We lived in Paris for three years . . .'

Over bacon and eggs at 3 a.m. she had said six years. With whom had she lived the other three years?

'The ambassador died last year. He was one of our greatest statesmen. He was eighty-four years old and he took a paternal interest in me. He was a widower for thirty years and he had no children of his own.'

Paternal, indeed! Not with Kay! If he had been ninety-four or even one hundred and four, she would not have been happy until she had him at her feet.

'At night he would often ask me to read to him. It was one of the few pleasures left to him.'

He wanted to shout vulgarly. 'Where were his hands?' but he restrained himself. He could imagine all sorts of salacious details, and the idea hurt him. He wished that she would hurry and get it all off her chest so they could forget the whole dirty business.

'Because of the ambassador, my husband claimed that the Paris air was bad for me, and we took a villa in Nogent. He got gloomier and gloomier and his jealousy went from bad to worse. Finally, I couldn't stand it any longer, and I ran away.'

All alone? Come, come. If she had run away like that of her own free will, would she have abandoned her child? And if it had been she who had sued for divorce, would she be where she was now. He clenched his fists. He wanted to hit her. It would be revenge for himself and the husband he despised.

'Is that when you went to Switzerland?' he asked, trying to suppress his sarcasm.

She caught it anyhow and she answered with sly spite.

'Not right away. First I lived on the Riviera and in Italy for a year.'

She didn't say with whom she had spent the year, nor did she specify that it was alone. He hated her. He wanted to twist her arm, to force her painfully to her knees to beg forgiveness. And she had the monumental gall to sit curled up in her chair and with wide-eyed candour declare: 'You see? I'm telling everything about my whole life.'

What about the things she didn't want to tell and he didn't want to hear? What about the way the old ambassador must have pawed and fondled her? He got to his feet and ordered, 'Come to bed.'

'May I finish my cigarette?' she asked, as he had expected.

He snatched the cigarette from her fingers, flung it to the floor, stamped it out on the rug.

'Come to bed.'

She turned her head and he was sure that she was smiling triumphantly. All her talk had been cleverly designed for its cumulative aphrodisiac effect. Well, he'd show her! He wouldn't touch her tonight. Then maybe she'd understand.

Understand what? It was absurd. But then wasn't the whole adventure absurd? What the devil were two strangers doing there in a room at the Ivy, above the neon sign that winked its welcome to transient couples?

He watched without excitement as she undressed. He had no trouble remaining cold and detached. She was not the beautiful, irresistible creature that she imagined herself. Her body, like her face, wore the patina of life.

As he contemplated her supreme self-assurance, he felt an overwhelming rage rising within him. He was carried away by a mad desire to wipe out everything, consume everything, possess everything. Furiously he bore down on her, his eyes staring and vicious. She watched him stupidly, paralysed with fright. He seized her, crushed her in his arms, swept her off her feet, plunged in deeply as though determined to root out forever the spell by which she had bewitched him . . .

When the peace of fulfilment had succeeded the storm of the senses, Kay wept. She did not cry like Winnie would cry beyond the wall, but like a little child. And it was the voice of a little child that stammered, 'You . . . you hurt me.'

Still like a little child, she fell asleep without transition. This time there was no vestige of the pathetic expression that had haunted her sleep their first night together. This time she had found release. She slept soundly, her lower lip puffing slightly with each breath, both arms stretched limply on the blanket, her hair an auburn tangle on the stark white of the pillow.

He did not sleep. He did not even try. Dawn was not far off, and when its first cold grey light touched the window, he arose, parted the curtains, and pressed his forehead against the coolness of the glass. The street was empty except for the trash cans lining the kerb with homely expectancy. Across the street a man was shaving at a mirror hooked to the window frame. For an instant their glances met.

What had their eyes said to one another? The man was about Combe's age, balding, with thick, worried eyebrows. Was there someone behind him in the room, a woman, perhaps, still sleeping? A man who got up so early must be leaving for work. What did he do? What star guided his life?

For months now, Combe had been following no star. But until two days ago he had at least been walking stubbornly in the same direction. On this chilly October morning, François Combe was a man without roots, a man nearing his fiftieth year, a man without ties to family, to profession, to country, to home; no ties – except to a strange woman asleep in the room of a hotel of dubious character.

The light in the window across the way reminded him that he had left his light burning in the Village two nights ago. Was it an excuse he had unconsciously been seeking? Sooner or later he would have to go home. Why not now? Kay would sleep all day; he was beginning to know her habits. He would leave a note on the night table telling her that he would be back soon.

As he dressed silently in the bathroom (he had closed the door so as not to wake her), his enthusiasm grew. He would straighten up his room in the Village; he might even get someone to give it a good cleaning. He would buy some flowers. He would buy a cheap crettone bedspread, a gaily coloured print to hide his grey blanket. Then he would order dinner delivered by the Italian restaurant that served J.K.C. and Winnie every Friday. After that he would have to telephone the radio studio about a broadcast he was scheduled to make the next day. He should really have called the studio before this . . .

Despite his fatigue he was thinking clearly and looking forward to a brisk walk alone, breathing the sharp morning air, hearing his footsteps echo on the empty sidewalks.

Kay was still sleeping soundly, puffing out her lower lip with her rhythmical breathing. He smiled a little condescendingly. She had taken a place in his life, certainly. There was no hurry to evaluate the importance of that place. If he had not been afraid of waking her, he would have kissed her gently and indulgently on the forehead.

On a blank page of his notebook he wrote, 'I'll be right back.' He tore out the page and slipped it under her cigarette case. That way she'd be sure to find it.

In the hallway he filled his pipe. Before lighting it he pushed the button for the lift. The night man was off already; a girl in uniform ran the car. He went out without stopping at the desk, paused at the kerb to fill his lungs. He almost sighed, 'At last'. He even half wondered if he would ever come back.

He walked a few steps, stopped, walked a little farther. He was suddenly worried, like a man who realizes that he has forgotten something, but can't remember exactly what. He stopped again at the corner of Broadway. The Great White Way looked very bleak without its blaze of lights. The empty sidewalks seemed unnecessarily wide . . .

What would he do if, when he returned to the hotel, the room should be empty?

No sooner did the idea strike him than he was seized with panic. A sinking feeling gripped his entrails. He turned quickly, looking back to see if anyone was coming out of the hotel. He walked very rapidly.

At the entrance to the Ivy he knocked out his still-lighted pipe against one heel.

'Eighth floor, please,' he told the girl who had just brought him down.

His heart pounded as he slipped the key into the lock.

Kay was still asleep. He took a deep breath.

He didn't know if she had seen him go out or come in. She seemed to be still asleep while he undressed. She didn't budge when he slid back into bed. Even when she snuggled against him, he could have sworn she was asleep.

She did not open her eyes, but her eyelids fluttered faintly like the wings of a bird learning to fly. Her lips moved. Her voice seemed to come from far away as she murmured, without a note of reproach, of sadness, or the slightest trace of melancholy, 'You tried to run away, didn't you darling?'

He almost answered her, and he would have spoiled everything. Luckily for him, she continued in the same voice, farther away than ever, 'But you couldn't do it!'

She was asleep again. Perhaps she had not really wakened, but was speaking from the depths of some dream. When they spoke together hours later, she made no reference to his absence or to her remark.

It was their most delightful hour. It was impossible to believe that this was only the second time they had awakened together in the same bed. The warm intimacy of flesh to flesh was so familiar they felt as though they had always been lovers and that there had been thousands of mornings like this. Even the drab bedroom of the Ivy was part of that familiarity.

'Do I get the bathroom first?' she asked. Then, with surprising perceptivity, 'Why don't you smoke your pipe? I don't mind, darling. In Hungary, lots of women smoke pipes.'

They were both very gay. There was something virginal, almost childish about their eyes on awakening. They were playing at life.

'When I think of all the things that I'll probably never see again because of Ronald. I have two trunks full of clothes and lingerie down there. And here I can't even change my stockings.'

She laughed about it. Standing at the threshold of a new day, without worrying about what was to go into it, generated a marvellous feeling.

The sun was shining when they went out, a laughing, sparkling sun, and they decided to have breakfast at a lunch counter not unlike the one in which they had first met.

'Shall we go for a walk in Central Park?'

'Why not?' he said. He tried not to be jealous so early in the day, yet every time she mentioned another place, he wondered with whom she had been there before. What memories would she find in Central Park?

She looked young this morning. Perhaps it was because she also felt young that she said solemnly, as they walked into the park, 'Do you know that I'm already quite an old woman, darling? I'm thirty-two. I'll soon be thirty-three.'

He calculated that her daughter must be about twelve, and he paid closer attention to the girls playing in the park.

'I'm forty-eight,' he confessed. 'Well, not quite. But I will be in another month.'

'Men have no age.'

Perhaps this was the moment to talk about himself. He hoped so. And he dreaded it, too.

What would happen when they finally decided to look reality in the face? Up to this moment they had been skirting the fringes of life, but the time must come when they would have to crash into the heart of the matter. Was she reading his mind, as usual? Her bare hand sought his, as it had once before, in the taxi. She squeezed gently but insistently as if to say, 'Not yet'.

He had made up his mind to take her home – if that was the word – to his cell in the Village, but he didn't dare – yet. She had not noticed that he had paid the bill at the Ivy when they left, and he had not mentioned it to her. That might mean many things, including, among others, the possibility that this would be their last walk together. In any case, it would be their last before they re-entered reality. Perhaps that was the reason she had suggested this stroll, arm in arm, in Central Park, where the last warmth of an autumn sun might bless them with a friendly smile.

She was humming as she walked – the silly little tune of the jukebox which had become their song. Her muted notes gave them both the same idea. The shadows were lengthening, the sun was swinging low over the towers of Central Park West, the wind was beginning to bite. By tacit, mutual agreement, they turned their steps towards Fifth Avenue.

He didn't hail a taxi. They walked, as though that was to be their destiny for all time – walking up or down Fifth Avenue, elbowing through the crowds that were not there or were without their consciousness. The moment was approaching when they would have to stop walking – and by tacit agreement, they were postponing it indefinitely.

'Listen . . .' There were times when, by the whole posture of her body, she could express a kind of naive joy. This happened instinctively when she felt that Fate was on her side – as when they walked into a little bar and the jukebox was playing their song, and there was a homesick sailor, in contrast, leaning his elbows on the bar and staring into space. Kay squeezed Combe's arm and favoured with a compassionate glance the man who had chosen her favourite melody to nurse his nostalgia.

'Give me a nickel,' she whispered.

She borrowed a second nickel, a third. The sailor turned his head and gave her a sad smile. Then he gulped his drink and staggered out, bumping into the doorjamb on the way.

'Poor guy!' she said.

He was almost jealous; maybe he was, just a little. He wanted to talk about himself; he wanted desperately to talk about himself, and still he could not overcome the block. What's more, she wasn't helping him. Was she doing this purposely?

She was drinking again. He didn't mind. He was matching her, drink for drink, mechanically. He was happy, and he was depressed. His emotions were so close to the surface that his eyes dimmed at a single phrase from the jukebox or a sentimental movement in the romantic half-light of the lounge.

They moved on. They walked on Broadway tonight. They pushed through the crowds and entered bar after bar – none of them as intimate as *their* bar. But the routine was the same.

'Two scotches.'

Then Kay would light a cigarette, nudge him, and whisper, 'Look'.

And she would nod at a couple obviously lost in unhappy thoughts, or a lonely woman seriously embarked on a roaring drunk. She seemed to be stalking the despair of others in the hope that the contact would immunize her against the virus that she herself had been fleeing.

'Let's go.' They looked at each other and smiled. It was a password they knew well – even though their intimacy had spanned only two nights. 'It's funny, isn't it?' she added.

He didn't have to ask her what was funny. They were thinking of the same thing, although they were little more than strangers who had met by some selective miracle in the world's biggest city and now clung to one another as if the cold of loneliness was about to close in on them again.

Combe thought, *Soon . . . a little later.*

There was a Chinese shop in Forty-second Street that advertised 'Baby Turtles'.

'Buy me one, will you, darling?'

They put it into a little cardboard box that Kay carried very carefully – and laughingly – for it was the only pledge of love that he had offered her.

'Listen, Kay.'

She stroked his lips with her finger, meaning silence.

'But Kay, I must tell you . . .'

'Not now. Let's get something to eat.'

They dawdled deliberately, because now they knew definitely

that they were really at home only in the street crowds of New York.

They ducked into a lunch counter, and again they dawdled. She ate with an exasperating slowness that no longer exasperated him. She said: 'There are so many more things that I want you to know, my darling. You see, I know what you think, and you are so wrong, my Frank.'

They were walking again. It was Fifth Avenue again, but in the other direction. Twice they had made the long trek uptown; tonight they were walking downtown.

'Where are you taking me?' She thought better of her question, and added, 'No, don't tell me.'

He wasn't sure what he was going to do or even what he wanted to do. He stared straight ahead as he walked, and she, for once, respected his silence. After a while this silent promenade down Fifth Avenue became so solemn that it struck them both as a bridal march. They edged closer together, not as lovers, but as two creatures who had been wandering blindly in the fog of solitude and who had finally been granted the unexpected favour of a human contact. For the moment they were scarcely aware of being male and female. They were two human beings, two beings who needed one another.

They were dead tired by the time they reached the tranquil surroundings of Washington Square. Combe knew that his companion must be wondering if he might not be taking her back to the lunch counter that was the fountainhead of their relationship, or perhaps to the house where Jessie lived, the house she had pointed out the night before.

He smiled to himself, a little bitterly, because he was afraid, very much afraid, of what he was going to do. He had never told her that he loved her, nor had she told him that she loved him. Why not? Superstition? Fear of the word *love*? Reserve?

Not far ahead Combe could see the house he had fled only forty-eight hours before, rather than submit to another night of torture by the love cries of his neighbours. Tonight he was walking right back into the torture chamber, solemnly erect because he was about to accomplish an act of great importance.

Once or twice he was on the point of turning back, of dragging

Kay back into the unreality of their vagabond days. He closed his eyes and saw as a safe harbour the flashing neon sign of the Ivy, the down-at-the-heel night clerk, the bed that was their bed . . . It would be so much easier.

He stopped at the entrance of the building he reluctantly called home. 'Come,' he said.

She did not underestimate the importance of the occasion. She realized that the moment was as solemn as if a resplendent Swiss guard had thrown open the portals of the church. She crossed the little courtyard valiantly, surveying the surroundings quietly and without surprise.

'How funny!' she said in her gayest voice. 'Here we've been neighbours all along, and yet we didn't meet for ages.'

They crossed the little lobby with its wall panel of names and buttons. Combe's name was not there, and he saw that she had noticed this.

'Come,' he said. 'There's no lift.'

'It's only four storeys,' she said. She must have counted from the street.

She climbed the stairs ahead of him. On the third landing she stepped aside to let him pass. The first door to the left was J.K.C.'s; the next was his. Before moving on, however, he looked at the woman for a long moment. Then he took her into his arms and pressed a long, slow kiss upon her lips.

'Come.'

The dimly lit hallway smelled of poverty. Grimy fingers had smudged the walls. Standing in front of the ugly brown door, he drew his key slowly from his pocket. Forcing a laugh, he said, 'The last time I went out I forgot to turn off the light. I noticed it from the street but I didn't have the courage to climb back up the stairs.'

He pushed open the door. The tiny foyer was cluttered with trunks and clothing.

'Come in,' he said. He didn't dare look at her. He said nothing. With trembling fingers he took her hand, drew her inside, and, anxious and half ashamed, pushed her gently into his life.

There was something unreal about the quiet of the room. He had expected that the lighted lamp would reveal a scene that was sordid; instead he saw only the tragic – the forlorn tragedy of loneliness: the unmade bed with the rumpled sheets that spelled insomnia; the dented pillow that still held the shape of his head; his slippers lying where he had kicked them off; his pyjamas and a soiled shirt thrown over the back of a chair; on the table an open book beside a paper plate on which lay a half-eaten sandwich, the sorry meal of a man alone.

He suddenly realized what he had escaped, even briefly, and he stood motionless in the foyer, not daring to speak. He didn't want to look at her, but he couldn't help noticing that she too was struck by the great depth of his loneliness. He had thought that she would be surprised and resentful. She was not resentful, although she may have been just a little surprised that his solitude had been even more complete than hers.

The first things she saw were the photographs of two children, a boy and a girl. She murmured, 'You too?'

It all went so slowly, exasperatingly slowly, that every second counted, each tenth of a second, the tiniest fraction of time enfolded so much of the past – and of the future.

Combe turned away from the photos of his children, which had become blurs and were growing even more indistinct. He was ashamed of himself and wanted to ask someone's pardon, whose or why he didn't know.

Kay slowly crushed out her cigarette in an ashtray. She stepped behind Combe to close the door he had left open. Then, touching him lightly between the shoulders, she said, 'Take off your overcoat, darling.'

It was she who helped him off with it, and she knew exactly where to hang it in the cupboard. When she turned to face him again, she seemed very human, very much at home. She smiled as though nurturing some secret joy that she was not quite ready to confess. As she wound her arms around him at last, she said, 'You see, darling, I've known it always.'

4

They slept that night as in a railway-station waiting-room, or in a stalled car by the roadside. They slept in each other's arms but they did not make love.

'Not tonight,' she had whispered prayerfully.

He had understood, or at least thought he did. They were both bone-tired and suffering from the sort of dizziness that is often the aftermath of a long voyage. Had they actually arrived somewhere? They had gone to bed at once, without touching the disorder of the room. And, like travellers home from the sea who feel the pitch and roll of the ship for the first few nights, they felt the impact of the great city's pavements in their legs that night as in their dreams they walked endlessly up and down Fifth Avenue.

For the first time they arose at the same hour as other people. When Combe opened his eyes, he saw Kay opening the door into the hallway. Perhaps the click of the latch had awakened him. He was startled, puzzled. She had her back to him. At first he was aware only of the silken tangle of her hair. Then he saw that she was wearing one of his dressing-gowns and that it dragged on the floor.

'What are you looking for?'

She didn't jump. She turned naturally towards the bed without a smile. She said, 'The milk. Don't you have milk delivered every morning?'

'I never drink milk.'

'Oh.' She stepped into the kitchenette, where a kettle was singing on the electric hot place. 'Do you drink tea or coffee?'

It was exciting to hear her familiar voice in this cubicle, which had never, during his occupancy, had a visitor. An instant earlier he had been a little put out because she had not kissed him good morning. But it was much better that she find her way around, making herself at home by daylight, opening drawers and cupboards. She brought him a navy-blue silk dressing-gown.

'Is this one all right?'

She was lost in his bedroom slippers, and the heels slapped the floor as she walked.

'What do you usually eat for breakfast?'

'That depends.' He leaned back, relaxed. 'When I'm very hungry, I go down to the drugstore.'

'I found some tea and a can of coffee. Since you're French, I took a chance and started the coffee.'

'I'll go downstairs for the bread and butter.' He was feeling very young. He was anxious to get out, but it wouldn't be like yesterday, when he had been unable to go more than a hundred yards from the Ivy. Today she was here, in his apartment. Today he was tempted to go out in bedroom slippers without even shaving, the way Parisians did in Montmartre or Montparnasse, but the well-groomed François Combe could not quite stoop to this.

There was spring in the air that autumn morning, and he hummed in his shower while she made the bed. She too was humming. He felt as though a great weight of years had slipped from his shoulders, a weight he had never been conscious of but that had nonetheless made him stoop.

'Aren't you going to kiss me?'

She gave him the ends of her lips before he closed the door. He started down the stairs, then came back. When he opened the door again she was still standing there.

'Kay!'

'What?'

'I'm happy.'

'So am I. Go on . . .'

He ran down the stairs two at a time. He mustn't let down now. It was all so new. Even the street was different. The drugstore, for instance, where he had so often eaten his solitary breakfast while reading the paper, now seemed an object to be regarded with joyous irony, tinged with pity. He stopped to watch an organ-grinder playing his heart out at the kerb – the first he had ever seen in New York, the first, in fact, he had seen since he was a boy. The Italian food shop was new too. He used to buy only for one, but today he ordered a dozen little things he had never wanted before but now seemed essential to stock the refrigerator.

He took the bread and butter, the milk and the eggs with him and had the rest delivered. On his way out he remembered something and came back.

'Please leave a quart of milk at my door every morning.'

Kay was at the window as he came down the street and she waved to him. She met him at the head of the stairs to take some of his packages.

'*Zut!*' he said. 'I forgot something.'

'What?'

'The flowers. Since yesterday morning I've been planning to put flowers in the room.'

'Don't you think it's better this way?'

'Why?'

'Because . . .' She groped for words, smiling but still serious. They were both a little bashful this morning. 'Because it doesn't seem so new this way. I'd rather feel that this has been going on for a long time.' Then, as though to avoid getting sentimental, she added quickly, 'Do you know what I was looking at when you saw me at the window? I was watching an old Jewish tailor just across the street. Haven't you ever noticed him?'

He vaguely remembered seeing an old man sitting cross-legged on a table in a window opposite. He had a long, untidy beard, and the fingers that plied the needle all day long seemed unhygienically dark.

'When I was living in Vienna with my mother – I told you, didn't I, that my mother was a famous concert pianist? Well, she was. But before she became famous, she had a hard time. When I was little, we lived in one room . . . Oh, not nearly as nice as this! There was no kitchenette, no bathroom, and no refrigerator. There wasn't even any running water, and we had to use the tap at the end of the hall to wash ourselves, like the rest of the tenants. If you only knew how cold it was in winter . . .

'What was I saying? Oh yes . . . When I was sick – I used to get the grippe – and had to stay home from school, I used to look out the window all day, when they didn't keep me in bed. And right across the street there was an old Jewish tailor just like this one, and when I looked out a little while ago and saw *this* man, I thought for a moment he was the same tailor.'

'Maybe he is.' Combe was teasing.

'Idiot! He would be at least a hundred years old. But don't you think it's a curious coincidence? It put me in a good mood for the rest of the day.'

'Did you need that?'

'No . . . but I still feel like a little girl today, and when I was young, I liked to make fun of people. I even feel like making fun of you.'

'What have I done now that's ridiculous?'

'Do you mind if I ask you a question?'

'I'm listening.'

'How does it happen that there are at least eight dressing-gowns in your cupboard? Maybe I shouldn't ask a question like that, but I must say that it's rather unusual for a man –'

'For a man who has so many dressing-gowns to live in a Village dump like this? Is that your question? Well, the answer is quite simple. I'm an actor.'

Why had he dropped those words so modestly, while avoiding her eyes? Why were they so careful of each other's sensibilities this morning, as they faced each other across the breakfast table (not yet cleared), and across the street from the old tailor with the rabbinical beard?

This was the first time, really, that they had been face to face without the supporting anonymity of the faceless New York street crowds, without the stimulus of scotch or a jukebox singer. They were, in a way, seeing each other for the first time. Kay had put on no lipstick – which gave her a new face – gentler, sweeter, with a touch of timidity; perhaps a little fearful. The change was striking. The eternal cigarette didn't quite fit the new Kay.

'Are you disappointed?' he asked.

'That you're an actor? Why should I be disappointed?' But she said it a little sadly, and because they understood each other without words, they both knew that this was serious. If he were an actor, and at his age had come down to a one-room kitchenette apartment in Greenwich Village . . .

'It's much more complicated than you think,' he sighed.

'But I wasn't thinking of anything, *mon chéri.*'

'I was quite well known in Paris. I might even say that I was famous.'

'I must admit that I don't remember your name. I know you told me, but only once, that night I first met you. Do you remember? I was so upset that I didn't dare ask you to repeat it.'

'François Combe. I used to play at the Théâtre de la Madeleine, at the Michodière, at the Gymnase. I've toured all Europe and South America. I have been the star of many films. Only eight months ago, I was offered an important contract . . .'

He watched her for some sign of pity that would have hurt him deeply. There was none.

'You are probably jumping to wrong conclusions,' he said. 'Any time I want to go home, a dozen producers will be after me with contracts.'

She poured him a fresh cup of coffee and he looked at her in surprise. It was such a natural gesture he could not believe that this homely, familial intimacy that had crept upon them unsuspected could be less than miraculous.

'It was very simple and very stupid,' he said. 'It's no secret. It was the talk of Paris. The newspaper columnists had a field day. My wife is also an actress – quite a fine actress in fact: Marie Clairois . . .'

'I know the name.' She was obviously sorry that she had pronounced those words, but it was too late. The fact that she had recognized his wife's professional name but not his was now a matter of record.

'She's not much younger than I am,' he went on. 'She's on my side of forty. She was seventeen when I married her. Our son will soon be sixteen.'

He spoke without passion, although he was looking at the photographs on the wall. He got up and began pacing as he continued: 'Last winter my wife abruptly announced that she was leaving me to live with a young actor who had just been engaged by the Théâtre-Français. He had just finished training at the

Conservatoire. He was twenty-one years old. I remember the night. I had just come home from the theatre. She was not home yet. It was in our house Saint-Cloud, a house I had built myself because I like houses. My tastes are rather bourgeois, you know.

'I was in the library when she came home. She announced her decision with poise, much kindness, quite a bit of affection, and I might say even tenderness. I had no way of knowing, of course, that the young upstart was waiting outside in a taxi, ready to carry her off as soon as she had finished her chore of making a clean breast to her husband. I must confess –'

He stopped and cleared his throat, suddenly aware that he was making an impersonal declaration, quite unsuitable to his present audience.

'I must confess, darling,' he resumed, 'that I was so stunned, so dumbfounded, that I asked her to think it over. I can see now how ridiculous I must have sounded when I said, "Go to bed, my girl. We'll talk this over tomorrow when you've had a chance to sleep on it."

'She said, "But François, I'm leaving you right this minute. Can't you understand?"

'What didn't I understand? Why she was in such a hurry that she couldn't wait until morning? I didn't understand, that much was true. I think today I might have understood. But that night I lost my temper. I must have said some pretty awful things to her.

'She never lost her quiet, patient manner, however. She was sweet and, I suppose, a little maternal. She repeated, over and over, "What a pity, François, that you cannot understand!"'

He stopped, and the silence was so tenuous, so delicate, that it was neither embarrassing nor distressing. He lighted his pipe with a self-assured gesture that he had used in several of his favourite stage roles.

'I don't know whether you've ever seen Marie in the theatre or on the screen,' he continued. 'She still plays young heroines, and she can still get away with it. She has a very sweet face, sensitive and a little sad, with big, innocent eyes that look out at you with such candour that – Well, like the eyes of a wounded fawn that can't believe the wicked hunter with the gun could possibly have meant any harm. That was the kind of part she always played, on the stage and in real life, and that was the part she was playing that night.

'Every paper in Paris told the story, some by insinuation, others cynically. The kid threw away the prestige of the Comédie-Française to join my wife in a new play opening on the *boulevards*. The Comédie sued him for breach of contract . . .'

'And your children?'

'The boy is in England. He's been at Eton for two years and I thought he ought to stay there. My daughter is living in the country with my mother, near Poitiers. I stayed there myself for two months. I suppose I could have stayed on.'

'Did you love her?'

He stared at Kay, uncomprehending. For the first time since they had met, words meant different things to each of them.

'They offered me a part in an important film, a star part. She was in it too, and I was sure that she would somehow get her lover a part as well. We can't get away from each other, in our business. For instance, since we lived in Saint-Cloud, and we drove home separately after our separate performances, we would frequently meet at Fouquet's in the Champs-Élysées . . .'

'I know Fouquet's.'

'Like most actors I know, I never used to eat before a performance, but I would have a hearty supper afterwards. I had my own table at Fouquet's and they knew exactly what to serve me. Well, believe it or not, only a few days after my wife's dramatic farewell, she turned up at Fouquet's after the theatre. And she wasn't alone, either. She came to my table and greeted me so simply, so naturally, that I had the curious feeling that the two of us – the three of us, rather – were playing a scene from something by Sacha Guitry.

'She said, "Bonsoir, François." The young interloper held out his hand, too, and stammered, "B-bonsoir, Monsieur Combe." I knew they expected me to invite them to sit at my table, and with fifty people watching breathlessly, could I afford to be ungracious? What's more, my supper was already being served.

'I saw there were several newspapermen in my audience, but I am not sure I realized the full consequences of my words when I announced, loudly enough for the audience to hear: "I think I'll be leaving Paris shortly."

'"Where are you going?" my wife asked.

'"I've been offered a contract in Hollywood, and now that there's nothing to keep me here . . ."

'Cynicism? Indifference? No. I don't believe she was very cynical. She believed what I said. She knew very well that I had received an offer from Hollywood four years before, and that I had turned it down, partly because she had not been included in the deal, and partly because I did not want to be separated from the children.

'She said to me, "I'm very happy for you, François. I have always been sure that everything would work out."

'I had left them standing in front of my table until that moment. Then I asked them to sit down – why, I still don't know.

'"What may I offer you?"

'"You know very well that I never eat supper, François. I'll have some fruit juice."

'"And you, young man?"

'The imbecile was in great need of a drink to restore his poise, but he thought it his duty to follow the lead of his mistress. He said, "Two fruit juices, Maître d'Hôtel."

'The two of them sat watching me while I ate my supper. My wife took her compact from her bag and asked, "Have you heard from Pierrot?" Pierrot was our boy's nickname. "I had a letter three days ago," I said. "He's still quite happy there." "So much the better," my wife said.

'Believe it or not, Kay –'

Why she chose that exact moment to interrupt he never knew. She said, 'Don't you want to call me Catherine?'

He reached out for her hand and squeezed it.

'Believe it or not, Catherine, all during my supper, my wife sat there giving encouraging glances to that young fool, as though to say, "See how simple it is? There was no reason to be frightened."'

'You still love her, don't you?' Catherine said.

He frowned. He got up and walked around the room twice, pausing at the window to stare at the old Jewish tailor across the way. Then he planted himself in front of her, his head turned slightly so that the light would flatter his profile. He paused an instant, as he did on the stage to give full effect to a particularly dramatic line he was about to deliver.

'No!'

He wanted no scene. He himself felt no emotion, and he was particularly anxious that Kay should not misinterpret his feelings. He began talking rapidly, sharply.

'I left Paris for the United States. A friend of mine, one of our top directors, had once said to me, "There's always a spot for you in Hollywood. A man of your talent and reputation doesn't have to wait for a contract. Go on out there. Go to see So-and-so. Or So-and-so. Tell them I sent you."

'I went. Everyone was very polite. They welcomed me with open arms – and not a single job offer. One producer said, "We're considering a story that has a fat part in it for you. If we decide to make the picture, we'll let you know." Another one said, "We'll have our production schedule set up in a month or so. Keep in touch." So you see, Kay –'

'I asked you to call me Catherine.'

'Forgive me. I'll get used to it. Some of my best Parisian friends were working in Hollywood. They were wonderful. They did their best to help me, but I turned out to be a dead weight. Rather than upset their busy lives, I came to New York. Contracts are signed just as easily here as in California.

'At first I lived in a swank Park Avenue hotel. Then I moved to a more modest hotel. And finally I found this place. For six months I've lived in New York alone. That's my whole story. Alone. Now you know why I have so many dressing-gowns, so many suits, so many pairs of shoes.'

His voice broke a little. He turned again to the window, pressed his forehead against the pane. He knew that she would come to him, silently, sympathetically. He expected the gentle touch of her hand on his shoulder. He didn't move. He stared at the bearded tailor across the street, smoking a porcelain pipe.

A voice whispered in his ear, 'Are you still very unhappy?'

He shook his head negatively, but he wouldn't, couldn't face her yet.

'Are you sure that you don't love her any more?'

At that, he lost his temper. He spun about, his eyes blazing.

'You idiot! Haven't you understood a word I've said?' Yet she must understand. It was too important, the most important thing in the world. And if she couldn't understand, who else could? It was so easy to follow the line of least resistance, to blame everything on a woman.

He paced the floor feverishly, so angry that he refused to look at her.

'Can't you see that my wife doesn't matter, that I'm the only one that counts? I . . . ! I . . . !' He almost screamed the word. 'I, alone, if you like. I, who found myself stripped naked before the world! I, who lived here alone, yes, for half a year, alone! And if you can't understand that, you . . . you . . .'

He stopped himself before he shouted, 'You aren't worthy of being here yourself.' He lapsed into silence, like a brat exhausted by a silly temper tantrum.

He wondered what Kay was thinking, whether her expression showed her reaction, but he stubbornly refused to look at her. He stood with his hands in his pockets, staring at the wall. Why didn't she help him? Wasn't this the time for her to make the first move? Did she really think that all his trouble arose from stupid sentimentality? Did she imagine that his suffering was that of a common cuckold? She made him sick. He was prepared to hate her all over again. He leaned his head to one side. When he was a small boy, his mother used to say that she could tell when he was slyly plotting mischief because he would lean his head towards his left shoulder.

He stole a glance at Kay with only one eye. She was smiling and crying, both at once. Although there were tears on her cheeks, there was happy compassion in her face, as if she was not sure which expression she should adopt.

'Come here, François.'

She was too intelligent not to realize what she was risking by summoning him at a moment like this? Was she that sure of herself?

'Come here.' She spoke to him as if she addressed a stubborn child. 'Come.'

He took a reluctant step towards her. She should have been a ridiculous figure in that borrowed dressing-gown that swept the floor, the slippers that dropped off her little feet each time she moved, her face free of make-up, her hair still sleep-tangled. But she wasn't. She drew him towards her as by some tropism. All he could do was look surly.

'Come.' She took his head between her hands, pressed it against her cheek. She did not kiss him. She held him close, so that her warmth would gradually make him aware of her presence. He did not melt easily; that last trace of bitterness was hard to give up.

Then she whispered, so softly that he would not have heard the words had not her lips been against his ear, 'You were not so lonely as I was.'

Did she feel him stiffen a little? She was sure of herself, however, or perhaps sure of their mutual loneliness that would forever make it impossible for one to dispense with the other.

'There's something I must tell you, too.' It was still a whisper, and, what was stranger still, a whisper in broad daylight, without muted incidental music, without any background more romantic than a window framing an untidily bearded, cross-legged old tailor sewing quietly across the way.

'I know that I'm going to hurt you,' she said, 'because you are jealous. I'm glad that you're jealous. But I have to tell you this anyhow. When we first met –'

She didn't say 'the day before yesterday', and he was grateful to her for the omission. He did not like to remember that they had known each other for so short a time.

'When we first met –' her voice was so low now he felt her words vibrating against his chest, rather than heard them '– I was so alone, so hopelessly alone, so darkly depressed that I was sure that I could never climb out to daylight again, that I had decided to go home with the first man who asked me, any man . . .' She paused. Then, 'François, I love you.'

She said it only once. She could not have repeated it anyhow, because she was so tightly locked in his arms that speech was impossible. Their embrace was so tight that everything seemed to stop – their breathing, perhaps even their heartbeats. What could either of them say after that? What could they have done? They could not even have made love. That would have ruined everything.

The man did not dare relax his embrace. They were so close now that any relaxation might have produced a fatal vacuum. It was she who freed herself, gently, simply, and smilingly. She said, 'Look across the street.' As he turned his head, she added, 'He saw us.'

A sunbeam slanted across their window and seemed to focus deliberately on the wall, a few inches from the photograph of his two children.

'François,' she said, 'you'll have to go out for a while.'

While there was still sunlight in the streets, sunlight in the city, sunlight in his heart, she knew that he would have to go out now, to get his feet on the ground, to re-establish contact with reality. It was essential for him – for them.

'I want you to change your clothes,' she went on. 'Yes, I insist. I'll pick the suit I want you to wear.'

There were so many things he wanted to tell her, after the confession she had just made. Why had she changed the subject? She had thrown open the cupboard and was fingering his suits, quite at home, humming to herself – and to him. It was their song, and she began to sing it as she had never sung it before, with a contralto that was at once solemn and gay, a voice that transformed the banal refrain into the quintessence of all they had just lived through.

She was still going through the wardrobe, switching from a song to a monologue: 'No, *monsieur*. No grey today. No beige, either. Beige is not becoming to you, whatever you may think. You're neither dark enough nor fair enough to wear beige.' She laughed. 'By the way, what colour is your hair? I've never noticed. Your eyes, yes. Your eyes change colour to fit your moods. A few minutes ago, when you were resigned to playing the role of victim – or almost resigned – your eyes were an ugly dark grey, like a heavy sea that makes all passengers seasick. I was wondering if you would be able to make the last few yards to shore, or whether I would have to come to your rescue.

'All right, *monsieur*. Mind Mamma, François. It will be navy blue. You will be magnificent in navy blue.'

He wanted to give her an argument, but he lacked the energy. Why, at this moment, was he again thinking, *She is not even beautiful?* And why had he not returned the compliment and told her that he loved her, too? He wished he had.

Perhaps he didn't love her, or at least was not sure. He needed her – that *was* sure – and he had a terrible fear of losing her and finding himself once more alone. As to what she had just confessed – he was grateful to her for being frank, and furious at her for what she might have done. Suppose it had been somebody else instead?

Condescending yet moved, he let her dress him as though he were a schoolboy. He knew that she wanted no more serious declarations, no more grave pronouncements that morning. He knew that she was playing at being a wife, a very difficult role to play if there is no love.

'I'll wager, Mr Frenchman, that you always wear a bow tie with this suit. Very well, to make you look even more French, I'm going to choose a blue bow with white polka dots.'

She was so right that he had to smile, even though he felt a little sheepish. He didn't want to appear ridiculous.

'And a white handkerchief for your breast pocket, right? Just a trifle mussed so you won't look like a store-window dummy. Where do you keep your handkerchiefs?'

It was silly. It was so idiotic. They laughed together. They were acting, both of them, with tears in their eyes, pretending they were not being softies.

'I'm sure you have people to see,' she said. 'Now don't deny it. Don't lie to me. I insist that you see them.'

'Well, there's the radio studio . . .'

'Then you're going to the studio. When you've finished, come home. I'll be here.' She felt that he was afraid. She was so sure of it that she sealed her promise by squeezing both his arms very hard. 'All right, François. *Hinaus!*' She had never used a German word before. She reverted immediately to French. '*Filez, monsieur*. And don't expect to find an elaborate luncheon when you come home.' They were both thinking of Fouquet's, but neither would have admitted it. 'And you must wear an overcoat. This one. And a black hat. Yes, I insist.'

She eased him towards the door. She had not yet had time to wash her face or comb her hair. He knew that she wanted to be alone, and he was not sure whether he should be angry or grateful.

'I'll give you two hours,' she said. 'Three at most.' She closed the door after him, but opened it almost immediately. She was obviously embarrassed, 'François!'

He came back up the few stairs.

'Forgive me for asking,' she said, 'but could you let me have a few dollars to get things for lunch?'

He blushed. Why had he not thought of this himself? He fished his wallet from his pocket. He had never felt more embarrassed in his life. Standing by the door with the green initials J.K.C., he drew out several bills – ones, fives, he didn't count them. He blushed even deeper.

'I'm sorry,' she said.

He knew. So was he. The question of money had never before come up between them. He wanted to go back into the apartment and tell her what was on his mind, but that would only make matters worse.

'Do you mind if I buy a pair of stockings?'

He understood, or thought he did, that this was a deliberate question, designed to restore his self-confidence, to restore him to his role of master of the house.

'Forgive me for not having thought of it,' he said.

'You know, I may be able to get back my luggage yet.' She was still smiling. All this had to be done with a smile, with the very special smile that had seen them through that morning. 'But don't worry. I won't spend it all on furs, darling.'

He looked at her. She was still without make-up, had no concern for the strange picture sketched by the too long dressing-gown and the too big slippers that were forever escaping her.

He stood two steps below the landing.

He climbed them at once.

There, in the anonymous no man's land of the dingy hallway, they exchanged their first real kiss of the day, perhaps the first real kiss of their acknowledged love. And they were both so much aware of all it implied, all the things it promised, that they prolonged the sweetness of its tender pledge until the sound of a door closing somewhere brought them back to reality. Their lips parted at last. She said simply, 'Go.'

As he went down the stairs, he felt like a new man.

5

François Combe's New York career had not been exactly brilliant. He had played the part of a Frenchman in a show that survived a Boston try-out but died after three weeks on Broadway. A French playwright named Laugier, who had been living in New York for two years, got him an occasional radio job.

This morning he felt no bitterness about his dismal American experiences. He walked to Washington Square to take a Fifth Avenue bus. The avenue was bathed in sunlight, giving the grey buildings a golden patina that was almost transparent at times. The sky was a pristine blue except for an occasional fluffy cloud like those which artists paint around saints and angels.

He was still lighthearted when he got off the bus but as he walked towards the radio studio, he began to feel a vague uneasiness, perhaps a foreboding.

A foreboding of what? The thought crossed his mind that when he got home Kay would no longer be there. He shrugged it off. He watched himself do the actual shrugging, for he had stopped in front of an art dealer's window and could see his reflection. Why did this uneasiness grow on him the farther he left the Village behind him?

He entered the studio building, took the lift to the twelfth floor, and strode down the long, familiar corridor. At the end was a large, well-lighted space in which a dozen men and women were working, set apart by partitions from the director of dramatic programmes, a pock-marked redhead named Hourvitch.

Combe suddenly remembered that Hourvitch was a Hungarian, which in turn reminded him of Kay. Henceforth everything that reminded him in the slightest of Kay would have a special significance.

'I was expecting you to call yesterday,' Hourvitch said, 'but sit down, it doesn't matter. You're all set for Wednesday. By the way, I'm expecting your friend Laugier in a few minutes. We'll probably broadcast his new play.'

The programme director's phone rang. Scarcely half an hour had passed since Combe had left Kay. She had chosen his suit, tied his tie, practically dressed him. He had thought then that they were living one of life's unforgettable moments that bind two people together forever, and now it already seemed far away and unreal.

He looked around the white walls, anchoring his gaze on a big black-rimmed clock. He was trying to remember what Kay looked like, and he was having little success. He could picture her more or less the way she had looked when he first met her, her little black hat perched forward almost over her eyes, her fur thrown back from her shoulders, her cigarette ringed with lipstick, but he was annoyed – no, he was worried – at not being able to visualize her as she had been that morning.

His nervousness must have been visible, for the Hungarian put his hand over the mouthpiece and said, 'Are you in a hurry? Aren't you going to wait for Laugier?'

Yes, he was going to wait for Laugier. But something had snapped inside him. All his calm had vanished, he could not tell at exactly what point, along with his self-confidence and a *joie de vivre* so new that he had hesitated to show it in public. And when Hourvitch at last put down the phone, Combe affected an air of nonchalance to cover up any sign of change in his mood.

'You're a Hungarian,' he said, 'so I suppose you know Count Larski.'

'You mean the ambassador?'

'Yes, I guess he must be an ambassador by now.'

'If he's the man I think you mean, he's a first-class diplomat. He's the present Hungarian Ambassador to Mexico. I knew him in Paris when he was First Secretary for a long time. I guess you know I worked in Paris for eight years with Gaumont. Larski's wife, if I remember correctly, ran away with a gigolo . . .'

He had expected this, and he was ashamed. Those were the very words he had been looking for, that he had in fact provoked, but that now he wanted to cut short.

'That's all I wanted to know,' he said.

But Hourvitch continued, 'I don't know what happened to the Countess. I met her once in Cannes when I was down there on location. I was an assistant director. I thought I saw her in New York once, but I lost her in a crowd and wasn't sure.' He smiled. 'It wouldn't surprise me, though. You run into everybody you ever knew in New York these days, the high and the low. I suspect she'd be among the low . . . Now about that broadcast. What I wanted to tell you was this . . .'

Was Combe still listening? He was sorry he had come, sorry he had opened his big mouth. He was conscious of having sullied something precious, and yet it was Kay that he blamed. Why hadn't she lied about *everything* instead of mixing truth with falsehood? Had he really believed that she had been the wife of a first secretary? He didn't know any more, but he was furious. He thought bitterly, *When I get home, she'll be gone. Isn't that her routine?*

The idea of coming home to an empty apartment was so intolerable that it hurt him physically. A sharp pain stabbed his chest. He wanted to run for the lift, to grab a taxi and hurry to the Village. Then almost instantly he thought, *I'm being silly. Of course she'll be there. Didn't she confess that the night we met, if I hadn't come along it would have been somebody else . . . ?*

A jovial voice broke into his consciousness.

'Well, well, little father, how are you?'

Combe forced a smile. He must have looked like an imbecile with that prop smile, because Laugier frowned as he shook hands.

'What's wrong, old boy? Off your feed?'

'No, not at all. Why?'

Laugier didn't frown often. Life for him was uncomplicated, or at least the complications were of his own devising. He must have been at least fifty-five, although he never admitted it. He was not married. He was constantly surrounded by pretty girls, none of them older than twenty-five, who seemed to be in constant rotation. He was like a juggler who could keep half a dozen balls in the air at once, none of which ever seemed to stay in his hands. The girls appeared and disappeared without a trace and without leaving a ripple on the calm of his bachelor's existence. And he was always ready to share his existence with a friend. He would telephone an invitation to dinner and add, 'Look, old boy, I've got a charming little girl coming to dinner too. If you're alone, I'll ask her to bring a friend . . .'

Was Kay in the apartment? He was still worried about not being able to remember how she looked that morning. Superstitiously he thought, *It must be because she's not there.* Perhaps because of the presence of Laugier, with his good-natured cynicism, he contradicted himself immediately. *Of course, she's there. And tonight she'll have another fairy story to tell me. Why should she stop lying now?* If only he could winnow the few grains of truth from her lies. He had begun to doubt everything, even the story of the Jewish tailor and the running water at the end of the hall, which she had told him to arouse his pity . . .

'You looked peaked, old man,' Laugier was saying. 'Come and have a hamburger with me. Yes, I insist. It will be my pleasure. I'll be through with Hourvitch in exactly three minutes.'

While the two men were settling their business, Combe found himself thinking of Kay and his wife at the same time, probably because of Hourvitch's phrase, 'She ran away with a gigolo.' People must have said the same thing about his wife. He didn't care. He had been sincere that morning when he declared that he no longer loved her. It was definitely not because of her that he had gone all to pieces. It was much more complicated.

Of course Kay would never understand. Why should she? It was ridiculous to put her on a pedestal just because he had been dying of loneliness the night he met her, when she was seeking, if not a man, at least a bed. Yes, it was the bed she wanted, no matter who might be in it.

'Ready, little father?'

Combe sprang up, smiling meekly.

'Hourvitch, my pretty prince,' said Laugier, 'you must consider our friend Combe for the part of the senator.'

A small part, no doubt, but it was good of Laugier anyhow. In Paris the situation would have been reversed. Seven years ago Laugier had breezed into Fouquet's, high as a kite, to seek his help at three o'clock in the morning.

'What a part, my precious one,' he had said. 'Made to order for you . . . Juiciest part you ever played . . . Three hundred performances on the *boulevards* guaranteed, to say nothing of the provinces and a road company for all Europe and the Americas . . . But only if you play the duke; otherwise the whole thing flops. Without you, there's no play . . . Leave everything to me . . . I told you the gimmick . . . Now read the script and get busy . . . If you take the script to the director of the Madeleine yourself and tell him you want to play the duke, it's in the bag . . . I'll phone you tomorrow . . . don't you agree, madame, that he ought to star in my play?'

For his wife had been with him that night. Laugier had slipped her the script with a sly smile, and next day sent her a huge box of Marquise de Sévigné chocolates . . .

And now, seven years later . . .

'You see, old bean,' Laugier was saying as the lift took them down, 'New York is like that. One day you're . . .'

Combe wanted to beg him, *Please stop. Shut up, for God's sake!* He knew the New York litany by heart, had heard it so many times. For him New York was finished. He was through thinking about it, or at least he wouldn't think about it until later. Right now there was only one thing that mattered: that there was a woman in his one-room apartment, a woman he knew practically nothing about but suspected much; a woman he could observe with eyes as cold, as lucid, as cruel as had ever looked upon any woman, a woman he could despise but, he was well aware, he could not do without.

'Hourvitch is a nice guy,' Laugier was saying. 'He pretty well knows he stands amid the alien corn, which is only proper. He has not forgotten that he got his start sweeping out the studios at Billancourt, and he has a few little accounts to settle. Otherwise, he's a good pal, particularly when you don't need him.'

Combe was on the point of stopping short, holding out his hand, and saying good-bye. If ever there was a body without a soul, he was there that day in Madison Avenue. Combe walked mechanically, but he lived and thought far downtown . . .

'You shouldn't take it so hard, old man. A month from now, maybe six weeks, you'll be the first one to laugh at the long face that's scaring the little children of Manhattan. Buck up, little old brother, if only to show the jealous no-good bastards who aren't even worthy of yapping at your heels that you're still on your feet. Why, I remember the night after my second play opened at the Porte-Saint-Martin . . .'

Why had she been so eager to let him go? She, whose intuition was infallible, must have known that this was not yet the moment . . . unless she herself needed the freedom . . . He wondered whether the story of Jessie was true? Those trunks locked up in Jessie's apartment and the key on the high seas, en route to the Panama Canal . . .

'What are you drinking?'

Laugier had guided him into a little bar rather like Kay's little bars. There was a jukebox in the corner . . .

'A manhattan.'

He thrust his hand into his pocket. While his fingers were seeking a nickel, he looked at himself in the mirror behind the glasses at the back of the bar. He certainly looked ridiculous. He smiled sarcastically at his reflection.

'What are you doing after lunch?'

'I have to go home.'

'Home where? I would have taken you along to a rehearsal . . .'

Combe knew those New York rehearsals: the cast crowded into a tiny studio on the twentieth or twenty-first floor of some tower above Broadway, everything so strictly scheduled that if the rehearsal ran over the hour or two hours allotted, another troupe would come barging in while the first crew was still hard at work. He had not been impressed by the *esprit de corps*. Each member of the cast knew his own lines but little about the production as a whole. Moreover they had little interest in their colleagues. Actors and actresses came and went without even a hello or good-bye to their fellow cast members, certainly never to him. They didn't even know his name – except perhaps for a few who had been part of the same cast in previous broadcasts. When the director gave the cue, he entered, approached the mike, delivered his lines, and departed without other recognition than a titter of laughter because of his French accent. He was suddenly frightened as he sipped his manhattan. He was even panic-stricken at the thought of returning to these anonymous rehearsals, facing an impersonal mike, afraid of the titters of snotty-nosed people who didn't even know his name. No. This was a loneliness even more intense than he had suffered in his cubicle during the Friday saturnalia of Winnie and J.K.C. behind the partition.

He was scarcely aware of the fact that he had walked to the jukebox, extracted five cents from his pocket, and slipped it into the slot . . . a slot he had chosen without even thinking.

Laugier had already signalled the bartender to refill the glasses. He was listening with one ear to the singer that Combe's nickel had brought into the room. He said: 'Do you know how much money that song has earned in the United States alone? One hundred thousand dollars, my little old man! That's royalties for both the composer and lyricist, of course. But when you consider that there are thousands of jukeboxes, orchestras, night clubs, restaurants, and the radio, still playing that tune . . . well, I sometimes think I should be writing songs instead of plays.' He raised his glass. 'Cheerio. Shall we go in and gnaw on an old bone?'

'Would you be offended if I left you now?'

He asked the question so solemnly that Laugier not only was surprised, but for an instant forgot his usual cynicism. There was genuine concern in his voice as he said, 'You really are in bad shape, aren't you?'

'Will you excuse me?'

'Of course, old man. But listen . . .'

No, he couldn't listen. He ran from the bar. Even the street noises tore at his nerves. His stupid jitters annoyed him. He stood at the bus stop for several minutes, but when a taxi came along, he flagged it down. He flung his address at the driver.

He wasn't sure which he feared the more – to find Kay at home or not to find her. He was furious with himself, furious with Kay, without knowing exactly why. He felt humiliated, terribly humiliated. The cross streets flashed past as the taxi raced downtown. He had no idea where he was, and he didn't care. He thought, *The little bitch got me out of there so she could run away without a scene.* Then, *What did she care? Me or another? Or the gigolo at Cannes?*

When the taxi stopped, he scanned the façade of the house, as though he expected to see a change. He was pale, and he knew it. His hands were icy and his forehead beaded with cold sweat.

She was not at the window, as she had been that morning, that morning when the day was young and the sun was gay, and she had waved to him affectionately.

He ran up the stairs. He paused on the third-floor landing. He was ashamed of his anger and hoped that, by pausing for breath, he might be able to laugh at himself.

As his hand touched the banister, slightly sticky, of the last flight, where he – and she – only two hours ago . . .

He couldn't wait any longer. He banged against the door. He had to know if she was still there. He stabbed his key at the lock, missed, tried again. He was still fumbling when the door swung inwards. Kay smiled at him.

'Come here,' he ordered, without looking at her.

'What's the matter, darling?'

'Nothing. Come here.'

She was wearing her black silk dress – the only dress she had. But she had added a little white embroidered collar he had never seen before – and it infuriated him.

'Come here.'

'You know, darling, lunch is ready.'

He knew that. He could see it through the open door. He could also see that the room was neat and clean for the first time in weeks. He could also imagine the bearded tailor across the street, but he preferred not to look.

Kay stared at him with even more concern than Laugier had shown. In her eyes he found the same eagerness to humour him. These fits of his apparently inspired respect. And why not? Didn't they realize that he had reached the end of his resources? If they didn't, let them say so and he would crawl off quietly to die alone in his corner. It was that simple. But he couldn't stand any more questions, any more waiting. He had had enough . . . Enough of what? Well, questions, for one thing, especially the questions he was asking himself, that were making him physically sick, yes sick – psychosomatic, if they insisted, but sick.

'Well?'

'I'm here, François. I just thought . . .'

She thought! She thought that she would fix him an intimate little lunch he would like. He knew that. He could see it. He wasn't blind. And after that? Was this the way he was supposed to love her, with the sanctimonious respect for the feelings of the young bride? Had they ever been able to stop before, either of them? Not he, at any rate.

'I think the hot plate . . .' she began.

The hell with the hot plate! Let it burn until they had time to think of it. Hadn't the light burned in his room for nearly forty-eight hours? Had he worried about the light?

'Come here.'

What was he so afraid of? Of Kay? Of himself? Of fate? Of one thing he was certain: he was desperately in need of carrying her with him again into the anonymous crowds of Manhattan. He had to walk with her, stop here and there in little bars, rub shoulders with strangers, beg their pardon when he jostled them or stepped on their toes. Perhaps he even needed to feel his nerves grow unbearably taut while she ringed just one more 'last' cigarette with her lipstick.

Did she really understand as they went down the stairs?

When they reached the sidewalk, it was he who wondered where they were going, and she who was not curious enough to ask where. So, as if resigned to whatever fate had in store for them at the moment she took his arm, he repeated dully: 'Come.'

The hours that followed were exhausting. With sadistic obstinacy he insisted on going back to all the places they had been together. At the Rockefeller Center cafeteria he saw that their trays contained the same dishes exactly. He scrutinized her fiercely, and he cross-examined her bluntly and without pity.

'With whom have you been here before?'

'What do you mean?'

'Don't ask questions. Answer me. When a women answers a question with a question, she is getting ready to lie.'

'I don't understand you, François.'

'You told me you came here often. You must admit that it would be unusual if you always came here alone.'

'I sometimes came here with Jessie.'

'That's all?'

'I don't remember.'

'With a man?'

'Possibly. Yes, once, with one of Jessie's friends.'

'One of Jessie's friends who just happened to be your lover?'

'Oh, now . . .'

'Admit it.'

'I mean . . . well, yes, if you want to call it that. Once in a taxi.'

He could picture the inside of the cab, the impersonal shoulders of the driver, the two pale blurs of faces in the darkness. He could taste the special savour of kisses stolen almost in the very heart of a crowd.

'Bitch!'

'It was so unimportant, Frank.'

Why did she have to call him Frank, all of a sudden?

'You mean it made no difference if it was he or another? One more or less?'

She shrugged. Why didn't she fight back? Her passivity, her humility, irritated him. He sprang up, seized her by the hand, dragged her from the cafeteria. Once in the street, he continued to cling to her hand as he pushed on and on, as though driven by some hidden force.

'Does this street bring back memories too? Did you walk here with a man?'

'No. I don't know any more.'

'Of course. New York is such a big city, isn't it? Still, you've been living here for years. You don't expect me to believe that you haven't gone to little bars like ours, with other men, and that you haven't endlessly played other records that were at that moment *your* song . . .'

'I've never been in love before, Frank.'

'You're lying.'

'Believe it or not, I've never been in love. Not the way I love you.'

'You used to go to the cinema. I'm sure you must have gone to the cinema with a man to sit in the last row and play dirty little games in the dark. Confess!'

'I don't know any more.'

'You see! It was on Broadway, wasn't it? Show me the cinema.'

'Maybe at the Capitol. Just once.'

The Capitol was scarcely a hundred yards ahead of them. He stared at the blazing marquee.

'Who was it?'

'A young naval officer. A Frenchman.'

'How long was he your lover?'

'One week-end. His ship was in Boston. He came to New York with a friend on week-end leave.'

'And you took on the two of them.'

'When his friend saw how things were going, he left us.'

'I'll bet you picked them up on the street.'

'That's right. I recognized the uniform. I overheard them speaking French. They didn't know I understood them until I smiled. Then they spoke to me.'

'Which hotel did he take you to? Where did you sleep with him? Answer me!'

She remained silent.

'Answer me!'

'Why do you have to know? You're torturing yourself for nothing, I assure you. It was so unimportant, Frank.'

'What hotel?'

She sighed resignedly. 'The Ivy,' she said.

He shouted with laughter. He dropped her arm. 'That does it!' he said. 'That takes the prize! Talk about the long arm of coincidence! So, on our first night – or first morning, rather, since it was nearly daylight – when I brought you to the –'

'François!'

'Yes, you're right. I'm being stupid. As you say so well, it's all so unimportant.' Then, after a few steps: 'I'll bet he was married, your naval officer. Did he tell you all about his wife?'

She nodded. 'And he showed me pictures of his children.'

He walked on, staring straight ahead, as though seeing the pictures of his own children on the wall of his bedroom. He was holding Kay's arm again. When they came opposite their little bar, he pushed her brusquely inside.

'Are you sure, absolutely sure, that you haven't come here before with another man? You'd better admit it now.'

'I've never been here with anyone but you.'

'It's possible, after all, that you may be telling the truth for once.'

She was not at all resentful. She was doing her best to remain her natural self. She held out her hand for a nickel and went meekly, as though performing a rite, to prod the jukebox into song.

'Two scotches.'

Another round, then another and another. He pictured her in other bars with other men, begging just one last drink, lighting one last cigarette, always the last. He pictured her on the sidewalk, waiting for the man, walking awkwardly because her heels were too high and her feet hurt, taking his arm . . .

'Don't you want to go home?'

'No.'

He wasn't listening to the music. He sat stolidly, apparently engaged in intensive soul-searching. Suddenly he got up and called for the bill.

'Come on.'

'Where are we going?'

'To look for other memories. We'll find them pretty much all over, won't we?'

As they passed a dance hall, he asked, 'Do you dance?'

She misunderstood. She asked, 'Do you feel like dancing?'

'I merely asked you if you dance.'

'I do, François.'

'Where did you go on nights when you wanted to dance? Show me. I want to know. You understand that, don't you? And if we should meet a man – are you listening to me? – a man you've slept with . . . and that is sure to happen one of these days, if it hasn't already happened . . . I want you to do me the honour of pointing him out and saying, "This one."'

He gave her a sidelong glance. Her cheeks were flaming and her eyes were unnaturally bright, but he was not sorry for her. He was too unhappy himself to feel pity for her.

'Tell me. Have we already met him?'

'Of course not.'

She was crying. She cried without really crying, like a little girl clinging to her mother's hand, being dragged through the crowd.

'Taxi!'

As they got in, he said, 'This should give more fond memories. Who was he, this taxicab lover of yours, assuming, of course, that there was only one? It's quite the thing in New York, isn't it – love in a taxi? Who was he?'

'I already told you – a friend of Jessie's. Or rather of her husband Ronald. We met him by accident.'

'Where?' He had to torture himself by visualizing everything.

'In a little French restaurant in the Forties.'

'And he bought you champagne. And then Jessie discreetly withdrew, like your sailor's friend. People can be so discreet, so understanding! Let's get out here.'

It was the first time since their meeting that they had come back to the corner of the all-night café.

'What do you want to do?'

'Nothing. A sentimental pilgrimage, as you see. And here?'

'What do you mean?'

'You know very well what I mean. Don't tell me that the other night was the first time you'd dropped in here for a late snack. It's just a stone's throw from where you lived with your Jessie. I'm beginning to know you well, the two of you, and I would be very much surprised if you hadn't struck up a conversation here with someone. You have quite a knack for engaging men in conversation, haven't you, Kay?'

He looked at her squarely. His face was so pale and drawn, his eyes so staring, that she didn't have the courage to protest. He tightened his grip on her arm until his fingers hurt.

'Come on.'

As they passed the house where Jessie lived, Kay stopped short in surprise. There was a light burning in one of Jessie's windows.

'François, look!'

'So what? So your girl friend has come home. Unless it's your Enrico. You'd like to go up, wouldn't you? Say it. You'd like to go up?' His voice threatened. 'Well, what are you waiting for? Are you afraid I might go with you and discover all the filthy little secrets that must be hidden away up there?'

This time it was she who said, in a voice heavy with unshed tears, 'Come on.'

She pulled him towards Fifth Avenue.

Once again they were walking up the long thoroughfare, heads down, silently, seeing nothing except the bitterness that lay between them.

'I'm going to ask you one question, Kay.' He seemed calmer, more nearly in control of himself.

'I'm listening,' she said, with just a hint of hope showing through her resignation.

'Promise me you'll answer me frankly.'

'Of course.'

'Promise?'

'I swear it.'

'How many men have there been in your life?'

'What do you mean?'

'Don't I make myself clear?' Again his tone was aggressive, hammering.

'That depends upon what you mean when you say that a man has been in the life of a woman.'

'How many men have slept with you?' He prompted her sardonically. 'A hundred? A hundred and fifty? More?'

'Oh no! Less, much less.'

'Which means?'

'I don't know. I've never counted. Let's see . . .' She seemed to be combing her memory. Her lips moved, but he couldn't tell whether she was producing names or merely figures. 'Seventeen. No, eighteen.'

'Are you sure you haven't forgotten anyone?'

'I don't think so. Yes, that's all.'

'Does that include your husband?'

'Sorry. No, I forgot my husband. That makes nineteen, my darling. But if you only knew how unimportant –'

'Come on.'

They turned around and started back down the avenue. They were both exhausted, physically and emotionally. They said nothing; what was there to say?

Washington Square . . . The side streets of Greenwich Village

. . . the light in the basement window, spotlighting a Chinese laundryman at his ironing table . . . The red-checked curtains of the Italian restaurant . . .

'Climb.'

He was close behind her in the stairway, so calm, so outwardly cold that she felt goose flesh rising on the back of her neck. He opened the apartment door.

'You may go to bed,' he said, as though pronouncing sentence.

'And you, darling?'

Oh yes. He. What *was* he going to do? He walked straight to the window, pressed his forehead against the pane. He heard her walking to and fro behind him. He heard the sigh of the bed-springs as she was apparently obeying instructions. He didn't move. For a long moment he remained safely protected by the armour of his bitter loneliness.

Suddenly he wheeled, strode to the bedside and stared at her. Not a muscle in his face moved – except the ends of his lips, which whispered, 'You . . .'

He repeated it, each time half a tone higher, until the word became a cry of despair.

'You . . . ! You . . . ! You . . .!'

He stared down at her face, his arm upraised. He paused, trying to regain control of himself.

'You!'

His voice broke, his arm slashed downwards, his hand – or his fist; he no longer could distinguish – made a sickening sound as he struck her face. Again, again, again . . . Until he collapsed on the bed, drained at last of all energy and all substance, sobbing, begging forgiveness.

As the salt of their tears mingled on their lips, she sighed. Her voice seemed to come from far, far away as she said: 'My poor darling . . .'

6

Without knowing it they awoke very early. They were both so sure they had been sleeping for ages that neither thought of looking at the clock. It was Kay who got up first to draw the curtains, and she said, 'Look, François.'

The Jewish tailor was, for the first time to their knowledge, no longer sitting cross-legged at his table. He was sitting in a chair like everybody else, a straw-bottomed chair that might have come from the hinterland of Poland or the Ukraine. He was quietly dunking thick slices of bread into some liquid in a flowered porcelain bowl. The dangling electric light, which he moved about to suit his needs, was still burning. He was eating slowly, solemnly, with no eyes for the scissors or the thick grey paper patterns hanging from his wall.

Kay said, 'He's my friend. I must find some way to make him happy.'

Combe nodded – because they were both happy.

'Do you know that it's only seven o'clock?' she said. No, he didn't, and neither did she. Neither of them felt any fatigue, only a profound sense of well-being that made them smile at one another for no sound reason.

She was dressing, and at the same time pouring boiling water into the coffee maker. As he watched her, he said, 'There must have been somebody in your friend's apartment last night, since the light was on.'

'I would be very much surprised if Jessie had come back.'

'You'd like to get your clothes back, wouldn't you?' he said.

She looked at him, surprised at this generous outburst, not yet quite ready to accept it.

'Listen,' he said. 'I'll go back there with you, and I'll wait downstairs while you go up and investigate.'

'You will?' He knew what she was thinking – that she might meet Enrico or even Ronald, Jessie's husband. 'All right, let's go.'

They went. The early-morning spectacle of the half-deserted streets they had not yet shared in the Village, with the provincial quiet of the thoroughfares, was not like the tired retreat of the barflies from the Times Square dawn. In the Village they seemed to be part of a fresh awakening, a cool shower for the soul, while the city was still washing its face.

'You see? There's a window open. Go on up. I'll wait here.'

'I'd rather you came with me, François. Please?'

The stairway wasn't elegant, but it was clean – a solid, middle-class stairway. There were door mats in front of nearly every door, and on the second floor a maid was polishing the brass doorknob with such energy that her ample breasts quivered like gelatin. He suspected that Kay was a little frightened, and that she considered this a mutual experiment. But to him the house was commonplace and without mystery.

She rang the bell. Her lips trembled. She looked to him for assurance, furtively squeezed his hand. They could hear the bell ringing inside, but there was no answer.

'What time is it?'

'Nine o'clock.'

She looked at the door of the neighbouring apartment and asked, 'Do you mind?' He said nothing. So she pushed the bell.

The door was opened by a man of about sixty, clad in a padded dressing-gown, his scant grey hair forming a crown around his pink scalp. He held an open book in one hand, and he bowed his head to peer over the rims of his glasses.

'Well,' he said. 'So it's you, my little miss. I thought you'd come by, sooner or later. Was Mr Enrico able to reach you? He stopped by last night. He asked me if you'd left your new address with me. He seemed to think you had some personal effects in the apartment that you might want to repossess.'

'Thank you, Mr Bruce. I'm sorry to have disturbed you, but I saw a light here last night, and I wanted to be sure that it was Mr Enrico.'

'No news from your little friend?'

Everything seemed so banal, so familiar.

When they were in the street again, she said, 'I don't know how Enrico happens to have a key, except – yes, that must be it. In the beginning, when her husband was sent to Panama and Jessie found out she couldn't stand the climate down there and had to come back, she took an apartment in the Bronx. She got a job as a switchboard operator with a firm on Madison Avenue, and after she met Enrico – whatever you may think, they went together for five months before anything happened – he was the one who insisted she live in the Village, much closer to her job. I don't know what arrangement they had between them, but I suspect now that he was the one who paid the rent and may even have had the apartment in his name. So naturally he would have a key . . .'

'Why don't you phone him?'

'Phone who?'

'Enrico, my girl. Since he has a key, and all your belongings are locked up in his apartment, what could be more natural?'

'You really want me to phone him?'

He squeezed her hand. 'Please do.'

He locked his arm in hers and marched her to the nearest drugstore – where she suddenly remembered that Jessie's lover never got to work before ten o'clock. So they sat at the counter, as unconcerned as an old married couple, waiting.

Twice she shut herself in the phone booth, and twice returned unsuccessful. On the third attempt she apparently made contact with her past. He could watch her through the glass door as she talked, and, although her past was at the other end of the wire, her eyes never left François Combe. She smiled at him continuously, timidly, as though she were thanking him and asking his forgiveness all at once.

'He's coming down,' she announced. 'I hope you don't mind. I couldn't put him off. He said he'd jump in a taxi and be here in ten minutes. He couldn't say very much because there was somebody in his office, but he said a messenger brought him the key in an envelope that had Ronald's name on it.'

So they waited on the sidewalk. He wondered if she would take his arm in the presence of the South American. She did – just as the taxi drew up. She looked at Combe squarely so that he could see the promise shining in her eyes. She wanted him to see that her eyes were clear and candid, and that the pleading pout of her lips asked his indulgence and his courage.

He needed neither. He felt suddenly so objective that he had a hard time keeping a straight face.

This Enrico, or Ric, as he liked to be called, was a little, unprepossessing fellow of whom nobody could be jealous. He was not ugly, exactly, but he was so commonplace, so obviously small potatoes, that he himself felt obliged to run up to Kay dramatically, to seize both her hands and exclaim effusively: 'My poor Kay! That all this should happen to us!'

Very simply she introduced the men. 'Enrico, I want you to meet a friend of mine, François Combe. You may speak freely, because I've told him everything.'

Combe noted that she addressed Enrico by the familiar 'tu'.

'Let's go right up,' said Enrico. 'I have an important appointment in my office in fifteen minutes. I'm keeping the cab.'

Enrico went up the stairs first, leaving a faint trace of perfume in his wake. He was quite a small man, perfectly groomed. And Combe thought he detected the marks of a curling iron in his well-pomaded hair.

Enrico looked for the key on an impressive-looking key ring – to Combe's delight; he hated men who carried key rings – and finally found what he was seeking in a jacket pocket. During the search his feet, in shoes as flexible as dancing pumps, beat a nervous tattoo on the floor. He spoke in a French of sorts: 'What a catastrophe when I came here and found nobody! Luckily I thought of ringing the bell of the nice old gentleman next door. He gave me the note she'd left for me.'

'For me too,' Kay said.

'I know. He told me. I didn't know where to find you.' He stole a glance at Combe, who smiled at him. Perhaps he was expecting an explanation from Kay. All he got was a happy smile.

'Then yesterday I got the key. Just the key, no explanation. So I came down last night.'

Lord, how simple it all was! And how prosaic! The open window was causing a draught, and Enrico closed the door as soon as they were all inside. It was a small, ordinary apartment, no different from thousands of others in New York, with the same overstuffed sofa, the same coffee table, the same ashtrays beside an armchair, the same record player, the same miniature library in a corner cabinet next to the window. It was here that Kay and Jessie . . .

Combe smiled unconsciously, a smile that seemed to come from deep inside. There may have been a trace of malice in his eyes, but just a trace, and he wondered if Kay was annoyed by it. What picture had he been building for himself of the life she had been leading here, of these men she was eternally calling by their first names, which made him wince? Well, one of the men stood before him now, and he could not help noticing that at ten o'clock in the morning he was wearing a pearl pin in his gaily coloured tie.

After closing the window Kay went into the bedroom. 'Would you give me a hand, François darling?'

The 'darling' was for Enrico's benefit; she wanted him to know how things stood between her and Combe.

She had glanced into an old trunk, then swung open a cupboard door.

'But Jessie didn't take any of her things with her!' was her surprised exclamation.

'Yes, I know,' Enrico said. 'This morning I got a letter she wrote on the *Santa Clara*.'

'Then she's already at sea?'

'He made her take the first boat to Panama with him. It wasn't as bad as I thought it might have been. When he arrived, he knew exactly what was going on. I'll let you read the letter. He didn't let her out of his sight. How she managed to write at all I'll never know. Anyhow, when he walked into the apartment, he said, "Are you alone?" She said, "You can see for yourself." "Aren't you expecting him any moment now?"'

Enrico was holding his cigarette in the self-conscious manner of so many American girls. He said, 'You know Jessie. She didn't say so in her letter, but she must have protested, grown indignant, thrown her arms around . . .'

Combe looked at Kay. They both smiled.

'It seems Ronald was very cold.'

Well, well! So Enrico called him Ronald too.

'I wonder if he didn't come to New York just to try to catch her in the act. I don't know who might have tipped him off. Anyhow, while Jessie was swearing to God that he was completely off his nut, he walked straight to the cupboard, grabbed my pyjamas and dressing-gown and threw them on the bed.'

They were still there. The dressing-gown was a thing of wonder, with huge floral patterns, and the pyjamas were of cream-coloured silk with initials embroidered in dark red.

'While she was crying,' Enrico continued, 'Ronald went through all her things. He picked out all the dresses that were hers three years before, when she came back from Panama. Those she could take with her. The rest she had to leave behind. You know Jessie . . .'

Combe himself was beginning to know Jessie. Furthermore, Kay herself was beginning to be more understandable, so much so that he felt a little sheepish.

'You know Jessie. She couldn't bear the idea of parting with some of the dresses and things she had acquired in the past three years. She said, "But I swear, Ronald, that I bought these things with my own money."'

Could it be that Enrico actually had a sense of humour?

'I don't know how she managed to write all this with her husband spying on her every minute of the day, as she said, but she did write six pages – in pencil. There was a message for you, too, Kay. She said that she was giving you everything that she couldn't pack, and that you were welcome to wear anything you needed.'

'Thank you, Enrico, but I couldn't do that.'

'The rent of the apartment is paid until the end of the month. I don't know yet what I'll do with all my stuff here. I can't take it home, as you know. If you want, I'll leave you the key. I'll have to leave it with you anyhow, since I have to go now. I really have some very important meetings this morning. I suppose that now they're on the high seas, Ronald will leave her in peace.'

'Poor Jessie!'

Did Enrico feel any guilt at all? He said, 'I wonder if there is anything *I* might have done. I had no idea that there was a crisis in the making. That night my wife was giving a big dinner, so I couldn't even telephone Jessie . . . Good-bye, Kay. Send the key to my office when you're through with it.'

Enrico didn't know exactly how he should treat this man he scarcely knew, but he shook his hand with exaggerated warmth, and then, as though his seal of approval was necessary, said, 'Take good care of this girl. She's Jessie's best friend.'

'What's the matter with you, François?'

'Nothing, my darling.'

It was the first time he had called her darling without a trace of sarcasm. Perhaps having found Enrico to be such a little man had reduced Kay's stature, too, but not unfavourably. In fact, he felt for her only an infinite tenderness.

The little man had gone, leaving behind only a faint, lingering scent, his pyjamas and dressing-gown on a bed, and his slippers on the floor of the open cupboard.

'Now do you understand?' Kay asked.

'I do indeed.' It was true. He was glad he had come. He finally saw her in her proper perspective, in her own setting, and all these men – the Enricos, the Ronalds, the sailors, these friends, with whom, indifferently, she used the familiar 'tu' – he saw them in their correct dimensions.

He did not love her any less for it. On the contrary, he loved her with deeper affection, with less strain and bitterness. He had almost lost his fear of her and of the future. Perhaps he had lost all fear and could let himself go at last.

'Sit down,' she said. 'You take up too much room.'

Had this bedroom she had shared with Jessie become smaller too, like everything else in his eyes? It was a gay, pleasant little room. The walls were off-white, the cretonne spreads on the twin beds were imitation Jouy print. So were the drapes, through which the sun was filtering. He sat down obediently on the bed next to the flowered dressing-gown.

'I was right, wasn't I, to refuse to take any of Jessie's things? Look, do you like this dress?'

It was an evening gown that seemed to him quite pretty, and she held it up in front of her like a Fifth Avenue salesgirl tempting a customer.

'Have you worn it often?' It was not a jealous question this time. He merely wanted to show his interest and his appreciation of her naive display of innocent coquetry.

'Only twice. And neither time, I swear, did anybody touch me. Nobody even kissed me.'

'I believe you.'

'Truly?'

'I believe you.'

'There are the shoes to wear with it. The gold is a little gaudy for my taste. I wanted some in old gold, but these were all I could find in my price range. Am I boring you with my fashion show?'

'No indeed.'

'Sure?'

'On the contrary. Come and kiss me.'

She hesitated, out of some sort of respect for his new mood. Then she bent over and quickly brushed his lips with hers.

'Do you know that you're sitting on my bed?'

'What about Enrico?'

'He only slept here about twice a month, sometimes less. He had to invent a business trip as an excuse for his wife. And it was complicated even then, because she always wanted to know the name of the hotel so she could phone him. She wouldn't have hesitated to call in the middle of the night.'

'Did she suspect something?'

'I think she did, but she pretended not to know. She took care of herself in her own way. I don't think she ever loved him, or at any rate she had stopped loving him, but that didn't stop her from being jealous. If she had tried to do anything rash, though, he was quite capable of divorcing her to marry Jessie.'

So the little fellow with the pearl tiepin would tolerate no nonsense? It was good to be able to listen calmly to all this now, and to be able automatically to give words and things their proper weight.

'He used to come over often to spend the evening. Every two or three days. He had to leave for home around eleven o'clock on those nights, and often I would go and see a film to leave them alone. I'll show you the cinema. It's very near here. Sometimes I would sit through the same film three times rather than take the subway uptown.'

'Aren't you dying to put on that dress?'

'How did you know?' She still held it in her hands. With a deft movement he had never seen before she slipped out of the black dress she had been wearing for days. He had the curious impression of seeing her for the first time in her underthings. In fact, had he ever really looked at her undressed?

Even better, he had not even been curious about her body. His body had known hers in the most intimate and violent contact. Only last night they had again wallowed in the abyss. His tactile knowledge of her could not be more complete. And yet he did not know how she was built; visually he could not have described her body.

'Should I change everything, darling?'

'Everything, *chérie*.'

'Go and lock the door.'

It was almost like a game, a most enjoyable game. This was the third bedroom they had entered together and in each he had found not only a different Kay but different reasons for loving her and a different way of loving her.

He sat down again on the edge of the bed and watched her undress. She was naked now, and her skin was very white except where the morning sun touched it with pale gold. She was digging in a drawerful of lingerie.

'I wonder what I should do about my things at the laundry,' she said. 'They'll bring it here and there'll be nobody at home. Maybe we'd better stop at the laundry. Do you mind?'

He liked the way she said '*We'd* better stop at', not just 'I', as though they were always to be together from now on.

'Jessie had much prettier lingerie than I have. Look at this.' She rubbed the flimsy silk with her fingers, held it out for him to feel. 'Jessie had a much better figure than mine, too. Do you want me to put on this slip? Or is it too pink for your taste? Oh, I've got a black slip and pants too. I always wanted black undies and I finally bought some. I've never had the courage to wear them, though. I've always been afraid it would make me feel like a tart.'

She was combing her hair. She knew exactly, without looking, where to reach for the comb. Her hand found the mirror automatically. She had a pin between her teeth as she said, 'Would you hook me up behind?'

She'd never asked him to do that before. What an amazing number of things they were doing for the first time this morning! For instance, it was the first time he had kissed the back of her neck, gently, without greediness, merely for the pleasure of breathing the fragrance of her hair, where it curled close to the nape. Then he went back to sit on the edge of the bed like a good boy.

'Do you like the dress?'

'It's very becoming.'

'I bought it in Fifty-seventh Street. It was very expensive, you know – at least for me.' She gave him a beseeching look. 'Maybe we could go out together one night. You could dress up and I could wear this dress . . .' then, without transition, while her lips were still smiling, two big tears rolled from under her eyelids. She turned her head away as she said, 'You've never asked me what I did for a living.'

It was a curious question from a woman in an evening gown, standing with bare feet in golden slippers.

'And I never dared talk about it myself,' she went on, 'because the subject was humiliating. I guess I was stupid, but I preferred to let you imagine things. In fact, I even did it on purpose at times.'

'Did what on purpose?'

'You know very well what! When I first met Jessie, I was working in the same building. That's how we met – we used to each lunch at the same drugstore downstairs. I'll show it to you some day; it's on the corner of Madison Avenue. I was hired as a translator, because I knew several languages.

'Only there's something you don't know. It's ridiculous and I'm ashamed of it. I told you a little about my life with my mother. When she began to be famous as a virtuoso and spent most of her time on the road, I practically stopped going to school. Oh, I spent a few months in this school or that, between seasons, but I didn't learn very much. Especially – now, don't you dare laugh! – I never learned to spell. Larski used to tell me – and I'm humiliated all over again every time I think of that cold voice of his – that I wrote like a scullery maid.

'So now you know. Unhook me at the back, will you, please?'

She offered him her back, pale, lean and appetizing between the dark shoulder straps. When his fingers stroked her skin, she begged: 'No, please, not right now. Do you mind? I'd like so much to continue talking.'

She stepped out of the evening gown. Clad only in panties and bra, she sought her cigarette case and her lighter, sat cross-legged on Jessie's bed, and pulled an ashtray within reach.

'They transferred me to the mailing department,' she went on. 'Two other girls and I worked all day long in a stuffy cell with no window, at the back of the offices, stuffing circulars into envelopes, sticking on addresses. The two girls were little animals. We had nothing in common. They hated me. We wore smocks because of the oceans of glue. I insisted on a clean smock every day . . . But I'm boring you. This is all ridiculous, isn't it?'

'Not at all.'

'You're just saying it. Well, you asked for it. Every morning, I'd find my clean smock already smeared with glue, even on the inside, where I'd get it on my dress. I had a real fight with one of them, a big Irish girl with a face like a Kalmuck. She weighed more than I did. She ruined a brand-new pair of stockings.'

'My poor Kay!' he said. His voice was at once pitying and gay.

'Maybe you think I was trying to be the wife of a first secretary. That's not true. I swear it. If Jessie were here, she could tell you.'

'But I believe you, darling.'

'I admit that I couldn't face it. I ran away from those two brats. I thought finding another job would be easy, but it wasn't. I was out of work for three weeks. That's when Jessie suggested that I move in with her. She was living in the Bronx then; I think I told you: a big barracks of an apartment block with iron fire escapes crawling up and down the brick walls. The building always smelled of cabbage cooking from top to bottom. For months we went to sleep and woke up with the taste of cabbage in our mouths . . . Still, I had no rent money and Jessie had the bed . . .

'I finally got a job in a Broadway cinema. Remember yesterday, when you were asking me about films . . .' There were again tears in her eyes. 'I was an usherette – not much of a job, you'll say. I know I'm not particularly strong, since I spent two years in a TB sanatorium. But the other girls had no more stamina than I. At night we were all ready to drop. Or sometimes it was just the vertigo produced by the maddening music, the magnified voices coming out of the walls, the endless walking up and down the aisles. Dozens of times I've seen the girls faint – but never on the floor. If they had the bad manners to pass out in public, they were out of a job. Bad public relations, you understand . . . Am I boring you?'

'No. Come here.'

She came closer to sit opposite him on the other twin bed. He caressed her, and was surprised to find her flesh so soft. Between the top of her pants and the line of her bra, there were contours that were new to him, shadows that stirred him strangely.

'I was very ill. Four months ago I had to go to hospital for seven weeks. Only Jessie came to see me. They wanted to send me away to another sanatorium, but I refused. Jessie begged me to stay home and rest for a while before trying to get work again. When I met you, I'd been job-hunting for about a week.' She smiled defiantly. 'I'll find one, too.' Then, without transition, 'Wouldn't you like a drink? There must be a bottle of whisky in the cupboard – unless Ronald drank it, which would surprise me very much.'

She went into the next room, returned with a bottle three-fourths empty. She put it down and disappeared into the kitchen. He heard her open the refrigerator and exclaim, 'Well, if that doesn't beat all.'

'What's wrong?'

'You'll laugh. Ronald remembered to turn off the refrigerator. It couldn't have been Enrico yesterday; he wouldn't have thought of it. It's just like Ronald. You heard what Jessie wrote. Always cool and collected. No scenes. He was the one who sorted her things and told her what she could take along. And you'll notice that he left nothing lying around, either. Everything put back in place – except Enrico's robe and pyjamas. Don't you think that's funny?'

No, he didn't think it was funny. He didn't think anything. He was happy. It was a new kind of happiness. If anyone had told him yesterday, or even this morning, that he would find pleasure in lolling about lazily, voluptuously, in this bedroom he had never seen before, he would not have believed it. He lay stretched on the bed that had been Kay's, squinting into a ray of sunshine, his hands clasped behind his head, gently drinking in the surroundings, detail by detail, like a painter labouring over the minutiae of a too specific canvas.

He was doing the same with Kay, unhurriedly, bit by bit, filling in her complete personality.

A little later, when he had energy enough to move, he would get up and take a look at the kitchen, even peek into the refrigerator, curious about what little clues he might find.

There were photographs on the bureau, Jessie's no doubt, among them a buxom, dignified old lady who was probably her mother. He would ask Kay about it. She could talk her head off now about the past and he would not be bored.

'Drink.'

She tipped up the glass with him, then withdrew it to drink from it herself.

'You see, François, it's not so glamorous after all. You were so wrong . . .'

Wrong about what? It was such a vague expression, and yet he understood it.

'Move over a little, will you?'

She slid down beside him. She was almost naked and he was fully clothed, but it seemed to make no difference. As he took her into his arms, their contact could not have been more intimate had they both been nude. Her lips were close to his ear as she whispered, 'You know, darling, nothing has ever happened to me here before, I swear it.'

He was without physical desire, without passion. He would have to go back a long way, even to his boyhood perhaps, to recapture a sensation that was of such unalloyed sweetness as the one that overwhelmed him now. He caressed her. It was not her flesh that he was caressing; it was all of her, a Kay whose whole being was becoming part of his, just as his was being absorbed in hers. They lay for a long time like this, not speaking, body and soul intermingled, their eyes half closed yet so near each other's that the glow of ineffable ecstasy was almost tangible.

For the first time he was not worried about possible consequences. He saw her pupils widen, her lips part slightly. He felt her breath on his cheek. He heard her voice, as from afar, saying, 'Thank you, darling.'

There was no fear this time that rancour or bitter afterthoughts might follow passion spent. When their bodies disentwined, they could look one another squarely in the eye without shame or regret. A wonderful weariness made their every gesture like something from a slow-motion film. The shaft of sunlight that lay across the bed was like a scarf of gold created especially for them . . .

'Where are you going, François?'

'To look in the refrigerator.'

'Are you hungry?'

'No.'

For half an hour or more he had been planning to inspect the kitchen. It was neat and clean, freshly painted. He opened the refrigerator. Inside were a slice of cold meat, some grapefruit, several overripe tomatoes, and a cube of butter wrapped in wax paper.

He picked up the meat with his fingers, dangled it above his mouth, and bit into it, grinning like a kid eating an apple stolen from a neighbour's orchard.

He was still grinning and still chewing when he followed Kay into the bathroom.

'You see? You *were* hungry,' Kay said.

Still grinning, he shook his head stubbornly. 'No.'

Then he laughed heartily at her puzzled expression.

7

Two days later he went to the studio for his broadcast. He was playing a Frenchman again, a faintly ridiculous part. Hourvitch did not even shake hands with him. The Hungarian was very much the busy director, every inch the big boss, rushing about the studio with his shirt sleeves rolled up, his red hair standing on end, his secretary rushing after him, notebook in hand.

'What do you expect me to do, old man?' he shouted at Combe. 'Get yourself a telephone, at least, and leave your number with my casting people so they can get in touch with you when a better part comes along. It's inconceivable that there are still people in New York without a phone.'

Combe was unruffled. Nothing could disturb his serenity. He had left Kay for the first time in . . . how many days had it been, incidentally? Seven? Eight? Numbers meant nothing. They were ridiculous. Whatever they were, they would add up to eternity.

He had wanted to bring her with him to the studio. She could sit in the waiting-room until after the broadcast. She had refused.

'No, *mon chéri*. It's all right for you to leave me *now*.'

They had both laughed over the *now*, which meant so much to them.

'I'll be home at six,' he had promised.

'It doesn't matter, François. Come home whenever you like.'

Why, then, since she had asked for no promise, had he persisted in repeating, 'Six o'clock at the latest'?

And here he was already breaking his promise. At least, he felt very guilty when, instead of waiting for his bus, he found himself walking into the gathering dusk in the direction of the Ritz Bar.

He knew what he was looking for at the Ritz and he was not very proud of it. Every evening around six Laugier held court at the Ritz Bar, surrounded by members of New York's French colony, Frenchmen passing through, or figures from the international artistic set on their way to or from Paris, London, Rome, Berlin, or Hollywood. The bar had something of the same atmosphere as Fouquet's. When he had first come to the United States, when he was not sure that he was going to stay or even that he would be able to make his living there, reporters had run him down at the Ritz Bar and had taken his picture.

He knew what he would find there, but he was not sure why he had come. Was it some inner need of betraying Kay, of giving full vent to the evil things that still fermented within him, of getting even with Kay? Getting even for what? During the days and the nights they had spent together, he had worked desperately to wall themselves off from the world, to create the absolute privacy he thought necessary to create complete intimacy between them, to annihilate the most elementary factors of shyness and modesty that exist between persons of the same sex, even in the promiscuities of the barracks. He had gone with her to do the shopping in the morning, he had helped her set the table, he had drawn the water for her bath, he had – He had done everything, fiercely determined to establish this absolute intimacy. Why, then, at the hour of six, when she was expecting him, when he had insisted that she should expect him, was he breezing into the Ritz Bar, instead of jumping on a downtown bus or getting a taxi?

'Hello, little father. Greetings. Draw up a chair.'

It was certainly not this easy familiarity that he was seeking. He had always detested this sort of thing. Was it to reassure himself that the leash was not too tight, that he still retained some freedom of movement, that, after all, he remained François Combe?

Half a dozen people were sitting at the two round tables that Laugier had pulled together. His offhand friendliness always made it difficult to distinguish his old cronies from people he had just met for the first time. It was just as difficult to keep track of who was buying the next round and whose hat was whose among those piled on top of the coat-rack.

'May I present . . .'

It was an American girl, quite pretty, a cover girl possibly, who had just imprinted her lipstick on a fresh cigarette.

Laugier was making the rounds, repeating at intervals, 'One of our most personable, charming, and celebrated actors of the Paris stage, whose name I'm sure you know, François Combe.'

One of those introduced was a rat-faced Frenchman – Combe didn't know why he disliked him instinctively, but he was sure that the man must be a crooked financier or a dubious industrialist – who couldn't keep his eyes off the actor.

'I had the pleasure of meeting your wife a few weeks ago, during a gala at the Lido. Wait. I just happen to have in my pocket . . .'

He produced a French newspaper that had just reached New York. Combe had not looked at a French newspaper for months. On page one there was a picture of his wife: 'Marie Clairois, charming and talented star of . . .'

Combe was not upset, no matter what Laugier thought. Laugier was giving him a series of eye and eyebrow signals, all calling for calm. He *was* calm. To prove it, after the courtiers had drunk their quota of cocktails and departed, and Combe was left alone with his friend, it was of Kay that he spoke:

'I want you to do me a favour. I want you to find a job for a girl I know.'

'How old is she, this girl?'

'I don't know exactly. Say, thirty, maybe thirty-three.'

'In New York, old man, that's no longer considered a girl.'

'Meaning what?'

'That the odds are against her. Forgive me for putting it so crudely, because I suspect a special interest. Good-looking?'

'That depends on your point of view.'

'The old story. She started out as a chorus girl fourteen or fifteen years ago, no? She grabbed the gold ring and she dropped it. Yes?'

Combe retreated into silence. Laugier may have been sorry for him at that instant, but Laugier's view of the world was exclusively a Laugier's-eye view.

'What can she do, your lovely virgin?'

'Nothing.'

'Now don't get steamed up, dear boy. I'm looking at this for your own good, as well as hers. In New York, there's no time to play hide-and-seek. Seriously, I'm asking you: what's her line?'

'And seriously, I'm telling you: nothing.'

'Can't she develop into a secretary? A phone operator? A model? A . . . I don't know what. Anything?'

Combe was going about this in the wrong way. It was his fault. He was already paying the price of his little betrayal.

'Listen to me, little father . . . Waiter, the same.'

'Not for me.'

'Shut up! I've got to talk to you, man to man, eye to eye, friend to friend. Understand? When you walked in here a little while ago with that undertaker's face of yours, I tuned you in right away. And the last time we met, when we left Hourvitch, don't you think I got your wavelength right off? So? Your girl has a New York age of thirty, thirty-three. That means thirty-five in good French . . . Do you want me to give you some good advice, which you will turn your back on so fast that you'll bust a gut? Well, here's the advice, right on the line: Get rid of her, little old brother!'

Combe was silent.

'And since I'm talking into the wind,' Laugier went on, 'may I ask you just where you two stand?'

Combe was stupidly furious, furious with himself, furious at feeling like a little boy as he stood in front of Laugier, who obviously felt seven feet tall.

'Nowhere,' he said.

'Then why are you getting yourself into such a stew? There's no brother, is there? No husband, no lover to blackmail you? There's no charge of kidnapping, is there?'

Why didn't he have the courage to get up and get out? Did those few drinks make a coward of him? If their love were to be at the mercy of four or five cocktails . . .

'Don't you want to talk seriously?' Combe asked.

'But I am talking seriously, my little old man. Or rather, I've been joking, but when I joke, that's when I'm the most serious. This little mouse of yours, this thirty-three-year-old mouse with no job, no profession, no talent, and no bank account – let's face it, she's through. I don't have to take you over to the Waldorf to prove my point. This is the men's bar, but just step through the door, cross the corridor, and you'll see fifty girls, one prettier than the other, all of them between eighteen and twenty, some of them even virgins, and every last one of them in the same shape as your old virago of thirty-three. In a little while, forty-eight of the fifty will walk out of here wearing a thousand dollars' worth of jewellery and smart clothes, they'll go to some Automat and dine on a fifteen-cent sandwich with maybe a nickel's worth of what they call here 'French fries' doused with free ketchup. Then they'll go home to bed, God knows where. Look, did you come to this country to work, or what?'

'I don't know.'

'Well, if you don't know, get the hell back to France and sign the first contract they offer you at the Renaissance or the Port-Saint-Martin. I know that you're going to do exactly what you want, that you'll never forgive me for trying to give you advice, that you already hate my guts. But you're not the first friend I've seen land here and take a nose dive.

'Now listen. If you make up your mind to hang on to the wheel and never mind the bumps, I'm with you. But if you insist on doing an amateur-night Romeo and Juliet, then I must bid you good-bye, old boy. Waiter!'

'No, wait. This is my –'

'Nonsense. I've been yelling at you enough to give me the right to buy you a few drinks. What story does she tell, your little mouse? She's a divorcee, of course. At that age, they've all been divorced at least once.'

Why, exactly, had Kay been divorced?

'She's been around, hasn't she? A rolling stone who's decided it's time to gather a little moss.'

'You're wrong, really.'

He didn't have the strength to go on betraying Kay.

'Can you swim?'

'A little.'

'Good. A little. Enough to reach shore if the sea is calm and the water not too cold. But if you had to save yourself *and* a panic-stricken madwoman who grabbed you, hung on for dear life, and fought furiously because she was afraid you would let her go down? Well, answer me?'

Combe said nothing. Laugier signalled the waiter for another round.

'Well, old boy, she's going to fight and flounder furiously, believe me! And you'll sink together like two stones. The day before yesterday when you left me, I didn't want to mention this, because you had a chip on your shoulder and you wanted to kick somebody's teeth in – anybody's. Today you seem more rational.'

Combe bit his lip.

'When I saw you march up to that jukebox like you were approaching an altar, stick your coin in the slot, and wait for the record to drop, with a look in your eyes like a *midinette* about to swoon at the sight of a matinée idol . . . No, old man, no! Not you! Not you or me; we live with that business and we know what makes it tick. So let me repeat for the last time, and I'm talking like an old chum who'd give the world to help you – François, you're sunk!'

Laugier counted his change, emptied his glass, calculated the tip, and stood up. 'Which way are you going?'

'I'm going home.'

'Home! Where there's not even a telephone. And you expect the producers to run after you?'

They went out in single file and stood on the Madison Avenue sidewalk, where the doorman held a taxi for them.

'You see, little brother, at home in Paris the lucky number comes up just once. Here you might get a chance to play it twice, three times. But don't stretch your luck too far. I can show you cuties who started out in a chorus line or behind a typewriter at sixteen, had a Rolls-Royce and a chauffeur at eighteen, and were back in the chorus at twenty-two – starting all over again at zero. I've known some who have hit the jackpot two, three times, and who went back to the footlights after losing a Park Avenue penthouse and a yacht in Florida – and who managed to get themselves still another husband.

'This gal of yours – has she managed to keep her jewellery, at least?'

Combe didn't deign to reply. What could he have said?

'If you listen to me, you'll try to get her a job as usherette in a cinema. And even that! Maybe with proper sponsors . . . You could kill me, couldn't you? Too bad. But much better for you. Everybody hates the surgeon who's just carved him up. You're too good for all this silly business, old ham bone, and when you realize it, you'll be cured. Bye-bye.'

Combe had had too much to drink. He had not realized it before because of the rapid rhythm of round after round, of the noise in the bar, and the suspense of his long wait for the chance to talk to Laugier alone.

He remembered his wife's photo on the front page of the Paris newspaper, the light making a blur of her hair, her head a little too large for her shoulders. The film people had always said that these were features that allowed her to play young roles – that and the fact that she had never had any hips . . .

Was Laugier blessed with second sight, or did he know about Kay? *Usherette in a cinema. And even that . . . !* Even that indeed! Poor Kay, with her strength still sapped by her long fight back to health!

Here you might get a chance to play it twice, three times . . .

The thought struck him as he walked through the patches of light that slanted down from the Madison Avenue shop windows. Kay had been gambling. He was her last chance. He was the lucky number that had come up at the very last minute. Had he come in fifteen minutes later, or perhaps sat down on another stool at the owl café, perhaps one of the drunken sailors would have . . .

Suddenly she was very dear to him. As a reaction against his cowardice, he hurried his homeward steps. He wanted to reassure her, to tell her that not all the Laugiers in the world, with their easy sophistication and their haughty cynicism, could prevail against the deep affection he shared with her.

He must be drunker than he thought, he reflected as he bumped a passer-by and raised his hat ridiculously high in apology. But he was sincere, anyhow. The rest of them, all the Laugiers – like the rat-faced Frenchman who after the second drink had made a triumphant exit with the American girl – the whole gang from the Ritz Bar, like the gang at Fouquet's – they were a bunch of assholes . . . !

He liked the phrase, which he had dug up from the depths of his memory. He liked it so well he repeated it aloud as he walked along: 'They're a bunch of assholes.' The sound made him even more furious. 'Assholes, that's all they are. I'll show them!'

What would he show them? He didn't know, but it mattered so little. He'd show them. He didn't need Laugier or Hourvitch – Hourvitch, who hadn't shaken hands and had barely seemed to recognize him – he didn't need any of them any more. Nobody . . . !

Assholes!

His wife, too. She had no need to play her number twice, three times. Her number had come up the first time, but it wasn't enough for her. She had to use her luck, to use him, to make a career for a gigolo! It was the truth. When he had promoted her to play opposite him, she was nothing. She didn't exist. She played walk-ons, or maybe a tiny part, like the maid who clumsily opens the sliding doors to the dining-room and stammers in a frightened voice, 'Dinner is served, *Madame la Comtesse*.'

And he had made her over into Marie Clairois. Even the name was his creation; he had made it up. Her real name was Thérèse Bourcicault, and her father sold shoes in the market place of a little town in the Jura Mountains. He remembered the night he had rechristened her. They were eating lobster *à l'américaine* in a little restaurant with red-checkered tablecloths in the Avenue de Clichy . . . La Crémaillère, that was it.

'Marie is such a French name,' he had said. 'Not only French, but universal. In fact, it's become such a common name that nobody but a nursemaid would use the name Marie these days. So now it has become original again. Marie.'

She had asked him to repeat the name.

'Marie . . . And now, Clairois . . .' He remembered that creating a rationale for Clairois had been more complicated. To make Clairois out of *clarion* was a little far-fetched . . .

Tonnerre de Dieu! What the devil was he thinking of? He didn't give a damn about La Clairois and her gigolo who was going to make a name for himself only because he had cuckolded the great Combe!

And the other one, the self-satisfied, condescending idiot who spoke of the jewellery Kay didn't have and of a nice little job as usherette . . .

If she had good sponsors!

It was only a few weeks ago that Laugier had asked him, with the monumental conceit of a man half convinced that he is God the Father, 'How long can you hold out, dear boy?'

'That depends on what you mean.'

'Enough to have your suits pressed every day, to pay your laundry, rent, and meals, with enough pocket money for taxis and a few cocktails.'

'Five months, maybe six. When my son was born, I took out an endowment policy that would pay for his college education when he reached eighteen. I suppose I could borrow on it, or maybe turn it in . . .'

Laugier wasn't interested in Combe's son.

'Five or six months, good! Get yourself a place to live, any place, even a dump, as long as it's got a telephone . . .'

And today Hourvitch had told him the same thing! But he wasn't going to be bothered by this coincidence. Not today. He should have taken the bus. The traffic wasn't so bad at this hour. And a few minutes more or less wouldn't make any difference if Kay were going to worry . . .

Kay!

What a different sound the name had then, and two hours ago, three hours, that morning, at noon when they were sitting face to face over lunch, smiling at the little tailor across the street to whom Kay had had delivered, anonymously, a beautifully roasted capon. They had been so happy! The name Kay made a happy sound. Even now it was soothing . . .

He decided to take a taxi. The sky had grown so black, so menacing as it shrouded the tops of the skyscrapers, even though it reflected the glow of the city. He leaned back gloomily against the cushions as he gave his address to the driver. He resented Laugier. He resented Rat-face. He resented everybody. He was not even sure but that he might resent Kay. He was still scowling as the cab drew up to his kerb, and he got out.

He had not had time to recapture a gayer mood and a lover's expression before he saw Kay. She was waiting for him on the sidewalk, out of breath, her face haggard.

'At last, François! Come quickly! Michèle . . .' Then without transition she began frantically to speak German.

He had been up and down the stairs three times, and it was

nearly midnight. Each time the street lights had seemed dimmer, the stairway dingier, his room more oppressive. His overcoat was soaked, his face cold and dripping with rain. The storm had broken suddenly.

The question of the telephone was still pursuing him. This time it was Kay who had said, testily, in fact, but he could hardly blame her, with the state she was in, 'Why don't you have a phone?'

It was because there was no phone in the apartment that Enrico had come himself to bring the telegram. Another coincidence: he had come at almost the very minute that Combe was entering the Ritz Bar and feeling a little guilty. If he had come right home, as he had promised . . .

This time he was not jealous of Enrico, even though Kay may have cried on his shoulder and he had probably tried to comfort her.

Another coincidence: the day before while they were shopping for dinner Kay had said, 'Maybe I ought to give my new address to the post office. It's not that I get much mail, you know, but . . .' She tried not to make him jealous. 'I ought to give Enrico the address, too, just in case . . .'

'Why don't you telephone him?' Combe had asked.

He could not then foresee the importance of his remark. They stepped into the drugstore, as they had done previously. He watched her through the glass panel. He could see her lips move but could not hear what she was saying.

He had not been jealous.

Just that day Enrico had gone to Jessie's place for his things. He found some mail for Jessie and the telegram for Kay. Since the telegram came from Mexico and was already a day old, he brought it to her. She was preparing dinner, and wore a pale-blue négligé that made her look like a bride.

MICHELE SERIOUSLY ILL MEXICO CITY STOP BANK OF COMMERCE AND INDUSTRY AUTHORIZED ADVANCE YOU TRAVEL EXPENSES IF NECESSARY

LARSKI

He was not telling her to come. He had left her free to make her own decision. Suspecting that she might be short of money, however, he had coldly and methodically made the proper arrangements.

'I didn't even know that he had sent for Michèle. I hadn't heard for four months.'

'Heard from whom?'

'From my daughter. She doesn't write often. I suspect that she's been forbidden to write to me and has to do it secretly, although she has never said so. Her last letter came from Hungary and said nothing about any trip. I wonder what's wrong with her? I'm sure it's not her lungs. We've had her examined regularly by the best specialists ever since she was a baby. Do you think she might have had an accident, François?'

Why had he drunk all those cocktails? When he had tried to console her after she had told him the news, he was ashamed of his breath. He was sure that she knew he had been drinking. He was sad. Even before he reached home, he had felt a great weight on his shoulders, heaviness he could not shake off.

'Eat, my poor François. You can telephone later.'

No, he wasn't hungry. He had gone downstairs to telephone from the Italian place, even though she had told him Enrico had already tried. If he had come home on time, Enrico would not have had to stick his nose into other people's business.

Enrico had been right.

'All flights to Mexico City are booked solid for ten days,' Combe had said when he came back upstairs. 'There's a train at seven-thirty in the morning.'

'I'll take it.'

'Then I'll try to get you Pullman seats.'

He went back downstairs to telephone. It was raining. The world was grey. The world was oppressive. His movements seemed unreal. He first telephoned the wrong station, of course. American railways mystified him.

The rain was coming down straight and hard, spattering noisily on the sidewalk. He dripped water on the stairs. When he bent his head to thrust his key into his door, water streamed from his hat-brim. Why did such ridiculous details affect him?

'There are no berths left on the morning train, but they told me if you come to the station half an hour before train time, there might be a cancellation.'

'I'm putting you to so much trouble, François.'

He studied her face carefully. Could it be that her forlorn expression was not due entirely to worry over her daughter? Wasn't Kay also thinking of them, and that they would be separated in a few hours?

There was calamity in that telegram, an evil destiny in that piece of yellow paper, that seemed the logical sequel to Laugier's lectures and the thoughts that had been running through Combe's head ever since. A man was tempted to believe that there was no escape, that Destiny would take care of putting things in order. The most disturbing thought was that he was almost resigned to whatever might happen. It was very depressing, this sudden weakness, this absolute lack of any reaction on his part.

She was packing. She said: 'I don't know what to do about money. The banks were already closed when Enrico came. I could take a later train, maybe.'

'There's none before evening.'

'Enrico wanted to – Now, don't be angry. Nothing really matters right now, you know. He told me that if I needed money, any amount, I could call him at home, even at night. I didn't know if you –'

'Could you get along with four hundred dollars?'

'Of course, François. Only . . .' They never talked about money.

'I can spare it. Truly.'

'Maybe I could give you a note or something, I don't know, that you could take to the bank tomorrow and they would give you the money instead of me.'

'We can wait until you get back.' He spoke as if he really believed that she was coming back, but he didn't look at her. He was afraid that she might not believe what he was saying.

'You'll have to get some sleep, Kay.'

'I couldn't.'

'Go to bed.'

'Do you think it's worth while? It's already two o'clock, and I'll have to leave here by six, in case we don't get a taxi right away. So that means I'll have to get up at five,' she went on. 'You want me to have a cup of coffee, don't you?'

She lay on the bed, fully dressed. He walked around for a moment, then lay down beside her. They didn't speak. They didn't close their eyes. They stared at the ceiling.

He had never in his life felt so depressed, so darkly desperate. It was a despair without words, without precise subject. It was a feeling of desolation against which there was no defence. He whispered in her ear, 'Will you come back?'

For an answer she sought his hand and squeezed it for a long moment.

'I wish I could die in her place.'

'Stop it. Nobody's going to die.' He wondered if she was crying. He touched her eyelids. They were dry.

'You'll be all alone, François. That's what hurts me the most. Tomorrow, when you come home from the station –'

She sat up suddenly, her eyes wide as she looked at François in alarm. 'You are taking me to the station, aren't you? You must! Forgive me for insisting, but I don't think I could go through with it alone. I know I must go, but you must send me, even if –'

She fell back again and hid her face in the pillow. They withdrew once more into silence, each wrapped in his own thoughts, rehearsing for the new loneliness they were both to face . . .

She slept a little. He dozed off in a series of cat naps. He arose first to make the coffee.

At five in the morning the sky was even darker than it was at midnight, and the street lights seemed unable to dispel the gloom. The rain continued to spatter down with a determination that promised to last all day.

'Time to get up, Kay.'

'All right.'

He didn't kiss her. They had not exchanged one kiss all night, perhaps because of Michèle, perhaps because each was afraid of breaking down.

'Dress warmly.'

'I've nothing warmer than my fur.'

'Wear a wool dress, anyhow.'

They managed to keep the conversation confined to the commonplace.

'Trains are always overheated, you know.'

She drank her coffee but couldn't eat anything. He helped her close her suitcase, which was too full. She looked around the room as she said, 'Do you mind if I leave the rest of my things here?'

'It's time to go. Come on.'

There were only two lighted windows in the whole street. More people catching an early train? Sickness?

'You stand in the doorway. I'll see if I can find a cab.'

'We'll lose time.'

'If I don't find one right away, we'll take the subway. You'll stay here, won't you?'

What a stupid question! Where would she go? He turned up the collar of his overcoat, ducked his head against the rain, and, hugging the buildings, ran for the corner. He had scarcely reached it when he heard her voice behind him: 'François! François!'

Kay stood in the middle of the sidewalk, gesticulating. A taxi had stopped two doors away, bringing a couple home from a night out. The night shift going off, so to speak; the day shift going on. Kay held the cab door open and spoke to the driver while Combe went after her suitcase.

'Pennsylvania Station.'

The seat was damp and sticky. Everything was wet around them. The air was raw. She snuggled against him. Neither of them spoke as they rode through the deserted streets.

'Don't get out, François,' she said when they reached the station. 'Go on home.'

She bore down on the word *home* to give him courage.

'You have an hour to wait.'

'It doesn't matter. I'll get something warm to drink. I'll try to eat a little.'

She tried to smile, but she made no effort to get out.

'I mean it, François. Don't come any farther.'

It wasn't cowardice on his part. He actually did not have the strength to follow her into the labyrinth of the station, to sit watching the huge hand of the monumental clock jump away the minutes, to live out the final seconds of their separation, to be caught up in the crowd surging forward when the gates were opened, to see her climb aboard the train that would carry her off.

She bent over him. There were raindrops on her fur. Her lips were burning hot. They clung to each other for a long moment, oblivious of the driver. He saw the glow in her eyes, heard her stammering as though in a dream: 'Now I don't feel any more that I'm going away. It's more like coming home, darling.'

She broke away from him, opened the door, signalled to a porter to take her suitcase. She took three quick steps, stopped and turned. She was pale, but she was smiling.

She held her bag in one hand. She raised the other, but not very high, no higher than the elbow. She waved good-bye with her fingers. Then she was swallowed up by the glass door.

He watched her through the glass, trotting off behind the porter, a picture he would remember always . . .

'Where to now, bud?' The taxi driver had turned around to break into his mood.

He gave his address. Automatically he filled his pipe. His mouth was fuzzy from his sleepless night.

She had said, '. . . like coming home . . .'

He sensed a vague promise.

But he still hadn't quite understood.

8

> Kay dear,
>
> I know Enrico has told you what happened to me, so you know that Ronald has really been very nice about it all, every inch the gentleman. He has preserved his usual calm which you know so well, and has not even gone into one of his cold furies which are his speciality. I don't know what would have happened if he had, in view of the state I was in . . .

Combe had not taken the nose dive he expected. Instead it had been a slow sinking, day by day, hour by hour, into the quicksands of solitude. During the first days he had even acted as a fairly reasonable human being. He had been borne up by the hope generated during the interminable hours of that very short final night.

'Will you telephone me?' It was a plea.

'Here?'

He had sworn that he would have a phone installed before she got to Mexico, and he had gone to work immediately, for fear that she might call before he had a number. After all, in France it sometimes took months.

'Will you telephone?'

'Of course, darling. If I can.'

'You can if you really want to.'

'I'll phone you.'

The formalities had been simple, so simple that he was almost annoyed. He had expected a complex, world-shaking operation. And his phone was installed the day after he had made an application. After that, he was afraid to leave the house, even though Kay had probably not yet reached Mexico City.

'I'll call information in New York,' she had said. 'They'll give me your number.'

He himself called information several times a day to make sure they were aware that he was now a subscriber and that they could furnish his number on request.

He didn't want to go out anyhow. Life was grey and grimy. The city was grey and grimy. The rain had turned into melted snow. The streets were so dark he could hardly see the little tailor in his cell of the honeycomb across the street.

Kay seemed to have dissolved in the rain and snow. All he could remember of her now was the last glimpse he had of her through the glass panel of the door at the railway station – a blurred, receding image he clung to desperately . . .

Letters came for her, forwarded from Jessie's address.

'Open them all,' she had said. 'I have no secrets from you, as you well know.'

Still, he had hesitated. It was not until there were half a dozen of them, and he noted one envelope bearing the house flag of the Grace Line that he opened one. It was a letter from Jessie, air-mailed from somewhere in the Caribbean.

> . . . in view of the state I was in . . .

He knew them all by heart now.

> . . . if I hadn't wanted to avoid a scene, at all costs . . .

It was all so far away. He had the impression of watching a scene in a topsy-turvy world through the wrong end of a telescope.

> I know very well that if Ric were driven into a corner, he would have left his wife without hesitation . . .

He repeated it to himself: driven into a corner!

> . . . but I chose to go away. It's going to be painful. And it will probably be long. This is a difficult moment to live through. How happy we were together, my poor Kay, in our little apartment!
>
> I wonder if those days will ever come back. I don't dare hope so. Ronald chills me and puzzles me, and yet there's nothing I can reproach him for. Instead of those terrible rages he used to go into

sometimes, he's so calm that he scares me. He doesn't leave me for a minute. I sometimes feel that he's trying to read my mind.

And he's so sweet, so considerate, more than he ever was before, even on our honeymoon. Do you remember the story of the pineapple that made you laugh so hard? Well, that could never happen again now.

Everybody on board thinks we're newly-weds, and sometimes it's funny. Yesterday we changed from woollens to linens because we're getting into the tropics. It's getting very warm. It seemed strange to see everybody in white all of a sudden, even the officers. There's one young officer (he has only one stripe) who can't keep his sheep's eyes off of me. Don't mention this to Ric, please; he might go into a decline.

I don't know how things are with you back there, my poor Kay, but I imagine they must be pretty awful. I can put myself in your place. I can picture your confusion and only hope you are making out somehow . . .

It was a strange sensation. There were times when he could see the world without shadows, without clouds, lucidly, objectively, in such raw, harsh colours that after a while he felt physical pain.

My dear Kay:

This letter came in an envelope bearing a French stamp and a Toulon postmark. Hadn't Kay told him to open them all?

I haven't heard from you for nearly five months now, but I'm not too surprised . . .

He read slowly, to get the full meaning of every word.

I found a rather disagreeable surprise waiting for me when we got back to France. My submarine had been transferred from the Atlantic to the Mediterranean Fleet. In other words, my home port was to be Toulon instead of our good-old Brest. It wasn't so bad for me, but for my wife, who had just rented a new villa and had barely finished getting settled, it was such a disappointment that she fell ill . . .

This was obviously the man who had slept with Kay. Combe knew it; he knew where and under what circumstances. He knew all the details. Hadn't he practically begged for them? He was hurt and he was pleased at the same time.

We're settled now in La Seyne, a not too pleasant suburb. But there's a bus that takes me right to the port and there's a park across the street where the children can play.

That's right, he had children too.

Chubby is fine and getting fatter than ever. He sends his regards.

Chubby!

Fernand is no longer with us. He has been assigned to the Naval Ministry in Paris, which is just the place for him. He's always had an air of high society about him, and he'll fit in very well with the parties in Rue Royale. As for your friend Riri, all I can say is that we have not spoken to each other, except in the line of duty, since we left the shores of wonderful America. I don't know whether he's jealous of me or I of him. He probably doesn't know either. It's up to you, my little Kay, to settle the argument . . .

He sank his fingernails into the palms of his hands, yet he was quite calm. He was so calm during those first days that he sometimes mistook the void he was living in as the irrevocable void. At such times he would tell himself, *It's all over*.

He was free again, free to drop in at the Ritz Bar any evening he liked at six, drink as many cocktails as he wanted with Laugier, talk all night if he felt like it. And if Laugier asked about his 'mouse', he was also free to say, 'What mouse?'

No doubt about it, he sometimes felt a certain relief. Laugier was right. This affair was bound to turn out badly. In any event, it could not turn out well. There were times when he wanted to see Laugier again. On several occasions he got as far as the entrance to the Ritz but his feelings of guilt never let him go into the bar.

Other mail came for Kay, mostly bills. There was a bill from the cleaner and one from a milliner who had done something to her hat, probably the hat she wore on the night they first met. He could see it now, perched over one eye, and the bill immediately assumed a sentimental value.

One dollar twenty-nine cents . . .

Not for the hat, but for doing something to the trimming – adding or subtracting a ribbon or some other silly feminine trifle.

One dollar twenty-nine cents . . .

He remembered the figure. He remembered too that the milliner's was in 260th Street. It was a long way to go, far up in the Bronx, and he pictured Kay walking there, the way they had trudged up and down Fifth Avenue together at night. They had certainly done a lot of walking . . .

Nobody had called him since his phone was installed, not surprising in as much as nobody but Kay knew that he had one. Kay had promised, 'I'll call you as soon as I can.'

But Kay had not called. He was almost afraid to go out, just in case the phone should ring while he was gone. For hours he would sit as though hypnotized, watching the bearded tailor across the street. He knew the routine of his life by heart – at what time he ate, at what time he assumed his sacerdotal pose, and what time he got down from his workbench. Solitude studying solitude.

He was almost ashamed of the capon that Kay had insisted on sending the old man. He could put himself in the other's place . . .

> My dear little Kay . . .

Everybody called her Kay. It made him furious. Why had she told him to open all her letters?

This one was in English, rather stiff and formal.

> I received your letter of August 14 and was glad to learn that you were in the country. I hope that the Connecticut air has done you some good. I myself was unable to get away from New York for as long as I wanted because my business kept me tied down. However . . .

However what? This one too had slept with her. They had all slept with her. Would he never get rid of that nightmare?

> . . . my wife would be delighted if you . . .

The bastard! No, he wasn't a bastard. It was Combe who was wrong. But he didn't have to be wrong any longer, since it was all over. All he had to do was write, 'Finished', period. Period, new paragraph. That was all he needed to end his suffering. Otherwise he would be suffering on her account until the end of his days.

That much was definite. He would suffer on her account to the end of his days.

And he was resigned to it.

Stupidly.

What would an imbecile like Laugier say if he confessed such a conclusion?

It was very simple, however, so simple that . . . Well, he could find no words for it. That's the way it was. Kay wasn't there and he needed Kay. He had seen himself as a tragic figure once because his wife, at the age of forty, wanted to experience a new love and feel young again. How childish he had been! Had it been of the slightest importance?

He knew now that it had not. The only thing that mattered now, the only thing in the world that was important, was Kay – Kay and her past, Kay and . . .

Kay and a phone call. That was all, just a phone call. He waited all day and all night. He set the alarm for one in the morning, to make sure he would not sleep through the first few rings and that the operator might stop ringing. Then he set the alarm for two, then three.

When the telephone persisted in its maddening silence, he would say to himself, *Good. Fine. It's all over. It couldn't end in any other way.* For he had the taste of catastrophe on his lips.

No, it couldn't end in any other way. He would be himself again. François Combe. They would welcome him at the Ritz like a man recovering from a serious operation.

'Well, is it over?'

'All over.'

'It didn't hurt too much? Are you still sore?'

And there was no one there at night to hear him begging his pillow: 'Kay, my little Kay, please telephone me. Please!'

The streets were empty. New York was empty. Even their little bar was empty. One day he went there for a drink and to bribe the jukebox to play their song, but he could not listen to it because a drunken Scandinavian sailor insisted on clinging to him while pouring out unintelligible secrets.

Wasn't it better this way? She was gone for good. She had known that she was going for good. They had both known it would be forever.

I don't feel any more that I'm going away . . . It's more like coming home, darling . . .

What had she meant by that? Why was it like coming home? Home to whom?

Dear Madam: You have probably overlooked our bill for . . .

Three dollars and some cents. For a blouse that he remembered having taken from Jessie's cupboard and handed to Kay, who was packing.

Kay was Kay – a menace to his peace of mind and to his future. Kay was Kay, whom he could no longer do without. He would reject her ten times a day, only to ask forgiveness ten times – to reject her again a few minutes later. And he avoided all contact with men, as though they were dangerous. He had not returned to the studio. He had seen neither Hourvitch nor Laugier. He disliked them heartily.

Finally on the seventh day, or rather the seventh night, while he was fast asleep, the telephone bell shattered the silence of his apartment. The alarm clock stood beside the instrument. It was two in the morning.

'Hello.' He could hear the long-distance operators exchanging service messages. One of them repeated stupidly, 'Hello, Mr Combe . . . ? Mr Combe . . . ? I have a long-distance call for Mr Combe, C – O – M – B – E.'

'Hello . . . this is Combe.' In the background he thought that he could hear Kay's voice saying hello, but she had not yet been put through.

'Mr François Combe?'

'Yes, speaking.'

'Just a moment. Go ahead, Mexico.'

She was there, at the other end of the night. She asked softly: 'Is that you?'

And he found nothing better to say than: 'Is that you?'

He had told her once – and she had laughed – that she had two voices: one was the commonplace, undistinguished voice of any woman; the other was deeper, a little husky, which he had loved the first time he had heard it.

He had never before heard her voice over the telephone and was delighted to find that it was the deeper one, a little lower-pitched than he remembered, warmer, with just a hint of a tenderly seductive drawl. He wanted to shout, *You know, Kay, I've given up. I'm not fighting it any longer.* He was eager to tell her the news, because he had just found it out a few seconds earlier.

'I couldn't call you any sooner,' she was saying. 'I'll tell you all about it later. But everything seems to be all right here. Michèle is getting the best of care. Only it has been very hard to telephone. It still is. But from now on I'm going to try every night.'

'Can I call you? At what hotel are you staying?'

There was a pause.

'François, I've had to move into the embassy, but don't imagine things, please. Nothing has changed, I swear. When I got here, Michèle had just been operated on. It was an emergency. It was critical. Acute appendicitis. And then peritonitis developed. Can you hear me?'

'Certainly. Who were you talking to?'

'The maid. A nice old Mexican woman, God bless her, who has a room on my floor. She heard me talking and she wondered if I needed something.'

He heard Spanish spoken in the background.

'Darling, are you still there? To go on with Michèle. She's had the best surgeons in the country. The operation was successful. But there is always the danger of complications for a few days. And that's that, my little sweetheart.'

My little sweetheart! She had never called him that before. It was a depressing term of endearment.

'I think of you all the time, you know. I worry about you, all alone in your little apartment. Are you very unhappy?'

'I don't know. Yes. No . . .'

'You sound so funny.'

'Really? That's because you've never heard my voice on the telephone before. When are you coming back?'

'I don't know yet. As soon as I can, I promise. Maybe in three or four days.'

'That's a long time.'

'What, darling?'

'I said, that's an awfully long time.'

She laughed. At least he thought he heard her laughing.

'I'm in my nightgown and my bathrobe, and I'm standing barefoot, because the telephone is near the fireplace and it's quite chilly tonight. Are you in bed?'

Where did she think he was? He said nothing. He had been looking forward with such enthusiasm to this call that now he hardly recognized her voice.

'Have you been a good boy, François?'

He said he had. Then he heard her humming, thousands of miles away at the other end of the line, so softly he could hardly hear her – their song.

Something warm surged up inside him, something that flooded his breast and welled up into his throat. He couldn't breathe, he couldn't open his mouth. Then the humming stopped, and there was a moment of silence. He wondered if she was crying, whether she too was speechless. Then she said: 'Good night, my François. Sleep well. I'll call you tomorrow. Good night.'

There was a faint sound that might have been a kiss winging its way from halfway to the equator. He must have stammered something that nobody understood. The operator was saying something he could not understand, something like 'Your three minutes are up . . .'

'Good night.'

That was all he could say. His bed was terribly empty.

'Good night, my François.'

He hadn't told her what he wanted to tell her. He hadn't given her the all-important news that had been screaming to be told. Only after he had hung up did the words form on his lips. *You know, Kay? . . . What, my sweetheart? . . . What you told me at the station. The last thing you said . . . Yes, my sweetheart . . . That you didn't feel as if you were going away . . . that you were coming home? . . .*

She would have been smiling, far away at the other end of the line, a million miles away. He could see her smiling, while he spoke aloud in the void of his lonely room.

I know what you mean now, finally. It's taken me a long time, hasn't it? But you mustn't be angry with me.

No, my sweetheart.

Because men, you know, are a little obtuse. And then there's always that masculine pride . . .

Yes, my sweetheart. It doesn't matter.

You got home first, but I'm with you now. We've both come home, haven't we. And isn't it wonderful?

Wonderful, my sweetheart.

Don't cry. You mustn't cry. I'm not crying either. But I haven't got used to this yet. Do you understand?

I understand.

But it's all over now. It's been a long, hard road, but I've come home at last. And I know now. I love you. Do you hear me, Kay? I love you . . . I love you . . . I love you!

He buried his damp, salty face in his pillow. His body was racked with sobs. Far, far away he could see Kay smiling at him. He could even hear her warmer, deeper voice murmuring in his ear, *Yes, my sweetheart.*

9

A letter came for him in the morning mail. Even without the Mexican stamp he would have known that it was from Kay. He had never seen her handwriting before, but it was the very essence of Kay, so much so that he was moved by merely looking at it. This was a Kay that, he was certain, nobody else knew – a somewhat childish Kay, at once timorous and terribly reckless.

He was probably being ridiculous, but he thought that he could imagine the curves of her body in the curves of certain letters. The very fine downstrokes were like the almost invisible lines in her face. There were sudden, unexpected marks of boldness, and there were signs of physical weakness. A skilled graphologist would doubtless discover marks of her illness in her hand, for Combe was convinced that she had never been completely cured, that she would carry her wounds with her all her life . . . He smiled at her retracings when she stumbled over a difficult word or was not sure of the spelling.

She had not mentioned the letter during her telephone call. She had so many other things to talk about she had probably forgotten all about it.

The monotonous grey of the city became, that morning, a soft, tender dove-grey. The continuous patter of the rain made a muted obbligato to his thoughts as he read:

> My great big darling,
>
> How alone and unhappy you must be! I've been here for three days now and I have found no time to write or a way to telephone. But I have never stopped thinking of my poor François, who must be worrying back there in New York.
>
> I'm sure that you feel lost and abandoned, and I still wonder what I could have done, what you can possibly see in me that has made my presence so necessary to you. If only you could have seen how

miserable you looked when our taxi reached the station. It took all the courage I had to keep from turning around and coming back to you. May I confess, though, that it made me very happy?

Perhaps I should tell you this, but you are never out of my thoughts, even when I'm with my daughter.

I'll telephone you tonight or tomorrow night, depending on how my daughter is getting along, for I've spent every night at the hospital since my arrival. They put up a bed for me in a room next to Michèle's. Since the door is always open, I haven't dared put in a call for New York, and I admit I'm afraid to call from the office because the vixen with glasses who runs it doesn't like me. If all goes well, this will be my last night at the hospital.

But I must hurry and tell you everything in detail, for I know that otherwise you will imagine all sorts of things, just to torture yourself. First of all, I must confess right away that I almost deceived you. But not in the way you think, my poor dear, as you will see in a minute. After I left you in the taxi and bought my ticket, I suddenly felt so forlorn that I rushed for the snack bar. I wanted so terribly to cry, my poor François! I could still see your face looking out through the taxi window, haggard and tragic.

There was a man next to me at the lunch counter. I couldn't tell you what he looked like, whether he was young or old. Whoever he was, I said to him: 'Speak to me, will you please? I still have twenty minutes before my train leaves. Say anything at all, anything, so I won't burst into tears right here in public.'

He must have thought I was an imbecile, I certainly was acting like one, as usual, I realized afterwards. But I had to talk. I had to pour out my heart to somebody, but I don't remember any more what I told this stranger for the next quarter hour. I talked of you, of us. I told him that I was going away and that you were staying behind. Then I thought that I'd have time to phone you before the train left. I didn't realize, until after I was in the booth, that you had no phone yet.

I wonder how I managed to get aboard the train but I did, and I slept all day. I didn't even have the courage to walk to the dining car. All I had to eat that day was an orange.

Am I boring you with all this? My daughter is asleep. The nurse has just gone out. She takes care of another patient on the floor and has to change an ice bag every hour. I'm in bed in a little white room like I had in the sanatorium, with one small light shining on the writing paper propped against my raised knees.

I think of you and of us. I still wonder how it's possible. I wondered all during the trip. I can't get rid of the feeling, you see, that I don't deserve you. And I'm so afraid of hurting you again. You know what I mean, my François, but I'm convinced now that one day you will realize that this is the first time I have ever been in love. Don't you begin to feel it? I hope so for your sake. I don't want you to be hurt any more.

I must stop writing about these things, or I might pick up the phone and call New York, whether my daughter overhears or not.

I was quite confused to find that Michèle was already quite a young lady. She looks much more like me now than she did when she was small, and everyone insisted that she was the image of her father. She has noticed this too, and she looks at me – forgive me if I seem just a little conceited to write this – she looks at me, as I said, with more than a little admiration.

As my train was not to arrive until nearly midnight, I sent Larski a wire from the border. An embassy car was waiting for me at the station. As we drove across the city, just I and the chauffeur, the chauffeur said, 'Madame need not worry about the little girl. She was successfully operated on yesterday, and the doctors say that she is out of danger.'

I was glad that Larski didn't come to meet me. He wasn't at the embassy, either. I was greeted by a sort of governess, very Hungarian and very much the great-lady-who-has-fallen-upon-unhappy-days. She showed me to the apartment I was to occupy and said, 'If you would like to go to the hospital tonight, an embassy car will be at your disposal.'

Can you imagine my state of mind, my sweetheart, all alone in that huge palace with just my poor little suitcase?

'The maid will run your bath, after which you will no doubt wish to eat something, perhaps?'

I don't know what I ate. They rolled the table into my room, all set, like in a hotel. They also brought me a bottle of tokay and I must confess (you can either laugh or scold me) that I drank it all.

The hospital was on a hill at the edge of town. Everything was quite formal. L. was in the waiting-room with one of the surgeons who had just examined Michèle. He bowed and introduced me to the surgeon: 'The mother of my daughter.'

He was in evening dress, which was not unusual for him; he had obviously just come from some diplomatic function; but it made him look more glacial than ever.

The doctor told me that while he was practically sure the crisis was past, the next three or four days would have to be carefully watched. Then he left me alone with L. in a sort of sitting-room that reminded me of the reception room of a convent. L., as calm and poised as ever, gave me the details.

'I hope you were not annoyed by the slight delay in my notifying you about Michèle,' he said, 'but I had some trouble in getting your last address.'

And you of course know, my darling, that it was not my last address, because I was already at our place. Forgive me for underlining those two words, but I have to write them, and I say them aloud to convince myself that it's true. I've been unhappy here, but I shouldn't tell you about it because you too are unhappy, and I should be with you. I know that's where I belong.

I'm trying to tell you everything that happened, but my ideas get a little mixed up. Do you know that I don't even know how long Michèle has been in Mexico? We haven't talked much. She's so intimidated by my presence that she hardly opens her mouth. And when I start asking questions, the nurse breaks in to tell me I mustn't tire the patient.

What was I saying, François? I've forgotten how many days I have been here. I sleep in the room next to Michèle's, as I told you, and she often talks in her sleep, almost always in Hungarian. She mentions names I have never heard before. In the morning I help the nurse with her toilet. Her little body reminds me of mine when I was her age, and makes me want to cry. She's just as modest and bashful as I was then. For part of her ablutions she won't even let me stay in the room, not even if I turn my back.

I don't know what she thinks of me or what people have told her about me. She looks at me curiously and with some astonishment. When her father comes, she looks at us both in silence.

And I, François, think of you all the time, even – and this is not a nice thing to write – even the other evening, at about ten o'clock, when Michèle fainted and scared everyone so that they telephoned the opera to have her father paged. Am I a heartless monster?

L. too looks at me with some astonishment. I sometimes wonder if something hasn't changed in me since I've known you and loved you, something that strikes even people who don't know me. You should see the looks I get from the dowager governess of the embassy . . .

Every morning the car comes to the hospital to take me back to the embassy. I go up to my apartment and have my meals there. I have never seen the great dining-hall. And the only glimpse I have had of the magnificent reception rooms was one morning when the cleaning women were in one of them and had left the doors open.

I have had only one real conversation with L. He telephoned me one day to ask if I could come to his office in the chancellery at eleven in the morning. Like all the others, he looked me over with some surprise. There may have been just a hint of pity in his expression, too; he could hardly fail to notice that my wardrobe is a little shabby, that I wear no jewellery, and that I have not bothered to use make-up since I have been here. But there is no getting around the fact that there was more than pity in his eyes. I don't know what it is and I can't explain it, but there is no doubt that being in love somehow gets through to people in a vague and confused manner, and the impression makes them feel ill at ease.

He asked me, 'Are you happy?'

I said yes so simply, while looking him straight in the eyes, that he was the first to look away.

'I am taking advantage, if that is the phrase,' he said, 'of the occasion that has thrown us together again accidentally, to inform you of my forthcoming marriage.'

'I thought you had already remarried.'

'I had. It was a mistake.' He disposed of the matter with a wave of his hand. Now don't be jealous, François, but he really has very distinguished hands. 'This marriage,' he continued, 'is the final one. I am recommencing my life. That is why I sent for Michèle. She will have her place in my new home.'

For a minute I thought I was going to faint. I'm sure I turned pale. I really don't know how I looked at the moment, but I swear – please believe me, darling – that the only thing I could think of was you. I wanted so much to say to him: 'As for me, I'm terribly in love.'

But he already knew it. He could feel it. People could not help sensing it.

'And that is why, Catherine,' he went on (excuse me once more, darling. I don't want to hurt you, but I must tell you everything), 'that is why you must not be vexed because I have excluded you from my daily life here, and why I hope your stay will not be unduly prolonged. I have merely done my duty.'

'I am very grateful.'

'There are several other matters that I have wanted settled for some time, but if I have not done so, it is only because I had been unable to find your address.'

I'll tell you all about it when I see you, François. I have not actually made any hard-and-fast commitments. But please believe that everything I have done I have done for your sake, with you in mind, and in the belief that we will always be together.

Now you know pretty much everything about my life here. You needn't think that I feel any humiliation. I am a stranger in the house. I speak to no one except the governess and the servants. They are polite but distant . . . all except one girl from Budapest. Her name is Nouchi. One morning she surprised me getting out of my bath, and she said, 'Madame has skin exactly like Mademoiselle Michèle's.'

Do you remember, my darling, the night that you told me that you loved my skin? Well, my daughter's is much softer, much whiter. And her flesh . . .

Here I am getting sentimental again. I swore I would not be sad tonight when I wrote to you. But I would so much like to be able to bring you something worth while! And I bring you nothing. On the contrary. You know what I am thinking about, what you are thinking about all the time, in spite of yourself, and the thought frightens me so that I wonder if I should return to New York. If I were a real heroine, like in the novels, I probably would not come back. I would disappear without leaving any address – and perhaps you would be quickly consoled. But I am not a heroine, my François. You see? I am not even a mother. I lie here in the room next to my daughter, and I think only of my lover, and it is to my lover that I am writing. For the first time in my life, I am proud of writing that word.

My lover!

Like in our song. Do you still remember it? Have you been listening to it? I hope not, because I can see your forlorn face as you listen, and I am afraid you would start drinking too much.

You mustn't. I wonder what you do with your days, your long days of waiting. You must spend hours and hours in our room and by now I'm sure you know every detail in the life of our little tailor. I miss him too. I must stop thinking of New York, or I will find myself risking a scandal and telephoning you right now, come what may. I hope you ran into no delay in having your phone connected.

I still don't know whether Michèle will be well enough tomorrow night or the night after so that I can sleep at the embassy with a clear conscience. There I have a phone in my bedroom. I've already said to L. in an offhand way, 'Will you mind if I have to make a phone call to New York?'

I could see his jaws tighten. Now don't start imagining things, darling. It's an old tic of his. It's about the only sign of emotion I've ever been able to discover in his face. I think he would have been quite happy to find that I was alone in the world, a castaway, even. Not for his own advantage, though. That's all over and done with. But to satisfy his own wounded vanity, which is incredible.

He bowed from the waist – another of his mannerisms he thinks is the mark of a great diplomat – and replied coldly: 'Whenever you wish.'

He knew what kind of call I wanted to make and I, my darling, was dying to put a name to his suspicion. I wanted to shout in his face, 'François!'

If I'm to stay here much longer, I'll have to find somebody who'll listen to me talk about you, anybody, like at the railway station. You're not angry with me, are you, because of that silly business at the station? It was only because of you, darling – I simply couldn't keep you shut up inside of me any longer.

I can still see the expression on your face the night you said to me. 'You just can't help turning on the charm, can you, even if it's just for the waiter in a cafeteria or a taxi driver? You are so hungry for the admiration of men that you expect it even from the beggar you give a dime to in the street.'

Well, I'm going to confess something else. No, I'd better not; you wouldn't understand. And yet . . . what if you don't? What if I told you that I almost told my daughter about you? In fact, I did mention you vaguely – oh, very vaguely – don't worry – as though I was talking to an old and trusted friend . . .

It's already four o'clock in the morning. I had no idea it was so late. I've run out of paper. I've already written in all the margins, as you can see. I hope you won't have too much trouble deciphering this.

I want so much for you not to be sad, or too lonely. I want you, too, to have confidence in us. I would give anything to prevent your being hurt any more on my account.

Tomorrow night or the night after I will telephone you. I will hear your voice, and I will be with you – in our home.

I am exhausted.

Good night, François.

He radiated so much genuine happiness next day he was sure that anyone coming near him must feel its warmth.

It was so simple. So simple!

And so simply beautiful!

Some of the old pain persisted, like the dull twinges of convalescence, but they were lost in the great serenity that enveloped him.

She would come back, and life would begin again. That was all. He repeated it over and over to himself: *She'll come back. She's coming back and life will start again.*

He had no urge to dance with joy, to laugh, or even to smile. He took his happiness with calm and dignity. And he was not going to give way to his doubts. Ridiculous little doubts, weren't they?

This letter was written three days ago. Much can happen in three days. Who knows if . . . ?

Just as his imagination had tried to re-create – inaccurately – the apartment she had shared with Jessie before he had seen it, so he now tried to conjure up a picture of the vast Hungarian Embassy in Mexico City, and of Larski, whom he had never seen. He could see Larski sitting across his ambassadorial desk from Kay, making this proposal she had accepted without really accepting it, and that she had postponed explaining.

Would she telephone him again tonight? At what time?

She must telephone, because he had something important to tell her. He had been so stupidly tongue-tied on the phone that she knew nothing of what had been going on inside him. She still did not know that he was in love with her. How could she know, since he himself had not known until a few hours ago?

So? What was going to happen next? Perhaps they would no longer be tuned in on the same wavelength when they met again. At any rate, he must tell her the big news. Since her daughter was out of danger, why didn't she come right home? Why was she dawdling down there anyhow, surrounded by hostile influences? And what about that silly idea of hers – disappearing without a trace, just because she had hurt him and would go on hurting him?

No, no! He must explain to her that everything was different now. He had to get through to her. She must be told. Otherwise she might do something stupidly rash.

His happiness suddenly became only potential happiness, like a promissory note payable in the future but on which the interest payments would be days of anxiety. He was terribly afraid now that he had lost his chance. He would tell her to hurry back by plane.

But suppose the plane should crash? He would tell her to return by train. Still, the train took days instead of hours. And trains, too, could be wrecked.

They would talk it over when she phoned. And since she said that she would not telephone before night, he could go out for a while.

Laugier had been idiotic. Worse. He had been perfidious. His long lecture the other evening had been nothing short of perfidy. Because Laugier too must have felt what Kay had been writing about – the aura of love, which infuriates people who are not in love.

In a pinch we might get her a job as usherette in a cinema . . .

Those weren't his exact words, but that was his plan for Kay.

Combe did not have a glass of wine all day. He did not want to drink. He wanted to enjoy his new-found calm and tranquillity because, in spite of everything, he was enjoying tranquillity. It was not before six in the evening that he made up his mind – although he knew all along that he was going to do it – to go and see Laugier at the Ritz Bar, not so much to annoy him as to display his peace of mind.

Perhaps if Laugier had teased him, as he had expected, or even if he had shown himself a trifle more aggressive, things might have turned out differently. Laugier was holding court at his usual table, surrounded by his usual crowd, including the American girl Combe had met before.

'How are things, old boy?' Laugier shook hands, perhaps a little more cordially than usual, and his expression seemed to say, *See? That's done it. What did I tell you?*

Did the idiot imagine that it was all washed up, that he had thrown Kay over? They wouldn't mention the subject again. The affair had been liquidated. Combe was once more a normal male . . . Did they really think that?

Well, Combe didn't want to be a normal male at the moment. He had an urge to give them all a pitying look. He suddenly missed Kay so much that a wave of dizziness swept over him. Was it possible that no one saw a change in him? Or was he really normal, like the others around him, the people for whom he felt only disdain?

He acted normally. He drank a manhattan, accepted a second, and talked to the American girl who was ringing a cigarette with lipstick as she asked him (in French) about the plays he had starred in in Paris.

He had a desperate, almost painful need of Kay's physical presence at that moment, and yet he was behaving like a normal male. He was a little surprised at himself, spreading his reputation like a peacock his tail, as he boasted, with perhaps more spirit than it deserved, of his stage career.

Rat-face was not there. Other people he had not met before claimed to have seen his films.

He wanted to talk of Kay. He had her letter in his pocket and at times he was ready to take it out and read it to whoever would listen – the American girl, for instance, whom he had hardly noticed the week before. *They don't know. They can't know.*

He drank his cocktails automatically as they were served. He thought: *Three more days. Four at most. She'll telephone me again tonight, and she'll hum our song.* He was in love with Kay, no doubt about it. He had never loved her as much as he did that night. And that very night he was going to discover a new shape of their love, perhaps its very roots.

But the present was still confused and would always remain confused, like a bad dream. For instance, the self-satisfied smile on Laugier's lips and the little spark of irony in his eyes. Why was Laugier suddenly making fun of him? Because he was talking to the American girl? Well, he would go on talking to the American girl – about Kay. She had given him his cue.

'You're married, aren't you?' she had asked. 'Is your wife with you in New York?'

And he had told her about Kay. He told her that he had come to New York alone and that loneliness had made him understand the inestimable value of a human relationship. His body as well as his spirit had ached with loneliness. He had met Kay. They had at once plunged as deeply into the intimacy of their beings as human nature would allow. Because they were starved for human contact.

The words seemed suddenly so heavy with meaning, there in the crowded, smoky din of the Ritz Bar, that they were like a revelation. He emptied his glass. Human contact!

'You wouldn't understand, of course,' he said. 'How could you understand?'

There was Laugier smiling cynically at him from the next table, where he was talking with a producer!

Combe was sincere. He spoke ardently. He was full of Kay, full to overflowing. He remembered the first time they had fallen into each other's arms, knowing nothing about one another except that they were both starved of human contact.

He repeated the phrase, tried to find its equivalent in English. The American girl watched him with eyes that grew pensive.

'She'll be in New York in three or four days,' he said. 'Maybe sooner, if she gets a seat on a plane.'

'How happy she must be!'

Time had slipped by. The bar was emptying. Laugier got up and held out his hand.

'I must leave you, my children,' he said. 'By the way, François, will you be a good boy and see June home?'

Combe had the vague feeling that he was the object of a conspiracy, but he was not willing to believe it.

Hadn't Kay given him everything that was possible for a woman to give? Here were two creatures, making their separate ways over the surface of the globe, lost in the great maze of thousands of New York streets. Yet Fate throws them together, and a few hours later they are so fiercely cemented to each other that the very idea of separation is intolerable. Isn't that a miracle? And it was this miracle that he was trying to explain to June, who was watching him with eyes in which he thought he saw a yearning for the new worlds he was opening for her.

'Which way are you going?'

'I don't know. I'm in no hurry.'

So he took her to his little bar. He felt that he had to go there that evening, yet he hadn't the courage to go alone.

June too was wearing a fur, and she too took his arm. It was a little like having Kay with him. After all, hadn't they been talking of Kay, and only of Kay, all evening?

'Is she very beautiful?'

'No.'

'But . . . ?'

'She's very exciting. She is handsome. You would have to see her. She is femininity personified. She is the universal woman, you understand. But I'm sure you don't understand. A woman who is rather sophisticated but who has remained a child. Let's go in here. I want you to hear . . .'

He fumbled in his pocket for nickels. He dropped several in the jukebox, watched June with the hope that she would immediately share *their* emotion.

'Two manhattans, bartender.'

He knew he shouldn't go on drinking, but it was too late to stop now. He was so moved by the music that tears came to his eyes. The American girl stroked his hand as if to comfort him. 'You shouldn't cry, since she's coming back.'

He clenched his fists. 'But can't you understand that I can't wait? Three days, four days are an eternity!'

'Shh! People are looking at you.'

'I'm sorry.'

He fed more nickels to the jukebox – three, four. Every time the record began again, he ordered another round of cocktails.

'At night we would walk up Fifth Avenue for hours.' He was tempted to walk up Fifth Avenue with June, just to show her, to make her feel what he had felt . . .

'I would love to know Kay,' she said, staring into space.

'You'll meet her. I want you to know her.' He meant it without reservation. 'There are so many places in New York now where I can't bear to go to alone.'

'I understand.' She took his hand again. She seemed to be quite as affected as he was. 'Let's go,' she said.

Go where? He had no idea of the time, but he certainly didn't want to go home to his lonely cubicle. He had a brain wave. 'All right,' he said. 'I'll take you to a place where Kay and I used to go.'

In the taxi she snuggled against him and reached for his hand. Then it seemed to him . . . No, it was difficult to put it into words, but it seemed to him that Kay . . . No, not Kay alone, but all humanity, all the love in the world . . .

He couldn't explain it to June. She wouldn't understand. She leaned her head against his shoulder. He breathed a strange fragrance . . .

'Promise me that you'll introduce her to me.'

'Of course.'

They walked into the bar at No. 1 Fifth Avenue. The pianist was still trailing his lazy fingers over the keys. She walked ahead of him with the same instinctive pride of a woman a man is following – just like Kay. She sat down and, like Kay, she pushed her fur back from her shoulders, opened her bag, found a cigarette, fumbled for her lighter. Was she too going to lecture the maître d'hotel?

At this time of night she began to show traces of fatigue under her eyes, just like Kay, and her cheeks had begun to sag under her make-up.

'Could you give me a light? My lighter has run out of fluid.'

He struck a match. She laughed smoke into his face. A moment later, as she whispered something into his ear, her lips brushed his neck.

'Tell me more about Kay,' she said. Then, obviously restless, she got up and added, 'Let's go.'

Go where? The same question – except that now they had both sensed the answer. They were in Greenwich Village. They were a few steps away from Washington Square. She was clinging to his arm, leaning against him with the limpness of abandon. He could feel her hip against his at every step . . .

And she was Kay. In spite of everything, it was Kay he was seeking. And it was Kay whose haunches pressed against his, it was even Kay's voice – the low-pitched one – when she spoke, and it was a voice that trembled on the edge of turbulence.

When they came to Combe's house, he stopped. For an instant he stood motionless, his eyes closed. Then, with a gesture that was both gentle and resigned, he took her arm. He did not know whether he was sorrier for her or for himself – or for Kay. He nudged her into the doorway.

She climbed the stairs a few steps ahead of him. She too had a run in her stocking.

'Is it still higher?'

True, she didn't know.

She stopped on the landing, and she didn't look at him. He opened the door and reached for the light switch. She clutched his arm.

'No, please. Don't. Do you mind?'

It took him a few seconds to adjust his eyes after the precise but anaemic light of the city streets. He lived for the moment in his sense of touch – the fur, the smoothness of silk, the warmth of a woman's body, the damp, eager pressure of the lips that sought to mould themselves to his.

He thought, *Kay* . . . !

Then he stopped thinking. They tumbled heavily to the bed.

They lay without speaking, without moving, body to body. Neither slept and each knew the other was awake. Combe's eyes were open, and his cheek almost touched the pale blur of her cheek in the darkness. He could see the faint sheen of perspiration on the outline of her nose. There was nothing to do but wait in silence . . .

The silence was rudely shattered by the ringing of the phone, a clangour so violent that they both jumped. Flustered, Combe fumbled in the dark, groping for the unfamiliar instrument that had rung only once before. It was June, ironically, who came to his aid by turning on the bedside lamp.

'Hello . . . yes . . .' He did not recognize the sound of his own voice. He stood stupidly in the middle of the floor, naked, holding the receiver in one hand. 'François Combe, yes . . .'

He saw June getting out of bed. She whispered, 'Do you want me to go?'

What for? Go where? She could hear just as well from the bathroom. He shook his head. She went back to bed, lying on her side. Her hair, fanned out over the pillow, was the same colour as Kay's – and in the same place.

'Hello.' His throat was tight and dry.

'Is that you, François?'

'Of course, my darling.'

'What's the matter?'

'Nothing. Why?'

'I don't know. Your voice sounds funny.'

'I woke up with a start.' He was ashamed of his lie, ashamed not only of lying to Kay, but of lying to her in the presence of the witness who was watching him from the bed. Why, since she had the tact to offer to leave the room, couldn't she be tactful enough to turn her back to him? She was watching him with one eye, and he stared back at that eye, fascinated.

'I have good news for you, darling. I'm leaving tomorrow, or rather this morning, by plane. I'll be in New York this evening . . . Hello!'

'Yes.'

'Haven't you anything to say? What *is* the matter, François? You're hiding something from me. You've been out with Laugier, haven't you?'

'Yes.'

'I'll bet you were drinking.'

'Yes.'

'I was sure that was it, my poor darling. Why didn't you say so? Will I see you tomorrow, then? I mean, this evening?'

'Yes.'

'The embassy got me a seat on the plane. I don't know exactly what time the flight is due in New York, but you can find out by calling the airline. Be sure you call the right one, though, because there are several. I'm flying Pan-American.'

'Yes.' There were so many things he had wanted to tell her. He had wanted most of all to shout out the great news. And instead he stood there dumbly, as though hypnotized by one eye.

'Did you get my letter?'

'This morning.'

'Did I make many mistakes in spelling? Did you have the courage to read it right through to the end? You know, I don't think I'll go to bed tonight, although it won't take me long to pack. I went out for an hour this afternoon, and I bought you a present. A surprise. But I'm keeping you up, darling. I can tell you're sleepy. Did you really have a lot to drink?'

'I guess so.'

'Was Laugier very disagreeable?'

'I don't really remember, darling. All I know is that I was thinking of you all the time.'

'See you this evening, François.'

'See you this evening.' He wanted to tell her. He tried, but it wouldn't come out. He should have tried harder. He should have confessed, *Listen, Kay, I've got somebody in the room. You understand now why I . . .* He would tell her when she got back. It must not be an act of treachery. There must never be anything underhanded between them.

'Go right to sleep.'

'Good night, Kay.'

Slowly he replaced the phone in its cradle. For a long moment he stood in the middle of the room, arms dangling, staring at the floor.

'Did she guess?'

'I don't know.'

'Will you tell her?'

He raised his head, looked her squarely in the eyes, and said, 'Yes.'

She was lying on her back, her erect breasts like twin pomegranates. After a while she sat up and tried to straighten her hair. Then she swung her legs off the bed, one after the other, and reached for her stockings.

He made no move to stop her. He too began dressing.

She said without bitterness, 'You don't have to see me home. I'll find my way.'

'I'll take you home.'

'It's better that you shouldn't. She might telephone again.'

'You think so?'

'If she suspects something, she'll call you back.'

'Please forgive me.'

'For what?'

'Nothing. For letting you go alone like this.'

'It's my fault.'

She smiled. When she had finished dressing, she lit a cigarette. She came up to him and planted a light, sisterly kiss on his forehead. Her fingers sought his and squeezed them warmly as she murmured, 'Good luck.'

He listened to her footsteps in the stairway. Then he sat down, half dressed, to wait out the night. Kay did not telephone again. The light went on in the little tailor's window across the street, announcing the start of a new day.

Was Combe wrong? Would it always be like this? Would he go on definitely discovering new depths of love to be attained? Not a muscle in his face moved. He was stiff and weary in body and mind. He did not feel capable of thought. But he had the conviction – it was a certainty that he felt with all his being – that it was only this night that he had loved Kay truly and totally; at least that he had been so truly and totally aware of it.

That was why, when dawn touched his windows and dimmed the lamp on his night table, he was no longer ashamed of what had happened.

10

She wouldn't understand. How could she? She couldn't know, for instance, that during the hour he had been waiting at the airport he had been wondering whether, without any romantic exaggeration, considering the state of his nerves, he would be able to withstand the shock.

Everything he had done that day, everything he had done up to the present moment, would be so radically new to her that he would, in a way, have to start training her all over again. And the burning question was whether they were still on the same wavelength, and if so, whether she could and would travel so far with him.

Worrying about this new development had kept him from doing the many things he had planned to do that morning. He had not bothered to change the pillow case on which June's head had lain; he had not even looked to see if she had left traces of lipstick. What was the use? He was so far beyond all that. It was all in the past.

He had not ordered dinner delivered from the Italian's, as he had been planning. He had not checked the refrigerator to see what there was to eat and drink.

She would never guess what he had actually been doing that day. He had drawn back the curtains and pulled a chair up to the window. The rain had turned to a fine drizzle, but the sky, despite the dull overcast, had a curious luminosity that hurt his eyes. The hard light was just what he needed. The week of rain had given the brick walls of the houses across the street a sickly colour, and the banality of the curtained windows was distressing.

Actually, he hardly saw the houses across the street. He was surprised to find later, that he had not even been watching the little tailor who had become their good-luck symbol. He was very tired. He had thought of going to bed for a few hours, but instead remained sprawled in his chair, his collar open, his legs extended, smoking pipe after pipe and dropping the ashes on the floor.

Towards noon he got up suddenly and went to the phone, called long-distance, and gave the operator a Hollywood number.

'Hello . . . that you, Ulstein?' Ulstein wasn't a friend. Combe had many friends in Hollywood, directors, French actors and actresses, but he was not calling them today. 'This is Combe . . . yes, François Combe . . . What? No, I'm calling from New York . . . Yes, I know that if you had something for me you would have written or wired me, but that's not why I'm calling . . . No, operator, I haven't finished talking . . .'

Ulstein was an awful man he had known in Paris, not at Fouquet's because he was not a regular there. But he was always prowling the streets in the immediate neighbourhood so that people might think he had just come from Fouquet's.

'Remember our last conversation before I came East, Ulstein? You told me that if I was willing to play second or third leads . . . to speak frankly, minor parts . . . you'd have no trouble at all getting work for me . . . What's that?' Combe smiled bitterly. At any moment now Ulstein would begin boasting. 'Figures, Ulstein, no generalities . . . I'm not talking about my career. How much a week? . . . Yes, to play any part . . . But damn it, that's my business, not yours! Just answer my question and leave the rest to me . . .'

The unmade bed on one side, the grey rectangle of the window on the other. Harsh white and cold grey. His voice, too, was harsh.

'How much? . . . Six hundred dollars? . . . Only for good weeks? . . . Good, five hundred . . . Are you sure of what you're saying? . . . Are you prepared to sign a six-month contract, say, at that rate? . . . No, I can't give you an answer today. Tomorrow, probably . . . No, no. I'll call you.'

Kay would know nothing of all this. She might expect to find the apartment filled with flowers. She would not know that he had thought of it but had shrugged it off scornfully. Wasn't he right in wondering, a little fearfully, whether they would still be on the same wavelength?

Perhaps he had been moving too rapidly. He realized that he had covered quite a distance at a dizzy speed in a very short time, a distance that some men take years to cover, others a lifetime.

He heard bells when he left the house; it must have been noon. He started walking, his hands in the pockets of his beige raincoat. Kay could not know that, except for the fifteen minutes it took to eat a hot dog at a lunch counter, he had been walking for eight hours when he reached the air terminal to wait for her plane. He had crossed Greenwich Village into the Lower East Side. He had found himself on the approach to the Brooklyn Bridge, and for the first time he walked across that historic iron span. He looked down.

It was cold. The drizzle had slackened off. The sky hung low over East River, dark and thick. The river was slashed with angry white wave crests. Tugs screamed angrily as they escorted ugly brown scows up and down the river.

Would she believe him if he told her the truth – that he had walked all the way from the Village to La Guardia, that he had stopped only three or four times in a neighbourhood bar, and that he had not put even one nickel in a jukebox? That was something he no longer needed.

Everything he saw about him on his pilgrimage through a world that was monotonously grey – the little dark men swarming like ants under the lights, the stores, the cinemas with their garlands of light, the hot-dog stands, the bakeries with their displays of nauseating pastries; the coin machines that played music for you or allowed you to play at rolling balls into little holes that rang bells and lit lights; everything a great city could invent to deceive man's loneliness – he would now contemplate without a sinking feeling and without panic.

She was coming home. She would soon be there.

He dragged his last anxious hours through the semi-urban desert of Queens, a desert of brick rectangles after brick rectangles with their iron zigzags of fire escapes. He wondered, not how people had the courage to live in such rectangular anthills, but where they found the courage to die there.

The buses passed him, loaded with faceless people, all with their own dark secrets. And the children, darkly silhouetted in the greyness, little people coming home from school, reaching desperately, they too, for some sort of gaiety.

The store fronts depressed him. The dummies in the show windows, holding out their too pink hands of wood or wax in unappealing gestures of appeal, revolted him.

Kay knew nothing of all this. How could she? How could she know that he had been pacing the terminal building at the airport for an hour and a half, eyeing the other pacers, some as tense and as anxious as he was, others gay or indifferent, all waiting. He wondered if he would be as calm as the calmest at the last minute.

That last minute was the moment of crisis. He wondered if, when he saw her again, she would be anything like herself, like the Kay that he loved. It was more subtle, deeper than that. He had promised himself that the moment he laid eyes on her he would say, 'It's all over, Kay.'

She wouldn't understand, of course; he knew that. It was a sort of a pun. She wouldn't know *what* was all over – that there would be no more pursuit, badgering, walking against infinity, chasing each other, taking or leaving – it was *that* which was over.

Yes, it was all over. It was his decision, and it was the reason why his day had been one of anxiety and soul-searching. Because it was still possible that she was not yet thinking and feeling on his plane, and that she might not want to go with him. And he had no more time to lose.

It was all over. That phrase summed it up. He had run the cycle. He had looped the loop to come back to the point where Destiny had been leading him, where Destiny, in fact, had first met him. In the all-night lunch counter, where they had been complete strangers to each other, their fate had already been decided over a plate of sausages and a plate of bacon and eggs. Instead of asking why, instead of groping blindly, resisting, rebelling, he now said with quiet humility and without shame: *I accept*.

He accepted everything. All their love and whatever its issue. Kay, just as she was, just as she had been, just as she might be. Would she really understand this when she saw him waiting in the anxious crowd behind the grey barriers of the airport?

She rushed towards him, trembling with excitement. She gave him her lips, unaware that at that moment he was not interested in her lips. She exclaimed: 'At last, François!' Then, because she was a woman: 'You're all wet!'

She wondered why he was staring at her with such a peculiar expression, the expression of a sleepwalker, and why he was dragging her through the crowd, making way with savage elbows. She almost asked, *Aren't you glad to see me?* Then she thought of her suitcase. She said: 'We'll have to wait for my luggage, François.'

'I'll have it delivered.'

'But I might need some of my things . . .'

'So what?' He took her luggage ticket, gave his address to a clerk, and hurried her towards the exits.

'It would have been so easy, with a taxi. I brought you something from Mexico, you know.'

'Come on.'

'Yes, François.' Her eyes were frightened, submissive.

'Greenwich Village,' he told the cab driver. 'Anywhere around Washington Square.'

'But –'

He hadn't asked her if she was tired or if she had eaten. He had not noticed the new dress she was wearing under her coat. She entwined her fingers in his fingers. He did not react. He was stiff, indifferent. Her heart sank.

'François?'

'What?'

'You haven't really kissed me yet, you know.'

It would have made no sense for him to kiss her here, not really kiss her, but he did it anyhow. He was condescending and she felt it. She was really frightened.

'Listen, François.'

'Yes?'

'Last night . . .'

He waited. He knew what she was going to say.

'I almost called you back last night. Forgive me if I'm wrong, but all the while I was talking to you, I had a feeling there was someone else in the room.'

He did not look at her. He did not want to be reminded of the other taxi, last night's taxi . . .

'Answer me. I won't be angry. Although . . . in *our* bedroom . . .'

He said nonchalantly, almost acidly, 'There was someone else there.'

'I was sure of it. That's why I didn't dare call you back. François . . .'

He wanted no scenes. He had gone so far beyond that sort of thing that he shrank from the hand that gripped his so frantically, from her sniffling, from the tears she was fighting so hard to hold back. He was impatient to be home. It was a little like a bad dream – the long, long road that never seemed to end because there was always one more hill to climb . . .

Would he have the courage to face it?

She should shut up. Someone should tell her to shut up, someone else. He could not do it himself. She had come back, and she thought that was enough. She had no idea what a long hurdle he had cleared while she was away.

She stammered, 'Did . . . did you really do that, François?'

'Yes.' He said it maliciously. He resented her impatience. Why couldn't she have waited for the marvellous moment that he had planned for her?

'I didn't think that I could ever be jealous again. I know very well that I have no right to be . . .'

He was watching the neon signs. He saw the all-night café where they had first met. He ordered the driver: 'Stop at the corner.'

It must be a disappointing homecoming for her. He knew that she was choking back the tears, but he couldn't help it. This was the way it had to be. He said: 'Come.'

She followed meekly, uneasily, tortured by this new mystery he had become for her.

'We'll have a bite to eat,' he said, 'and then we'll go home.'

As he stepped into the lighted doorway, he looked every inch the man of mystery, the international adventurer, with his damp trench coat, his rain-soaked hat, and his pipe, which, for the first time in her presence, he had lighted in the taxi.

It was he who ordered bacon and eggs for her without asking what she wanted. He also ordered her brand of cigarettes without waiting for her to dig into her handbag for her cigarette case. He opened the pack and offered her one.

Was she beginning to guess what it was that he had not yet been able to tell her?

'What I can't understand, François, is that it had to be just last night, the night when I was so happy because I could tell you I was coming home . . .'

She might have found that he was looking at her coldly, that he had never looked at her so coldly, even on that first day, or first night, rather, when they had met on this very spot.

'Why did you do it?'

'I don't know. For your sake.'

'What do you mean by that?'

'Nothing. It's too complicated.' He was very solemn, almost distant. She had to talk, if only to move her lips.

'I must tell you right away,' she said, 'unless of course you don't want me to, what Larski did. Like I told you, I haven't accepted anything yet. I wanted to talk to you first.'

He knew what she was going to say. Anyone observing them that night would have taken him for the most thick-skinned, inconsiderate man on earth. All this was so unimportant in relation to the decision he had made, in relation to the great human truth that had at last dawned upon him.

She was digging into her handbag. It was an error of taste and timing. She was so anxious in her quest that he forgave her.

'Look.' She held up an impressive oblong of paper, a sight draft for five thousand dollars. 'I want you to understand exactly . . .'

Yes, of course. He understood.

'He didn't do this in the spirit that you think, really. It was due me by the terms of our divorce, but I never wanted to bring up the question of money, any more than I wanted to bring up my right to have my daughter so many weeks a year.'

'Your eggs are getting cold. Eat.'

'Am I annoying you?'

'No.' He said it sincerely.

Had he foreseen the routine? Almost. He was so far ahead that he had to wait for her to catch up, for he had reached the top of the hill long ago. He said, 'Waiter. The salt.'

This is where they had come in. The salt. The pepper. Then the Worcestershire sauce. Then a light for her cigarette. Then . . . He was not impatient. He did not smile. He remained as solemn as he had been at the airport, and that was what baffled her.

'If only you knew him, and especially if you knew his family, you wouldn't be surprised.'

Surprised? Why should he be surprised? By what?

'For centuries the Larskis have been landowners, with estates as big as the Alpes-Maritimes. At one time the land produced enormous revenues. I don't know if it still does, but the family is immensely wealthy. They had an eccentric old scholar, maybe he was crazy, maybe he was just smart, I wouldn't know, who lived in one of their castles, just cataloguing the library. He would read all day, make a few notes on bits of paper, and toss the paper into a box. After ten years, the box caught fire. I'm sure he set fire to it himself.

'In that same castle there were three nurses, three old women. I don't know whom they were supposed to nurse, because Larski was an only child. They were housed in the outbuildings, did nothing all day, and lived off the fat of the land. I could go on like this for hours, but – What's the matter, darling?'

'Nothing.'

He had just caught sight of her reflection in the mirror as he had on their first night, rather unflattering, a little distorted. This was the final test; he need hesitate no longer.

'Do you think I should keep the money?'

'We'll see about it.'

'It's only for your sake that I'd accept it. I mean – now don't get angry – so I would not be just a dead weight around your neck. Do you understand?'

'Of course, *chérie*.'

He almost wanted to laugh. It was so nearly grotesque. Her poor little love was so far behind his own, which he was about to offer but about which she still knew nothing!

And she was so frightened! She was so bewildered! She resumed eating with deliberate slowness as though to put off the unknown that lay ahead. Then she lit the inevitable cigarette.

'My poor Kay!'

'What? Why do you say poor?'

'Because I have hurt you a little bit. I hasten to add that I did not do it deliberately, even though I think that it was necessary. It happened because I am a man, and therefore it may happen again.'

'In our bedroom?'

'No.'

She gave him a grateful look. She was still in the dark. She could not know yet that the bedroom in question was already becoming part of the past.

'Come.'

She fell in step beside him. June too had adjusted her step so well to that of the man that their haunches had moved as one.

'You know, you've really hurt me deeply. I'm not angry with you, but –'

He stopped her under a street light and kissed her. It was the first time he had kissed her out of pity; the time had not yet come for the other kind.

'Would you like to go to our little bar for a drink?'

'No.'

'What about Number One? It's not far.'

'No.'

'Very well.'

She followed meekly, although perhaps not reassured, as they approached their house.

'I would never have thought that you would bring her here.'

'I had to.'

He wanted to get to the point quickly. He nudged her into the stairway, the way he had done with June the night before, but only he knew that no comparison was possible. Her fur trailed from her shoulders ahead of him. The pale legs came to a stop on the landing. He came abreast of her, opened the door, switched on the light.

There was no welcome for Kay. There was only the empty room, chilly and in a mess. He knew that she wanted to cry.

Perhaps he even wanted to see her cry. He took off his trench coat, his hat, his gloves. He took off her hat and jacket. Just as her lower lip was beginning to form a pout, he said: 'You see, Kay, I have made an important decision.'

She was still afraid. She looked at him with the wide, terrified eyes of a little girl, and he wanted to laugh. What a state to be in for making such a momentous declaration!

'I know now that I love you. Whatever the future may bring, whether it should be happiness or unhappiness, doesn't matter. I accept all of it in advance. That's what I wanted to tell you, Kay. That's what I wanted to shout into the phone, not only the first time you called, but again last night, in spite of everything. I love you. And I will love you whatever happens, whatever I may have to go through, whatever –'

It was his turn to be perplexed. Instead of falling into his arms, as he had expected, she remained frozen in the centre of the room, pale, very cold. Hadn't he been right to worry about their being on the same wavelength?

He called to her, as though she was a long way off.

'Kay!'

She did not look at him. She remained speechless.

'Kay!'

She did not come to him. On the contrary, she turned her back to him, ran into the bathroom, and closed the door.

'Kay!'

He stood dumbfounded in the middle of the room he had deliberately left in disorder, his arms outstretched, his love at the tips of his empty fingers.

11

For a long time he sat deeply ensconced in his armchair, his eyes fixed on the bathroom door. No sound came from behind it. As the minutes dragged by, his calm returned. Impatience and perplexity slipped from him as confidence enveloped him gently with its insinuating warmth.

It seemed an eternity before the bathroom door opened without any preliminary sound. He saw the knob turning silently. Then the door swung out and Kay was there. They looked at each other without a word.

Something about her had changed, but he could not tell what. Her face, her hair were not the same. She wore no make-up. She had been travelling all day, yet her features were relaxed and her complexion blooming. She smiled timidly, a little awkwardly, and walked towards him. He had a strange, almost sacrilegious feeling that he was witnessing the birth of happiness.

She stopped in front of his chair and held out her hands for him to rise. At that solemn moment they must both be standing.

They stood very close together, cheek to cheek, but they did not embrace. The silence hung almost tangibly about them. It was she who dared break it at last. She breathed: 'You've come home.'

He was ashamed, for he had a premonition of the truth.

'I didn't think you would come, François,' she continued, 'and I didn't even dare hope for it. Sometimes I hoped you wouldn't. Do you remember our taxi in the rain and the last words I said to you at the station, words I thought you would never understand? "I don't feel any more as though I'm going away . . . It's more like coming home."

'I was speaking for myself.'

'And now . . .'

He felt her go limp in his arms. He was just as weak and clumsy as she was as the result of this wonderful thing that had happened to them, but he tried to lead her to the bed before she collapsed. She protested feebly: 'No.'

The bed was not their place that night. The two of them were wedged into the big, threadbare armchair, so close that their pulses pounded in unison and each could feel the other's breath upon their cheek.

'Don't say a word, François. Tomorrow . . .'

Tomorrow with the dawn they would enter into their new life forever. Tomorrow they would be lonely no longer, they would never be lonely again. He felt her shiver, and at the same moment he felt a tightening in his throat like some old, forgotten affliction. At the same instant they had both looked back for the last time at their past solitude. And both wondered how they had managed to live through it.

'Tomorrow,' she repeated.

Tomorrow there would be no more beds, no more bedrooms in Manhattan. They would need them no longer. Nor would they need a jukebox in a little bar. Tomorrow and from tomorrow on they could go anywhere, be at home anywhere.

What was the meaning of that tenderly mocking smile that crossed her face the moment the little tailor across the way turned on the electric light that hung from a cord? He squeezed her hand to ask the question, for words were no longer needed.

She stroked his forehead as she said, 'You thought that you had passed me, didn't you? You thought that you were far, far ahead of me, and all the while, poor darling, you were far, far behind.'

Dawn of the new day was not far off. They could already hear the distant sounds of the city coming to life. Why should they hurry? This day would be theirs, as would all the others to follow, and the city – this one or another – could no longer frighten them. In a few hours this apartment, this bedroom, would exist no longer. There would be luggage on the floor and the armchair that now held them in its embrace would resume its shabby role as just furniture for a run-down Village apartment. They could look back without fear. Even the pillow with its mould of June's head had lost its dread . . .

The future, said Combe, was up to Kay. Either they would return to France, if she wanted to, and with Kay by his side, he would quietly take his old place on the Paris stage. Or they would go to Hollywood and he would start again from scratch. It didn't matter to him. Weren't they starting from scratch anyway?

'I understand now,' she said, 'why it was you couldn't wait for me.'

He opened his arms to embrace her, but she slipped from him, and, with a fluid movement, slid from the chair. In the half-light of dawn he saw her kneeling before him on the rug. She seized his hands and kissed them fervently. She whispered: 'Thank you.'

They could draw back the curtains all the way now, to let the raw, sunless daylight outline the bare poverty of the room. As the new day began, they, calmly, fearlessly, and only a little awkwardly because it was so new, began the business of living.

They were smiling at each other across the room, and he could find no other phrase to express the happiness that welled up within him except: 'Good morning, Kay.'

Her lips trembled as she replied, 'Good morning, François.'

After a long silence, she turned from him to the window.

'Good-bye, little tailor.'

They locked the door as they left.

MAIGRET AND THE GHOST

Translated by Eileen Ellenbogen

1

Inspector Lognon's Nocturnal Activities and His Wife's Infirmities

On the night in question, it was past one o'clock when the light went out in Maigret's office. The Chief Superintendent, his eyelids swollen with fatigue, opened the door communicating with the inspectors' room. Bonfils and young Lapointe were the officers on duty that night.

'Good night, lads,' he mumbled.

Outside, the cleaning women were sweeping the vast lobby. He raised his hand in greeting. As always at this late hour, there was a draught, and the stairway was damp and freezing cold as he and Janvier went down together.

It was the middle of November. Rain had been falling all through the day. Maigret had not once set foot outside his overheated office since eight o'clock the previous morning, and before stepping out into the forecourt he turned up his coat collar.

'Can I give you a lift?'

A taxi, ordered by telephone, was waiting outside the main gate on the Quai des Orfèvres.

'Just as far as the nearest metro station, Chief.'

The rain was coming down in sheets and bouncing off the paving stones. The Inspector got out at the Châtelet.

'Good night, Chief.'

'Good night, Janvier.'

They had parted like this hundreds of times before, with the same sense of somewhat jaded satisfaction.

A few minutes later Maigret, without making a sound, was creeping up the stairs to his flat in the Boulevard Richard-Lenoir, groping in his pocket for the key, then turning it carefully in the lock. Almost immediately he heard Madame Maigret turning over in bed.

'Is that you?'

How often had he come home in the middle of the night to hear her call out these same words, her voice drugged with sleep, as he groped in the dark for the switch of the bedside lamp? Hundreds if not thousands of times. Then, in her nightdress, she would get out of bed and take a look at her husband, to see what sort of a mood he was in.

'Is it over?'

'Yes.'

'Did the boy talk in the end?'

He nodded.

'Are you hungry? Would you like me to get you something?'

He hung his wet coat on the coat-stand, and loosened his tie.

'Is there any beer in the fridge?'

On the way home, he had almost stopped the taxi in the Place de la République, with the intention of going into one of the all-night brasseries and ordering a half.

'Did it turn out as you expected?'

A dull case, if one can talk of dullness where the fate of three men is in the balance. One newspaper had managed to introduce a hint of sensationalism with the headline: THE MOTORCYCLE GANG.

On the first occasion, in broad daylight in the Rue de Rennes, two motorcycles had drawn into the kerb in front of a jeweller's. The first motorcycle had been carrying two men, the second, one. The three men had tied red scarves over their faces and gone into the shop. They had emerged a few minutes later, carrying guns, and a quantity of jewellery and watches snatched from the display window and counter.

At first the crowd had been too stunned to react, but when the first shock had subsided, a number of passers-by in cars had driven off in pursuit of the thieves, causing such a snarl-up in the process as to help rather than hinder the escape of the wanted men.

'They'll try again,' Maigret had predicted.

It had been a pretty meagre haul, for the shop, owned by a widow, stocked only very cheap stuff.

'This was by way of being a dress rehearsal.'

It was the first time that motorcycles had been used in a hold-up.

The Chief Superintendent had guessed right, for, three days later, the scene was re-enacted, only this time at a luxury jeweller's in the Faubourg Saint-Honoré. The outcome was the same, except that on this occasion the thieves got away with jewellery worth millions of old francs, two hundred million, according to the newspapers, a hundred million according to the insurance company assessors.

However, one of the thieves had dropped his scarf while escaping, and was arrested the following day at his place of work, a locksmith's in the Rue Saint-Paul.

By the evening of that same day, all three were under lock and key. The eldest of them was twenty-two years of age, and the youngest, Jean Bauche, nicknamed Jeannot, barely eighteen.

He was a tall, fair-haired youth, who wore his hair too long. He was also employed in the locksmith's workshop. His mother worked as a cleaning woman in the Rue Saint-Antoine.

'Janvier and I have been taking it turn and turn about all day,' Maigret, looking glum, said to his wife.

Drinking beer and eating sandwiches the while.

'See here, Jeannot, you think you're tough, don't you? They talked you into believing you were. But it wasn't you or your two little friends who thought up either of those jobs. There's someone behind all this, someone who engineers things, while taking great care not to soil his own hands. He's only been out of Fresnes Prison two months, and he's none too keen to find himself back inside. You might as well admit it, he was in the vicinity in a stolen car, and he covered your retreat by a dazzling display of clumsy driving.'

Maigret undressed, pausing from time to time to take a sip of beer. Disjointedly, he brought his wife up to date on the case.

'Those kids are as stubborn as they come . . . They have their own peculiar code of honour . . .'

He had ordered the arrest of three old lags, among them a man named Gaston Nouveau. As was only to be expected, he had a cast-iron alibi, having produced two witnesses ready to swear that, at the time of the hold-up, he was in a bar in the Avenue des Ternes.

There had been hours of fruitless interrogation. The eldest of the three motorcyclists, Victor Sidon, familiarly known as Granny because he was inclined to plumpness, kept darting sly glances at the Chief Superintendent. Saugier, nicknamed Squib, wept and denied all knowledge of the affair.

'Janvier and I decided that our best course was to concentrate on young Bauche. We sent for his mother, who pleaded with him:

'"Talk, Jeannot! Can't you see that these gentlemen are not out to get you? They know perfectly well that you were led astray . . ."'

Twenty hateful hours spent in leaning on a young lad, pushing him remorselessly to the limits of human endurance. It was not pleasant, either, to see him suddenly crack up without warning.

'Very well! I'll tell you everything. You were right, it was Nouveau who brought us together at the Lotus and set up the job.'

The Lotus was a small bar in the Rue Saint-Antoine, much frequented by teenagers, attracted by the music of the jukeboxes.

'And because of you, he'll have me beaten up by his mates the minute I get out of prison . . .'

At last! The end of the day. Maigret, his head aching, got into bed.

'What time do you have to be at the office?'

'Nine.'

'Couldn't you have a lie-in, just for once?'

'Wake me at eight.'

As far as he was concerned, there had been no interval. He felt as if he had not slept at all. It seemed to him that he had no sooner shut his eyes than the doorbell rang, and his wife was creeping out of bed to answer it.

He could hear whispering in the entrance lobby. The voice seemed familiar, but he thought he must be dreaming, and buried his face in his pillow.

He could hear his wife's footsteps approaching the bed. Would she get back into bed? Had someone rung their doorbell by mistake? No. She touched him on the shoulder, and drew the curtains. Without having to open his eyes, he realized that it was daylight. Drowsily, he asked:

'What time is it?'

'Seven.'

'Is there someone there?'

'It's Lapointe. He's waiting for you in the dining-room.'

'What does he want?'

'I don't know. Don't get out of bed yet. I'll bring you a cup of coffee.'

Why did his wife sound as if she had just had some bad news? Why hadn't she given him a straight answer to a straight question. The sky was a dirty grey, and it was still raining.

Maigret's first guess was that Jean Bauche, realizing with terror all that he had admitted, had hanged himself in his cell at the Préfecture. Without waiting for his coffee, Maigret slipped on his trousers, ran a comb through his hair and, still feeling fuddled, after having been woken from a deep sleep, went into the dining-room.

Lapointe was standing at the window, wearing a black overcoat and carrying a black hat. After a night on duty, his chin was bristly.

Maigret looked at him inquiringly.

'I'm so sorry, Chief, to disturb your sleep only to bring you bad news. Something happened last night . . . It concerns someone you're fond of . . .'

'Janvier?'

'No . . . It's not one of our own men . . .'

Madame Maigret came in, bearing two large cups of coffee.

'It's Lognon . . .'

'Is he dead?'

'No, but he's very seriously hurt. He's been taken to Bichat for an emergency operation. One of their top surgeons, Mingault, has been at work on him for the past three hours. Knowing what a heavy day you'd had yesterday, I felt you needed your rest. That's why I didn't come earlier or phone . . . Besides, at first they didn't think he had much chance of pulling through . . .'

'What happened to him?'

'He was shot twice, in the stomach and just below the shoulder blade . . .'

'Where did this happen?'

'On the pavement, in the Avenue Junot.'

'Was he alone?'

'Yes. For the time being, his colleagues in the 18th *arrondissement* are handling the case . . .'

Maigret was drinking his coffee in small sips. He was not enjoying it as much as he usually did.

'I thought you'd probably want to be there when he regained consciousness. I've got a car waiting downstairs . . .'

'Is anything more known about the incident?'

'Almost nothing. They don't even know what he was doing in the Avenue Junot. A concierge nearby heard the shots, and rang the police emergency number. A stray shot penetrated her shutters, shattering a window pane and lodging in the wall above her bed . . .'

'I'd better get dressed . . .'

He went into the bathroom. Madame Maigret was laying the breakfast, and Lapointe, having taken off his coat, was seated at the table.

Although Inspector Lognon, much as he had longed to be, was not a member of the Crime Squad, nevertheless he and Maigret had often worked together, almost every time, in fact, that a sensational case had come up in the 18th *arrondissement*. He was what is popularly known as a plain-clothes detective, one of twenty plain-clothes inspectors with headquarters in the Town Hall of Montmartre, on the corner of the Rue Caulaincourt and the Rue du Mont-Cenis.

He was known to some as Inspector Grumpy, because of his churlish manner, but Maigret had nicknamed him Inspector Hapless, for it seemed to him that poor Lognon had a positive gift for bringing upon himself every kind of misfortune.

He was small and thin, and never without a head-cold from one year's end to the next, so that, in spite of being probably the most abstemious man in the Force, he looked, with his red nose and watering eyes, the very picture of a drunkard.

He was afflicted with an ailing wife, who spent her time trailing between her bed and an armchair near the window, so that Lognon, when he went off duty, was burdened with the housework, the shopping and the cooking. He could just about afford to pay a cleaning woman to turn out the rooms once a week.

He had sat the competitive examination for admission to the Police Judiciaire on four separate occasions, and he had failed each time, through some trivial slip or omission. And yet he was outstandingly good at his job, a sort of bloodhound who, once he was on the scent, would never give up. He was stubborn and punctilious to a fault. He was one of those men who had only to pass a dubious character in the street to sense that something was amiss.

'Is there any hope of saving his life?'

'Apparently the doctors at Bichat think he has a thirty per cent chance.'

As applied to a man who had earned the nickname of Hapless, this was not very encouraging.

'Was he able to speak?'

Maigret, his wife and Lapointe were eating the croissants which had just been delivered to the door by the baker's boy.

'No one in his section mentioned it, and I didn't want to press them for information.'

Lognon was not the only one with an inferiority complex. Most of the District Inspectors keep a wary eye on the Big House, as they call the Quai des Orfèvres, and when they are on to anything important which is likely to hit the headlines, they hate having it taken away from them.

'Let's go,' sighed Maigret, putting on his coat, which was still damp from the previous night.

He caught his wife's eye, and knew that there was something she wanted to say to him. He guessed that she had just been struck with the same idea as he had.

'Do you think you'll be in to lunch?'

'I very much doubt it.'

'In that case, don't you think . . . ?'

She was thinking of Madame Lognon, alone and helpless in her flat.

'Hurry up and get dressed! We'll drop you at the Place Constantin-Pecqueur.'

The Lognons had lived there for the past twenty years, in a red brick building with a surround of yellow brick to every window. Maigret could not recall the number of the house.

Lapointe sat at the wheel of the little Police Judiciaire car. Only twice in as many years had Madame Maigret driven with her husband in one of these cars.

They drove past crowded buses. On the pavements, people were hurrying along, leaning forward and clutching their umbrellas, for fear that they should be snatched away by the wind.

They reached the Rue Caulaincourt in Montmartre.

'This is it.'

In the middle of the square stood a stone sculpture of a man and a woman. The woman was swathed in drapery, but for one exposed breast. On the side where it had been lashed by the rain, the figure was black.

'Give me a ring at the office. I hope to be back there before lunch.'

Having barely had time to complete one case, he was now embarked on another, about which as yet he knew nothing. He was fond of Lognon. Often, in his official reports, he had stressed his good qualities, and had even gone so far as to attribute to Lognon successes which were really his own. All to no avail. Poor old Inspector Hapless!

'Bichat Hospital first . . .'

A staircase. Corridors. Open doors, revealing rows of beds, from which rows of eyes stared at the two strangers as they went past.

They had been misdirected, and so were forced to return downstairs to the courtyard and go up another staircase, where at last they found, on guard outside a door marked 'Surgical Wing', an inspector from the 18th *arrondissement* whom they knew. His name was Créac, and there was an unlit cigarette between his lips.

'I think you'd be wise to put your pipe away, Chief Superintendent. There's a right dragon in there, and she'll come down on you like a ton of bricks, as she did on me when I tried to light my cigarette . . .'

Nurses were going to and fro, carrying enamel jugs and bowls, and trays loaded with little bottles and nickel-plated surgical instruments.

'Is he still in the operating theatre?'

The time was a quarter to nine.

'They've been at work on him up there since four o'clock this morning.'

'Have you heard anything?'

'I went into that office over there on the left to inquire, but the old bag . . .'

It was the Matron's office, and the Matron, according to Créac, was a dragon. Maigret knocked at the door. An unfriendly voice called out to him to come in.

'What do you want?'

'I'm sorry to disturb you, madame. I am the Chief Superintendent in charge of the Crime Squad of the Police Judiciaire . . .'

Her frigid stare said 'What of it?' as plainly as if she had spoken aloud.

'I was wondering if you could tell me how the Inspector is standing up to the operation.'

'I shan't know until the operation is over . . . All I can say is that he is alive, seeing that the surgeon is still in there . . .'

'When he was brought in, was he able to talk?'

This time she looked at him with contempt, as if he had asked a stupid question.

'He'd lost more than half the blood in his body. He had to be given an emergency transfusion.'

'How long before he regains consciousness, do you think?'

'You'll have to ask Professor Mingault.'

'If you have a private room available, I'd be obliged if you would keep it for him. It's important. An inspector will be in attendance at his bedside . . .'

Her attention was distracted by the opening of the door of the operating theatre. A man appeared in the passage, wearing a white cap and a bloodstained apron over his white overall.

'Professor, this person here is . . .'

'Chief Superintendent Maigret . . .'

'Pleased to meet you.'

'Is he still alive?'

'For the moment . . . Unless there are unforeseen complications, I hope to be able to pull him through.'

His forehead was running with perspiration, and his features drawn with fatigue.

'Just one more thing . . . It's important to us that he should have a private room . . .'

'See to that, please, Matron . . . Now, if you'll excuse me . . .'

He strode off towards his office. Once again, the door opened. A surgical bed on wheels appeared, propelled by an orderly. Under the sheet could be traced the outline of a body, Lognon's body, stiff and drained of blood, with only the upper part of his face showing.

'Take him to number 218, Bernard.'

'Very good, Matron.'

She walked behind the bed, with Maigret, Lapointe and Créac close on her heels. It was a dismal procession, in the wan morning light coming from windows high above them. The sight of the straight rows of beds in the wards as they went past was scarcely cheering. It was like living through a bad dream.

A house-surgeon emerged from the operating theatre and tagged on behind.

'Are you a member of his family?'

'No . . . I'm Chief Superintendent Maigret . . .'

'Ah! So it is you!'

He looked at him searchingly, as if anxious to confirm that the Chief Superintendent really did look as he had imagined him to be.

'The Professor says there's a chance that he may pull through . . .'

It was a world apart, where voices lacked the resonance normal elsewhere, a world without echoes.

'If he said so . . .'

'Have you any idea how long it will be before he regains consciousness?'

Was Maigret's question so absurd that he deserved such a look as he got? The Matron stopped the police officers at the door.

'No. Not now.'

The wounded man had to be made comfortable and no doubt given treatment, since two nurses were wheeling in a variety of equipment, including an oxygen tent.

'You can wait out here, if you insist, but I'd rather you didn't. There are regular visiting hours.'

Maigret glanced at his watch.

'I think I'd better be on my way, Créac. I'd like you to be present, if possible, when he regains consciousness. If he's able to talk, take down verbatim everything he says.'

He did not feel humiliated. No. All the same, he was a little ill-at-ease, not being accustomed to such disrespectful treatment. With these people, whose attitude to life and death was different from that of the ordinary man, his reputation cut no ice.

It was a relief, outside in the forecourt, to be able to light his pipe. Lapointe, at the same time, took the opportunity to light a cigarette.

'As for you, you'd better go home to bed, after you've dropped me at the Town Hall in the 18th *arrondissement*.'

'Would you mind very much if I stayed with you, Chief?'

'You were up all night . . .'

'Oh! Well, you know, at my age . . .'

The Town Hall was no distance away. In the Inspectors' Duty Room, there were three plain-clothes detectives engaged in writing reports. Crouching over their typewriters, they looked a thoroughly conscientious bunch.

'Good morning, gentlemen . . . Which of you is conversant with the facts?'

He knew them, too, if not by name, at least by sight, and all three had stood up as he came into the room.

'All of us, and none of us . . .'

'Has anyone been to break the news to Madame Lognon?'

'Durantel is attending to it.'

There were damp footmarks on the wooden floor, and a lingering smell of tobacco smoke about the place.

'Was Lognon on to something?'

They looked at him, hesitating. At last, one of the three, a small fat man, began:

'That's just the question we've been asking ourselves . . . You know Lognon, Chief Superintendent . . . He had a way of making a mystery of it when he was on the trail of something . . . Often he would work for weeks on a case before saying a word about it to any of us . . .'

And no wonder, considering the number of times others had been given the credit for his achievements!

'He's been very secretive for the past fortnight at least. And sometimes, when he came into the office, he looked as if he was working up to something big, that he intended to spring on us as a terrific surprise.'

'Did he drop any hints?'

'No. But he had himself transferred more or less permanently to night duty . . .'

'Do you know where he spent his time?'

'He was seen once or twice by the night patrols in the Avenue Junot, not far from the spot where he was attacked . . . But not recently . . . He used to leave here about nine at night, and wouldn't get back until three or four in the morning . . . Sometimes he would be out all night . . .'

'Didn't he put in any reports?'

'I've looked in the register. He just wrote "Nothing to report".'

'Have you any men at the scene of the shooting?'

'Three. Chinquier is in charge.'

'What about the press?'

'It's not easy to hush up an attempt on the life of a detective inspector . . . Would you like a word with the Superintendent?'

'Not just now . . .'

With Lapointe still at the wheel, Maigret had himself driven to the Avenue Junot. The last of the autumn leaves were falling from the trees and sticking to the wet pavements. The rain, which was still pelting down, had not deterred a crowd of about fifty people from gathering in the middle of the road.

A square section of the pavement had been cordoned off, and there were uniformed policemen on guard. When Maigret got out of the car to thread his way among spectators and umbrellas, cameras clicked all around him.

'Just one more, Chief Superintendent . . . Could you move forward a little?'

He glared at them as balefully as the Matron had glared at him in the hospital. On the small stretch of pavement protected from trampling feet, the rain had not entirely washed out the blood-stains, though they were gradually being diluted, and, since it had not been possible to use chalk, the position of the fallen body had been outlined with twigs.

Inspector Deliot, yet another member of the 18th *arrondissement* Division, removed his sopping hat in deference to Maigret.

'Chinquier is inside, talking to the concierge, Chief Superintendent. He was the first of us to arrive on the scene.'

The building was fairly old, but very clean and well maintained. The Chief Superintendent went in and pushed open the glass door of the lodge, just in time to see Inspector Chinquier putting his notebook back in his pocket.

'I was expecting you. I was surprised to find no one here from the Quai.'

'I went to the hospital first.'

'How did the operation go?'

'Quite successfully, I gather. The professor thinks he may pull through.'

The lodge was clean and neat. The concierge, aged about forty-five, was still an attractive woman, with a pleasing figure.

'Please sit down, gentlemen . . . I've just been telling the Inspector everything I know . . . Look over here, on the floor . . .'

The green linoleum was strewn with slivers of glass from a broken window pane.

'And here . . .'

She pointed to a hole about three feet above the bed, which stood at the far end of the room.

'Were you alone in here?'

'Yes. My husband is night porter at the Palace Hotel in the Avenue des Champs-Élysées. He doesn't get back here until eight in the morning.'

'Where is he now?'

'In the kitchen.'

She pointed to a closed door.

'He's trying to get some rest, because, in spite of everything, he'll have to go on duty tonight as usual.'

'I am taking it for granted, Chinquier, that you have asked all the necessary questions. So don't be offended if I ask a few questions of my own.'

'Will you be needing me?'

'Not for the moment.'

'In that case, if you don't mind, I'll take a look round upstairs.'

Maigret frowned, wondering what the Inspector had in mind to do up there, but he didn't pursue the point for fear of causing offence to the local man.

'I'm sorry to have to bother you, madame . . .'

'Madame Sauget. The tenants all call me Angèle.'

'Do please sit down.'

'I'm so used to standing!'

She drew the curtain across the bed. It was usually kept closed during the day, thus turning the main area into a small sitting-room.

'Can I get you anything? A cup of coffee?'

'Thank you, no. So, last night, after you went to bed . . .'

'Yes, I heard a voice call out: "Please release the catch."'

'Did you notice the time?'

'My alarm clock has a luminous dial. It was twenty past two.'

'Was it one of the tenants asking to be let out?'

'No. It was that gentleman . . .'

She looked embarrassed, as if she felt she had been trapped into committing an indiscretion.

'What gentleman?'

'The one who was shot at . . .'

Maigret and Lapointe exchanged bewildered glances.

'Inspector Lognon, do you mean?'

She nodded, and went on: 'One shouldn't keep anything back from the police, should one? I'm not one to gossip about my tenants, as a rule. I never talk about their comings and goings, or the company they keep. Their private lives are no concern of mine. But after what has happened . . .'

'Have you known the Inspector long?'

'Yes, for years . . . Ever since my husband and I came here to live . . . But I didn't know his name . . . I used to see him go past, and I knew he was a police officer, because he came into the lodge a few times on identity checks . . . He never said much . . .'

'When did you get to know him better?'

'When he started coming in to call on the young lady on the fourth floor.'

This time Maigret was struck speechless. As for Lapointe, he looked as if he had been hit over the head. Not all policemen are necessarily saints. Maigret knew that there were men in his own section who were not above indulging in extra-marital adventures.

But Lognon! He just could not imagine old Hapless slinking out at night to visit a young woman in a building barely two hundred yards from his own flat!

'You're quite sure we're talking about the same man?'

'He's not the sort you'd forget in a hurry, is he?'

'How long has he been in the habit of . . . calling on the lady?'

'About ten days.'

'I take it, then, that the first evening, he came in with her?'

'Yes.'

'Did he try to hide his face as he went past the lodge?'

'That was the impression I got.'

'Did he come back often?'

'Almost every night.'

'Was it very late when he left?'

'At the beginning, that's to say the first three or four nights, he left round about midnight . . . After that he stayed longer, until two or three in the morning.'

'What is this woman's name?'

'Marinette . . . Marinette Augier . . . She's a very pretty girl. She's about twenty-five, and ladylike in her manners.'

'Was she in the habit of entertaining men?'

'I think I can answer that with a clear conscience, because she never made any secret of her private life . . . For a whole year, a handsome young man used to visit her two or three times a week. She told me they were engaged . . .'

'Used he to spend the night with her?'

'You're bound to find out in the end . . . Yes . . . After he stopped coming, she looked sad, I thought . . . One morning, when she called in to collect her mail, I asked her if the engagement was broken off, and she said: "You're a good soul, Angèle, but I don't want to talk about it. It's no good upsetting oneself over a man. They just aren't worth it."

'She must have succeeded in putting him out of her mind, because not long afterwards she was her old, cheerful self again . . . She's a very lively girl, and bursting with health.'

'What does she do for a living?'

'She's a cosmetician, so she tells me. She works in a beauty salon in the Avenue Matignon . . . That probably explains why she is always so well groomed and tastefully dressed . . .'

'What about her boyfriend?'

'The fiancé who stopped coming? He was in his thirties. I don't know what his occupation was. I don't even know his surname. I always called him Monsieur Henri, because that was how he announced himself, when he went past the lodge at night.'

'When was the relationship broken off?'

'Last winter, round about Christmas.'

'Which means that for nearly a year, this young woman . . . What's her name . . . ? Marinette . . . ?'

'Marinette Augier.'

'Are you, then, saying that for the best part of a year she has had no one up there with her?'

'Except for an occasional visit from her brother. He lives in the suburbs somewhere, and he's married, with three children.'

'And about a fortnight ago, she came home one evening in company with Inspector Lognon?'

'As I have already told you.'

'And since then, he's been here every night?'

'Except Sundays, unless he managed to slip in and out without my seeing him.'

'Did he never come during the day?'

'No, but I've just thought of something. One evening, when he arrived as usual at nine o'clock, I ran after him as he was starting to go upstairs, and called out: "Marinette isn't in!"

'"I know," he said. "She's at her brother's."

'But he went on up just the same, without explanation, which, now I think of it, suggests that she had lent him her key.'

Maigret now understood why Inspector Chinquier had gone up there.

'Is your tenant in her flat now?'

'No.'

'Has she gone to work?'

'I don't know, but when I went up to break the news to her as gently as I could . . .'

'What time was this?'

'After I had telephoned for the police . . .'

'In other words, round about three in the morning?'

'Yes . . . I thought she couldn't have failed to hear the shots . . . All the other tenants did . . . Some were leaning out of their windows . . . Others were coming down the stairs in their dressing-gowns, to find out what was going on . . .

'It wasn't a pretty sight, what was out there in the street . . . So I ran upstairs, and knocked at her door . . . There was no answer . . . I went in, and found the flat empty . . .'

She gave the Chief Superintendent a somewhat smug look, as if to say: 'I dare say you've come across a good many peculiar things in the course of your career, but I defy you to cap this!'

She was right. All Maigret and Lapointe could do was to gape blankly at one another. Maigret thought of his wife, who, at this very moment, was with Madame Lognon, whose christian name was Solange, offering consolation, and doubtless doing all the housework for her!

'Could she have left the building at the same time as he did?'

'I'm sure she didn't. I have very sharp ears, and I'm certain only one person went out, and that was a man.'

'Did he call out his name as he went past?'

'No. He was in the habit of simply saying: "Fourth floor."

'I recognized his voice. And besides, he was the only one to announce himself in that way.'

'Could she have gone out before he arrived?'

'No. I only once released the catch last night, at 11.30, to let in the third-floor tenants, who had been to see a film.'

'So she must have gone out after the shots were fired?'

'It's the only possible explanation. As soon as I saw the body lying on the pavement, I rushed back here to ring Police Emergency . . . I was reluctant to shut the front door. I couldn't . . . I would have felt I was deserting the poor man . . .'

'Did you bend over him, to see if he was dead?'

'It was dreadful . . . I have a horror of blood, but I did.'

'Was he conscious?'

'I don't know . . .'

'Did he say anything?'

'His lips were moving . . . I could see he was trying to speak . . . I thought I caught just one word, but I must have been mistaken, because it doesn't make sense . . . Maybe he was delirious.'

'What was the word?'

'Ghost . . .'

She flushed, obviously fearful lest the Chief Superintendent and the Inspector should laugh at her, or accuse her of romancing.

2

Lunch at Chez Manière

One might have been forgiven for thinking that the man had chosen this particular moment in order to create the maximum dramatic effect. Had he, perhaps, been listening at the door? Scarcely had the word 'ghost' been spoken than the doorknob was seen to turn, the door to open a crack, and a head without a body to appear through the gap.

The face was pale, the features indeterminate, the eyelids and mouth drooping. It took Maigret a second or two to realize that the man's lugubrious expression was largely due to the absence of dentures.

'Why aren't you asleep, Raoul?'

And, as if they didn't know, she introduced him: 'My husband, Chief Superintendent.'

He was much older than she, and was wearing a hideous purple dressing-gown over crumpled pyjamas.

In his gold-braided uniform, behind his desk at the Palace Hotel, he might pass muster, but here and now, unshaven, his body slumped, and wearing the peevish look of one who has been deprived of sleep, he seemed both ludicrous and pathetic.

With a cup of coffee in his hand, he acknowledged Maigret's presence with a vague nod, and then turned his gaze towards the lace window-curtains, beyond which could be seen a mass of dark shapes, gathered together in the still persisting rain, in spite of the efforts of the uniformed constables to hold them back.

'How long is this going on?' he groaned.

Sleep, which he needed and had a right to, was being denied him, and, to look at him, one might have supposed that he was the true victim in the case.

'Why don't you take one of those pills the doctor prescribed?'

'They give me stomach-ache.'

He retired into a corner, sat down, and began drinking his coffee, his slippers dangling from his bare feet. During the remainder of the interview, he never once opened his mouth, except to emit a sigh.

'I'd be grateful, madame, if you would try and remember in detail exactly what happened from the time when you were asked to release the catch.'

Why such an attractive woman should have married a man at least twenty years older than herself was no concern of his. Presumably, at that time she had never seen him without his dentures.

'I heard someone call out: "Please release the catch."

'And then the same voice, which I knew well, added: "Fourth floor!"

'As I have already told you, I looked at the clock automatically. It is a habit with me. It was half-past two. I put out my hand to press the button. There's no cord to pull nowadays, as there used to be, just an electrically operated catch.

'It was just then that I thought I heard a car engine, as if a car had drawn up, not in front of this building but the one next door, leaving the engine running. I actually thought it was the Hardsins, who live next door and often get home very late.

'It all happened so quickly, you see. I heard Monsieur Lognon's footsteps in the hall. Then the door banged. Immediately after that the engine revved up, the car moved off, and three shots were fired, one after the other . . .

'The third shot seemed to go off right inside the lodge itself, what with the shock of the impact on the shutter, the shattering of the glass, and the strange noise above my head . . .'

'What happened to the car? Did it drive on? You're sure there was a car?'

The husband, with lowered head, looked at each of them in turn, while at the same time absently stirring his coffee.

'I'm quite sure. The street is on a slope. To go up it, cars have to accelerate. That particular car roared away at full tilt, in the direction of the Rue Norvins . . .'

'Do you remember hearing anyone cry out?'

'No. At first, I was so scared I couldn't move. But you know what we women are. We just have to know, to find out what's going on. I switched on the light, grabbed my dressing-gown, and rushed out into the hall.'

'Was the street door shut?'

'I told you, I heard it slam. I pressed my ear against it, but I could hear nothing but the rain. Then I opened it a crack, and saw the body lying barely six feet away.'

'Which way was it facing? Up or down the street?'

'It looked as if he'd been making for the Rue Caulaincourt. The poor soul was clutching his stomach with both hands, and his fingers were dripping with blood. His eyes were open, and he stared at me fixedly.'

'And you went out and bent over him, and it was then that you heard or thought you heard the word "ghost". Is that right?'

'I could swear that was what he said. Windows were flung open. There are no private telephones in the flats. All the tenants have to use the one in the lodge. Two of them have been on the waiting list for a phone of their own for over a year.

'I went indoors, and looked up the police emergency number in the telephone book. One ought to carry a number like that in one's head, but one doesn't think of these things, especially in a respectable place like this . . .'

'Was there a light on in the hall?'

'No. Only in my lodge. The policeman asked me several questions, to satisfy himself that it wasn't a hoax, so that it took some time . . .'

The telephone was fixed to the wall. Anyone using it would not be able to see out into the hall.

'Some of the tenants had come downstairs . . . But I've told you all that . . . It wasn't until I had replaced the receiver that I thought of Marinette, and rushed up to the fourth floor . . .'

'I'm much obliged to you. I wonder if I might use your telephone?'

Maigret rang through to Headquarters.

'Hello! Is that you, Lucas . . . ? I dare say you've seen Lapointe's note about Lognon . . . ? No, I'm not ringing from the hospital . . .

They can't say for sure yet whether he's going to pull through . . . I'm in the Avenue Junot . . . I want you to go to Bichat . . . Yes, in person, if you can manage it . . . You'd better pull rank for all you're worth, because the people there haven't much time for interlopers.

'Try and have a word with the house-surgeon who was present during the operation. I don't suppose Professor Mingault will be available at this hour . . . I presume they've extracted at least one bullet, if not both . . . Yes . . . I'd like to have as many details as possible, in advance of the official report . . . As to the bullets, you'd better get them straight off to the Lab . . .'

Formerly, this sort of work was done by an outside consultant, a man called Gastienne-Renette, but the Police Judiciaire now had their own ballistics expert in the Forensic Laboratory, up in the attics of the Palais de Justice.

'I'll be seeing you later this morning or in the early afternoon . . .'

The Chief Superintendent turned to Lapointe.

'Don't you think you really ought to go home to bed?'

'I don't feel in the least sleepy, Chief . . .'

The night porter of the Palace Hotel gave him a look of mingled envy and reproof.

'In that case, off with you to the Avenue Matignon. It shouldn't be too difficult to locate the beauty salon where Marinette Augier works . . . There can't be all that many of them . . . I shouldn't think there's much hope of finding her there . . . Try and find out all you can about her . . .'

'Very good, Chief.'

'As for me, I'm going upstairs . . .'

Maigret was a little annoyed with himself for not having thought of the bullets earlier, when he was actually at the hospital. But this was not just any ordinary case. Somehow, because it concerned Lognon, it had assumed the character almost of a private investigation.

While he was there, his thoughts were almost wholly occupied with the Inspector, and he had allowed himself to be overawed by the Matron, the Professor and the wards full of rows of watching patients.

There was no lift in the building in the Avenue Junot. There was no stair-carpet either, but the wooden treads, worn smooth by use, were well polished, and the banisters gleamed. There were two flats to each floor, and beside some of the doors brass plates could be seen, inscribed with the names of the tenants.

When he reached the fourth floor, he found the door ajar. He pushed it open, and crossed a rather dark entrance lobby leading to a living-room, where he found Inspector Chinquier smoking a cigarette in an armchair covered in flowered chintz.

'I've been expecting you . . . Has she told you all about it?'

'Yes.'

'Did she mention the car . . . ? That's what struck me the most . . . Take a look at this . . .'

He stood up, and took from his pocket three shining, spent cartridges, which he had wrapped in a scrap of newspaper.

'We found these in the road . . . If the shots were fired from a moving car, as seems likely, then the man who fired them must have held his arm out through the window . . . As you will have noticed, they're ·763s . . .'

Chinquier was a conscientious police officer, and knew his job.

'The weapon was probably a Mauser automatic, a heavy gun, that, which couldn't be slipped into a handbag or a trouser pocket . . . Do you see what I'm getting at? Everything points to a pro, and he must have had at least one accomplice, because he couldn't possibly drive and aim at the same time. A jealous lover wouldn't be likely to rope in a pal to help him get rid of a rival . . . And besides, Lognon was shot in the stomach.'

A marksman would indeed stand a better chance by aiming at the stomach rather than the chest, for the victim seldom recovers with his intestines perforated in a dozen places by a large-calibre bullet.

'Have you been round the flat?'

'I'd be glad if you would have a look round yourself.'

There was another aspect of this case that made Maigret uneasy. It was the local inspectors themselves who had handled it in its early stages. They might not have thought much of Lognon when he was able to stand on his own two feet, but he was still their colleague, and now the victim of attempted murder. In such circumstances, the Chief Superintendent could scarcely elbow them out of the way and take charge himself.

'Quite a pleasant room, don't you think?'

On a bright day, no doubt, it would be even pleasanter. The walls were painted a vivid yellow, the floor was highly polished and spread with a paler yellow carpet. The furniture, more or less contemporary in design, was tastefully chosen. The room, which served both as a sitting-room and dining-room, was equipped with every comfort, including a television set and a record player.

The first thing Maigret had noticed on coming in was the table in the centre of the room, on which stood an electric percolator, a cup with a little coffee left in it, a sugar basin and a bottle of brandy.

'Only one cup,' he mumbled. 'You haven't touched it, have you, Chinquier? You'd better ring the Quai, and ask them to send along some of the forensic chaps . . .'

He had not taken off his coat, and he now put his hat back on his head. One of the armchairs was turned to face the window, and beside it stood a small occasional table, with an ashtray containing seven or eight cigarette stubs.

There were two doors opening off the living-room. One led into the kitchen, which was clean and neat, and looked more like an Ideal Homes set-up than the sort of kitchen usually to be found in old buildings in Paris.

The other door opened on to the bedroom. The bed was unmade. The pillow, the only pillow, still showed the dent where a head had lain.

A pale blue dressing-gown was carelessly thrown over the back of a chair, the jacket of a matching pair of women's pyjamas lay in a heap on the floor, and the trousers against the wardrobe.

Chinquier was back already.

'I've had a word with Moers on the phone. His men are on their way. Have you had time to look around? Have you seen inside the wardrobe?'

'Not yet . . .'

He opened it. There were five dresses on hangers, a fur-trimmed winter coat and two tailored suits, one beige, the other navy.

There were suitcases stacked in a row on the top shelf.

'Do you see what I'm getting at? It doesn't look as if she's taken any luggage with her. And if you look in the chest of drawers, you'll find all her underwear tidily folded away.'

From the window could be seen quite an extensive view of Paris, but today in particular the grey sky, dripping rain, dominated the buildings. Beyond the bed was a door leading to a bathroom. Nothing was missing there either, not even a toothbrush or any beauty preparations.

If the flat were anything to go by, Marinette Augier was a home-loving girl, with excellent taste and a liking for her creature comforts.

'I forgot to ask the concierge whether she did her own cooking, or went out for her meals,' admitted Maigret.

'I asked about that. She almost always had her meals here . . .'

The refrigerator contained, among other things, half a cold chicken, a quantity of butter and cheese, some fruit, two bottles of beer and one of mineral water. There was another bottle, opened, on the bedside table.

But of greater interest to the Chief Superintendent was an ashtray, also on the bedside table, containing two cigarette stubs stained with lipstick.

'She smoked American cigarettes . . .'

'Whereas the stubs in the living-room are all Caporals. Is that what you're getting at?'

The two men exchanged glances. They had both been struck with the same thought.

'If the state of the bed means anything, it couldn't have been used for any amorous frolics last night . . .'

In spite of the tragic circumstances, Maigret had difficulty in suppressing a smile at the thought of Inspector Grumpy in a clinch with a lovely young beauty consultant.

Had they quarrelled? Had Lognon stumped off into the other room to sulk and chain-smoke, leaving his mistress alone in bed?

There was something that didn't quite ring true in all this, and, once again, Maigret was reminded that from the beginning he had not approached the problem with his usual clear-headedness.

'I'm sorry to have to ask you to go downstairs again, Chinquier, but there's just one thing I forgot to ask the concierge. Could you find out whether, when she came up here, she found the light on in the living-room?'

'I can tell you that. The bedroom door was open, and there was a light on in there, but the rest of the flat was in darkness.'

Together, they went back into the living-room, with its two french windows opening on to a balcony which ran right round the building, a common feature of the top storeys of so many old buildings in Paris.

In spite of the overcast sky, it was still just possible to see, in misty outline, the Eiffel Tower above the gleaming wet slates of hundreds of rooftops, with a smoking chimney here and there.

Maigret remembered the Avenue Junot as it had been at the start of his career. It had scarcely been an avenue then, with only a few large buildings, interspersed with gardens and patches of waste ground. The first person to build a private house there had been a painter, and daringly modern it had seemed at the time!

Others followed his lead, among them a novelist and an opera singer, and before long the Avenue Junot had developed into a fashionable address.

Standing at the french windows, the Chief Superintendent looked down, and observed that many of the houses below were squeezed right up against each other. The one opposite, judging from the architecture, must have been about fifteen years old. It was built on three floors.

Was it the home of a painter? The top floor, built almost entirely of glass, seemed to suggest it. Dark curtains had been drawn across these picture windows, leaving a gap of no more than eighteen inches.

If anyone had asked the Chief Superintendent what he was thinking about, he would have been hard put to it to reply. He was simply registering impressions. Haphazardly, as they struck him. At times he stared out of the windows, at other times he roamed about the flat. Sooner or later, he knew, all these impressions would coalesce and become meaningful.

He could hear sounds, traffic in the streets, heavy footsteps on the stairs, voices, banging. The team from the Forensic Laboratory had arrived with their equipment, led by Moers, who had taken the trouble to come in person.

'Where's the body?' he asked, his blue eyes, as usual, looking a little puzzled behind the thick lenses of his spectacles.

'There is no body. Hasn't Chinquier put you in the picture?'

'I didn't want to waste time . . .' explained the local Inspector apologetically.

'It concerns Lognon. He was shot just as he was leaving this building . . .'

'Is he dead?'

'He's been taken to Bichat. There's just a chance that he may pull through. He spent part of last night in this flat with a woman. I'd very much like to know whether he left any prints in the bedroom, besides those you will find in here. Fingerprint everything you can. Are you coming down with me, Chinquier?'

He waited until they were in the hall on the ground floor to murmur softly: 'It might be as well to find out what the other tenants and the neighbours have to say. It's not very likely that any of them were leaning out of their windows when the shots were fired. Not in this weather. But you never can tell.

'The girl Marinette may have taken a taxi, in which case it shouldn't be too difficult to trace the driver. She probably went down the street towards the Place Constantin-Pecqueur, where there are fewer taxis than there are at the top of the hill . . . You and your colleagues know the district better than I do . . .'

Shaking Chinquier by the hand, he sighed: 'The best of luck to you!'

And he pushed open the glass door of the lodge. The husband, it seemed, had at last decided to go to bed, judging from the sound of steady breathing coming from behind the curtain.

'Is there anything more I can do to help?' murmured Angèle Sauget.

'No. I want to make a phone call, but I won't do it from here. I don't want to disturb his sleep.'

'You mustn't think too badly of him. When he doesn't get his regular hours of sleep, he's impossible. I've given him a sleeping pill, and it's just started to work.'

'If anything comes back to you that you have forgotten to tell me, be sure and ring me at the Quai des Orfèvres.'

'I doubt if anything will, but if it does, I promise I'll let you know. If only those wretched reporters and photographers would go away! They're the ones that are drawing the crowds . . .'

'I'll see if I can get them to move further off.'

As was only to be expected, in spite of the attempts of the policemen to hold them back, they mobbed him the minute he set foot outside the door.

'May I have your attention, gentlemen! At this stage of the case, I know no more than you do. Inspector Lognon was attacked by persons unknown, in the execution of his duty . . .'

'Duty?' someone called out, waggishly.

'I said in the execution of his duty, and I repeat it. He was gravely wounded, and has been operated on by Professor Mingault at Bichat Hospital. However, he is not likely to be in any condition to talk for some hours, possibly even for some days.

'Until that time, there is no point in speculating. In any case, there is nothing more to see here. However, if you care to call at the Quai des Orfèvres this afternoon, I may have further news for you . . .'

'What was the Inspector doing inside the building? Is it true that a young woman has disappeared?'

'See you this afternoon!'

'Have you nothing more to say?'

'I've told you all I know.'

With his collar turned up and his hands in his pockets, he plodded away down the avenue. Two or three clicks told him that, for want of a better subject, they were photographing him from behind, and, when he looked back, the pressmen were beginning to disperse.

When he reached the Rue Caulaincourt, he went into the first bistro he came to, and, because he felt a little shivery, ordered a hot toddy.

'Would you be so good as to let me have three telephone *jetons*?'

'Did you say three?'

He gulped down a generous mouthful of his toddy before going into the telephone box. His first call was to the hospital. As he had expected, he was switched from one extension to another, before being put on to the Matron of the Surgical Wing.

'No, he's not dead. One of our house physicians is with him at present, and one of your inspectors is waiting outside in the corridor. There is still no firm prognosis. Ah! here's another of your men just coming into my office . . .'

Resignedly, he hung up, and dialled the number of Police Headquarters.

'Has Lapointe come in yet?'

'He's been trying to reach you at the Avenue Junot. I'll put him on to you.'

Through the glass panes of the box Maigret could see the zinc counter, and the proprietor in his shirtsleeves pouring two large glasses of red wine for a couple of workmen.

'Are you there, Chief? I had no difficulty in finding the beauty salon, as it's the only one in the Avenue Matignon. It's very luxurious. Apparently, there's a man working there of the name of Marcellin, whom all the ladies speak of with bated breath . . . Marinette Augier didn't come into work today, which surprised her colleagues, as she is usually so very punctual and conscientious . . .

'She never confided in anyone about her relationship with the Inspector . . . She has a married brother, who lives in Vanves, but they don't know his address. He works for an insurance company, and Marinette sometimes used to phone him at his office. The firm is the Fraternal Assurance . . . I looked it up in the telephone book . . . It has offices in the Rue Le Peletier . . .

'I thought I ought to ask you before going there . . .'

'Is Janvier there?'

'He's busy typing a report.'

'Ask him if it's urgent. I'm most anxious that you should get some rest, so that you'll be fresh when I need you . . .'

A brief silence at the end of the line. Then Lapointe's voice, sounding resigned: 'He says it's not urgent.'

'In that case, put him in the picture, will you? I want him to go to the Rue Le Peletier and see if he can get a lead on where Marinette might be hiding herself . . .'

The little café was filling up, mostly with regulars. They were served with their usual drinks, without having to order. Several of the customers had recognized him, and were darting inquisitive glances towards the glassed-in phone box.

He had to look up Lognon's number. As he had expected, it was Madame Maigret who answered.

'Where are you?' she asked.

'Shh! . . . For heaven's sake, don't tell her that I'm within a few yards of her flat. How is she?'

His wife hesitated. He could guess why.

'I suppose she's in bed, and feeling worse than her husband?'

'Yes.'

'Have you got a meal ready for her?'

'I had to go out and do some shopping first.'

'So she can be left?'

'Not if she can help it!'

'Whether she likes it or not, tell her I need you here, and meet me as soon as you can at Chez Manière . . .'

'Are you inviting me out to lunch?'

She could scarcely believe her ears. They did occasionally go out for dinner at the weekend, but hardly ever for lunch, and certainly not when he was busy on a case.

The Chief Superintendent, returning to the bar to finish his drink, noticed that the spontaneity had gone out of the voices around him. This was the price of all the publicity foisted on him by the press, and which was so often a handicap in his work.

Someone, avoiding his eye, said: 'Is it true that Old Grumpy has been shot by gangsters?'

Another voice, deliberately trying to sound mysterious, replied:

'If it really was gangsters.'

So, rumours were already rife in the district regarding the Inspector's relationship with Marinette. Maigret paid for his drink and, with all eyes upon him, went out of the bistro, and made his way to Chez Manière.

It was a brasserie, adjacent to a flight of stone steps. It had once been a popular haunt of local celebrities, and was still patronized by actresses, writers and painters. It was too early for the regulars to show up. Most of the tables were vacant, and there were not more than four or five customers leaning on the bar.

He took off his wet coat and hat, and collapsed with a sigh of relief on to the bench nearest the window.

Looking about him dreamily, he lit his pipe, and had smoked it almost to the end when he spotted Madame Maigret, holding her umbrella like a shield, crossing the road.

'It feels so strange, meeting you like this . . . It must be at least fifteen years since we were here last . . . It was one evening, after the theatre . . . Do you remember?'

'Yes . . . What will you have?'

He handed her the menu.

'I don't need to ask what you're going to have . . . It will be the *andouillette* I'm sure . . . I wonder if I might venture to let myself go, and have lobster mayonnaise?'

They sat in silence until the hors d'oeuvre and a bottle of Loire wine were brought to the table. The atmosphere was intimate, with the windows misted, and the tables around them empty.

'I feel almost as if I were one of your colleagues . . . When you rang to say you wouldn't be home to lunch, I could picture you eating in a place like this with Lucas or Janvier . . .'

'It's just as likely that I would have stayed in my office, and had sandwiches and a glass of beer . . . Tell me all about it . . .'

'I don't want to sound catty . . .'

'Just be your own truthful self.'

'You've often spoken to me about her and her husband . . . He was always the one you were sorry for, and I've sometimes wondered whether you weren't being a little unfair . . .'

'And now?'

'I'm not as sorry for her as I was, though I dare say she can't help herself . . . I found her in bed, attended by the concierge and a neighbour, an old woman who never stops fiddling with the beads of her rosary. They had sent for the doctor because, to look at her, you'd have thought she was dying . . .'

'Was she surprised to see you?'

'You'll never guess what her first words to me were! She said: "Well, now at any rate, your husband will have to stop persecuting him. I dare say he's sorry now that he obstructed Charles's promotion to a job at Headquarters . . ."

'At first, I felt very uncomfortable . . . And then, the doctor fortunately arrived . . . He's small, elderly and placid, and he has a mischievous twinkle in his eye . . .

'The concierge returned to her lodge. The old lady, still fidgeting with her beads, followed me into the dining-room.

'"Poor soul!" she said. "What sorry, weak creatures we are, when it comes down to it! When one thinks of all that is going on around us, one is almost afraid to set foot outside one's own door . . ."

'I asked her how serious Madame Lognon's illness was, and she said that her legs were so weak that she could scarcely stand. It was something to do with her bones, she thought.'

They couldn't help exchanging smiles. The contrast between lunching at home in the Boulevard Richard-Lenoir and in the intimate atmosphere of the little restaurant struck them both at the same time. Madame Maigret especially was tremendously thrilled by it. Her eyes sparkled and her colour rose as she spoke.

Lunching or dining at home, it was usually Maigret who did all the talking, since she had little of interest to relate. On this occasion, she was relishing the opportunity of being useful to him.

'Is all this really of interest to you?'

'Very much so. Go on.'

'After he had finished examining her, the doctor beckoned me to follow him to the entrance lobby, and we stood there talking in whispers. He began by asking me if I really was the wife of Chief Superintendent Maigret. He seemed very surprised to find me there.

'I explained . . . Well, you can guess what I said to him . . .

'"I understand how you feel," he mumbled. "It's most generous of you . . . But allow me to give you a word of warning . . . While I don't claim that she has the constitution of an ox, I can assure you that she is very far from being seriously ill . . . I have attended her for ten years . . . And I'm not the only one!

'"She is forever calling in one or other of my professional colleagues, hoping against hope that one of them will find something seriously wrong with her . . . But, whenever I dare to suggest that she should consult a psychiatrist or a neurologist, she grows indignant, and says she is not mad, and that I don't know the rudiments of my job . . .

'"Perhaps her marriage has not turned out as she had hoped? At any rate, there is no doubt that she is deeply resentful of the fact that her husband has not made more progress in his career . . .

'"And, by way of revenge, she plays the helpless invalid, so as to force him to attend to all her needs, do the housework, and, in general, lead a life which, by any standards, is intolerable . . .

'"You came to see her this morning . . . All well and good . . . But if you show yourself too willing, she'll latch on to you with all her strength . . .

'"I telephoned Bichat in her presence, and I was able to assure her that her husband's chances of recovery were excellent . . . I laid it on a bit thick . . . But it made no difference . . . She had no sympathy to spare for her husband, only for herself . . ."'

The *andouillette* and chips, and a half-lobster coated with mayonnaise, were brought to the table. Maigret refilled their glasses.

'After you rang me, I told her that I should have to leave her for an hour or two, and she retorted, sourly: "Naturally, your husband needs you. All men are the same . . ."

'Then, abruptly changing the subject, she went on: "When I am a widow, my pension won't even stretch to keeping on this flat, where I have lived for twenty-five years."'

'Did she make any mention of there being another woman in Lognon's life?'

'Only obliquely. She remarked that police service was a degrading occupation, involving, as it did, hobnobbing with riff-raff of every sort, prostitutes included.'

'Did you try and find out whether she'd noticed any change in him of late?'

'I did, and her reply was: "Ever since I was fool enough to marry him, he's told me periodically that he's on to something really big, which will at last bring him the recognition and promotion he deserves . . . At first, I believed him and rejoiced with him . . .

'"But it was always the same, either the big case would fizzle out, or someone else would get the credit."'

Madame Maigret, looking more playful than Maigret could ever remember seeing her, added: 'I may as well tell you that, judging by the look she gave me as she said this, I was left in no doubt that you were the one she blamed for stealing all the credit . . . As to recent events, her main complaint is that lately he's been burdened with more than his fair share of night duty. Is that true?'

'It was at his own request.'

'He didn't admit that to her . . . Apparently, for the past four or five days, he's been very full of himself, saying that something big was about to happen, and that, this time, the papers would have no choice, whether they liked it or not, but to print his picture on the front page . . .'

'Didn't she try to get any more out of him?'

'She didn't believe him, and I dare say she just sneered. Wait a minute, though! She did say something else that struck me as odd. She told me he had said: "People aren't always what they seem, and if one could see behind the façade, one would find a good many things one wasn't expecting . . ."'

They were interrupted at this point by the proprietor, who came to their table to pay his respects, and offer them a liqueur on the house. When they were alone again, Madame Maigret asked, a little anxiously: 'Will you be able to make use of any of this, or have I been wasting your time?'

As he was in the middle of lighting his pipe, he made no immediate reply. Besides, he was preoccupied with the germ of an idea, which was beginning to take shape in his mind.

'Did you hear me?'

'Yes. I fancy that what you have just told me alters the whole complexion of the case . . .'

She stared at him, torn between incredulity and delight. For the rest of her life, that lunch at Chez Manière was to remain one of her happiest memories.

3

The Loves of Marinette

The rain was beginning to abate a little. It was no longer pelting down like stair-rods, beating upon the backs of the unwary. Maigret, gazing out of the window, was in no hurry to break up this exceptionally heart-warming lunch-hour tête-à-tête.

If Lognon had been able to see them, it would merely have inflamed his bitterness.

'Here am I, lying on my bed of pain, while they take advantage of my plight to meet for lunch like young lovers at Chez Manière, and talk of my poor wife as an old bitch or a half-wit . . .'

A thought struck Maigret, which he would not have claimed to be either original or profound: 'It's odd the way a man's susceptibilities can often cause more complications than his actual shortcomings or the lies he tells . . .'

This was particularly true of his own profession. He could recall inquiries which had dragged on for days longer than necessary, sometimes even for weeks, because he dared not put a blunt question to a colleague, or because that colleague was inclined to shy away from certain topics.

'Are you going back to your office?'

'I'll be calling in at the Avenue Junot first. What about you?'

'I think, don't you, that if I leave her on her own, she'll accuse you of neglect, of letting her lie there unattended, while her husband, as a result of his devotion to duty, is dying.'

It was true. Madame Lognon, who did not live up to her christian name of Solange, was quite capable of complaining volubly to the reporters who would soon be thronging to her door, and heaven alone could tell what the newspapers would make of it.

'Still, you can't possibly spend all your days and nights with her until such time as he may recover. You'd better see if you can come to some arrangement with the old girl with the rosary.'

'Her name is Mademoiselle Papin.'

'I dare say that, for a small consideration, she could be persuaded to spend a few hours a day in the flat. If the worst comes to the worst, you could always engage a nurse . . .'

By the time they left the restaurant, only a few sparse drops of rain were falling. They parted in the Place Constantin-Pecqueur. Slowly, Maigret walked back along the Avenue Junot, and spotted Inspector Chinquier coming out of one house and ringing the bell next door.

This was another delicate job, often with disappointing results. One disturbed people in the peace of their own homes, people to whom the very word 'police' was unsettling and harassing, to probe into their little private concerns.

'Would you mind telling me whether, last night . . .'

Everyone already knew that there had been an attempted murder in their own street. Doubtless they felt themselves to be under suspicion. Besides, it was not always pleasant to have to tell a perfect stranger what one had been up to the previous night.

In spite of all this, Maigret would have liked to be in Chinquier's shoes, because a closer acquaintance with the Avenue and its inhabitants, a better understanding of their private lives, would at least have provided him with a context for the dramatic climax, and perhaps even a solution to the puzzle.

Unfortunately, it was a task which, as a Chief Superintendent, he could not permit himself to carry out in person, especially as he was already under censure for his propensity to wander off here, there and everywhere, instead of staying in his office to supervise his subordinates.

Only one solitary constable remained on duty outside Marinette's building. Traces of blood were still visible on the pavement. The reporters and cameramen had disappeared, but the occasional passer-by was still stopping to take a brief look.

'Anything fresh?'

'Nothing, Chief Superintendent. It's all been very quiet.'

In the lodge, the Saugets were still lingering over their lunch.

The night porter of the Palace Hotel was still unshaven and still wearing his hideous dressing-gown.

'Don't let me disturb you . . . I'm just going up to the fourth floor for a minute or two, but first there are a couple of things I'd like to ask you . . . Did Mademoiselle Augier, by any chance, own a car?'

'She bought herself a moped a couple of years back, but, after she'd had it only a few months, she was run into by a car, and decided to get rid of it . . .'

'Where did she usually go for her holidays?'

'Last summer she went to Spain, and she was so brown when she got back that I didn't recognize her at first . . .'

'Did she go alone?'

'With a girl friend, or so she told me.'

'Did any of her girl friends visit her here?'

'No. Apart from the fiancé I mentioned, and the Inspector who took to dropping in recently, she was mostly on her own.'

'What about Sundays?'

'She would often go away on the Saturday evening – she had to work on Saturday afternoons – and come back on the Monday morning. Hairdressing salons are mostly closed on Monday mornings.'

'I presume she didn't go very far?'

'All I know is that she went swimming. She often talked of the hours she had spent in the water . . .'

He plodded up the four flights of stairs, spent a quarter of an hour or more opening drawers and cupboards, examining the dresses and underclothes and all the other small possessions that reveal the tastes and personality of their owner.

Although none of her things were in the top price bracket, every item had been chosen with care. He found a letter, posted in Grenoble, which he had missed earlier on. The handwriting was that of a man, and the letter was lively and affectionate in tone. It was not until towards the end that the Chief Superintendent realized that the writer was Marinette's father.

'Your sister is pregnant again, and that engineer husband of hers is more cock-a-hoop than if he had built the world's largest dam . . . As for your mother, she's still coping with those forty-odd infants of hers, and comes home to us at night smelling wholesomely of wet babies . . .'

He found a wedding photograph, presumably of her sister's wedding, which was obviously some years old. Flanking the bridal couple were their parents, looking stiff and awkward as they always do in such photographs, a young man and his wife with a little boy of about three, and lastly a girl with expressive, sparkling eyes, who could only have been Marinette.

He put the photograph in his pocket. A few minutes later, he was in a taxi on his way to the Quai. He returned to his office, which he had not left until one o'clock that same morning, after many hours of persistent effort to arrive at the exact circumstances of the hold-up.

He barely had time to take off his coat before Janvier was knocking at his door.

'I've seen the brother, Chief. I got him in his office in the Rue Le Pelletier. He's quite a bigwig in the firm.'

Maigret showed him the wedding photograph.

'Is this him?'

Unhesitatingly, Janvier pointed to the father of the little boy.

'Had he heard about what happened last night?'

'No. The papers were only just out. At first he insisted that there must be some mistake. His sister was not the sort to take flight or go into hiding, he said.

' "She's so outspoken that I've had to tick her off about it more than once, because some people don't like it . . ." '

'Did you get the impression that he had something to hide?'

Maigret had sat down and was fidgeting with his pipes. Finally, he picked the one he wanted, and filled it slowly.

'No. I was very favourably impressed. He told me all about his family, without reservation. His father teaches English at the Lycée in Grenoble, and his mother is matron of a day nursery. There is another sister living in Grenoble. She's married to an engineer, and he fathers a child on her every year . . .'

'I know . . .'

Maigret forbore to add that his source was a private letter found in a drawer.

'After passing her *baccalauréat*, Marinette decided to move to

Paris. Her first job was as a short-hand typist in a lawyer's office, but she didn't care for office work, so she took a course in beauty care. Her dream, according to her brother, is to open a beauty salon of her own.'

'What about the fiancé?'

'She really was engaged. The young man, whose name is Jean-Claude Ternel, is the son of a Paris industrialist. Marinette introduced him to her brother. She was intending to take him to Grenoble to meet her parents . . .'

It is always discouraging, in a criminal case, to come across so many decent, ordinary people. One can't help wondering how and why they ever got themselves mixed up in it.

'Does the brother know that Jean-Claude used often to spend the night in her flat?'

'He hadn't much to say about it, but he did give me to understand that, although, as her brother, he couldn't openly give his blessing, he was well enough up in present-day mores not to be too censorious . . .'

'In other words, an ideal family!' groaned Maigret.

'I thought he had considerable charm . . .'

The flat in the Avenue Junot, which must be a reflection of Marinette's personality, also had charm.

'Be that as it may, I want her found as soon as possible. Has her brother seen her recently?'

'Not this last week, but the week before. Whenever she wasn't away in the country, she spent her Sunday afternoons with her brother and sister-in-law. They live in Vanves, overlooking the park, which, as François Augier says, is very convenient for the children . . .'

'Did she have anything special to tell them?'

'She mentioned in passing that she'd met the most extraordinary man, and that, quite soon, she might have an equally extraordinary story to tell. Her sister-in-law teased her about it.'

'Was she referring to a new fiancé?'

Janvier looked quite crestfallen at having so little of interest to tell.

'She swore not, saying that once was enough.'

'Why did she break it off with Jean-Claude?'

'She woke up, in the end, to the fact that he was a weakling, incapable of standing on his own feet, and, besides, she had come to realize that he wouldn't be all that sorry to get out of the engagement. He twice failed his *baccalauréat.* His father then sent him to stay with friends in England. The experiment didn't turn out too well. In the end, his father found him a job of sorts in the Paris office of his firm, but his performance proved far from satisfactory . . .'

'Would you mind finding out the times of trains to Grenoble last night and early this morning?'

Nothing came of this. If Marinette had taken the early train, she could have been at her parents' by now. But neither her father, whom he had finally managed to reach at the Lycée, nor her mother had seen her.

Once again, he had had to tread very warily, to spare these good people as much anxiety as he could.

'Oh! no . . . I'm sure nothing has happened to her . . . Don't worry, Madame Augier. By sheer chance, your daughter just happened to be a witness to an attempted murder last night . . . No! Not in her flat. It happened outside, in the Avenue Junot . . . For some reason that is not yet clear to me, she decided to disappear for a short time . . . I thought she might have taken refuge with you . . .'

Having replaced the receiver, the Chief Superintendent turned to Janvier.

'Phew! What else could I say to her . . . ? Lapointe interviewed the girls at the beauty salon this morning, and none of them knows where Marinette used to spend her Sundays . . . She went out into the rain with no luggage, not even a change of clothing. She must have known that she couldn't book in to a hotel without arousing suspicion.

'So she must either be staying with a girl friend in whom she has complete trust, or she's gone to some quiet little place that she knows well, a secluded retreat of some kind, some rural inn on the outskirts, perhaps . . .

'She's passionately fond of swimming . . . It's not very likely, on her salary, that she could afford a day by the sea every week-end . . . But there are lots of possible places on the river, any river nearby, the Seine, the Marne or the Oise . . .

'I suggest you go and see this Jean-Claude character, and try and find out from him where they used to go together . . .'

Moers was awaiting his turn in the next-door office. He had with him a small cardboard box, containing the bullets and the three spent cartridges.

'The ballistics expert agrees with us, Chief. The gun used was a ·763, almost certainly a Mauser.'

'What about finger-prints?'

'I wonder what you'll make of this. Inspector Lognon's prints were all over the living-room, even on the knobs of the radio . . .'

'None on the television set?'

'No. In the kitchen, his prints were on the handle of the fridge, and on a tin containing ground coffee . . . He had also used the electric percolator . . . Why are you smiling? Am I talking nonsense?'

'No. Go on.'

'Lognon drank from the glass and the cup. As for the bottle of brandy, it is covered with his prints and those of the girl . . .'

'What about the bedroom?'

'No trace of Lognon. Not a single hair of his on the pillow, only one of hers. Not a speck of mud anywhere, either, though I understand it was pouring with rain when Lognon arrived at the Avenue Junot.'

Moers and his men could be trusted not to miss a thing.

'It looks as if he sat for a long while in the arm-chair facing one of the french windows. It was during that time, I dare say, that he turned on the radio. At some time or other, he opened the french window. I found some splendid prints on the handle, and one of his fag ends tossed out onto the balcony. I see you're still smiling . . .'

'Only because what you say confirms an idea that I've been mulling over ever since my wife told me about her visit to Madame Lognon . . .'

Surely everything pointed to the conclusion that Old Grumpy, reduced by his wife to a state of abject servitude, had at last broken his chains, and found compensation in an amorous adventure for his dismal home life in the Avenue Constantin-Pecqueur?

'My dear fellow, I'm smiling at the thought of all his colleagues buying the notion that Lognon was transformed overnight into some sort of Don Juan. Now I'd stake my life on it that there was nothing of the sort between those two. For his sake, I could almost wish there had been.

'He spent his nights in the front room, the living-room, most of the time sitting facing the french window, and the girl, Marinette, trusted him enough to retire to bed, in spite of his presence next door . . .

'Did you find anything else?'

'Traces of sand in the girl's flat-heeled shoes, the ones she must have worn on her trips to the country. It's river sand. We have hundreds of different samples upstairs, but it will take hours of work and a good deal of luck to match it . . .'

'Keep me in the picture . . . Is there anyone else next door waiting to see me?'

'An inspector from the 18th *arrondissement*.'

'Has he a little brown moustache?'

'Yes.'

'It must be Chinquier. On the way out, send him in to me.'

It was beginning to rain again, a fine rain, more like a scotch mist, which softened the light. The clouds in the sky were almost motionless, though coalescing imperceptibly to form a canopy of unrelieved grey.

'Well, Chinquier?'

'I've left my men to complete the door-to-door questioning. It's a blessing there aren't more than forty houses on each side! Even so, that entails questioning two hundred people, at least.'

'It's the houses opposite I'm most interested in.'

'With your permission, Chief Superintendent, I'll come to that in a minute. I guessed what you had in mind. I began by questioning the tenants of the building which poor Lognon is known to have visited. There's only one flat on the ground floor, occupied by an elderly couple, the Guèbres, who have been away for a month, visiting their married daughter in Mexico . . .'

He drew from his pocket a notebook, several pages of which were covered with lists of names and diagrams. He, too, had to be handled with kid gloves, to avoid giving offence.

'There are two flats to each of the other floors. On the first floor, there are Madame Faisant, a widow who is a saleswoman in a couture house, and a couple called Lanier, who have private means. They rushed to the window as soon as they heard the shots, and saw the car drive off, but unfortunately, weren't able to read the number plate . . .'

With eyes half-closed, Maigret, occasionally puffing at his pipe, listened abstractedly to the Inspector's painstaking report, which came across to him as a prolonged droning sound.

He pricked up his ears, however, when mention was made of one Maclet, who lived on the second floor of the neighbouring building. According to Chinquier, he was a creaking old gentleman, who had shut himself up in his flat once and for all, and whose only recreation was to sit at his window, watching the antics of the world outside with sardonic amusement.

'He's crippled with rheumatism, and just manages, with the aid of two sticks, to hobble about his filthy flat, where no cleaning woman is permitted to set foot. He orders the food he needs each day by means of a note left under the doormat, and the concierge takes up the food and leaves it outside his door.

'He has no radio, and never reads a newspaper. The concierge claims that he's a rich man, for all that he lives like a pauper. He has a married daughter, who has tried more than once to get him committed to a mental hospital . . .'

'Is he really mad?'

'Judge for yourself. I had the greatest possible difficulty in persuading him to open the door. It wasn't until I threatened to come back with a locksmith that he finally let me in. When, at last, he did so, he inspected me lingeringly, from head to foot, and then said with a sigh: "You're rather young for this sort of job, aren't you?"

'I told him I was thirty-five, and he retorted, two or three times over: "A boy! A mere boy . . . What does anyone know at thirty-five? Understanding comes with experience . . ."'

'Did you get anything of interest out of him?'

'He talked mostly about the Dutchman who lives opposite, in that house we saw from the balcony this morning, the little private house with the top floor glassed in like an artist's studio . . .

'It seems that this house was built fifteen years ago, by a man called Norris Jonker, who still lives there. He is now sixty-four, and is married, it seems, to a fine-looking woman much younger than himself.'

Once again, Maigret regretted not having been able to carry out this work himself. He would have enjoyed meeting the rheumatic old misanthropist, who lived the life of a hermit in the heart of Paris, in the heart of Montmartre, and who spent his time observing the comings and goings of the people across the way.

'Suddenly he was positively garrulous, and owing to his habit of jumping from one subject to another, and interspersing the narrative with his own comments, I'm afraid I may not be able to report verbatim everything he said . . .

'Later, I went to see the Dutchman, and I think I ought to tell you about him first. He's a pleasant man, cultured and stylish. He's a member of an extremely rich and well-known family in Holland. His father owns a bank in Amsterdam, Jonker, Haag & Co . . . He has never shown any interest in banking, and he spent much of his early life travelling the world.

'When he discovered that he was never so happy as in Paris, he built his present house in the Avenue Junot, leaving his brother Hans to run the bank after his father's death . . .

'Norris Jonker was quite content to receive his share of the dividends, and invest it in pictures . . .'

'Pictures?' repeated Maigret.

'Apparently he owns one of the finest collections in Paris . . .'

'Just a second! Presumably you rang the doorbell . . . Who answered it?'

'A manservant with very fair hair and pink cheeks, youngish . . .'

'Did you say you were a police officer?'

'Yes. He didn't seem surprised. He showed me to a seat in the entrance hall . . . I'm no expert on paintings, but even I had heard of some of the signatures I was able to read, such as Gauguin, Cézanne and Renoir. A lot of naked women . . .'

'Were you kept waiting long?'

'About ten minutes. There are double doors leading from the

hall into the drawing-room. They were open, and I caught a glimpse of a young woman with black hair. She was still in her dressing-gown, at three in the afternoon! I may have been mistaken, but I had the feeling that she'd come down specially to take a look at me . . . A few minutes later, the manservant led me through the drawing-room into a study lined with books from floor to ceiling . . .

'Monsieur Jonker received me wearing flannel trousers, an open-necked silk shirt and a black velvet jacket . . . He has pure white hair, and a complexion almost as rosy as his manservant's . . .

'There was a tray with a decanter and glasses on his desk.

'"Please sit down and state your business," he said, without a trace of an accent.'

It was plain to see that Inspector Chinquier had been impressed equally by the luxuriously appointed house, the pictures and their distinguished Dutch owner.

'I confess, I didn't know where to start . . . I asked him whether he had heard the shots, and he replied that he hadn't, adding that his bedroom was at the back of the house facing away from the Avenue Junot, and that, anyway, the walls were so thick as to be almost soundproof.

'"I have a horror of noise . . .' he said, and proceeded to pour me a glass of a liqueur that was not familiar to me. It was very strong, and tasted faintly of orange . . .

'I said: "Still, you must be aware of what occurred last night just across the street from your house?"

'"Carl told me about it when he brought me my breakfast. That was round about ten. Carl is my manservant. He's the son of one of our tenant farmers. He said the Avenue Junot was in turmoil, because a policeman had been shot by a gang of thugs."'

'How did he seem?' asked Maigret, fidgeting with his pipe.

'Cool and smiling, and surprisingly courteous for a man who had been intruded upon without warning.

'"If you wish to speak to Carl, he is at your disposal, but his room also faces the garden, and he has assured me that he heard nothing either."

'"Are you married, Monsieur Jonker?"

'"Yes, indeed. My wife was very upset to learn what had occurred only a few yards from our door."'

At this point in his narrative, Chinquier began to show signs of uneasiness.

'I don't know whether I did the right thing, Chief Superintendent. I would have liked to ask him a lot more questions, but I hadn't the nerve, and I consoled myself with the thought that my first consideration should be to put you in the picture . . .'

'Very well, then, let's get back to the old cripple.'

'Just so. It's because of what he told me that I would have liked to discuss a number of things with the Dutchman. Almost the first thing Maclet said was: "What would you do, Inspector, if you were married to one of the most beautiful women in Paris . . . ? Ha! Ha! . . . You don't answer, I see . . . And you are a long way short of your middle sixties! Let me put it another way . . . How would you expect a man of that age to behave, with a glorious creature like that always at his disposal . . . ?

'"Well now, the gentleman opposite must have rather peculiar views on this subject . . . I sleep very little . . . I'm not much interested in current affairs, nor in the various disasters of which the press and the radio make so much . . .

'"I spend my time thinking . . . Do you see what I mean . . . ? I look out of the window and I think . . . Few people seem to appreciate the entertainment value of thought . . .

'"Take the Dutchman and his wife, for instance. They seldom go out, once or twice a week at most, she wearing a long dress and he in a dinner jacket. They seldom get home later than one in the morning, which suggests that they enjoy nothing better than dining with friends or going to the theatre . . .

'"They themselves never entertain in the evening. Nor do they give luncheon parties . . . In fact, they seldom sit down to lunch before three in the afternoon.

'"You see . . . One gets one's fun where one can . . . One watches . . . One makes guesses . . . One endeavours to make sense of the scraps of information one has gathered . . .

'"Consequently, when one notices that, two or three times a week, a pretty girl rings the doorbell round about eight in the evening, and doesn't leave the house until much later, often as late as the early hours of the following morning . . ."'

Maigret was decidedly sorry not to have been able to interview this eccentric old gentleman himself.

'"But that's not all, officer . . . Ah! my ramblings are beginning to interest you, I see . . . You'll be even more interested when I tell you that it's a different young woman each time.

'"They usually arrive in a taxi, but occasionally one comes on foot . . . From my window, I watch them peering at the numbers of the houses . . . And that too is significant, wouldn't you say?

'"It means they have a prearranged appointment with someone at a specific address . . .

'"You see, I haven't always been an old sick animal gone to ground in his lair. There was a time when I knew quite a lot about women.

'"Do you see that standard lamp a few yards from their door . . . ? In the course of your work, you must have learned to recognize on sight the sort of woman who makes her living out of love, isn't that so . . . ? And you must also be able to recognize the kind of girl who is on the fringes of the profession, night-club entertainers, for instance, or bit-part actresses in films or the theatre, who are not above earning extra money that way, if the occasion arises . . ."'

Maigret sprang to his feet.

'See here, Chinquier, do you get the point of all this?'

'What point?'

'How Lognon got involved in the first place. He often spent the night in the Avenue Junot, where he was on speaking terms with most of the people living there . . . Let's suppose that he had several times spotted women such as you describe being admitted to the Dutchman's house . . .'

'I thought of that, too. But there's no law against a man, even an elderly man, having a taste for variety.'

And, indeed, it didn't offer an adequate explanation of why Old Grumpy had sought and found a place from which to spy on that particular house, without being seen.

'I can think of another possibility.'

'What?'

'That he was waiting for one of these late visitors to leave. He could have spotted one particular prostitute he'd had dealings with before . . .'

'I see . . . All the same, everyone is free to . . .'

'That depends on what was going on in the house, and what the girl had witnessed there . . . What else did your nice old gentleman have to say?'

For Maigret was becoming more and more intrigued by the queer old man at the window.

'I asked him every question that came into my head, and made a note of his replies.'

Once more, Chinquier referred to his notebook.

'Question: "Are you sure it wasn't the manservant that these women came to see?"

'Answer: "For one thing, the manservant is in love with the girl in the dairy at the end of the road. She's a podgy little thing, always ready to burst out laughing . . . She comes and waits for him outside, several nights a week. She stands in the shadows, ten yards or so away from the house – I could point out the exact spot – and it's never very long before he comes out to join her . . ."

'Question: "About what time would this be?"

'Answer: "Tennish . . . I presume he has to wait at table, and that his employers dine late . . . The two of them go for a walk arm-in-arm, stopping occasionally to exchange a kiss, and, before parting, they retire into that little recess over there, and cling to one another for quite a long time . . ."

'Question: "Doesn't he see her home?"

'Answer: "No. She skips off happily down the road by herself . . . Sometimes she looks for all the world as if she's going to break into a dance . . . And there's another reason why those women I told you about can't be there for the manservant . . . On several occasions, they've come while he was out . . ."

'Question: "Who answered the door?"

'Answer: "That's just it! How's this for an odd twist? Sometimes it's the Dutchman himself, and sometimes his wife . . ."

'Question: "Do they own a car?"

'Answer: "Yes. One of those big American cars."

'Question: "Do they employ a chauffeur?"

'Answer: "Carl does the driving, wearing a chauffeur's uniform."

'Question: "Are there any other living-in servants?"

'Answer: "A cook and two housemaids . . . The maids never stay long . . ."

'Question: "Do they have many visitors, apart from the ladies you mentioned?"

'Answer: "A few . . . The most regular visitor is a man in his forties, an American, I should guess. He drives a yellow sports car, and generally calls in the afternoon."

'Question: "Does he stay long?"

'Answer: "An hour or two."

'Question: "Doesn't he ever call in the evening or at night?"

'Answer: "He did so twice, about a month ago, in company with a young woman. He was in and out in no time, leaving his companion behind in the house."

'Question: "Was it the same woman on both occasions?"

'Answer: "No!"'

Maigret could picture the old man's smile, sardonic, perhaps even faintly salacious, as he watched these mysterious comings and goings.

'Answer: "There is also another man, bald though quite young, who arrives at dusk in a taxi, and leaves carrying several parcels."

'Question: "What kind of parcels?"

'Answer: "They could be pictures . . . But then again they might be anything . . . Well, Inspector, I think I've told you pretty well all I know . . . It must be years since I last talked at such length, and I hope it may be years before I am called upon to do so again . . . I'd better warn you, it would be a waste of time to summon me to a police station or a judge's chambers . . .

'"Still less can you depend on me to appear as a witness at the Assizes, if things should ever get that far . . .

'"We've had our little chat . . . I've told you what I think . . . Make whatever use of it you like, but I'm not going to allow myself to be put to further trouble on any pretext whatsoever . . ."'

Whereupon Chinquier proceeded to prove to Maigret that the local inspectors were well up to their job.

'After I had seen inside the Dutchman's house, I began to wonder whether the old man hadn't been leading me up the garden path. I thought to myself that, if I could confirm one of his assertions, I could more readily believe the rest.

'After I left the old man I called in at the dairy. I waited outside until the assistant was alone in the shop. She was exactly as he had described her, a plump, country girl, looking as if she'd arrived so recently that she still hadn't got over her delighted astonishment at finding herself in Paris.

'I went in and asked her point blank: "Do you know anyone called Carl?"

'She blushed, looked uneasily towards an open door at the back, and murmured: "Who are you? What business is it of yours?"

'"I'm just making routine inquiries. I'm a police officer."

'"What have you got against him?"

'"Nothing. It's a simple matter of checking a statement. Are you engaged?"

'"We may get married some day, but he hasn't actually proposed to me yet . . ."

'"You see him several times a week, don't you?"

'"Whenever I can . . ."

'"I believe you wait for him a few yards away from the house in the Avenue Junot?"

'"Who told you?"

'At this point, an enormously fat woman suddenly emerged from the back room, and the girl had the presence of mind to raise her voice and say: "No, sir. I'm afraid we're out of Gorgonzola, but we have Roquefort . . . Roquefort and Gorgonzola taste very much alike . . ."'

Maigret smiled.

'Did you have to buy some Roquefort?'

'I told her my wife wouldn't eat anything but Gorgonzola . . . Well, that's the lot, Chief Superintendent . . . I can't say, of course, what my colleagues may have to report tonight . . . Any fresh news of poor Lognon?'

'I got someone to ring the hospital a short while ago. The doctors still won't commit themselves, and he hasn't yet regained consciousness. They fear that the second bullet, which hit him below the shoulder, may have damaged the tip of his right lung, but he's in no fit condition to be X-rayed at present . . .'

'I wonder what he could have found out to provoke an attempt at murder . . . You'll be as baffled as I was when you meet the Dutchman . . . I just can't believe a man like that . . .'

'There's just one more thing I'd like you to do, Chinquier . . . When your men get back, and especially when the night-duty chaps come on, put them all on to finding out everything they can about the young women. Some of them, you tell me, arrived on foot in the Avenue Junot, which suggests that they may live locally . . .

'Tell the men to go through all the night spots with a fine-tooth comb . . . From your old gentleman's description, those girls don't sound the sort to walk the streets. Do you see what I'm getting at?'

'You think we may dig up one of the women who went to the Avenue Junot . . .'

No doubt, he would learn more from Marinette Augier, if he could find her. Would it be Moers and his lab assistants, with their samples of sand, who would finally put him on her track?

4

A Visit to the Dutchman

'Netherlands Embassy at your service.'

The voice, which was young and fresh, with a slight accent, brought to mind windmills dominating a landscape, such as are sometimes depicted on cocoa tins.

'I should like to speak to the First Secretary, please, mademoiselle.'

'Who is that?'

'Chief Superintendent Maigret of the Police Judiciaire.'

'One moment. I'll just see if Monsieur Goudekamp is in his office.'

After a brief pause, he heard the same voice again: 'Monsieur Goudekamp is in conference, but I'll put you on to the Second Secretary, Monsieur de Vries . . . Hold on . . .'

A man's voice, less fresh than the girl's, needless to say, and with a stronger accent.

'Hubert de Vries speaking, Second Secretary at the Netherlands Embassy.'

'Chief Superintendent Maigret here, Head of the Crime Squad.'

'What can I do for you?'

Maigret could imagine Monsieur de Vries at the other end of the line, stiff and mistrustful. After all, he was only the Second Secretary as yet. No doubt he was fair, and a little too correctly dressed, as northerners so often are.

'I should like some information about a fellow countryman of yours, who has been living in Paris for a long time, and whose name is probably familiar to you . . .'

'Where are you speaking from, Monsieur Maigret?'

'From my office at the Quai des Orfèvres.'

'I hope you won't take it amiss if I ring off, and call you back.'

Five minutes elapsed before the telephone rang.

'Forgive me, Monsieur Maigret, but we get rung up by all sorts of people, some of them assuming an identity other than their own. You wanted to talk to me about a citizen of the Netherlands living in Paris?'

'A Monsieur Norris Jonker . . .'

What was it that gave Maigret the impression that his invisible informant had suddenly been put on his guard?

'Yes . . .'

'Do you know him?'

'Jonker is a very common name in Holland, almost as common as Durand in France. And Norris is not an unusual christian name.'

'This particular Norris Jonker is related to the Amsterdam banking firm.'

'The firm of Jonker, Haag and Company is one of the oldest in the country. Old Kees Jonker died some fifteen years ago and, if I am not mistaken, was succeeded by his son, Hans.'

'And Norris Jonker?'

'I don't know him personally.'

'But you know of his existence?'

'Of course. I believe he's a member of the Saint-Cloud Golf Club. I may have seen him there without knowing who he was . . .'

'Is he married?'

'To an Englishwoman, according to my information. Permit me to ask you a question, Monsieur Maigret. What is your interest in Monsieur Jonker?'

'He may have a very remote connexion with a case I'm working on.'

'Have you been to see him?'

'Not yet.'

'Don't you think it would be simpler to put your questions to him direct? I could probably let you have his address.'

'I have it.'

'Norris Jonker hardly ever attends Embassy functions. He is a member of a family which is not merely respectable but highly distinguished, and I have every reason to believe that he himself is irreproachable. He is best known for his collection of paintings.'

'What do you know of his wife?'

'I could answer more freely if I understood the drift of your questions. According to my information, Madame Jonker was born in the South of France, and subsequently married an Englishman, Herbert Muir of Manchester, a manufacturer of ball bearings.'

'Have they any children?'

'Not to my knowledge.'

Maigret, realizing that this was not getting him any further, brought the conversation to an end, and dialled another number, that of a licensed valuer, who frequently appeared in the courts as an expert witness.

'Monsieur Manessi? Maigret here . . .'

'Hang on a minute, while I shut the door . . . Right . . . Carry on . . . Dealing in pictures now, are you?'

'I don't know whether I am or not! Do you know a Dutchman of the name of Norris Jonker?'

'The one who lives in the Avenue Junot? Not only do I know him, but I've been consulted by him regarding the authenticity of some of his purchases. He owns one of the finest collections of late nineteenth- and early twentieth-century paintings in existence . . .'

'In other words, he's a very rich man?'

'His father was a banker and was himself a collector of paintings. Norris Jonker grew up surrounded by Van Goghs, Pissarros, Manets and Renoirs. It's not surprising that he has no interest in banking. He inherited the greater part of his father's collection, and his income from the bank, which is now run by his brother, is sufficient to enable him to add to the collection . . .'

'Do you know him personally?'

'Yes. Do you?'

'Not yet.'

'He's more in the style of the English gentleman than a typical Dutchman. If I remember right, he got an Oxford degree and stayed on in England for many years afterwards. I've been told, in fact, that by the end of the last war he had attained the rank of Colonel in the British Army.'

'What about his wife?'

'She's a gorgeous creature. She was first married, very young, to an Englishman from Manchester.'

'The manufacturer of ball bearings, yes, I know . . .'

'I can't imagine why you should be taking so much interest in Jonker. I trust none of his pictures have been stolen?'

'No.'

It was the Chief Superintendent, now, who was being evasive.

'Do they go out much?'

'Not as far as I know.'

'Does Jonker move in artistic circles?'

'He attends the sales, of course, and is always in the know when anything good is coming up for auction at the Hôtel Drouot or Galliéra's or Sotheby's or in New York . . .'

'Does he bid in person?'

'That's more than I can tell you. I know he used to travel a great deal, but whether he still does, I can't say. It's not necessary to be present to buy a picture at auction. Quite the contrary, it's becoming more and more common for the big buyers to bid through an agent . . .'

'In other words, he's a man to be trusted?'

'With one's eyes shut.'

'Thanks.'

That didn't make things any easier. Reluctantly, Maigret got up and went to the cupboard to get his hat and coat.

The better known people are, the more important and highly-regarded, the trickier it is to ring at their doorbells and ask them questions. Such people are liable to complain to higher authority, which may result in unpleasant consequences for the police officer.

He considered asking one of his inspectors to accompany him, but in the end decided to go alone to the Avenue Junot. He did not want his visit to look too official.

Half-an-hour later, he stepped out of a taxi at the door of the private house. Having presented his card, he was ushered into the hall by Carl, the white-jacketed manservant, just as Inspector Chinquier had been, but, perhaps owing to the Chief Superintendent's senior rank, he was kept waiting only five minutes, instead of ten.

'This way, if you please.'

Carl led him across the drawing-room, where, much to Maigret's disappointment, the beautiful Madame Jonker was not on view, and opened the study door. To all appearances, the Dutchman had not moved from his chair, nor changed his clothes, since Chinquier's visit. He was seated at an Empire desk, studying engravings with the aid of an enormous magnifying glass fitted with a light.

He stood up at once, and Maigret was able to observe that he was exactly as he had been described to him. In his grey flannel trousers, his soft silk shirt and black velvet jacket, he was the very model of the casually dressed Englishman at home. He also had a good deal of British phlegm.

Showing no surprise or emotion, he inquired: 'Chief Superintendent Maigret?'

He waved his guest into a leather arm-chair on the other side of the desk, and sat down again.

'I am highly flattered, believe me, to receive a visit from a man as famous as yourself . . .'

He spoke slowly as if, even after so many years, he still thought in Dutch, and had to translate every word.

'At the same time, I am a little surprised. This makes the second time I have been visited by the police . . .'

He paused, staring down at his plump, well-kept hands. Although he was by no means fat, he was what used to be called 'a fine figure of a man', and, in 1900, would have been much sought after as a model for drawings in *La Vie Parisienne*.

His face was a little flabby, and his blue eyes glinted behind rimless spectacles, supported by thin, gold side-pieces.

Maigret, feeling not altogether at ease, began: 'Inspector Chinquier did, in fact, tell me that he had been to see you. He is a local man, and is connected only indirectly with my own branch of the Force . . .'

'Do you mean that you have come to check up on his report?'

'Not exactly. But it may be that he did not ask you as many questions as he might have done.'

The Dutchman, fidgeting with his magnifying glass, gave Maigret a straight look. There was more than a hint of mischief in his pale eyes, and also, perhaps, a touch of disingenuousness.

'See here, Chief Superintendent. I am sixty-four years of age, and I have seen a good deal of the world in my time. I settled in France many years ago, and built my house in Paris, because I felt so much at home here.

'I have no police record, as they say here, and I've never so much as set foot in a police station or court room.

'I understand that last night shots were fired in the street, opposite my house. As I told the Inspector, neither I nor my wife heard anything, as our bedrooms are on the other side of the house.

'Come now, tell me, how would you react if I were in your place and you in mine?'

'I shouldn't exactly welcome these visits. It is never very pleasant to have uninvited strangers charging into one's house.'

'Come now, that's not what I'm complaining about. On the contrary, I welcome the opportunity of meeting someone of whom I have heard so much. My objection, as you must know, is on quite other grounds.

'Your inspector asked me a number of questions verging on the indiscreet. It might have been worse, I admit, given his occupation. I don't know what questions you intend to ask, but I confess it does surprise me that a man of your seniority should have thought fit to come in person.'

'What if I were to tell you that it was out of respect for your position . . . ?'

'I should be flattered, but not necessarily convinced. Perhaps it would be wiser of me to ask what legal right you have to be here.'

'I have no objection to that, Monsieur Jonker, and you are perfectly free to consult your lawyer. I may as well tell you that I have no warrant, and that you have every right to show me the door. On the other hand, you are no doubt aware that, should you refuse to cooperate, you would be taking the risk of being regarded as a hostile witness, if not as one who had something to hide . . .'

The Dutchman, leaning back in his arm-chair, smiled, and stretched out his hand towards a box of cigars.

'You do smoke, I believe?'

'Only a pipe.'

He himself chose a cigar, which he held against his ear and pinched, before snipping off the end with a gold cigar cutter. Then very slowly, making something of a ritual of it, he lit it.

'One more question,' he said, between two puffs of fine blue smoke. 'Am I to understand that, of all the people living in the Avenue Junot, I am the only one to be honoured by a visit from you, or do you attach so much importance to this investigation that you propose to conduct all the house-to-house inquiries yourself?'

Maigret, in his turn, weighed his words with care.

'You are not the first person in the avenue whom I have thought fit to visit myself. As you surmise, house-to-house inquiries in general are being conducted by my inspectors, but in your case I felt I owed it to you to take the trouble . . .'

The Dutchman nodded his thanks, but still looked unconvinced.

'In that case, I will do my best to answer your questions, but only in so far as they don't probe into my private life.'

Maigret was opening his mouth to reply, when the telephone rang.

'Excuse me.'

Jonker picked up the receiver and, frowning, proceeded to talk curtly in English to his caller. Maigret's schoolboy English was far from adequate. It had been of little use to him in London, and still less on the two occasions when he had visited the United States, although the people with whom he had come in contact there had been more than eager to follow his words.

All the same, he was able to gather that the Dutchman was saying that he could not talk freely, adding, in reply to a question from his invisible caller:

'From the same firm, yes . . . I'll call you back later . . .'

What could he mean by this remark, but that the Inspector's earlier visit had been followed up by another from someone else in the same profession?

'Sorry about that . . . I'm all yours . . .'

He settled himself more comfortably, leaning back a little in his chair, and resting his elbows on the arms. Every now and again, he would examine the gradually lengthening white ash on his cigar.

'You asked me, Monsieur Jonker, what I should do if I were in your place. I can only reply to that by asking you to try and put yourself in mine. Whenever and wherever a crime is committed, there are always people in the neighbourhood who, with prompting, are able to recall some odd little occurrence, the significance of which escaped them at the time.'

'Tittle-tattle, do you mean?'

'Call it that, if you like. At any rate, we can't ignore such snippets of information. Admittedly, many turn out to be without foundation, but occasionally one such snippet may prove to be a vital clue.'

'Can you give me an example?'

But the Chief Superintendent had no intention of blundering straight in. He was as yet unable to make up his mind whether the Dutchman was simply an honest man with a mischievous sense of humour, or a very shrewd and devious character, hiding his true self behind a show of candour.

'You are a married man, Monsieur Jonker?'

'Is that so surprising?'

'No. I am told that Madame Jonker is a very beautiful woman.'

'I repeat, is that so surprising? Admittedly, I'm not as young as I was, some might describe me as an old man, but they would have to add, in fairness, that I was well preserved.

'My wife is only thirty-four, which means that there is a difference of exactly thirty years in our ages. Do you imagine that ours is a unique case? I assure you that there are lots of couples like us, not only in Paris but everywhere. I see nothing especially remarkable in our situation.'

'Is Madame Jonker a Frenchwoman by origin?'

'You are well informed, I see. Yes, she was born in Nice, but I first met her in London.'

'I believe she has been married before?'

Jonker betrayed a hint of impatience, appropriate surely to any gentleman, righteously shocked at such an intrusion into his private affairs, and particularly at the mention of his wife's name.

'She was a Mrs Muir before she became Madame Jonker,' he said, sounding more curt than hitherto.

He stared for some little time at his cigar, then added: 'I should tell you, moreover, since you have thought fit to raise the subject, that she didn't marry me for my money, as she was already, as they say, rich in her own right.'

'For a man in your position, Monsieur Jonker, you very seldom go out.'

'Is there anything wrong with that? Remember that the greater part of my life has been frittered away in going out and about, here, and in London, in the States, in India, in Australia and a lot of other places besides. When you get to my age . . .'

'I'm not so very far off it . . .'

'I repeat, when you get to my age, you will probably feel happier at home than at fashionable parties, or gambling clubs, or night clubs . . .'

'Your attitude is the more understandable in that you must be very much in love with Madame Jonker . . .'

This time, the former British Army Colonel stiffened. He responded merely with a nod, which dislodged the ash of his cigar.

The awkward moment, which Maigret had postponed as long as he could, was approaching. He allowed himself a brief respite, in which to relight his pipe.

'You used the expression "tittle-tattle", and I am prepared to concede that some at least of our information falls into that category . . .'

Was not the Dutchman's hand shaking a little? Be that as it might, he stretched out for the cut-glass decanter, and poured himself a drink.

'Would you care for a Curaçao?'

'No, thanks.'

'Would you prefer a whisky?'

Not waiting for a reply, he rang the bell. Almost without delay, Carl appeared.

'A bottle of scotch, please . . . With soda or plain water?'

'Soda . . .'

During this brief interval both men were silent, and Maigret looked about him at the bookshelves, which covered the walls from floor to ceiling. Mostly, they were filled with art books, not only on painting but also on architecture and sculpture, from their earliest beginnings to the present day. Besides these books, there were bound volumes of all the important sales catalogues, going back forty years or so.

'Thanks, Carl . . . Have you told Madame that I am busy?'

Out of politeness, he addressed the manservant in French.

'Is she still upstairs?'

'Yes, Monsieur.'

'And now, Chief Superintendent, I drink your health, and await your account of the tittle-tattle you mentioned . . .'

'I don't know whether the same is true of Holland, but Paris is full of people, mostly elderly people, who spend a good deal of their time looking out of their windows . . . In this way, it has come to our notice that you frequently receive visitors at night. According to our information, two or three times a week sometimes, a young woman, always a different one, rings at your doorbell late at night, and is admitted to your house . . .'

The Dutchman's ears had suddenly turned red. Instead of replying, he drew deeply on his cigar.

'I might have concluded that these visitors were friends of Madame Jonker, but for the fact that they were all women of somewhat dubious reputation. It would have been insulting to your wife to infer that they could have been her friends . . .'

He had seldom had to choose his words with such care. Indeed, he had seldom found himself in a more awkward position.

'Do you deny that these visits took place?'

'Since you have taken the trouble to come yourself, Chief Superintendent, I must assume that you are sure of your facts. Come now, don't prevaricate. Admit that if I were so foolish as to contradict you, you would confront me with one or more witnesses.'

'You haven't answered my question.'

'What exactly were you told about these young women?'

'I ask you a question, and you fob me off with another.'

'Well, I am in my own home, aren't I? If I were in your office, our respective positions would be different.'

The Chief Superintendent thought it prudent to concede the point.

'Let us say, then, that the visitors in question could all be described as women of easy virtue. They don't merely go in and out, but spend the greater part, if not the whole, of the night in this house . . .'

'That is so.'

His glance did not waver. Quite the reverse, but his blue eyes had clouded over, so that they were now almost grey.

Maigret might not have found the courage to pursue the matter, had he not thought of Lognon lying in hospital, and of the unknown man who had viciously aimed a murderously powerful gun at his stomach.

Jonker gave him no help. His face was as impassive as a poker player's.

'If I am in error, please feel free to say so. I believed at first that the young ladies came to see your manservant, but then I learned that he had a steady girl friend, and that, on several occasions when the visitors in question called, he and she were out together.

'Would you mind telling me where exactly your manservant sleeps?'

'Upstairs, next door to the studio.'

'Do the cook and housemaids also sleep on that floor?'

'No. The three women sleep in an annexe built out into the garden.'

'You often go to the door yourself, to admit your visitors at night . . .

'Forgive me for mentioning that, according to my information, Madame Jonker, too, has been seen to open the door to them . . .'

'It would appear that we have been under close surveillance. Our old village crones in Holland could scarcely do better. And now, perhaps, you would be so good as to tell me what possible connection there could be between the visits of these young women and the shots fired in the street?

'It is beyond belief to me that I personally should be a suspect, or that, for some reason as yet obscure, someone is attempting to involve me in this unsavoury business . . .'

'There's no question of that, and, to prove it, I will lay my cards on the table. The course of events last night, the type of weapon used, and other indications which I am not at liberty to disclose, all lead me to the conclusion that the marksman is a professional criminal.'

'Are you suggesting that I would have dealings with anyone of that sort?'

'Let me put a hypothetical case. You are known to be a very rich man, Monsieur Jonker. There are more works of art in this house than in many a provincial museum, no doubt of incalculable value . . .

'Have you installed a burglar alarm in the house?'

'No. The real professional criminal, as you call him, can circumvent the most sophisticated of security equipment. If you want proof of this, you have only to refer to your own recent criminal records. I prefer to be well insured.'

'Have you never been the victim of an attempted burglary?'

'Not to my knowledge.'

'Are your servants trustworthy?'

'Carl and the cook, who have been with me for twenty years, most certainly are. I'm not so sure about the housemaids, but my wife never engages anyone without taking up their personal references. You have still not explained the connection between what you call my lady visitors and . . .'

'I'm just coming to that.'

So far, Maigret had managed to hold his own quite creditably. He rewarded himself with a gulp of whisky.

'Supposing a gang of art thieves, of which there are several scattered about the world, were planning to steal your pictures . . . Supposing a local inspector of police had got wind of the plan, but had insufficient evidence to enable him to take direct action . . . Supposing this inspector was watching this house from across the road last night, as he had done every night for the past few weeks, in the hope of catching the thieves in the act . . .'

'Surely, that would have been rather reckless of him?'

'In our job, Monsieur Jonker, we are sometimes obliged to take risks.'

'Sorry.'

'These gangs of art thieves, even though a killer may sometimes be found in their midst, are usually made up of clever, cultured people, who wouldn't dream of acting without the most careful preliminary investigation . . . Since you tell me that you have every confidence in your servants, I can only suppose that one of those young women . . .'

Did Jonker accept the Chief Superintendent's reasoning at face value, or did he suspect a trap? It was impossible to tell.

'Many young women who work in night clubs and such are known to have contacts in what we in France call *le milieu*, in other words, the underworld.'

'Are you asking me for the names, addresses and telephone numbers of all the young women who have been to this house?'

His tone was not merely ironic now, it was acid.

'That might be a help, but what I would really like to know is what they come to your house to do.'

Phew! This was the crunch. Jonker, motionless, his burnt-out cigar between his fingers, was still looking him unblinkingly in the eye.

'Very well!' he said, at last, rising to his feet.

And, having dropped his cigar stub in a blue ashtray, he took a step or two towards the middle of the room.

'I warned you at the outset of this interview that I was prepared to answer any question you might care to put to me, unless it was concerned with my private life. I admire you and congratulate you on the remarkable skill with which you have contrived to bring my private life into the discussion, by linking it with last night's unhappy events.'

He stopped in front of Maigret, who was now also on his feet.

'I imagine you have been in the Police Force for a long time?'

'Twenty-eight years.'

'I dare say your experience has not been wholly confined to the criminal classes. Is this really the first time you have encountered a man of my age and in my position who is a slave to his instincts? And do you regard it as entirely reprehensible?

'Paris can hardly be described as a puritan city, Chief Superintendent. In my own country, I would be pointed out in the street, perhaps even repudiated by my own family.

'There are many foreigners living here and on the Riviera who have chosen to make their home in France, precisely because of the Frenchman's tolerant attitude in such matters . . .'

'May I ask whether Madame Jonker . . .?'

'Madame Jonker is a woman of the world, and no puritan. She knows that some men of my age need the stimulus of variety . . . You leave me no choice but to speak of these extremely intimate matters. I trust you are satisfied . . .'

He seemed to think that the interview was at an end, judging from the way he was looking towards the door.

But Maigret, speaking gently and in a very low voice, returned to the charge.

'Just now, you made some reference to names, addresses and telephone numbers . . .'

'You're not expecting me to provide a list, surely? People of that sort, though their lives may not be above reproach, are not required to give an account of themselves to the police. It would be a gross impropriety on my part to place them in an equivocal position . . .'

'You have admitted that you seldom go out, and that you are not in the habit of visiting night clubs. May I ask, therefore, how you make contact with your lady visitors?'

Another long pause for reflection.

'Do you really not know how these things are done?' he said at last, with a sigh.

'Needless to say, I am aware of the existence of pimps and procuresses, but their activities are illegal.'

'Are their clients also in breach of the law?'

'At a pinch, a charge of complicity might be brought, but as a rule . . .'

'As a rule, their clients are not subject to harassment. Isn't that so? In which case, Chief Superintendent, I have no more to say to you.'

'But I still have a favour to ask of you.'

'Do you really mean a favour, or is that just a euphemism?'

The two men had now almost reached the point of open conflict.

'Heavens above! Well, if you must know, I might, if you were to refuse, be obliged to resort to the processes of the law.'

'Well, what is it you want?'

'I should like to see over your house.'

'Don't you mean search it?'

'You are forgetting that, up to now, I have proceeded on the assumption that you were an intended victim.'

'And you are trying to protect me? Is that what you're saying?'

'Perhaps.'

'Very well. Come with me.'

Jonker was no longer the courteous host, offering drinks and cigars. His manner was suddenly very haughty indeed, quite that of the lord of the manor.

'You have already seen this room. I spend a good deal of my time in here. Do you wish me to open the drawers for you?'

'No.'

'I should point out that there is an automatic in the right-hand drawer, a Lüger, which I acquired during the war.'

He showed it to Maigret, adding: 'It's loaded . . . I keep another gun, a Browning, in my bedroom. That too is loaded. I'll show it to you later . . .

'This is the drawing-room . . . I know you haven't come to admire my pictures. All the same, you might like to take a look at this Gauguin here. Many people consider it the artist's greatest work, and it will go to the museum in Amsterdam after my death . . .

'Follow me . . . Do you know anything about carpets? . . . There's nothing of interest to you here . . . This is the dining-room. The picture on the left of the chimneypiece is Cézanne's last painting . . .

'This door here leads to a little room which my wife uses as her private sitting-room. As you see, I have striven to create an atmosphere which is at once intimate and very feminine . . .

'This is the pantry . . . As you see, Carl is engaged in cleaning the silver . . . It's seventeenth-century English silver. Its only drawback is that it is heavy to handle . . .

'The kitchen is in the basement . . . So is the cook . . . Do you wish to see them?'

Whether intentionally or not, there was a touch of insolence in his easy manner.

'Very well, we'll go upstairs . . . The staircase comes from an old château near Utrecht . . . My own suite of rooms is on the left . . .'

He opened doors in the manner of an estate agent conducting a prospective purchaser round a house.

'Another study, you see, like the one downstairs. I am fond of books, and find them very useful . . . Those card-indexes on the left-hand side record the individual histories of several thousand paintings, including a list of their successive owners, and the prices paid when any of them changed hands.

'Here is my bedroom . . . The revolver I mentioned is in the drawer of the bedside table . . . It's a common ·635, not a very efficient offensive weapon . . .'

Everywhere, even on the staircase, there were pictures, hung so close together as to be almost touching, and the best of them were to be found not in the drawing-room but in the Dutchman's bedroom, a very dark room full of English furniture and deep, leather armchairs.

'My bathroom . . . If you will give me a moment to make sure that my wife is not there, I'll show you her rooms across the passage . . .'

He knocked, opened the door, and stepped inside.

'You may come in . . . Her dressing-room, with the two Fragonards that I chose specially for her. The armchairs once belonged to Madame de Pompadour. If only you were here as an art-lover instead of a policeman, Chief Superintendent, it would give me the greatest pleasure to linger over all our treasures with you . . . My wife's bedroom . . .'

The walls were covered in crushed strawberry satin.

'Her bathroom . . .'

The Chief Superintendent did not go in, but he caught a glimpse of the bath, which was a sunken pool of black marble, with steps cut into the side.

'Let's go up to the top floor . . . You have a right to see everything, isn't that so?'

He opened another door.

'Carl's bedroom . . . His bathroom is through that door there . . . As you see, he has his own television set . . . He prefers black and white moving pictures to the works of the great masters . . .'

He knocked on the door opposite, a heavy door richly carved, which had probably once adorned some château.

'May we come in, darling? I am showing Chief Superintendent Maigret over the house. He is the Head of the Crime Squad . . . That's right, isn't it, Chief Superintendent?'

Maigret received a shock. In the middle of the glass-walled studio, facing an easel, stood a figure all in white, which vividly recalled to his mind Lognon's words: 'The ghost . . .'

It was not an ordinary painter's smock that Madame Jonker was wearing. It was more like the habit worn by Dominican friars, and seemed to be made of some thick, soft material, such as turkish towelling.

And, to cap it all, the Dutchman's wife's head was swathed in a white turban of the same material.

She had a palette in her left hand and a paintbrush in her right. Her black eyes were turned inquiringly on the Chief Superintendent.

'I have often heard about you, Monsieur Maigret, and I am delighted to meet you. Forgive me if I don't shake hands . . .'

Having got rid of the paintbrush, she wiped her right hand on the white robe, leaving smears of green paint.

'I hope you're not a connoisseur of the arts . . . But if you are, I beg you not to look at what I'm doing . . .'

After having seen so many masterpieces hanging on the walls downstairs, it was a shock to Maigret to find himself looking at a bare canvas, spattered here and there with shapeless blobs of colour.

5

The Graffiti

At that instant something occurred which Maigret could not quite define, a change of tone, or rather a sort of gear-shift, as a result of which words, gestures and attitudes took on a weightier significance. Was this due to the presence of the young woman, still draped in that peculiar garb, or had it something to do with the atmosphere of the room itself?

Logs were burning and crackling in the vast, white stone fireplace, and the flames seemed to have an impish life of their own.

The Chief Superintendent now understood why the curtains which could be seen from the windows of Marinette Augier's flat were almost always kept drawn. The studio was walled with glass on two sides, so that light could be let in from one side or the other, according to preference.

These curtains were of thick, black hessian, now greyish from frequent washing, and they had shrunk, so that they no longer met in the middle.

The view on one side was of rooftops stretching as far as Saint-Ouen; on the other, with the sails of the Moulin-de-la Galette in the foreground, almost the whole of Paris could be seen, including the lay-out of the boulevards, the large open space of the Champs-Élysées, the windings of the River Seine, and the gilded dome of the Invalides.

All Maigret's senses were alert, but it was not the view which fascinated him. It is difficult for anyone finding himself suddenly in an unfamiliar environment to grasp the whole of it, but Maigret felt that he was on the way to doing so.

Everything impinged on him at the same time, the two bare walls, for instance, painted a harsh white, with the vibrant flames of the fire flickering in the middle of one of them.

Madame Jonker had been engaged on a painting when the two men had come into the room. Did it not follow, therefore, that there should have been other paintings hanging on the walls? And also, as in any artist's studio, canvases stacked one against another on the floor? The expanse of polished boards, however, was as bare as the walls.

Next to the easel was a small table, on which stood a box full of tubes of paint.

Another table further off, a table of white unvarnished wood, the only undistinguished object he had so far seen in that house, was covered with a jumble of pots, tins, bottles and rags.

The only other furniture in the studio consisted of two antique wardrobes and two chairs, one upright, the other, an armchair, upholstered in fading brown velvet.

He could sense that something was amiss, though he could not say what, but he was very much on the alert, so that he was the more struck by the Dutchman's next words, addressed to his wife: 'The Chief Superintendent has not come to admire my pictures, but, strange as it may seem, to discuss the subject of jealousy. Apparently, he is surprised to learn that not all women are jealous . . .'

It sounded a commonplace enough remark in spite of its ironic tone. But to Maigret's ears it was a clear warning from Jonker to his wife, and acknowledged by her with a flicker of the eyelids.

'Does your wife suffer from jealousy, Monsieur Maigret?'

'To tell you the honest truth, madame, she has never shown the slightest sign of it.'

'Still, you must have interviewed a great many women at your office in your time.'

He thought he had intercepted another signal, but this time addressed to him. Could he have been wrong?

The impression was so strong that he began to search his memory. Had he seen this woman before? Had she ever been up before him at Headquarters? Their eyes met. Her beautiful face still wore the vague smile of a hostess receiving a guest. But was there not something more to be read in those great brown eyes, with their long, flickering lashes?

'Please don't interrupt your work on my account . . .' he murmured.

For she was laying her palette down on the table. When she had done so, she unwound the white turban from her head, and shook her black hair into its natural loose waves.

'I believe you are French by origin?'

'Norris told you, I suppose?'

It was a harmless enough question. Was he imagining things, or did it really suggest some other hidden meaning?

'I already knew before I came here.'

'So you've been making inquiries about us?'

Jonker was less relaxed than he had been in his study on the ground floor, or when, looking somewhat contemptuous, he had taken Maigret on a lightning tour of the house, explaining each room as if he were an official guide, showing a visitor over an old château.

'You must be tired, darling. Why not go and rest?'

Another signal? An order?

She took off the white *burnous* which enveloped her, and emerged wearing a clinging black dress. At once, she seemed taller. She had the well-rounded figure of an attractive woman of mature years.

'When did you first take up painting, madame?'

Instead of replying directly, she explained: 'Living in a house full of pictures, and married to a man whose only passion is art, one could scarcely avoid the overwhelming temptation to try one's own hand with a paintbrush. I could hardly attempt to compete with the great masters, whose works look down on me from morning to night, so I had to content myself with abstract painting. But please don't embarrass me by asking what this daub of mine is supposed to mean . . .'

All the years she had spent in England and in Paris had not wholly wiped out her southern accent, and Maigret noted every nuance of her speech with ever closer attention.

'Were you born in Nice?'

'So they told you that, too?'

It was his turn to look into her eyes and signal a message.

'I greatly admire the church of Sainte-Réparate . . .'

She didn't blush, but almost imperceptibly flinched.

'I see you know the town.'

By naming the church, he had evoked the whole of the old quarter of Nice, the poorest part of the town, with its narrow streets where the sun did not often penetrate, and where lines of washing were strung between the houses from one year's end to the other.

He was now almost sure that she had been born in that district, in one of the crumbling tenements which each housed fifteen or twenty families, their staircases and back yards swarming with kids.

It even seemed to him that she had implicitly admitted as much, and that, unknown to her husband, who was blind to these subtleties, he and she had exchanged what almost amounted to a masonic sign.

Chief Superintendent and Head of the Police Judiciaire Crime Squad Maigret might be, but he was still a man of the people.

As for her, live as she might among paintings worthy of the Louvre, buy her clothes as she might from the top couture houses, glitter as she might have done in diamonds, rubies and emeralds at innumerable grand evening parties in Manchester and London, she had still grown up in the shadow of the church of Sainte-Réparate, and he would not have been surprised to learn that she had haunted the terraces of the Place Masséna with an armful of flowers to sell.

Both were now playing a role, as if beneath the words spoken between them flowed other words which were no concern of the son of the Dutch banker.

'Did your husband build this magnificent studio specially for you?'

'Oh! no . . . He hadn't even met me when he built the house . . . He had a very dear friend, who was a real artist . . . She still exhibits at various art galleries . . . I can't think why he didn't marry her. Maybe he wanted someone younger . . . What do you say, Norris?'

'I don't remember . . .'

'Well! How's that for good manners and delicacy?'

'I asked you just now when you started painting.'

'I don't know . . . A few months ago.'

'I presume you spend part of each day up here in the studio?'

'This really is a grilling!' she said, banteringly. 'Anyone could tell from the questions you ask that you are neither a woman nor a housewife. If you were to ask me, for instance, what I was doing at this time yesterday, I should probably find it difficult to answer . . . I'm lazy, and it's my belief, contrary to what is usually said, that time passes more quickly for lazy people than for others.

'I get up late . . . I dawdle . . . I gossip with my maid . . . The cook comes up to my room to get her orders . . . It's lunch time before I have really woken up to the fact that the day has begun . . .'

'You're very chatty all of a sudden, my dear.'

Maigret intervened: 'I didn't realize that it was possible to paint at night.'

This time, it was impossible to miss the look that passed between husband and wife. The Dutchman forestalled whatever reply his wife had intended to make.

'It wouldn't have been, I dare say, for the Impressionists, obsessed as they were with the interplay of sunlight and shade, but I know several modern painters who claim that artificial light brings out some colours better than daylight . . .'

'Is that why you paint at night, madame?'

'I paint whenever I happen to feel the urge.'

'And you usually feel the urge after dinner, and often work on at your easel until two in the morning . . .'

She forced a smile.

'Well, really! I don't seem to be able to hide anything from you . . .'

He pointed to the black curtains which covered the glass bay overlooking the Avenue Junot.

'Look at those curtains over there. They no longer meet in the middle. In my experience, there is at least one insomniac to be found in every residential street. I mentioned this to your husband, when we were talking just now. The more educated among them read or listen to music. The others look out of their windows . . .'

Jonker had by now surrendered the initiative to his wife, as if he felt that he was out of his depth. He was nervous, but pretended to be listening to the conversation with only half an ear. Two or three times he went to the window, to gaze at the panorama of Paris spread out below.

The sky was growing lighter and lighter. It was white all over, and becoming more and more luminous, especially to the west, where it was almost possible to discern the sun dipping towards the horizon.

'Do you keep all your canvasses in these cupboards?'

'No . . . Would you like to check? . . . I don't object to your prying . . . After all, you're only doing your job . . .'

She opened one of the cupboards, which contained rolls of drawing paper, and more tubes of paint, bottles and tins, all in a muddle, like those on the table.

The other cupboard was empty, except for three blank canvasses bearing the label of a supplier in the Rue Lepic.

'You look disappointed. Were you hoping to find a skeleton?'

She was referring to the English saying, to the effect that every family has a skeleton in its cupboard.

'Skeletons don't occur overnight,' he said, frowning. 'For the present, Lognon is still alive in his hospital bed . . .'

'Lognon? That's an odd name. Who is he?'

'An inspector of police . . .'

'The one who was shot last night?'

'Are you quite sure, madame, that you were in your bedroom when the shot was fired, or rather, I should say, the three shots?'

'I think, Chief Superintendent,' interposed Jonker, 'that this time you really are going too far . . .'

'In that case, you may prefer to answer for her. Madame Jonker spends a good deal of her time painting, especially at night, often until very late . . . And yet I find her in a virtually empty studio.'

'Is there any French law which obliges a householder to fill his studio with furniture?'

'One would at least expect to find a great many paintings, some in progress, some completed. What do you do with your paintings, madame?'

Once again, she and her husband exchanged glances. Was she not, in effect, telling him to answer for her?

'Mirella doesn't claim to be a serious artist . . .'

It was the first time Maigret had heard her referred to by name. No doubt she had originally been called Mireille.

'Most of her paintings she destroys after she's finished them . . .'

'One moment, Monsieur Jonker . . . I'm sorry to have to be so persistent. I've met one or two painters in my time . . . How would they set about destroying a painting?'

'They'd cut it into strips and burn it, or put it in the rubbish bin . . .'

'I mean before that.'

'I don't understand you.'

'And you such an expert! You surprise me. Are you suggesting that they throw away the stretchers as well? Look, there are three stretchers in this cupboard, all brand new . . .'

'If my wife isn't too dissatisfied with a picture, she will sometimes give it to a friend . . .'

'Are you referring to the paintings that are collected from here at night?'

'At night, or during the day . . .'

'If those are your wife's work, then she's more prolific than she has led me to believe . . .'

'They're not all hers . . .'

'Is there anything else you need me for?' inquired Madame Jonker. 'Why don't we all go downstairs and have a cup of tea?'

'Not just now, madame. Your husband has been kind enough to show me over the house, but I have not yet seen what is behind this door, here . . .'

It was a massive door of blackened oak, at the far end of the studio.

'Who knows? We might even find one or two of your elusive paintings in there . . . ?'

The tension in the air was like a charge of electricity. The voices, though more muted, sounded sharper.

'I'm afraid not, Chief Superintendent.'

'How can you be so sure?'

'Because that door hasn't been opened for months, if not for years . . . It belonged formerly to the person my wife spoke of . . .

She used to go in there to rest between sessions at her easel . . .'

'And you have kept it as a shrine for all these years?'

He was deliberately pressing home the attack, in the hope of provoking an unguarded response from his adversary. The time had come, he felt, to exploit his advantage to the limit, and this time, by exception, the climax had been reached, not in his office in the Quai des Orfèvres but in an artist's studio, from which could be seen a panoramic view of Paris.

The Dutchman's fists were clenched, but he still did not lose his self-control.

'I am quite sure, Chief Superintendent, that if I were to burst unexpectedly into your home, rooting in corners and harrying your wife with question after question, I should discover a great many things which would strike me as peculiar, if not inexplicable. Surely you must realize that everyone has his own personal habits, his own special way of looking at things, which are incomprehensible to any outsider . . .

'This is a fairly big house . . . Practically all my time is taken up with my pictures . . . Our social life is severely restricted, and my wife, as she has told you, likes to amuse herself with a paintbrush. Is it so very surprising that she should attach little importance to what becomes of her paintings, whether they are burnt, thrown in the rubbish bin or given away to friends . . . ?'

'What friends?'

'You leave me no choice but to repeat what I said earlier in my study. It would be most improper of me to forget myself so far as to involve a third party in the sort of unpleasantness which my wife and I are now having to put up with, because shots were fired in our street by persons unknown . . .'

'To get back to the question of this door . . .'

'I don't know how many rooms you have in your flat, Chief Superintendent, but there are thirty-two in this house. There are four servants always coming and going. We have occasionally had to dismiss one of the maids for improper conduct . . .

'Given these conditions, it is surely not surprising that a key should occasionally get lost?'

'And you haven't had a new one made?'

'It never occurred to me.'

'Are you sure the key is not in the house?'

'Not as far as I know. If it is, I dare say it will turn up one day in the most unlikely place . . .'

'Do you mind if I make a phone call from here?'

There was an extension telephone on the table. Maigret had noticed that there was one in almost every room in the house. No doubt they could be used for both internal and external calls.

'What do you intend to do?'

'Send for a locksmith . . .'

'I don't think I can allow that. It seems to me you're exceeding your authority . . .'

'Very well, I'll ring the Department of Public Prosecutions, who will issue a warrant, duly signed, and deliver it to me here . . .'

Once more, husband and wife exchanged glances. It was Mirella who made the first move. She went across to the cupboard, carrying the stool which had been standing in front of the easel. She climbed onto it, stretched out her arm, and ran her hand along the top of the cupboard. When she lowered her arm, she was holding a key.

'You see, Monsieur Jonker, there was something that struck me as odd, or rather, I should say, two related things. There is a bolt on the door of this studio, but, contrary to the usual practice, it is fixed to the outside of the door.

'Just now, while you were talking to me, I noticed that the same is true of this other door . . .'

'You're perfectly entitled to express surprise, Chief Superintendent. Indeed, you have done little else since you came into this house. Your way of life is so very different from ours that you couldn't be expected to understand.'

'I'm doing my best, as you can see . . .'

He took the key that Madame Jonker held out to him, and went across to the locked door. While his two companions stood motionless, as if rooted to the floor in the middle of the vast studio, he tried the key in the lock.

'How long did you say it was since this door was last opened?'

'What does it matter?'

'I won't ask you to join me here, madame, and I'm sure you can guess why, but I should be obliged if your husband would do so . . .'

The Dutchman came forward, determined to keep his end up.

'To begin with, please note that this floor is clean. There isn't a speck of dust anywhere, and, if you touch it, you will see that it is damp in places, as if it had been scrubbed down very recently . . . In fact, the room was cleaned last night or this morning. Who did it?'

It was Mirella who spoke, her voice coming from behind him.

'It certainly wasn't me . . . You'd better ask the maids . . . unless my husband gave instructions to Carl . . .'

It was quite a small room. The window, like the glass bay in the studio, looked out on the panoramic view of Paris, and the shabby flowered curtains were spattered with paint. It looked, in fact, as if someone, after having been painting with his fingers, had wiped his hands on them here and there.

There was an iron bedstead in one corner, with a mattress on it, but no sheets, blankets or counterpane.

The most striking aspect of the room was what Maigret could only call the graffiti. On the dirty white walls, someone had amused himself by delineating obscene figures in outline, such as one sometimes sees in public lavatories. The only difference was that these were not pencil drawings, but were done with oil paints in green, blue, yellow and violet.

'I will not make so bold, Monsieur Jonker, as to ask you whether you think these murals were done by your former friend. Indeed, this sketch here rules out any such supposition . . .'

It was a portrait of Mirella, executed by means of a few bold strokes, and it was a good deal livelier than many of the paintings hanging in the drawing-room.

'You are waiting for an explanation, no doubt?'

'Does that surprise you? As you said yourself, your life-style and mine are very different. Perhaps I do find it a little difficult to understand your behaviour. Be that as it may, I am none the less convinced that your own friends, members of your own social class, would be very much surprised if they were to discover these – er – let's call them frescoes, under your roof . . .'

Not only had someone portrayed, with a wealth of detail, those parts of the human body normally kept covered, but there were also scenes of unbridled eroticism. In contrast, the wall near the bed was covered in vertical lines, which reminded the Chief Superintendent of those drawn on prison walls to mark the passage of time.

'Why did the person who lived here count the days so impatiently?'

'What do you mean?'

'Didn't you know of the existence of these graffiti?'

'I did take a look round in here some time ago.'

'How long ago?'

'Several months, as I told you . . . I was shocked by what I saw, so I double-locked the door and put the key on top of the wardrobe . . .'

'In the presence of your wife?'

'I don't remember.'

'You have seen these murals, have you not, madame?'

She nodded.

'What were your feelings when you saw the portrait of yourself?'

'I don't call that a portrait. It's just a rough sketch, a doodle such as any painter might draw . . .'

'I'm waiting for one or both of you to tell me what this is all about.'

There was a long silence, during which Maigret, without waiting for permission, took his pipe out of his pocket.

'I wonder whether it wouldn't be best,' murmured the Dutchman, 'for me to call in my lawyer. I am not sufficiently familiar with French law to know whether or not you have the right to interrogate us like this.'

'If you choose to call in your legal adviser now, rather than to give me a straight answer, I suggest you arrange for him to meet you at the Quai des Orfèvres, because, if that is your decision, I must ask you to accompany me there at once.'

'Without a warrant?'

'With or without a warrant. If necessary, I can have a warrant delivered here within half an hour . . .'

The Chief Superintendent went towards the telephone.

'Wait!'

'Who occupied that room?'

'It's an old story . . . Why don't we go downstairs and have a drink while we talk? I could do with a cigar myself, and I haven't got one on me . . .'

'On condition that Madame Jonker comes with us.'

She went first, looking weary and perhaps resigned. Maigret followed, with Jonker close on his heels.

'In here?' asked Mirella, when they reached the drawing-room.

'I'd rather we went into my study . . .'

'What can I offer you, Monsieur Maigret?'

'Nothing for the moment . . .'

She looked towards the glass from which he had drunk earlier, standing next to her husband's on the desk. Was it because the situation had changed that the Chief Superintendent had this time refused a drink?

The room was darker now. The Dutchman switched on the lights, and poured himself a glass of Curaçao. He looked inquiringly at his wife.

'No. I'd rather have whisky . . .'

He was the first to decide to sit down, assuming almost the identical posture in which he had sat an hour earlier. His wife remained standing, with a glass in her hand.

'Two or three years ago –' began the art-lover, snipping the end of his cigar.

The Chief Superintendent interrupted him.

'I wish you would be more precise. Ever since I got here, you have not mentioned a single date or name, unless we are to include the names of painters long since dead . . . You talk in terms of several weeks, several months or several years . . . Instead of stating the time, you say early evening or late at night.'

'Maybe it's because I don't take much account of time. Remember, I have no office to go to or leave at any particular time, and, until today, I have never been called upon to give an account of myself to anybody.'

He was overdoing the aggressive arrogance. It didn't ring true any more. Maigret caught a look of mingled anxiety and disapproval on his wife's face.

You, my dear, he thought, know from experience that that particular line cuts no ice with the police . . .

Was it in Nice, when she was a mere girl, or in England that he had had dealings with her?

'It's up to you whether you believe me or not, Chief Superintendent . . . I repeat that, two or three years ago, I was told of a talented young painter who was so down on his luck that he sometimes had to sleep under the bridges, and forage for food in dustbins . . .'

'You say you were "told" of this young man. Who by? A friend, an art dealer?'

Jonker made as if to brush away a fly.

'What does it matter? I don't remember. At any rate, I felt a twinge of guilt when I thought of that studio up there going to waste . . .'

'This was before your wife took up painting, then?'

'Yes . . . I wouldn't have had him here . . .'

'What is the name of this graffiti merchant?'

'I never knew his surname.'

'What was his first name?'

A slight pause: 'Pedro.'

It was plain to see that this was pure invention.

'A Spaniard? An Italian?'

'Believe it or not, I never bothered to ask. I put the studio and adjoining bedroom at his disposal, and gave him enough money to buy paints and canvas.'

'And at night, you locked him in to prevent him from going on the town?'

'I didn't lock him in.'

'What, then, was the point of the bolts on the outside of the doors?'

'They were put there when the house was built.'

'What for?'

'For a very simple reason. As you are not a collector, it would probably not occur to you. For a long time, I used the studio as a storeroom for such paintings as I had no room to display on my walls. It's quite natural that I should bolt the door from the outside, since I could hardly do so from inside.'

'I thought you said that the studio had been built for the use of your former artist friend . . .'

'Let's say the bolts were put on after she had ceased to live here . . .'

'Including the bolt on the bedroom door?'

'I'm not even sure that it was on my instructions that it was put there . . .'

'To return to Pedro . . .'

'He lived in the house for several months . . .'

'*Several!*' exclaimed Maigret, stressing the word. Mirella could not help smiling.

The Dutchman was growing restive. He must have exercised a great deal of self-control to keep his temper.

'Was he genuinely talented?'

'Very much so.'

'Did he make a success of his career? Did he achieve recognition?'

'I don't know . . . I used occasionally to go up to the studio, and I admired his work.'

'Did you buy any of his pictures?'

'How could I buy pictures from a man who was dependent on me for bed and board?'

'So you don't possess a single one of his works . . .? Did it not occur to him to make you a present or two before he left?'

'Have you seen a single painting in this house which is less than thirty years old . . .? A love of paintings often turns a man into a collector . . . And collectors as a whole prefer to specialize in one particular field . . . My own special field begins with Van Gogh and ends with Modigliani.'

'Did Pedro have all his meals upstairs?'

'I suppose so.'

'Did Carl take them up to him?'

'I leave all that sort of thing to my wife.'

'Yes, it was Carl,' she said, without conviction.

'Did he go out much?'

'No more than any other young man of his age.'

'How old was he, by the way?'

'Twenty-two or twenty-three. Towards the end of his stay he

had made a good many friends, young men and women of his own age. At first, he never entertained more than one or two at a time.

'Then he began overdoing it. Some nights, there would be as many as twenty of them up there, making a fearful racket just above my wife's bedroom, preventing her from getting to sleep . . .'

'Did it never occur to you, madame, to go upstairs yourself and find out what was going on?'

'I left that to my husband.'

'And what was the outcome?'

'He threw Pedro out, but not, mind you, before he had put him in funds.'

'And it was then that you discovered the graffiti?'

Jonker nodded.

'And you too, madame? If so, you must have realized, when you saw that portrait of yourself, that Pedro was in love with you. Did he ever make a pass at you?'

'You'd better not take that tone with my wife, Chief Superintendent, otherwise I'll be regretfully compelled to make a formal complaint to my Ambassador,' said Jonker, sternly.

'You won't forget to tell him, will you, about the young women who used to slink into the house after dark, and stay the whole night?'

'I thought I understood the French character . . .'

'I thought I understood the Dutch character . . .'

Mirella intervened.

'Would you two kindly stop bickering? I can understand that my husband should be irritated by some of your questions, especially those concerning me. But I also understand that it is hard for the Chief Superintendent to approve of the sort of life we lead . . .

'As far as those women are concerned, Monsieur Maigret, I've always known about them, even before we were married. You'd be surprised to learn how many husbands there are who share his tastes . . . Most of them keep it dark, especially if they move among high-minded people. My husband prefers to be open about it, and I take that as a tribute to my intelligence and my affection for him . . .'

He noticed that she didn't say 'love'.

'If some of his answers seem imprecise and apparently self-contradictory, I believe it is because he has nothing to hide . . .'

'Very well, then, let me now put a question to you which requires a precise answer. Until what time, exactly, did you remain in your studio last night?'

'Let me think. I don't bother with wearing a watch when I'm working, and you yourself will have noticed that there are no clocks up there . . . It was about eleven when I told my personal maid that she could go to bed . . .'

'At that time, were you still up there?'

'Yes. She came in to ask me if I should be needing her help in getting ready for bed . . .'

'Were you working on the painting that is still on the easel?'

'I spent a long time with a stick of charcoal in one hand and a rag in the other, trying to think of a subject.'

'What is the subject of the painting . . . ?'

'Let's call it Harmony . . . Abstract paintings are not mere daubs . . . Possibly, they require more thought and entail more false starts than figurative paintings . . .'

'Let's get back to the time . . .'

'It could have been as late as one in the morning when I went downstairs to my room.'

'Did you switch off the light in the studio?'

'I think so. It's the sort of thing one does automatically.'

'Were you wearing the same white robe and turban as you wore today?'

'To tell you the truth, it's only an old bath robe and a turkish towel. As I only paint for recreation, it would have been pretentious of me to buy a real painter's smock.'

'Had your husband gone to bed? Didn't you go in and say good night to him?'

'I never do, if he goes to bed before me.'

'Because you're afraid one of his lady visitors might be with him?'

'If you say so.'

'I think we've almost reached the end . . .'

He could feel a relaxation of tension, but he was only up to one of his favourite tricks. Slowly, he relit his pipe, apparently searching his memory for anything he might have overlooked.

'Earlier this evening, Monsieur Jonker, you made a point, as tactfully as you were able, of the fact that I lacked experience of the thought processes, actions and behaviour of an art connoisseur. I see from your library shelves that you keep abreast of all the important sales. You obviously buy lavishly, as there are times when you have to store some of your pictures in the studio, because you have no room to hang them . . .

'Am I to deduce from this that you sometimes sell pictures when you have grown tired of them?'

'For the last time, let me try and explain. I inherited a number of paintings from my father, who was not only a financial genius, but also one of the first men to discover those artists whose works are now sought after by every museum in the world.

'My income, large though it is, is insufficient to enable me to buy every picture I covet *ad infinitum*.

'As all collectors do, I started with the second-rate, or perhaps I should say with the minor works of the great painters . . .

'Little by little, as these paintings appreciated in value and I became more selective in my tastes, I began to sell some of those lesser works, and replace them with better ones . . .'

'Forgive me for interrupting. Have you continued this practice up to the present day?'

'And shall do, till I die.'

'These paintings you sell, do you put them up for auction at the Hôtel Drouot, or do you entrust them to an art dealer?'

'I do occasionally, but not often, sell a picture at public auction. But most of the items that come up for auction form part of estates which are being wound up. A collector prefers to set about things in a different way . . .'

'How do you mean?'

'He studies the market. He knows, for instance, that such and such a museum in the United States or South America is on the look out for a Renoir, say, or a blue period Picasso. If he has such a painting to dispose of, he sets about making the right contacts . . .'

'Which would explain how some of your neighbours happened to see pictures being taken away from your house . . . ?'

'Those, and my wife's paintings . . .'

'I wonder, Monsieur Jonker, if you would be willing to let me have the names of some of the buyers. Let's confine ourselves, say, to the past twelve months . . .'

'No.'

It was a cold and emphatic 'no'.

'Am I then to understand that these were clandestine transactions?'

'I don't care for the word "clandestine". Such transactions are always conducted discreetly. Most countries, for instance, have laws regulating the export of works of art, with a view to protecting their national treasures.

'It's not only that the museums have pre-emptive rights, but that export permits are not readily granted.

'There is, in the drawing-room next door, one of Chirico's most important works, which was illegally smuggled across the Italian frontier, not to mention a Manet which, incredible as it may seem, came to me from Russia.

'Surely you must see that I can't possibly name names? Someone buys a picture from me. I hand it over to him, and he pays me. It's no concern of mine what becomes of it after that . . .'

'You don't know?'

'I don't want to know. It's none of my business, any more than it is to find out where one of my own purchases comes from . . .'

Maigret stood up. He felt as if he had been in this house for an eternity, and the luxurious trappings, so remote from real life, were beginning to oppress him. Besides, he was thirsty and, as things now stood between Jonker and himself, he was precluded from accepting a drink from him.

'Please forgive me, madame, for having disturbed you at your work, and for having ruined your afternoon . . .'

Was there not an unspoken question in Mirella's eyes?

Surely this is not the end? they seemed to say. I know how the police go about their business. You don't intend to let us alone, and I'm wondering what trap you have in store for us . . .

Turning to her husband, she seemed about to speak, hesitated, then murmured lamely to Maigret: 'It's been a pleasure to meet you . . .'

Jonker, standing up, put out his cigar, and said in his turn: 'I'm sorry if I seemed short-tempered at times. One should not forget one's duty as a host . . .'

The manservant was not summoned to see him out. The Dutchman himself preceded him to the door, and opened it. Outside it was cool, and the air was damp and acrid with dust. Haloes were beginning to form around the standard lamps.

In the building opposite, Marinette Augier's windows were dark. So were the windows on the first floor of the house next door, but there was a face pressed against one of the window panes, the face of an old man.

Maigret was tempted to give a friendly wave to old Maclet, still faithfully at his post. He even felt inclined to go across and knock on his door, but he had more urgent matters to attend to.

These, however, did not prevent him from returning to the bistro which he had patronized that morning and gulping down two large glasses of beer, before getting into a taxi at the corner of the Rue Caulaincourt.

6

The Barefoot Drunkard

Habits are formed rapidly in local bistros. Because Maigret had had a hot toddy that morning the proprietor, wearing his sleeves rolled up, seemed surprised that he should now order beer. And when Maigret asked for a *jeton* for the telephone, he said: 'Only one?'

The man who had used the telephone before Maigret must have drunk a great deal of Calvados, because not only the telephone box but the instrument as well reeked of fermented apples.

'Hello! Who is that speaking?'

'Inspector Neveu.'

'Isn't Lucas there?'

'I'll get him . . . One moment . . . He's speaking on another line . . .'

The Chief Superintendent waited patiently, looking absently about him at the reassuring furnishings of the little café, the zinc counter, the bottles, with their familiar shapes and labels. The newspapers were much given to expressing complacency or anxiety about the dizzying speed of change in the modern world, yet here displayed before his very eyes, after so many years, including those of the Second World War, were brands of aperitif which he used to see on the shelves of the village inn when he was a child.

'Sorry, Chief . . .'

'There's a man of the name of Norris Jonker, who lives in the Avenue Junot. I want the house put under surveillance as soon as possible. It's opposite the building Lognon was leaving when he was shot. You'd better send at least two men with a car . . .'

'I'm not sure there are any left in the forecourt . . . I'm afraid not . . .'

'You'll manage somehow . . . Not only do I want the Jonkers followed if they go out, but I want a tail put on anyone who calls at the house . . . Be as quick as you can . . .'

In the taxi, as it wound its way through the lighted streets, Maigret was in a strange mood. He ought to have felt pleased that he had not allowed himself to be overawed by the Dutchman, with all his pride and wealth, nor by the mature beauty of Mirella.

Seldom had he gathered so much information in a single day about a case of which he had known nothing when he had got up that morning. Not only had he shaken a great many little secrets out of the art collector and his wife, but he had learned much that he would never have suspected about the Avenue Junot itself.

Why, then, was he still not satisfied, but rather prey to an indefinable anxiety? He forced these questions upon himself, but it was not until they were crossing the Pont-au-Change and were in sight of the old Palais de Justice, so familiar to him, that he thought he had found the cause of his uneasiness.

Although he had spent more time in Norris Jonker's study than anywhere else, and had been shown over the house from top to bottom, and although the drama had reached its climax in the studio at the top of the house, it was not any of these rooms that had made the greatest impression on him.

The scene that had etched itself on his memory, like the chorus of a song, was the little bedroom with its iron bedstead, and he suddenly understood why he had felt uneasy.

He saw again, but magnified as on a cinema screen, the obscene pictures daubed on the white walls with thick brush-strokes in red, black and blue. When he tried to conjure up a picture of Mirella Jonker, it was her portrait, rapidly sketched with a few bold strokes, that came most vividly to his mind.

The man or woman who had made that sketch in a transport of passion, and surrounded it with so many nightmarish sexual symbols, must surely have been mad? He had seen paintings by certified lunatics which had had the same powerfully mesmeric and evocative effect on him.

The room had been recently occupied, there was no doubt about that. Otherwise, why should it have been thought necessary to scrub it down so thoroughly within the last few hours? And why had they not, at the same time, ventured to slap a fresh coat of whitewash on the walls?

Slowly he went up the great staircase at Police Headquarters. Often he would not go straight to his office, but look in on the inspectors in their Duty Room. He did so now. Each sat working at his desk under the lighted ceiling globes, like a class of students at night school.

He was not looking for anyone in particular. It was just that he found it reassuring to resume contact in this way with his working surroundings.

Just as school children do not look up when the teacher passes by, neither did they; and yet there was not one who did not know that he was looking grave and anxious, and that his face showed signs not merely of weariness but of exhaustion.

'Has my wife telephoned?'

'No, Chief.'

'Try and get her at my home number. If she's not there, try Lognon's flat.'

Perhaps not a certified lunatic, confined in a psychiatric hospital, but certainly a violent man, with little or no self-control . . .

'Hello! Is that you?'

She was back in their flat, and was no doubt making preparations for dinner.

'Have you been back long?'

'Over an hour. Actually, I don't think she was all that keen for me to stay . . . She was flattered that I had put myself out for her, but she doesn't feel comfortable with me . . . She is much more at home with the old girl with the rosary . . . Alone together, they can have a good moan, and spend endless time totting up all their little misfortunes . . .

'I went out to the shops again, and bought her a few little treats . . . And I slipped some money into the old girl's hand – she took it as if it was her due – and promised to look in again tomorrow morning . . . And what about you? Do you expect to be in to dinner?'

'I'm not sure yet, but I doubt it.'

'How is Lognon?'

'The last I heard, he was still alive, but I've only just got back here.'

'See you this evening, I hope.'

'I hope so, too.'

They never addressed each other by name, nor were they in the habit of exchanging endearments. What was the point, since both felt that, in many ways, they were one person?

He replaced the receiver and opened the door.

'Is Janvier there?'

'Coming, Chief.'

And Maigret, now seated at his desk and rearranging his pipes, said: 'First of all, what news of Lognon?'

'I rang Bichat ten minutes ago . . . The Matron is getting pretty fed up with us . . . No change . . . The doctors weren't expecting any until tomorrow at the earliest . . . He's still in a coma, and when he opens his eyes, he doesn't know where he is or what's happening to him, and he doesn't recognize anybody . . .'

'Have you seen Marinette Augier's ex-fiancé?'

'I found him in his office, and he seemed scared to death that his father might find out that I was a policeman . . . Apparently, his father is a holy terror, and has all the staff shivering in their shoes . . . Jean-Claude is a bit of a dandy, and he seems pretty feeble and flabby . . . He took me outside and went through a long rigmarole in front of the receptionist, pretending that I was a customer . . .'

'What does the firm make?'

'Metal tubing and all that sort of thing, in copper, iron and steel. It's one of those great big sinister boxes that one sees so often round about the Avenue de la République and the Boulevard Voltaire. He took me to a café a long way from his office. The afternoon papers mention the shooting and Lognon's injuries, but Marinette's name doesn't appear. Anyway, Jean-Claude hadn't seen a paper.'

'Was he cooperative?'

'He's so terrified of his father, and of getting involved in anything that might cause trouble for him, that he would gladly have confessed all the sins of his youth, if I'd let him . . . I told him that Marinette had suddenly vanished from her flat, and that we needed her urgently as a witness . . .

'"You were engaged to her for nearly a year . . ."

'"Engaged? Well, that's pitching it a bit high . . ."

'"Or a bit low, considering you spent a couple of nights a week in her flat?"

'He was terribly upset that we should have found out about that.

'"At any rate, if she's pregnant, it's not my fault. I haven't set eyes on her for longer than nine months . . ."

'You can tell the sort he is, can't you, Chief? I asked him about the week-ends.

'"I dare say there were some places you liked better than others . . . Have you a car?"

'"Of course."

'"Used you to go to the sea or just to the outskirts of Paris?"

'"To the outskirts . . . Not always to the same place . . . We'd stop at some little inn or other, usually on the river, because Marinette was nuts about swimming and boating. She didn't care for hotels, they were too smart and sophisticated for her. To tell you the truth, she had rather low tastes . . ."

'In the end, I managed to get half-a-dozen or so addresses out of him, places they'd been to more than once, the Auberge du Clou at Courcelles in the Vallée de Chevreuse, Chez Mélanie at Saint-Fargeau, midway between Corbeil and Melun, Félix et Félicie at Pomponne, on the Marne, not far from Lagny . . . She had a specially soft spot for that particular bistro, because that's all it is, a country bistro with a couple of bedrooms above. It doesn't even have running water . . .

'Then in Créguy, on the outskirts of Meaux, there's a sort of teagarden. He can't remember its name, only that the proprietor is deaf . . . La Pie Qui Danse, right out in the country between Meulan and Apremont . . . And on one occasion they had lunch at the Coq Hardy in Bougival.'

'Have you checked?'

'I thought it was better that I should stay here, to coordinate all the information as it comes in. I could have phoned through to the various local police stations, but I was afraid they might bungle things, and frighten the girl into running away . . . I know it's a bit irregular, as none of these places are in the Seine region, but I knew you were anxious to get things moving . . .'

'Well?'

'I've sent a man to each district: Lourtie, Jamin and Lagrume . . .'

'Did you assign a car to each of them?'

'Yes,' admitted Janvier, uneasily.

'So that's why, as Lucas has just informed me, there are no cars available?'

'I'm sorry . . .'

'You did the right thing . . . Any results yet?'

'Only at the Auberge du Clou. No news yet from nearer home . . . The others should be reporting in any time now . . .'

Maigret smoked his pipe in silence, as if he had forgotten that the inspector was still there.

'Can I help you at all?'

'Not for the moment. Don't leave without letting me know. You'd better tell Lucas to stay on as well . . .'

He was eager to get on with it. Ever since his long afternoon session with the Dutchman and his wife, he had had the feeling that someone was in danger, though he could not have said who.

Of course, the whole episode had been stage-managed for his benefit. No doubt the pictures on the wall were genuine, but he was sure that everything else that he had seen and heard was phoney.

'Put me through to the Aliens Office . . .'

It took them about ten minutes to find out Madame Jonker's maiden name for him. Her original christian name had not been Mireille, as he had supposed on account of her southern origins. No, Mirella Jonker had been christened with the much more common name of Marcelle, Marcelle Maillant.

'Get me the Police Judiciaire in Nice, will you? I'd like to speak to Superintendent Bastiani, if he's available . . .'

Rather than sit doing nothing, he was pursuing at random every possible lead.

'Hello! Bastiani? How are you, old man . . . ? Basking in the sunshine? Here we've had two solid days of rain. It didn't stop until this afternoon, and the sky is still overcast . . . I say, could you do me a favour . . . ? I'd be obliged if you could put a couple of your men on to rooting among some of your old files . . . If they find nothing in your section, maybe they could try the Palais de Justice . . . It's about a woman named Marcelle Maillant. She was born in Nice, probably in the old quarter, somewhere near Sainte-Réparate.

'She's aged thirty-four. She was formerly married to an Englishman named Muir, a ball-bearings manufacturer from Manchester. She lived in London for several years, and there met and married a rich Dutchman, Norris Jonker. They are now living in Paris . . .

'She's a magnificent woman, the sort people turn round to look at in the street . . . She's tall, dark and well groomed . . . Very much a woman of the world, but there's something about her that doesn't ring true . . . Do you see what I'm getting at? There's something wrong somewhere, though I don't know what . . . I can tell by the way she looks at me . . .

'Yes. It really is urgent . . . There's something very nasty brewing up, I'm certain, and I want to prevent it if I can . . . By the way, did you, by any chance, know Lognon, when you were in the Rue des Saussaies? Inspector Grumpy, yes . . . He was shot last night . . . He's not dead, but it's touch and go . . . There is a connection, yes . . . I'm puzzled as to exactly how she is involved, and how deeply . . . Your information may help me there . . .

'I'll be staying in my office, all night if necessary . . .'

He was well aware that, knowing it to be connected with the attempted murder of a colleague, Bastiani and his men would go to work with a will. It would be a point of honour with them.

For fully five minutes he sat slumped, as if in a dream, then stretched out his hand to the telephone.

'I want a call put through to Scotland Yard . . . Top priority . . . Inspector Pyke . . . Hang on a minute . . . No! Chief Inspector Pyke . . .'

They had met in France, when the worthy Mr Pyke had come to study the Police Judiciaire's methods in general, and Maigret's in particular. He had been surprised to discover that Maigret had no method at all.

They had met twice more after that, in London, and had

become good friends. Maigret had been told of Pyke's promotion some months ago.

Although it took no more than three minutes to get through to Scotland Yard, it took nearly ten to reach his friend, and they wasted a few more in mutual congratulations, Pyke speaking in bad French and Maigret in bad English.

'Maillant, yes . . . M for Maurice, A for Andrew . . .'

He had to spell out the names.

'Muir . . . M for Maurice again . . . U for Ursula . . .'

'Now that's a name I know . . . Are you referring to Sir Herbert Muir? . . . of Manchester? He was knighted three years ago . . .'

'The second husband's name is Norris Jonker . . .'

He spelt that out too, and went on to mention that the Dutchman had served in the British Army, and had reached the rank of Colonel.

'There may have been other men between the two marriages . . . Apparently she lived in London for quite a while, and I can't see her living on her own . . .'

Maigret was careful to add that his inquiries were connected with the attempted murder of a police officer, and Chief Inspector Pyke said solemnly: 'In this country, the criminal, whether a man or a woman, would be sentenced to death. The murder of a policeman is always punishable by death . . .'

Like Bastiani, he promised to ring him back.

It was half past six. When Maigret opened the communicating door to the Duty Room, only four or five inspectors were still there.

'Nothing from Chez Mélanie in Saint-Fargeau, Chief. Nothing from the Coq Hardy or La Pie Qui Danse either . . . I wasn't really expecting anything . . . That leaves only the Marne region, now that we've drawn a blank in the Vallée de Chevreuse and the Seine . . .'

Maigret was just about to return to his office when Inspector Chinquier burst into the room in a state of intense agitation.

'Is the Chief Superintendent in?'

Almost before the question was out of his mouth, he saw him.

'I've got news for you . . . I decided to come myself, rather than telephone . . .'

'Come into my office.'

'I've brought a witness . . . I've left him outside in the waiting-room, in case you should want to question him yourself . . .'

'First of all, sit down and tell me about it.'

'Do you mind if I take off my coat? I've been rushing around so much today that I'm sweating like a pig. Well, here goes! In accordance with your wishes, the men of the 18th *arrondissement* have been going through the Avenue Junot and all the streets near by with a fine-tooth comb. Except for old Maclet, they couldn't find anyone at first who was able to help. Then out of the blue I received information which I judged to be of the utmost significance . . .

'That particular building had already been visited this afternoon. The concierge had been questioned, and also those tenants who were there at the time, not many, women mostly, because the men were still out at work . . .

'I'm speaking of a block of flats right at the top of the avenue . . .

'Just as one of my colleagues arrived there for the second time – less than an hour ago – a man was going into the lodge to collect his mail. His name is Langeron, and he's a door-to-door salesman of vacuum cleaners . . . I've brought him with me . . .

'He's not the most cheerful of men, being more used to having the door slammed in his face than to being received with open arms . . . He lives alone in rooms on the third floor. He works irregular hours, in the hope of discovering the most favourable time for calling on his potential customers . . .

'Most of the time he cooks his own meals, but whenever he has a successful day, he treats himself to a meal in a restaurant . . . That's what happened last night . . . Between six and eight in the evening, when most people are at home, he sold two vacuum cleaners, and, after having an aperitif in a brasserie in the Place Clichy, he had a huge meal in a little restaurant in the Rue Caulaincourt.

'A little before ten in the evening, he returned to the Avenue Junot, carrying his demonstration model, and saw a parked car outside the Dutchman's house. It was a yellow Jaguar, and he was struck by the registration number, because the letters TT were painted in red.

'He had gone on only a few yards when the door opened . . .'

'Is he sure it was the door of the Jonkers' house?'

'He knows all the houses in the Avenue Junot like the back of his hand, having, needless to say, tried to sell a vacuum cleaner to practically everyone in it . . . Now listen to this . . . Two men came out, supporting a third who was so drunk he couldn't stand upright . . .

'When the two men, who were virtually carrying the other man to the car, caught sight of Langeron, they looked as if they were minded to return indoors, but then one of them said, crossly: "Come on, you idiot, move! You ought to be ashamed of yourself, getting into this state!"'

'Did they drive away with him?'

'Just a minute. That's not all. In the first place, my friend, the vacuum cleaner salesman, says that the man who spoke had a strong English accent . . . And furthermore, he says, the drunk wasn't wearing any shoes or socks . . . Apparently, his bare feet were dragging along the pavement . . . He was bundled into the back seat, followed by one of the two men . . . The other took the wheel . . . And the car drove off at high speed . . .

'Would you like to see my witness?'

Maigret hesitated, haunted by the conviction that time was getting very short.

'Take him in next door, and have him dictate a statement. Make certain he leaves nothing out. One can never be sure that some quite trivial detail may not turn out to be important . . .'

'What shall I do with him after that?'

'Come and see me again when you've finished.'

The previous night, at this very same hour, he had been leaning on young Bauche, nicknamed Jeannot, and it had been one o'clock in the morning before he had wrested a confession from him, which had enabled him to arrest Gaston Nouveau.

He was beginning to fear that tonight, also, there would be a light burning in his office until God knows what time. It was unusual for him to be working so late two nights in succession. There was almost always an interval between cases, and, paradoxically enough, there was nothing like a prolonged interval to make Maigret feel thoroughly restless and disgruntled.

'Get me Motor Vehicle Registrations . . . And hurry!'

He could not remember ever having seen a yellow Jaguar, a colour which was anyway uncommon for a British car. The letters TT indicated that the car had been brought to France by a foreign owner who intended to stay only for a short while, and was therefore not required to pay any import duty.

'Who in your department deals with TT registrations? . . . Rorive? . . . He's not there? . . . Everybody has gone home? Well, you're still there, aren't you? . . . Listen to me, laddie . . . You'll just have to manage on your own . . . It's absolutely vital . . . You can do one of two things: go into Rorive's office and look up the information I require, or ring him at his home and tell him to come back at once . . . I don't give a damn if he is in the middle of dinner . . . Understood? . . . It's about a Jaguar . . . Yes, a Jaguar . . .

'It was seen being driven in Paris as recently as yesterday evening . . . It's yellow, and fitted with TT plates . . . No! . . . I don't know the number . . . That would be too much to hope for . . . But there can't be all that many yellow Jaguars with TT plates in Paris . . .

'Put your skates on, and as soon as you have the information, ring me here at the Quai . . . I want the name of the owner, his address, and the date of his arrival in France . . . I hope it won't be long before I hear from you . . . Oh! and if you have to disturb Rorive, apologize to him from me . . . I hope to be able to repay him sometime . . . Tell him it's a lead to the fellow who shot Lognon . . . Yes, the inspector from the 18th *arrondissement* . . .'

He went across and opened the communicating door, and called Janvier in.

'Nothing yet from the Marne district?'

'Not yet. Maybe Lagrume has had a puncture . . .'

'What's the time?'

'Seven o'clock.'

'I'm thirsty . . . Have them send up a few halves of beer . . . And, while you're about it, you may as well order some sandwiches . . .'

'For how many?'

'I've no idea . . . A pile of sandwiches . . .'

With his hands behind his back, he paced up and down for a while, then once again picked up the telephone receiver.

'Could you get me my wife, please . . .'

To tell her that he would certainly not be home for dinner.

No sooner had he hung up than the telephone bell rang.

Hastily, he picked up the receiver.

'Hello! . . . Yes . . . Bastiani . . . So it turned out to be easier than you thought? . . . A stroke of luck? . . . Good! . . . Go ahead . . .'

He sat down at his desk, notebook in hand, and picked up a pencil.

'What name did you say? . . . Stanley Hobson . . . What's that? . . . A long story? . . . Well, cut it as short as you can, but don't leave anything out . . . Of course not, my dear fellow . . . It's just that I'm a bit on edge this evening . . . I have a feeling that we need to move fast . . . I'm plagued by the vision of a barefoot drunk . . . OK . . . I'm listening . . .'

The incident went back sixteen years. It concerned a man of the name of Stanley Hobson, who was staying in Nice at one of the big hotels on the Promenade des Anglais. On a tip from Scotland Yard, he was arrested and charged with a number of thefts of jewellery from villas in Antibes and Cannes, and also from one of the rooms in the hotel where he was staying.

At the time of his arrest he was with a girl who was not quite eighteen, and who had been his mistress for several weeks past.

They had arrested her at the same time. Both were held for questioning for several days. Their hotel room had been searched, and so had the girl's mother's flat in the old quarter. The girl, it seemed, had earned her living by selling flowers in the market.

No jewellery was found. For lack of evidence the couple were released, and two days later they had crossed the frontier into Italy.

In Nice, nothing more was ever heard of Hobson, nor of Marcelle Maillant, for it was indeed she who was the girl in the case.

'Do you happen to know what became of her mother?'

'For several years now she's been living in a comfortable flat in the Rue Saint-Sauveur on a private income. I've sent one of my men to see her, but he hasn't got back yet . . . I presume she gets an allowance from her daughter . . .'

'Thanks, Bastiani. You'll be hearing from me again soon, I hope.'

The wheels were beginning to turn, as Maigret was fond of saying, and at a time like this he could have wished that all the offices in the building had been manned night and day.

'Come in here a minute, Lucas . . . I want you to go down to Licensed Lettings . . . I hope you won't find everyone gone . . . Make a note of this name . . . Stanley Hobson . . . According to Bastiani he must, by now, be between forty-five and forty-eight years old . . . I don't have a description, but, fifteen years ago or more, he was suspected of being involved in a number of international jewel robberies, and at that time Scotland Yard issued his description to every Police Force in Europe . . .

'If necessary, go upstairs and see if they've got anything on him in Records . . .'

When Lucas had gone, Maigret looked reproachfully at the telephone, as if he felt it was letting him down by not ringing incessantly. Then there was a knock on his door. It was Chinquier.

'Here you are, Chief Superintendent . . . Here is Langeron's statement, duly typed and signed. He says can he go and have some dinner. Do you really not want to see him?'

Maigret was satisfied with a mere glimpse of the man through the half-open door. He looked very ordinary and insignificant.

'Tell him he's welcome to go out to dinner, but that he's to be sure and come back here afterwards. I don't know when I may need him, if at all, but there are too many people in this case already scattered about all over the place . . .'

'What should I do next?'

'Aren't you hungry? Do you never have dinner?'

'I'd like to help in any way I can . . .'

'The best thing would be for you to go back to your own office, so that you can keep me informed of any new developments in your district.'

'Are you hoping for a breakthrough?'

'If I weren't, I'd go straight home to my wife, and we'd have dinner together and watch television . . .'

The waiter from the Brasserie Dauphine was just putting down a tray laden with sandwiches and glasses of beer, when the telephone rang.

'Splendid! . . . Congratulations . . . Ed? . . . Just Ed? An American? . . . Yes, I see . . . Even their presidents are familiarly known by a diminutive . . . Ed Gollan . . . Two l's . . .? Do you have his address? . . . Eh! What's that? . . .'

Maigret's brow clouded over. The man in question was the owner of the yellow Jaguar.

'Are you sure it's the only one of its kind in Paris? . . . Good . . . Thanks, old man . . . I'll follow it up at once, but I wish he was staying anywhere but at the Ritz . . .'

Once more, he looked in on the inspectors' room.

'I hope there are some cars left in the forecourt, because I want two of you to go and get hold of one . . .'

'Two cars have just driven in.'

A few seconds later, he was on the telephone again.

'Is that the Ritz? . . . Would you put me on to the Head Porter please, mademoiselle . . . ? Hello! Is that the Head Porter? Is that you, Pierre . . . ? Maigret speaking . . .'

Maigret had more than once conducted an investigation at the Ritz in the Place Vendôme, one of the most select hotels, if not *the* most select, in Paris, and had always proceeded with the utmost discretion.

'The Chief Superintendent, that's right . . . Now listen carefully, and don't mention any names . . . At this time of the evening, the foyer must be crowded . . . Have you anyone staying there of the name of Gollan, Ed Gollan . . . ?'

'Do you mind holding on a moment? I think I'd better get this call transferred to one of the cubicles . . .'

No sooner was this done than the Head Porter was able to give Maigret the information he wanted: 'Yes, he is here . . . He stays here quite often . . . He's an American from San Francisco. He travels a lot, and comes to Paris three or four times a year . . . As a rule, he stays about three weeks . . .'

'How old a man is he?'

'Forty-eight . . . Not one of your business types at all . . . More of an intellectual, I'd say . . . According to his passport, he's an art critic, and I've heard it said that he has an international reputation as an expert in his field . . . He's entertained the Director of the Louvre on several occasions, and all the big picture dealers call on him when he's here . . .'

'Is he in his suite now?'

'Let me see . . . What time is it . . . ? Half-past seven . . . ? He's probably in the bar . . .'

'Would you check on that . . . ? As discreetly as you can, of course . . .'

Another pause.

'Yes, he's there . . .'

'Alone?'

'He's got a good-looking woman with him.'

'Is she staying at the hotel?'

'She's not quite the type . . . It's not the first time she's had a drink with him in the bar . . . Later, he'll probably take her out somewhere for dinner.'

'Could you let me know, as soon as they show any sign of leaving?'

'I'll be glad to, but I won't be able to stop them . . .'

'Don't worry about that . . . Just give me a ring . . . And thanks!'

He called Lucas into his office.

'Listen carefully. This is urgent, and you'll have to handle it with great discretion. I want you and another inspector to go to the Ritz straight away . . . Tell the Head Porter I sent you, and ask him if Ed Gollan is still in the bar . . . If he is, as I'm hoping he will be, leave your colleague in the foyer and, very discreetly, go and have a word with Gollan and his companion . . .

'Don't show your badge, or announce yourself in a loud voice as a police officer . . . Just tell him it's about his car, and that we want the answers to one or two questions. Insist on his coming with you . . .'

'What about the woman? Is she to come too?'

'Not unless she's tall and dark and very beautiful, and answers to the name of Mirella . . .'

Lucas cast a longing glance at the still frosted glasses of beer, then turned and went out without a word.

'Remember, speed is of the essence . . . Get there as fast as you can . . .'

The beer was good, but Maigret was not tempted by the sandwiches. He was too agitated to eat. Nothing seemed to hang together in this case. No sooner did he evolve a theory than new evidence turned up to belie it.

And, except for the mysterious Stanley Hobson, everyone concerned seemed, on the face of it, to be thoroughly respectable.

Having given the matter some thought, he decided to telephone Manessi, the Official Valuer, at his home.

'It's me again, yes . . . I hope you're not in the middle of a party . . . You are . . . ? Then I'll be brief . . . Does the name Gollan mean anything to you . . . ? One of the most respected of American art valuers . . . ?'

As he listened to what Manessi had to tell him, he sighed more than once.

'Yes . . . Yes . . . I might have known . . . Just one more question . . . I was told this afternoon that the real connoisseurs of painting often prefer to resell under the counter, so to speak. That's right, is it . . . ? Naturally, I won't ask you to name names . . . No, the case I'm working on has no connection with works of art, or if it has, I don't know what the connection is . . . One last word . . . Is it conceivable that a man like Norris Jonker could have any fakes in his collection . . . ?'

Manessi, at the other end of the line, laughed heartily.

'It's just about as likely as looking for fakes in the Louvre . . . Admittedly, there are those who claim that the Mona Lisa in the Louvre is a copy . . .'

The door burst open and Janvier appeared, looking highly excited, indeed radiant. He could hardly wait for Maigret to ring off.

'I'm much obliged to you . . . Now you can go back to your guests . . . I hope I'm wrong, but I think I may have to come back to you . . .'

Janvier could not contain his news for another second. He exploded: 'We've done it, Chief . . . ! She's been found . . .'

'Marinette?'

'Yes . . . Lagrume is driving her back to Paris . . . It wasn't a puncture that held him up, it's just that it took him a long time to find the inn, Félix et Félicie. It's on the far side of Pomponne, at the end of a dirt road that leads nowhere.'

'Has he got anything out of her?'

'She swears she knows nothing. When she heard the shots, she thought immediately of Lognon. She was afraid they might be gunning for her as well.'

'Why?'

'She didn't offer any explanation . . . She made no difficulties about coming back with Lagrume, not after he'd shown her his badge, that is . . .'

They would be arriving at the Quai des Orfèvres within the hour. Before that, all being well, Ed Gollan would have arrived, fuming no doubt, and threatening to complain to his Embassy. It was amazing, the number of people who were prepared to bother their Embassies!

'Hello . . . ! Yes . . . Chief Inspector Pyke, my dear fellow! Yes, it's me in person . . .'

The recently promoted Scotland Yard Chief Inspector said his say in a leisurely manner, sounding as if he were reading from a prepared text, and, whenever anything of importance came up, he repeated the words.

And a great deal of his information was extremely important. For instance, that the marriage between Mirella and her first husband, Herbert Muir, had lasted only two years. The young woman had been sued for divorce as the guilty party, and the co-respondent, to use the English term, had been none other than Stanley Hobson.

Not only had the pair been caught *in flagrante delicto*, in the somewhat dubious district of Manchester where Hobson was living at the time, but it was further established that, throughout the two-year duration of the marriage, Mirella and Hobson had never ceased to meet.

'I have not yet been able to find out whether Hobson was in London at all during the intervening years. I hope to be able to tell you more about that tomorrow. I'm putting two of my men on to the job of having a word with some people in Soho, who know everything that goes on in the criminal fraternity . . .

'Oh! there's one other thing . . . Hobson is best known by his nickname of Bald Stan. At the age of twenty-three or twenty-four, following some illness or other, he lost all his hair, and his eyebrows and eyelashes . . .'

Maigret, who was feeling overheated, went across and opened the window a little. He was just finishing one of the glasses of beer when he heard, outside in the corridor, someone speaking in French with an American accent. He couldn't hear the words, but it was clear from the tone of the voice that the speaker was beside himself with anger.

Accordingly, Maigret, assuming his most friendly, affable and smiling manner, opened the door, and said: 'Please come in, Monsieur Gollan, and forgive me for putting you to all this trouble . . .'

7

Mirella's Choice

Ed Gollan had very short, brown, bristle-cut hair. In spite of the overcast sky and the cold air, he had not bothered to put on a coat, and his light-weight suit, with its unpadded shoulders, made him look even taller than he was.

In spite of his fury, he was not at a loss for words, and his French was both fluent and grammatical.

'This gentleman,' he said, pointing to Lucas, 'came on the scene at a most inopportune moment. It was embarrassing not only for me, but also for the lady who was with me . . .'

Maigret signalled to Lucas to leave the room.

'I'm extremely sorry, Monsieur Gollan. You mustn't think too badly of him, though. He was only doing his job.'

The art critic got the point.

'I presume it concerns my car?'

'You are the owner of a yellow Jaguar, are you not?'

'I was.'

'What do you mean?'

'That this morning I went in person to the Divisional Police Headquarters in the 1st *arrondissement* to report that it had been stolen.'

'Where were you yesterday evening, Monsieur Gollan?'

'With the Mexican Consul, at his home in the Boulevard des Italiens.'

'Did you dine there?'

'Yes. With a party of about a dozen people.'

'Were you still there at ten o'clock?'

'Not only was I there at ten, I was still there at two in the morning. You can check if you like.'

Noticing the tray loaded with glasses of beer and sandwiches, he looked surprised.

'I'd be obliged if you would tell me right away . . .'

'One moment. I am pressed for time myself, more pressed than you are, believe me, but it's essential that we should take things in their proper order. Did you leave your car in the Boulevard des Italiens?'

'No. You know as well as I do that it's virtually impossible to find a parking space there.'

'Where was it when you saw it last?'

'In the Place Vendôme, where a certain amount of parking space is reserved for residents of the Ritz. I only had a few hundred yards' walk to get to my friend's house.'

'Were you away from his flat at any time during the evening?'

'No.'

'Did you receive a telephone call?'

He hesitated, apparently surprised that Maigret should know.

'From a woman, yes.'

'From someone whom you would no doubt prefer not to name? The call was from Madame Jonker, wasn't it?'

'It might have been. As it happens, I do know the Jonkers.'

'When you got back to the hotel, didn't you notice that your car was no longer there?'

'I used the Rue Cambon entrance, as most of the residents do . . .'

'Do you know Stanley Hobson?'

'It is not my intention, Chief Superintendent, to allow myself to be interrogated, until I know what this is all about.'

'It concerns some friends of yours who happen to be in trouble.'

'What friends?'

'Norris Jonker, for one . . . I presume you have sold pictures to him, and perhaps bought from him as well . . . ?'

'I'm not a picture dealer . . . I am occasionally commissioned by museums and private collectors to find them a painting by a specific artist, representing a specific period in his development, and of greater or lesser importance in the canon of his works . . . If, in the course of my travels, I happen to learn that a painting of the right sort is on the market, I merely pass on the information to those concerned . . .'

'Without taking any commission?'

'That's no business of yours. It's between me and the Revenue Department in my own country.'

'I presume I can take it for granted that you have no idea who stole your car. Did you leave the key in the dashboard?'

'It was in the glove compartment. I'm so absent-minded that if I carried it on me, I'd be sure to lose it.'

Maigret was listening with half an ear for sounds in the corridor. He seemed to be asking questions at random, without any real sense of purpose.

Well, Gollan was the first fish in his net, wasn't he?

'I presume I am now free to rejoin the lady I have invited to dine with me?'

'Not quite yet, I'm afraid. I may need you again later . . .'

Maigret had heard footsteps, then the opening and shutting of a door, followed by the sound of a woman's voice in the adjoining office. This was the night of the clicking doors, or so it came to be called later.

'Janvier, would you mind coming into my office for a minute. It would be discourteous to leave Monsieur Gollan all on his own . . . We've already caused him to miss his dinner, so if he would care for a sandwich . . .'

The few inspectors whom Maigret had asked to stay on, including Lagrume, who was bursting with pride at the success of his mission, were all looking with interest at a charming young woman wearing a blue tailored suit, and she, in her turn, was taking note of her surroundings.

'You're Chief Superintendent Maigret, aren't you? I've seen your picture in the papers. Please tell me at once, is he dead?'

'No, Mademoiselle Augier. He is still on the danger list, but the doctors hope to be able to save him.'

'Was he the one who told you about me?'

'He's in no condition to speak, and won't be for hours yet, perhaps not for two or three days. I'd be obliged if you would come with me.'

He led her into a little side-office, and shut the door.

'I think you will understand what I mean when I say that we have no time to lose. That's why I won't ask you now to tell me all you know in detail. There will be time enough for that later. I just want to ask you a few questions. Was it through you that Inspector Lognon learnt of the strange things that were going on in the house opposite?'

'No. I hadn't noticed a thing, except that there was often a light on in the studio at night . . .'

'Where did you meet?'

'In the street, one evening, when I was on my way home from work. He told me he'd found out that the flat I was living in was an ideal place from which to keep watch on someone, and asked if he might spend the next two or three nights looking out of my sitting-room window. He showed me his police badge and identity card. I wasn't too happy about it, and even thought of ringing the police station.'

'What made you change your mind?'

'He seemed so miserable. He told me he'd always been dogged by bad luck, but, if only I would help him, all that would change, because he was on the track of something really big . . .'

'Did he say what?'

'Not the first night.'

'Did you watch with him, that first night?'

'For a time, yes, in the dark. The curtains of the studio opposite didn't quite meet, and, from time to time, we could see a man moving across the gap, holding a palette and paintbrush.'

'Was he dressed all in white? With a turban wound round his head?'

'Yes. I laughed, and said he looked for all the world like a ghost.'

'Did you ever see him at work?'

'Once. On that particular night, he had set up his easel in a position where we could see it, and he was painting away furiously . . .'

'How does one paint furiously?'

'I don't know, but he gave the impression of being a man possessed.'

'Did you ever see anyone else in the studio?'

'A woman. She was undressing, or rather, I should say, he almost tore the clothes off her . . .'

'Was she tall and dark?'

'It wasn't Madame Jonker. I know *her* by sight.'

'Have you ever seen Monsieur Jonker?'

'Not in the studio. The only other person I ever saw there was an elderly, bald man.'

'What happened last night, exactly?'

'I went to bed early as usual. I come home from work very tired, especially when the salon stays open later than usual because of some fashionable ball or gala performance.'

'Was Lognon in the living-room?'

'Yes. We got on very well together in the end . . . He never tried to make a pass at me, and he was always very kind, in a fatherly sort of way. Sometimes he'd bring me some chocolates or a bunch of violets as a thank-you present . . .'

'Were you asleep at ten o'clock?'

'I was in bed, but I hadn't yet fallen asleep. I was reading the paper . . . He knocked on my door . . . He seemed wildly excited. He told me there had been a new development, that they had just abducted the painter, but it had happened so quickly that he had had no chance of getting downstairs in time . . .

'"I'd better stay here a little longer . . . At least one of the men is almost sure to come back . . ."

'He returned to his post at the window, and I went to sleep . . . I was woken by the sound of shots . . . I looked out of my window . . . Then I leaned forward, and saw a body lying on the pavement . . . I hadn't, at that stage, decided what to do, but I began to get dressed . . .'

'Why did you run away?'

'I was afraid the thugs might know who he was and what he was up to in the building, in which case they might have it in for me as well . . . I didn't know where I was going . . . I just didn't stop to think . . .'

'Did you take a taxi?'

'No. I walked as far as the Place Clichy, and went into a café that was still open. I stayed there for a while, during which time I was examined from head to foot by all the prostitutes in the place . . . Then I remembered an inn where I used occasionally to go and stay with a friend, some time ago . . .'

'Yes, with Jean-Claude . . .'

'Was he the one who told you?'

'See here, mademoiselle. Everything that concerns you interests me, and I should be happy to hear the full story of your adventure. But I have a feeling that there are more urgent matters to be dealt with . . . I'd be greatly obliged if you'd be good enough to wait for me in the Inspectors' Duty Room. I'll show you the way . . . In the meantime, Inspector Janvier will be pleased to take down your statement in writing . . .'

'Lognon wasn't mistaken, then?'

'No! Lognon knows his job, and seldom jumps to the wrong conclusion . . . As he told you, he's been unlucky, one way and another . . . Either the ground is cut from under his feet, or he gets himself shot just when he's on the point of making his mark . . . Come with me!'

He left her in the adjoining office and returned to his own, to find Janvier waiting for him.

'I'd be grateful if you would take down the young lady's statement.'

At this, Gollan, who had been seated up to now, sprang to his feet.

'You don't mean to say you've brought her here?'

'We're not talking about your friend, Monsieur Gollan . . . This one is a real lady . . . Do you still maintain that you've never met Stanley Hobson, better known as Bald Stan?'

'I don't have to answer that.'

'As you please . . . Sit down . . . I'm about to make a telephone call . . . You may find it helpful . . . Hello . . . ! Get me Monsieur Jonker, will you . . . ? Norris Jonker, Avenue Junot . . .

'Hello . . . ! Monsieur Jonker . . . ? Maigret speaking . . . Since I left your house, I have found the answers to a number of the questions I put to you . . . The real answers, if you take my meaning . . .

'For instance, I have Monsieur Gollan with me, here in my office, and he's none too happy about it, especially as he still hasn't found his missing car . . . A yellow Jaguar . . . The one that was seen outside your house at ten o'clock last night, and which drove away with your lodger, among others, inside . . .

'Your lodger . . . That's right . . . And in very poor shape, it seems . . . Wearing no shoes or socks . . .

'Now, listen carefully, Monsieur Jonker . . . I could, if I so wished, have you arrested tonight or tomorrow morning on charges relating to certain illegal activities, the details of which are more familiar to you than to me . . . I'd better warn you, in any case, that there is a police guard on your house . . .

'I am asking you to come and see me here at once, accompanied by Madame Jonker, so that we may continue our conversation of this afternoon . . . If your wife is inclined to make difficulties, tell her we know the whole of her history . . . It's possible that, in addition to Monsieur Gollan, she may meet another friend here, a man generally known as Bald Stan.

'That's enough, Monsieur Jonker . . . ! For the present, I'm doing the talking . . . Your turn will come very soon now . . . I dare say it is embarrassing to be mixed up in a case of forgery, but it is surely less so than if I had charged you with being an accessory to murder . . .

'I am convinced that the attack on Inspector Lognon came as a surprise to you, and probably to Monsieur Gollan as well . . . But I'm very much afraid that plans are afoot for another murder, which concerns you more closely, since the intended victim is the man who for some time lived in your house, virtually as a prisoner . . . Where is he . . . ? Where has he been taken, and by whom? Tell me that . . . No, not when you get here . . . Not in half-an-hour's time . . . Now, Monsieur Jonker, do you hear me?'

He could hear the murmur of a woman's voice. Mirella must be leaning over her husband's shoulder. What was she advising him to do?

'I swear to you, Chief Superintendent . . .'

'And I repeat that there is no time to lose . . .'

'Hold on . . . ! I don't know the number off-hand . . . I'll have to look it up in my book . . .'

At this point, Mirella openly intervened: 'He's looking up the address, Monsieur Maigret . . . The man's name is Mario de Lucia. He has a furnished flat somewhere near the Champs-Élysées . . . Ah! here's my husband . . .'

Jonker read out: 'Mario de Lucia, 27B Rue de Berry . . . I have entrusted Frédérico to his care . . .'

'I take it Frédérico is the painter to whom you lent your studio?'

'Yes . . . Frédérico Palestri . . .'

'I shall be expecting you, Monsieur Jonker . . . And be sure to bring your wife with you . . .'

Maigret did not spare a glance for the American art critic. He had already picked up the receiver again.

'Get me the Superintendent of the 9th *arrondissement* . . . Hello . . . ! Who is that speaking . . . ? Dubois . . . ? I want you to go to an address I shall read out to you . . . Take three or four men with you . . . Yes, I did say three or four . . . I want you all armed, because the man is dangerous . . . The address is 27B Rue de Berry. The man – his name is Mario de Lucia – has a furnished flat in the building . . . If he's at home, as I think he will be, arrest him. Yes, in spite of the lateness of the hour . . .

'You'll find another man being held prisoner there; his name is Frédérico Palestri . . . I want both these men brought here as soon as possible . . . I repeat, be very careful . . . Mario de Lucia is armed with a ·763 Mauser . . . If he hasn't got it on him, find it . . . !'

He turned to Ed Gollan.

'You see, Monsieur, it would be unwise of you to make difficulties . . . It's taken me a long time to work it all out, because I know very little about the traffic in paintings, genuine or faked . . . And besides, your friend Jonker is a gentleman who is not easily thrown off balance . . .'

The telephone rang and, once again, he grabbed the receiver.

'Yes . . . Hello . . . ! Is that you, Lucas . . . ? Where are you . . . ? Quai de la Tournelle . . . ? Hotel de la Tournelle . . . ? I see . . . He's having dinner in a nearby bistro . . . ? No, not alone . . . Get a couple of the local inspectors to go along with you. After all, we can't be sure he isn't the one who likes playing around with large-calibre guns. It would surprise me, but it would be just poor Lognon's luck . . .'

He went across to the door communicating with the Inspectors' Duty Room and opened it.

'I'd like some more chilled beer sent up . . .'

He returned to his seat, and began filling his pipe.

'Well! there it is, Monsieur Gollan . . . ! I hope your painter friend is still alive. I don't know Mario de Lucia personally, but I dare say we have him on our books under one name or another . . . If not, we shall get in touch with the Italian police . . . It shouldn't be more than a few minutes before we get some definite news. You might as well admit it, you're as worried as I am.'

'I refuse to say anything, except in the presence of my lawyer, Maître Spangler. His telephone number is Odéon 18.24 . . . No, that's not right . . .'

'It's of no consequence, Monsieur Gollan . . . As things are at present, your statement can wait. It's a pity a man like you should have allowed himself to become entangled in this business, and I hope Maître Spangler will be able to put forward sound arguments in your defence.'

The beer had not yet arrived before the telephone rang again.

'Yes . . . Dubois?'

He listened for some time without saying a word.

'Right . . . ! Thanks . . . It's no fault of yours . . . You'd better report direct to the D.P.P. . . . I'll look in there later . . .'

Maigret got up, avoiding the unspoken question in the eyes of the American, who had turned pale.

'Has something happened? I swear to you that if . . .'

'Sit down and be quiet.'

He went next door and beckoned to Janvier, who was engaged in typing Marinette Augier's statement, to join him in the corridor.

'Anything wrong, Chief?'

'I don't yet know exactly what has happened . . . The painter has been found hanging from the lavatory chain in the bathroom where he was being kept prisoner. Mario de Lucia has disappeared . . . You'll probably find a file on him upstairs . . . Put out a general alert to all railway stations, airports and frontier posts . . .'

'What about Marinette?'

'She can wait . . .'

A man and a woman were coming up the stairs, discreetly followed by a uniformed constable from the 18th *arrondissement*.

'I'd be obliged if you would wait in that room there, Madame Jonker . . .'

The two women, who knew one another by sight but had never before met face to face, eyed each other with interest.

'And you, Monsieur Jonker, please come with me . . .'

He led him into the little side-office where he had interviewed Marinette Augier.

'Please take a seat . . .'

'Have you found him?'

'Yes.'

'Alive?'

The Dutchman had lost both his rosy complexion and his self-assurance. In the course of a few hours, he had become an old man.

'Has Lucia . . . killed him?'

'He was found hanged in the bathroom . . .'

'I always said it would end badly . . .'

'For whom?'

'For Mirella . . . And others . . . But especially for my wife . . .'

'How much do you know about her?'

It was hard for him to make the admission, but with bowed head he managed it.

'Everything, I think . . .'

'Do you know about Nice and Stanley Hobson?'

'Yes.'

'And that he was the co-respondent in the divorce suit brought by Herbert Muir in Manchester?'

'Yes.'

'Did you meet her in London?'

'At a country house near London, where I was staying with friends . . . She was very popular in her own particular social world . . .'

'And you fell in love with her . . . ? Was it you who proposed marriage?'

'Yes.'

'Did you know about her, even then?'

'You may find this hard to believe, though a fellow-countryman of mine would understand . . . I had hired a private detective to find out more about her . . . I discovered that she and Hobson, nicknamed Bald Stan, had lived together for some years. I also discovered that the British police had only managed once to make a charge stick, and that he had served a two-year sentence . . .

'By the time he found her again, in Manchester, she was married to Muir . . . When she moved to London, they had ceased to live together, but he used to visit her at intervals, to extort money . . .'

There was a knock at the door.

'Would you like some beer, Chief?'

'You, Monsieur Jonker, I dare say, would prefer a brandy . . . I'm sorry I can't offer you your favourite brand of liqueur. Send someone to fetch the bottle of cognac from the cupboard in my office . . .'

Soon they were alone together once more. The spirits, swallowed at one gulp, had brought a little of the colour back to the Dutchman's cheeks.

'You see, Chief Superintendent, I can't live without her . . . Falling in love at my age is a very dangerous thing to do . . . She told me that Hobson was blackmailing her, but said that he was prepared to be bought off if the price was right, and I believed her . . . I paid up . . .'

'How did the picture racket start?'

'You'll find this hard to believe, but then you are not a collector . . .'

'I collect people . . .'

'I wonder how you would classify me in your collection . . . As a fool, perhaps? As you have been making inquiries about me, you will undoubtedly have been told that I am genuinely an expert on the paintings of a specific period . . . When one has immersed oneself, for so many years, in one particular branch of learning, one is bound to acquire a great deal of specialized knowledge, isn't that so?

'I am often asked for my opinion on this painting or that . . . And it is enough that a picture should have formed part of my collection for a time, for it to be accepted without question . . .'

'A hall-mark of authenticity, in fact . . .'

'The same is true of any major collection . . . As I told you when you came to my house, I sometimes sell a picture in order to replace it with a finer and rarer example of the artist's work . . .

Once one has started, it is difficult to stop . . . Once, I made a mistake . . .'

His voice sounded listless, as if he no longer cared what happened to him.

'The painting in question was a Van Gogh, no less. Not one of those I inherited from my father, but one I bought through an agent. I could have sworn it was genuine . . . I kept it for a while in my drawing-room . . . A South American collector offered me a sum so large for it that it would have enabled me to replace it with a picture that I had had my eye on for a long time . . .

'The sale was concluded . . . A few months later, the man Gollan, whom I knew only by name, came to see me . . .'

'How long ago was this?'

'About a year ago . . . He mentioned the Van Gogh, which he happened to have seen in the home of the Venezuelan purchaser, and was able to convince me that the painting was a clever fake . . .

'"I didn't say a word to the owner," he stated . . . "It would make it most unpleasant for you, wouldn't it, if anyone were to find out that you had passed on a fake . . . Others who had bought pictures from you might start feeling uneasy . . . Indeed it would throw doubt on your entire collection . . ."

'I repeat, you are not a collector . . . You can't possibly imagine what a fearful blow this was to me . . .

'Gollan came to see me again . . . One day, he announced that he had found the artist who had forged the Van Gogh . . . He said he was a pleasant young man, who claimed to be able to imitate, equally convincingly, the style of Manet, Renoir or Vlaminck . . .'

'Was your wife present on that occasion?'

'I don't remember . . . It's possible that I may have told her about it afterwards . . . Possibly she urged me to agree to his proposition . . . Possibly I would have agreed anyway . . . I am known as a rich man, but wealth is a relative term . . . Though I have the means to buy some pictures, there are others which are beyond my resources, however much I may want to own them . . . Do you understand?'

'I think I understand this much: it was essential that you should retain the forgeries for a while, to establish their authenticity beyond dispute.'

'That's about it . . . I would hang one or two forgeries among my own pictures, and . . .'

'One moment! At what stage did you actually meet Palestri?'

'A month or two later . . . I had already sold two of his works, with Gollan acting as agent . . . Gollan preferred, if he could, to sell to South American collectors or obscure little out-of-the-way museums . . .

'Palestri was giving him a lot of trouble . . . He was a sort of crazy genius, with an insatiable sexual appetite . . . You could see that, when you went into his bedroom, couldn't you . . . ?'

'Light began to dawn when I saw your wife standing at the easel . . .'

'We had no choice but to try and put you off the scent . . .'

'When and how did you discover that someone was taking an interest in the goings-on in your house?'

'It wasn't I who noticed it, it was Hobson . . .'

'Hobson had come back into your wife's life?'

'They both swear not . . . Hobson just happened to be a friend of Gollan's . . . It was he who put him on to Palestri . . . Do I make myself clear . . . ?'

'Yes.'

'I was trapped . . . I agreed to let him work in the studio, where no one would think of looking for him . . . He slept in the room you went into . . . He was quite prepared to stay indoors, provided we procured women for him . . . Painting and women were his only passions . . .'

'I was told that he "painted furiously" . . .'

'Yes . . . Two or three fine originals would be propped up in front of him . . . He would circle round them like a matador with a bull, and a few hours or a few days later, he would come up with a painting so akin in feeling and texture to the original that everyone was taken in . . .

'It wasn't any too pleasant having him living on the premises . . .'

'You mean on account of his insatiable appetite for women?'

'And his gross manners. Even towards my wife . . .'

'Is that as far as it went?'

'I prefer not to dwell on that . . . There may have been more to it . . . You saw that sketch he made of her with a few bold brush-strokes . . .

'One overriding passion is enough for any man, Chief Superintendent . . . I should have stuck to paintings and kept my collector's fever within reasonable bounds . . . But it was my misfortune that I should happen to meet Mirella . . . And yet none of this is her fault . . . What were we talking about?

'Oh! yes . . . Who discovered that we were being watched . . .? It was a woman – I can't even remember her name – a strip-tease artiste in a night club in the Champs-Élysées, I think, whom Lucia had brought to the house for Palestri . . .

'The next day, she rang Lucia and told him that, on leaving my house, she had been followed by an odd little man, who had accosted her and asked her all sorts of questions . . . Lucia and Stan kept a look-out, and discovered that there was a skinny, shabbily dressed little man, who made a habit of roaming up and down the Avenue Junot at night . . .

'Some days later, they saw him go into the building opposite, in company with a young girl . . . He used to sit up there in the dark by the window . . . He thought no one could see him, but, as he was a compulsive smoker, the glowing tip of his cigarette was visible from time to time . . .'

'Did it never occur to anyone that he might have been a policeman?'

'Stan Hobson said that, if it had been a police operation, the man would have been relieved at intervals . . . whereas in this case, there was only the one man, which convinced Stan that he must be a member of a rival gang, on the look-out for evidence that could be used to blackmail us . . .

'It was becoming a matter of urgency to get Palestri out of the house . . . Lucia and Hobson undertook to arrange it, using Gollan's car . . .'

'Gollan was in the know, I take it?'

'Palestri refused to go. He was convinced that, having made use of him for the best part of a year, we now intended to eliminate him . . . There was no choice but to bash him over the head . . .

Not, however, in time to prevent him from throwing his shoes out into the garden . . .'

'Were you present?'

'No.'

'And your wife?'

'No! We were waiting for him to go, so that we could tidy up the studio and his bedroom . . . Stan had already removed the painting he was working on, the night before . . . One thing I can assure you, if I have not forfeited the right to ask you to believe me, I knew nothing whatever of their intention to shoot the inspector . . . It wasn't until I heard the shots that I realized . . .'

There followed a long silence. Maigret was weary, and looked with helpless compassion at the old man facing him, as he hesitantly stretched out his hand towards the bottle of brandy.

'May I?'

Having drained the glass, Jonker gave a forced smile.

'In any event, it's all over for me, isn't it? I wonder what I shall miss most . . .'

His pictures, which had cost him so dear? His wife, about whom he had never had any illusions, but whom he needed so much?

'You'll see, Chief Superintendent, no one will ever believe that an intelligent man could have been so naive . . .'

He added, after a moment's reflection: 'Except perhaps another collector . . .'

In another office, Lucas had begun interrogating Bald Stan.

For the next two hours there was much coming and going from one room to another, and a great many questions and answers, accompanied by the chatter of typewriters.

As on the previous night, it was nearly one in the morning before the lights were switched off.

'I'll drive you home, mademoiselle . . . Tonight you will be able to sleep without fear in your own bed . . .'

They were sitting together in the back of a taxi.

'Are you angry with me, Monsieur Maigret?'

'Why should I be?'

'If I hadn't lost my head and run away, it would have made things a lot easier for you, wouldn't it?'

'We might have cleared up the case a little sooner, but it wouldn't have made any difference to the outcome . . .'

He seemed none too happy with the outcome, however, and was even prepared to spare a not unsympathetic glance for Mirella as she was led away to the cells.

A month later, Lognon was discharged from hospital, thinner than ever, but with a gleam in his eye, because he was now something of a hero to his colleagues in the 18th *arrondissement*. Better still, it was not Maigret's picture but his that had featured in all the newspapers.

That same day, he and his wife left for a village in the Ardennes, where they stayed for the two months of his convalescence, as ordered by his doctors.

He spent most of those two months, as Madame Maigret had foreseen, dancing attendance on Madame Lognon.

Mario de Lucia had been arrested at the Belgian frontier. He and Hobson were both sentenced to ten years' hard labour.

Gollan denied all knowledge of the attempted murder in the Avenue Junot, and got off lightly with a mere two-year sentence for fraud.

Jonker, sentenced to only one year's imprisonment, left the court a free man, having been in custody for six months while awaiting trial, which, according to French law, corresponded to a year's detention after sentence.

Mirella, having been acquitted for want of evidence, went with him, clinging to his arm.

Maigret, who had been standing at the back of the court-room, was one of the first to leave, so as to avoid meeting them face to face, and also because he had promised to ring Madame Maigret as soon as the verdict was announced.

The trial caused very little stir. It was already stale news, and besides it took place in June, a time of the year when no one talks of anything but where they are going on holiday.

Noland, 23 June 1963

MORE ABOUT PENGUINS AND PELICANS

For further information about books available from Penguins please write to Dept EP, Penguin Books Ltd, Harmondsworth, Middlesex UB7 0DA.

In the U.S.A.: For a complete list of books available from Penguins in the United States write to Dept CS, Penguin Books, 625 Madison Avenue, New York, New York 10022.

In Canada: For a complete list of books available from Penguins in Canada write to Penguin Books Canada Ltd, 2801 John Street, Markham, Ontario L3R 1B4.

In Australia: For a complete list of books available from Penguins in Australia write to the Marketing Department, Penguin Books Australia Ltd, P.O. Box 257, Ringwood, Victoria 3134.

In New Zealand: For a complete list of books available from Penguins in New Zealand write to the Marketing Department, Penguin Books (N.Z.) Ltd, P.O. Box 4019, Auckland 10.

Also in Penguins by Georges Simenon

MAIGRET'S CHRISTMAS

Here are nine entrancing stories featuring that laconic pipe-puffing detective, Chief Superintendent Maigret. Some are set in Paris, some deep in the provinces – there are memorable scenes in Maigret's office at the Quai des Orfèvres, a remote country inn and the bustling streets and cafés of Paris.

Maigret's patience, ingenuity and compassion are put to the test and, as we follow him through the various stages of his career, and even into a not uneventful retirement, we catch a rare glimpse of Maigret at home as well as at work.

MAIGRET STONEWALLED

A simple enough case . . . on the face of it. A commercial traveller killed in a hotel bedroom on the Loire. But Maigret sensed falseness everywhere: in the way the witnesses spoke and laughed and acted and, above all, in the manner of M. Gallet's death, under a false name, from a shot that nobody heard, with his own knife plunged into his heart. And behind the falseness, as Maigret discovered, the pathos of a man for whom nothing had ever gone right – not even death.

and

MAIGRET AND THE ENIGMATIC LETT
MAIGRET AND THE HUNDRED GIBBETS
MAIGRET AT THE CROSSROADS
MAIGRET MEETS A MILORD
MAIGRET MYSTIFIED
THE FIRST – FOURTEENTH SIMENON OMNIBUSES

G. K. Chesterton

'It may seem odd to class a man who has difficulty in rolling his umbrella and does not know the right end of his return ticket among the Supermen of detection, but Father Brown belongs among them' – Julian Symons in *Bloody Murder*

G. K. Chesterton's Father Brown must be the most lovable amateur detective ever created. This short, shabby priest, with his cherubic, round face, attracts situations that baffle everyone – except Father Brown in his, rather naïve, wisdom.

THE INCREDULITY OF FATHER BROWN
THE INNOCENCE OF FATHER BROWN
THE SCANDAL OF FATHER BROWN
THE SECRET OF FATHER BROWN
THE WISDOM OF FATHER BROWN

Dashiell Hammett

'Dashiell Hammett gave murder back to the kind of people that commit it for reasons, not just to provide a corpse; and with the means at hand, not with handwrought duelling pistols, curare, and tropical fish' – Raymond Chandler

THE BIG KNOCKOVER AND OTHER STORIES
THE THIN MAN

Julian Symons

THE BLACKHEATH POISONINGS

'A superb detective novel of an original kind, which, while offering the reader as much information as anyone, ends with a surprising and totally unexpected conclusion. At the same time his evocation of this late Victorian epoch – a kind of black *Diary of a Nobody* – seems to ring true in every respect' – *The Times Literary Supplement*

THE TELL-TALE HEART

THE LIFE AND WORKS OF EDGAR ALLAN POE

'Mr Symon's analysis of Poe's divided self is uncondescending, and does not simplify his subject. On the contrary, he rescues Poe from Freudians, symbolists, moralists and other simplifiers. By indicating the ramifications of the two selves, he restores to Poe his depth and mystery. He manages to be both incisive and finely circumspect . . . And he even makes you like Poe most of the time' – John Carey in the *Sunday Times*

BLOODY MURDER

'An urbane and scholarly account of the crime novel . . . from its beginnings with Poe and Vidocq down to the immediate present' – Michael Gilbert in the *Sunday Telegraph*

'Can be heartily recommended to anyone who has ever enjoyed a detective story or a crime novel' – Kingsley Amis in the *Spectator*

Also published by Penguins

THE PENGUIN COMPLETE SHERLOCK HOLMES

Here, in four novels and fifty-six short stories, is every word Sir Arthur Conan Doyle ever wrote about Baker Street's most famous resident:

A STUDY IN SCARLET
THE SIGN OF FOUR
THE ADVENTURES OF SHERLOCK HOLMES
THE MEMOIRS OF SHERLOCK HOLMES
THE RETURN OF SHERLOCK HOLMES
THE HOUND OF THE BASKERVILLES
THE VALLEY OF FEAR
HIS LAST BOW
THE CASE-BOOK OF SHERLOCK HOLMES

All these stories are also published by Penguins in separate volumes.